THE W

Sonia Prentice (née Bowring) was born in Liverpool in 1922. Her family soon moved to Surrey, where with short interruptions she has lived ever since. She was educated at Benenden School in Kent. In the 2nd World War she worked in the Naval Section at Bletchley Park. In 1948 she married Ronald Prentice (d. 1984). She has three children and five grandchildren.

SONIA PRENTICE

THE
WAGER

HOLLYTREE BOOKS

HB

First published in Great Britain in 2001 by Hollytree Books,
Henhaw Farmhouse, Coopers Hill Road, South Nutfield,
Redhill, Surrey, RH1 5PD

ISBN 0-9541174-0-9

This book is a work of fiction. Names, characters,
places and incidents are either a product of the author's
imagination or are used fictitiously. Any resemblance to
actual people living or dead, events or locales
is entirely coincidental.

Typeset/data conversion by Avonset, Bath
Printed and bound by
The Cromwell Press, Trowbridge, Wiltshire.

ACKNOWLEDGEMENTS

This book would not have been possible without the help and encouragement of all my family, especially at first from my husband and latterly from my daughter, Caroline.

For Ronald

CHAPTER I

The appearance of the fashionable gentleman leaning against the mantel-piece was in direct contrast to his surroundings. The room, large and well proportioned, had an indefinable air of gloom and decay and the shafts of sunlight coming through the tall windows only served to emphasize the faded curtains and covers and the film of dust upon the once handsome furniture. Clearly, however, no expense had been spared in the dressing of Sir Richard Harding; his well-cut coat of olive green superfine proclaimed the man of fashion, and there was evidence of an inclination to dandyism in the length of his coat tails and the exaggerated points of his shirt collar.

He was reading a letter with frowning attention, his mouth a little agape as his eyes followed the lines of careful script. Suddenly an expression of astonishment appeared upon his face, his prominent eyes widened. He read the sentence again, then looked up, staring before him as one thunderstruck. A slow smile spread over his face as he murmured under his breath, "Good God! Who would have thought it possible?" Now there was no mistaking his excitement, he took a few turns about the room, re-read the letter to the end, then, dropping heavily onto a chair beside the fireplace, gazed before him as one surveying in his mind's eye an intensely pleasing prospect.

He sat for some time in contemplation, a more thoughtful and serious mood succeeding his previous elation. He seemed oblivious of his surroundings and even when the flames died out and the fire grew dull he did not trouble to stir the logs. All at once he drew in his breath sharply, an ugly gleam in his eyes. He read the letter again, nodded to himself with satisfaction, then slowly rose and going to the bureau that stood by one of the windows, he placed the letter in the top drawer, carefully locked it and put the key in his pocket. For a while he stood before the window looking out into the garden where, across the unkempt lawn, the slight figure of a girl could be seen gathering flowers and his eyes, as they followed her movements, seemed to contemplate with gloating satisfaction some future event.

Unaware of her half-brother's regard, Emma was rejoicing in the May sunshine and fresh warm air, so delightful after a dismal spring, with day succeeding day of cold, wet weather. Indeed ever since she had come to live in Richard's house in early April there had hardly been a day fit for walking in the garden. Now, at last, the melancholy, which had followed her acute grief at the sudden death of her father was lifting and she felt a welcome return of the cheerful optimism natural to her temperament. Life must surely have more to offer than this dismal existence. The future, she felt confident, must show at least some degree of improvement – it was not possible that it should continue in the same dreary way.

As she laid in her basket the last of the tulips and wallflowers to have survived the onslaughts of wind and rain, she resolved to set herself the task of putting the household linen in order. The sorting and darn-ing would occupy her hands and she knew that she must turn her mind away from the past and make the best of her situation. A wistful thought that a ride in Richmond Park on such a lovely morning would be vastly more to her liking was resolutely put aside. Richard had not offered to provide her with a mount and she was far too conscious of her dependent position to express any wishes for her own diversion.

As she drew near the house she could see her half-brother standing at the window of the drawing-room and at that moment he tapped on the glass and beckoned to her to come in.

Setting aside her basket and shawl, Emma entered the room reluc-tantly; her previous encounters with the man her father had designated in his Will as her guardian had not led her to expect any pleasure from his society and conversation, but on this occasion she was surprised to discover him to be in an affable mood.

"I fear, Emma, that you have been having a deuced dull time of it here!" he said in a jovial voice, "But now I'm happy to say that I have some news that I believe will afford you some pleasure! Lady Fraser – she's my aunt, y'know, is holding a rout-party tonight and she has

10

particularly requested that you should accompany me to it – wishes to make your acquaintance – says everything that's civil. It's high time, my girl, that you had some distractions! She's a member of the ton, knows all the right people – it will prove an excellent opportunity to introduce you to society!"

He was smiling as he spoke but his eyes were watchful. Perhaps for the first time he considered her appearance as others might see her; her round gown of black crepe and bombazine was not perhaps in the latest mode but she had a light, graceful figure and the white ruff at the high neckline set off a lively countenance, with large, very expressive hazel eyes, a small straight nose and a delicately curving mouth.

"Why, how kind of her! I should like it above all things!" Her eyes were shining, her cheeks faintly flushed with excitement, as she replied, but hardly had she spoken than her face fell. She said reluctantly, "But, Richard, I fear it will not possible, for Lady Fraser can scarcely be aware that I am still in mourning for my father – I believe it would be most improper for me to attend such a function at present ...."

Richard's reply surprised her by its vehemence. "Come, Emma, this is being foolish beyond permission – there cannot be the least impropriety in your attending a private party. Family too! After all, it is now nearly a year since your father died – it would be folly to contemplate missing such an opportunity!"

"You really think so?" she surveyed him with anxious eyes, "Oh, I should like to believe it! But then, what in Heaven's name could I wear? For you must know that I have not a dress in my wardrobe which would be suitable for such an occasion!"

"No need to worry your head on that score. I have already decided to ask Mrs Steadman to lend you one of her evening gowns. She will find something for you and," he added expansively, "she can assist you to dress and give the finishing touches to your appearance."

Emma thought of Mrs Steadman, whose position in the household even she, ignorant of the world as she was, felt to be somewhat curious despite that lady's claim to be a distant cousin of Richard. Would that bold-mannered widow possess a dress evenly remotely suitable for her to wear?

He saw that she was looking doubtful and concluded hastily, "Well, that's settled then! We shall leave here between eleven and midnight. You'll have to accustom yourself to town hours now, you know!" and turning from her dismissively, picked up a journal, adding as he did so, "Some friends of mine dine here today – we shall be playing cards afterwards until it is time to leave for my aunt's house, and as you will not be dining with us, you will have plenty of time to prepare yourself."

Emma left Richard with her mind in a turmoil and as she arranged the flowers she thought wistfully of her father and hoped devoutly that he would not have regarded as sinfully worldly her growing excitement at the prospect of the evening's festivities. Was this the beginning of the change in her life for which she had been wishing only a few moments ago.

The Reverend William Stanton, a widower since Emma was scarcely more than an infant, had been a devoted father and an exemplary parish priest. At Hinton St Anne, in Wiltshire, she had been taught to regard the welfare of her fellow creatures as a matter of supreme importance. Too young to have entered society before her father's fall from his horse had rendered her an orphan, she could not help hoping that Lady Fraser's rout party would provide her with an entrée into a new and exciting world, of which, at present, she was totally ignorant.

It had not taken her long to realise that Richard had not been best pleased to find himself her guardian and the sole administrator of the pathetically small sum that was all her father had had to leave to his daughter. Indeed, it had been the cause of considerable surprise to Emma that her austere, scholarly parent's choice should have fallen upon such a man.

A considerable period of time had elapsed after his death before the lawyers had been able to contact Richard in Paris, where he had been continuing in the way of life that he had so disastrously begun in England; a passion for gambling and a succession of expensive mistresses having led him inexorably to the brink of ruin. Dilatory in answering their letters, he had, moreover, allowed eight months to elapse before returning to England.

It had been a fortunate chance for Emma that the new incumbent at Hinton St. Anne had been only too happy that she should continue to reside at the Rectory. Very conscious of the awkwardness of her position, Emma had assisted Mrs Ludworth with the care of her numerous offspring and had felt herself to be an object of pity.

Richard had not even troubled himself to be at Gresham House to welcome her when she had arrived and she seldom saw him. She had been profoundly shocked to discover how much he had changed since she had last seen him and not even the utmost exertions of his tailor could conceal the growing stoutness of his figure. He had been perfectly polite, but there had been a cold look in his pale blue eyes, and something in his manner towards her that had made her wish to avoid his company as much as possible.

Thinking now of his thoughtfulness in promoting her debut in society and the pleasure that it seemed to afford him, Emma wondered hopefully whether she had misjudged him. Perhaps the evening's events would usher in a new relationship between them. Ever optimistic, she began to visualise the prospect of a new and less monotonous existence.

Later that morning Mrs Steadman was summoned to the book-room. Although the running of Richard's household had been in her care for the past eight years or more, there was little of the house-keeper in her appearance: a fashionable lace cap, tied with ribbons under her chin, was set upon her black curls and only the bunch of keys dangling at the waist of her striped silk dress proclaimed her office. When Richard had first met her she had been a dashing widow, existing on the fringes of society and not overnice in her notions of propriety. Their relation-ship had been intimate, if not, perhaps, cousinly and although a succession of younger members of her sisterhood had succeeded her in Richard's favour, she had continued to live there, part house-keeper, part confidante and ever ready to assist him in any of his amorous adventures.

Richard looked up as she entered the room and said with a grin, "Come and sit down, Bella. I need you to help me."

She sat down opposite him and, folding her hands on her lap, shot him a shrewd glance from her round, dark eyes and said knowingly, "Who's the beauty this time?"

He laughed, looking a trifle sheepish, and said, "Nothing like that, my dear! I want you to do something for me but, fact of the matter is, I don't intend to tell you my reasons – the less you know the better!"

She nodded, "You know your business best, Richard!"

He fidgeted with his quizzing-glass before he spoke again, then, avoiding her eyes, said awkwardly, "This evening I want you to lend m'sister one of your most revealing dresses – one that will display her figure to best advantage." He looked up and saw her amazement and gave a coarse laugh, adding, "Not to put too fine a point on it, she is to be made to look like a charming little barque of frailty! You know – none better – how to accomplish it: help her dress, paint her face – whatever tricks you women get up to! Use your best endeavours, Bella, my dear!"

"Good God, have you run mad!" She stared at him as if he had taken leave of his senses. "Where in the world are you taking her, and what in Heaven's name are you about?"

"All these questions, my dear! Matter of fact, *I'm* not taking her anywhere, but Emma understands that she is to accompany me to a rout-party tonight at my aunt's house. That's all you need to know!"

"Dressed in that fashion? My dear Richard, surely even she would be sensible that such an appearance would be quite improper? Impossible to believe that she would consent!"

"Come, use your wits, Bella! She's quite ignorant of the world! Contrive that she does not see herself clearly in a looking-glass – make her think your gown is quite in the latest mode."

Mrs Steadman looked at him thoughtfully, then she gave a malicious chuckle, "If you're not the most complete hand I ever knew!" She stood up, "I'll do it! I've no love for your sister. Sets me all on edge with her polite, finicky ways. After all, it's no concern of mine what Canterbury tales you tell her!"

"I knew I could count on you, my dear!" There was an air of suppressed excitement about Richard. "She's to be dressed by eleven this evening, mind, and to wait for me in the drawing-room. You must bear her company until I come to fetch her." He kissed her roughly on the cheek, saying exultantly, "By God, Bella, if my plan succeeds we shall come about famously – you'll see!"

It was approaching midnight when play stopped for the moment. Six men sat around Sir Richard's table. The atmosphere was heavy with tobacco smoke and the candles had burned down almost to their sockets and shed only a fitful light on the baize-covered table, on the dice and wineglasses. That there had been heavy drinking was evident in their flushed faces and raised voices.

Only the Earl of Ware, sprawled in an armchair with his long legs stretched out before him, showed no obvious sign of having drunk deep, though anyone intimately acquainted with his lordship would have recognised from the reckless gleam in his hard grey eyes that my lord had been imbibing freely. A pile of guineas and notes of hand lay in front of him upon the table but seemed to afford him little if any satisfaction.

He had arrived at Richard's house that evening in a black mood. Summoned earlier in the day to his uncle's residence in Mount Street, he had been obliged to endure, grim-faced, Lord Rupert Vane's animadversions on his character and mode of life.

"Good God, Robert, I never thought to hear one of our family described to me as a libertine!" Lord Rupert's voice had been full of indignation. "I say nothing to a few discreet affairs ...."

"Indeed, I should say not, sir!" His disrespectful nephew had interjected, a smile for an instance lightening his expression as he had recollected a certain charming little lady living in a house in St. John's Wood where Lord Rupert was a frequent visitor.

His interruption had been waved aside with a wave of a plump white hand; in full flow, Lord Rupert had continued, "You positively flaunt your mistresses in the face of society! It will not do, sir! You owe something to your name. You are nearly thirty and it is more than time that you settled down and married and ensured the succession. Do you intend that that miserable second cousin of yours should succeed to the title?"

"You have scarcely set me a good example, sir, by remaining a bachelor!" Ware had objected.

"That is neither here nor there. I have no patience with you! I tell you to your face, it is your duty to marry, sir!"

Looking back later on the interview, Lord Rupert had had to admit to himself that nothing in his nephew's words or attitude could have encouraged him to feel that the least heed would be paid to his strongly worded advice.

If his uncle's strictures had had any effect on Ware there was certainly no evidence of it that evening, unless a furious determination to follow his own inclinations and appetites could be counted as a result.

Seated on his left, Horace Brownlow, a sharp-featured young man dressed in the extreme of fashion, was scrawling his signature with a careless flourish to a note of hand to be added to the pile that lay before Ware, saying indignantly as he wrote, "Confound you, Robert, you have the devil's own luck!"

"And not only the devil's own luck at play!" added an older man who was slumped in his chair opposite. He turned his blood-shot eyes towards his host, a sly grin on his florid face as he said, "Damme man, it's only a month or so ago that Ware stole that charming little ladybird away from *you*, Richard, just as she was about to succumb to your advances! Ain't that so, my lord?"

Ware, taking snuff from an elegant gold and enamel box, looked up at Sir James Kent and said cynically, "The face of an angel and the temper of a fiend! She enacted me too many scenes, my dear Kent, so, alas, I fear it had to end." He glanced around the table with raised brows, "Do we continue to play, gentlemen?"

Sir Richard, his normally pale face flushed with wine, poured himself another glass of brandy with a hand that trembled. He rose ponderously to his feet, took the dice-box in his hand and announced truculently, "It ain't a usual wager – that I'm bound to say – but I'm finished – done up!" He looked around at the faces turned towards him, then continued in a lowered voice with more than a hint of lewdness in his manner, "I've a new beauty in keeping now, living here at this very moment and a deucedly compliant female into the bargain, thank God!" he paused, then said with a coarse laugh, "I'll be damned if I don't stake *her*! What say you, gentlemen?"

In the stunned silence that followed this announcement, he looked challengingly across the table at Ware and demanded, with a sneer, "Will you cover that stake, my lord?"

There was a startled exclamation from Horace Brownlow, "Dash it all, man, can't wager a female! Ain't the thing at all!"

Meanwhile an unpleasant smile had appeared on Sir James Kent's face as he looked from Richard to Ware and back again, saying nothing, but clearly enjoying the situation.

Next to Richard, the Honourable Mathew Tilgate, who had been gazing owlishly before him, his head supported on his hands, turned to Richard and spoke with the simplicity of one deep in his cups, "By Jupiter, you're m'mad, Harding! Or d-devilish castaway!"

On Ware's right, a slim young man, the perfection of whose intricately tied neck-cloth proclaimed a Pink of the Ton, said urgently, consternation written upon his youthful countenance, "For God's sake, Cousin, don't be a fool! Dammit, man, you haven't even set eyes on the girl!"

Ware looked around the circle of faces and a faint smile lightened the look of devilment in his eyes. He leaned forward and pushed the pile of coins and crumpled notes into the centre of the table with a careless gesture, saying in a seemingly bored voice, "I believe I must satisfy my curiosity, Edward. I'll cover your bet, Richard – for that reason if for no other!"

"Good God, there's m'more than ten thousand pounds there! You're both mad!" Horace Brownlow struggled up from his chair and stood clutching at its back to support himself, swaying slightly, adding with surprising clarity, "Jove, what famous sport though – wouldn't have missed it for the world! Call a main, Richard! Call a main!"

Sir Richard's eyes had narrowed greedily. He cast the dice. Brownlow called out, "A three and a six! Nine's the main!" Richard cast again and said, "I take seven!" He picked up the dice-box and shook for the third time. As the dice tumbled onto the table everyone pressed forward eagerly except his lordship who remained leaning back in his chair.

There was a moment of tense silence; someone drew in his breath sharply…. the five and the four lay uppermost upon the table!

In the babble of voices that followed, Edward Wyndham cried out, "My God, you win again, Robert!"

Richard was looking at Ware, a curious expression on his face. He said slowly, "I should have known better than to try and break your luck!"

17

Ware drained his glass and there was a wicked gleam in his eyes as he stood up. "A most delightful evening's play, Richard." A cynical smile curved his mouth. "And a decidedly unexpected but charming ending! I believe I should leave at once – anything else would be in the nature of an anti-climax, don't you think? Would you be so obliging as to present to me this charmer whom I have just won, so that she and I can depart at once?"

"Have you no fear, my lord, that this female may show herself to be unwilling?" Sir James Kent's flushed face seemed to express pleasure at the thought.

Mathew Tilgate answered him, struggling to focus his eyes on the company. "She wouldn't go with you, K-Kent, too ugly!" he pronounced, "Wouldn't go with Horace, no m-money! Wouldn't go with m-me, too drunk! But she'll go with Ware, d-devilish handsome fellow and rich enough to buy an abbey!" He nodded his head wisely, content at his own sagacity.

Richard went to the door. He seemed to have no difficulty in concealing any chagrin that he might have been expected to have felt, merely saying briefly, "Very well, I will order your carriage, Robert, and tell Miss Stanton to be ready to prepare to leave immediately."

To Emma, seated in the shabby drawing-room with Mrs Steadman, her feelings fluctuating between excitement and apprehension, the sound of Richard's footsteps came as a welcome end to what had seemed to be an interminable wait.

It had been several hours earlier that Mrs Steadman had helped her to dress. Conducted to that lady's own apartment, her hair had been curled and caught up into a loose knot at the back of her head from which several light ringlets fell onto her bare shoulders in the Roman style. The dress that Mrs Steadman had finally selected was one which she had worn several years earlier, when her figure had been slighter and more closely resembling Emma's slim form. It had the added advantage, to fulfil Richard's requirements, of dating from a time when it was fashionable to expose the shape of the body. The white gauze of which it was composed was semi-transparent and clung revealingly to Emma's figure; while the neckline of the high-waisted bodice was cut amazingly low and wide.

There had been only a few candles lit in Mrs Steadman's bed-chamber and it had contained no long looking-glass. Emma was only able to see her head and shoulders in the dim light. She had expressed grave doubts about the immodest neckline but Mrs Steadman had laughed her to scorn, mendaciously assuring her that such a dress was quite in the latest fashion and that her appearance was both elegant and proper.

"You look delightful, my dear – quite '*comme il faut*' if you'll pardon my French! But you've not a mite of colour in your cheeks. That'll be the excitement I'll be bound ...." and before Emma could have had had time to remonstrate if she had so desired, she had swiftly applied a quantity of rouge to her cheeks.

When Richard entered the drawing-room and saw her, a faint smile of satisfaction touched his lips. Before him stood no longer the innocent-looking, dowdily dressed seventeen-year-old he had last seen, but a highly-coloured, attractive young woman whose openly displayed charms fitted her to be the *chère-amie* of the most exacting lover.

"You look charmingly, my dear Emma," he said admiringly, managing by a supreme effort to conceal his semi-inebriated condition, "I regret profoundly that you have had to wait so long – however, we shall leave immediately."

He picked up her cloak and, as he put it around her shoulders, added casually, "You will be travelling in the Earl of Ware's carriage. We will meet at his house in Grosvenor Square before we proceed together to my aunt's rout-party." He saw her astonishment and continued, with a rueful smile, "That way you will be more comfortable, for I fear that more than one of my guests are badly foxed and I must see that they reach their homes safely! Lord Ware is a most sober and respectable married man – I have no fear in entrusting you to him for the journey."

As he spoke, he caught Mrs Steadman's eye, saw the incredulous expression on her face and gave her a triumphant smile. He seemed not to feel the least compunction in carrying forward his design and wore an air of suppressed excitement, like a gambler, who having staked his all, awaits the turn of a card or the fall of the dice.

Emma could not, indeed, feel easy at the notion of travelling alone to London with a complete stranger, and a member of the male sex at that. She thought it decidedly odd but entertained no doubts but that Richard had her best interests at heart; she was in any case rather more apprehensive at the thought of appearing for the first time in Polite Society and wished for the thousandth time since that morning that she might have had some female relation to bear her company.

She followed Richard into the hall and saw, in the dim light, a very tall man in a long, many-caped coat, with his hat and gloves in his hand, standing by the book-room door. As she approached with Richard, she could see other men within the open doorway; one looked out and saw her and other faces appeared, she heard low voices and a coarse laugh rang out.

A little in awe of this tall stranger, Emma curtsied shyly as Richard presented the Earl of Ware to her and, looking up, found a pair of hard grey eyes regarding her. There was something in his gaze which made her feel oddly uncomfortable; but when he asked, "Miss Stanton, are you willing to come with me?" she replied simply, "Yes, my lord!" in her soft clear voice.

He stared at her for a moment from under frowning brows and then, with what seemed to Emma a scornful smile, offered her his arm and led her out to the waiting carriage.

The chaise and four was at the door with the postillions already mounted, a gleaming equipage with a crest upon the door. The Earl handed Emma up into the carriage, then mounting up himself, sat down beside her and the door was closed.

She experienced a momentary sensation of disquiet; she had never before been alone in such close quarters with a man and a stranger at that. In almost complete darkness, in the confined space of the chaise, he seemed larger and taller than ever. She sat well back in her corner and drew her cloak closely around her.

Ware, after one glance at her, settled himself comfortably against the soft back cushions, stretching his long legs before him as far as was possible, and said sardonically, "We shall have plenty of time in due course to become better acquainted, Miss Stanton. I therefore suggest that we strive to get what sleep we can now." and promptly closed his eyes.

It was certainly not a very courteous remark but to Emma it was a relief not to be obliged to make polite conversation. The journey had suddenly presented itself to her in an alarming light. After surreptitiously regarding her companion's face in the pale moonlight – he was without doubt a startlingly handsome man – she gazed out of the window at the dark countryside passing by and hoped that, in spite of her present misgivings, the evening would prove to be the beginning of a happier future.

CHAPTER 2

She must have fallen asleep and awoke with a start as the chaise stopped; outside were many lights and the sound of voices.

A footman opened the chaise door and let down the step and the Earl descended, then, holding up his hand, assisted Emma to alight. She saw wide steps leading up to immense double doors; flambeaux were burning at either side and light streamed out from the house into the street.

They entered a vast hall with a staircase rising from it to the dimly lit floor above; many candles were burning in their sconces, their points of light reflected in the tall pier glasses. Emma looked around her with astonishment; with its marble floor and painted ceiling, the hall was grander than anything she had ever seen before.

Having been directed by his lordship to conduct Miss Stanton to the library, one of the tall stiff-backed footmen ushered Emma into a large room where a fire burned brightly at its farther end. The walls were lined from floor to ceiling with leather-bound books and over the mantel-shelf was a magnificent oil-painting of a chestnut mare and two foals standing beneath a tree.

Emma laid aside her cloak and gazed around her with interest. She had been familiar with her father's much-used book-room with its modest contents, and recognising that the owner of this vast collection must be a man of considerable learning, she found her opinion of his lordship rising imperceptibly.

She was admiring the painting and warming herself at the fire when she heard the door close and, turning, said with shining eyes, "What a remarkably beautiful picture, my lord!"

Ware's gaze, as he approached, was not fixed however upon this work of art, but upon the female figure standing before it – his first sight of the fruits of Mrs. Steadman's labours – for until this moment

Miss Stanton's person had been partially concealed by her cloak, an unremarkable garment. He raised his quizzing-glass and his appreciative eyes beheld a slight figure attired in a chemise dress of a thin, clinging, white material embellished with a quantity of gold braid. The neckline was cut low with a total disregard for propriety and showed a marked tendency to slip off Miss Stanton's shoulders; it was moreover perfectly apparent that her petticoat, if she was indeed wearing such an article of apparel, must have been one of the 'invisible' variety.

"Indeed a delightful picture!" There was a note of sarcasm in Ware's voice, and Emma, conscious of his eyes upon her, looking her up and down in an insultingly open fashion, felt the colour mount to her cheeks.

"May I pour you a glass of wine, Miss Stanton?" he continued and, without waiting for a reply, crossed the room to a side-table where a tray had been placed and poured out two glasses of champagne.

As he handed her the glass he asked curiously, "How long, Miss Stanton, have you been living in Richard's house?"

"Since early April, my lord, almost two months."

"And you did not cavil at coming with me tonight in spite of our being unacquainted?"

"Oh yes, my lord!" She tried to speak lightly, wishing that he did not stand so close, "But Richard assured me that I should be vastly more comfortable with you."

She took a sip from her glass and choked a little from the unexpected bubbles.

"Indeed!" He raised an eyebrow, his eyes fixed upon her face.

She added hastily, fearing that she had been guilty of impoliteness, "He said that you would take good care of me."

A cynical smile lifted the corners of Ware's mouth. Here was frankness indeed! This little game bird was clearly like all her sisters. He had been puzzled by a certain quality in Miss Stanton's voice, a lack of coquetry in her manner most unlike that of Richard's previous mistresses; but her words left him in no doubt that she was fully alive to the advantages of bestowing her favours upon so wealthy a protector. He was at the same time becoming increasingly aware of the seductive quality of those charms, so boldly displayed, and it was with a warm look and a glint in his eyes that he said softly, "I am sure we shall deal together extremely!"

He received no reply. Emma, afraid to look up, was wishing most fervently that her brother would soon arrive. Ever since his lordship had entered the room she had been horribly conscious that no-one possessing even the most vivid imagination could describe this tall reckless-looking man, with his hard, gleaming eyes and careless dress, as a *respectable* person.

It was at this moment that Ware tossed back the contents of his glass and, removing Emma's from her unresisting hand, placed them upon a nearby table. She felt her heart begin to beat wildly but before she could speak Ware said in a low voice, "By God, you're a damnably bewitching creature!" and as he stepped forward she found herself locked in a cruelly crushing embrace, his mouth came hard down upon hers, kissing her savagely, expertly, his hands moving over her body, touching her intimately, frighteningly and holding her so tightly against his person that she could scarcely breathe. For a moment Emma was too shocked and terrified to move, then panic seized her and she began to struggle desperately in his arms – striving to turn her face away, pushing against his chest with all her strength, in a state of terror.

Such unexpected resistance in one who could only be presumed to be, at the very least, acquiescent, took Ware by surprise and he at once loosened his embrace. As he did so, Emma took a hasty step backwards, her foot caught in the rug and she fell heavily, striking her head on the corner of the brass fender with such force that she lay motionless at his feet.

His lordship stood frowning down at her, his expression compounded more of vexation than alarm; then, picking her up in his arms, he laid her down upon a sofa near the fire and, taking a heavy silver candelabra from the mantelpiece, brought it to stand on the table by her head.

In the all-revealing light of the many candles she looked astonishingly young and fragile. Her closed eyelids with long, dark lashes, her smooth cheeks and gently curving mouth had the innocence of extreme youth; for now the patches of rouge on her deathly pale face gave her the appearance of a child who plays the part of a grown person and her immodest dress, in disarray, had slipped at one shoulder and revealed even more shockingly her youthful figure.

There was a grim look now on Ware's countenance, a growing anger in his eyes; but it was with gentle fingers that he re-arranged the flimsy material to cover her breast, then tenderly felt the side of her head where a large lump had formed, finding, to his relief, that the skin was scarcely broken. Crossing to the side-table, he moistened his handkerchief in a jug of water and coming again to her side, laid it on her forehead. As her eyelids began to flicker, he stepped back and stood leaning against the mantelshelf watching her intently. At last her eyes opened and she looked around her in a bemused way, puzzled at her unfamiliar surroundings.

As full consciousness returned, she turned her head, saw his lordship watching her, and, with an exclamation of fright, struggled to sit up. But the sudden movement made her senses swim, she became aware of a violent throbbing in her head and sank back against the cushions. Surely Richard must soon arrive and deliver her from this madman! His passionate embrace had shocked her profoundly. Her last recollection had been of falling; now, lying on the sofa, she became conscious with growing dismay that he alone must have laid her there.

Ware did not move from his position. He was frowning now as he looked down at her white, strained face and said grimly, "You must allow that I was not aware that Richard had chosen a mistress from the schoolroom!"

Emma gazed back at him blankly for a moment, seeking to make sense of his words, then, as full realisation of their meaning came to her, a faint colour rose to her cheeks, her eyes flashed as she replied furiously, "How dare you say such a thing, my lord! That is a monstrous suggestion! I – I am Richard's half-sister!"

Ware stared at her through narrowed eyes, "Impossible! Good God, if that were so, why should you willingly come away with me ....?"

She saw with alarm his growing anger. He said harshly, "If it be true, is this some trick that you and your brother have devised? Believe me, if it is – by God, you will live to regret it"

Emma was eyeing him warily now; the man must be either mad or drunk! In either case, how could Richard have entrusted her to such a person. She said stiffly, "I do not understand you, my lord. There is no trick!"

"If, then, you are Richard's sister," he demanded, "Why in God's name did you come with me tonight?"

"Did you not know? Because we are going to Lady Fraser's rout-party. Richard bade me travel in your carriage and will join me here." With horror she saw disbelief on Ware's face and added desperately, "Surely he must arrive soon!"

Now there was biting sarcasm in his voice, "My dear Miss Stanton, do you really expect me to believe that you had the intention of attending a rout-party in such a dress as the one that you are now wearing? I assure you I am not such a fool as to be taken in by that!"

She looked down doubtfully at her dress and said ingenuously, "Is it so very unsuitable? Mrs Steadman lent it to me and *she* said it was in the latest mode but there was so little light in the room that I was not able to see myself clearly."

"Annabel Steadman! That abbess!" He looked angrier every moment.

"I do not think Mrs Steadman has any religious connections." Emma faltered.

To her amazement this strange man stared at her for a moment, then actually laughed. When he spoke again it was in a softer tone but his words were uncompromisingly direct. "That dress is most shockingly improper, Miss Stanton! Not to put too fine a point upon it, you have been dressed as a whore!"

She blushed vividly, looking down at the offending garment, and stammered, "I d-don't understand .... s-so that is why ...." words failed her and she lay silent, staring at him with growing fright in her soft brown eyes.

"Miss Stanton, if you are indeed Richard's sister, you have been wickedly deceived! There is no rout-party – Richard has no intention of coming to this house! Tonight he staked, as his last wager at Hazard, 'the lady living under his protection' – I won the wager and you were that lady! And so I brought you here."

There was a long silence: the colour drained from Emma's face as she repeated in a horrified voice, "No rout-party! Richard staked me at play!" In a frightened whisper she added, "But why? Why should he do such a terrible thing?"

Ware raised an eyebrow and regarded her consideringly. "I think, Miss Stanton, it would be as well if you acquainted me with some facts about yourself and your family. You say that *you* cannot comprehend this deception, but *I* certainly am not able to do so. Have you no parents to protect you?"

She looked at him helplessly, then, in a low voice, she told him of her circumstances since her father's death and how she had come to live in Richard's house. In faltering tones she described the events of that day. It was only when she told of Richard's instructions to travel in the Earl's carriage that Ware interrupted her contemptuously.

"How came you to agree to such an improper arrangement? You seem to have some very odd notions of propriety!"

"Richard assured me that you were a sober and respectable married man." she retorted indignantly.

He gave a short laugh, then his brows drew together in a frown, considering her words.

"I am neither married nor respectable! Have you no notion of my reputation, Miss Stanton? Have you never heard of the 'wicked' Earl of Ware?"

She eyed him doubtfully. "I know nothing of Polite Society, my lord – your name was quite unknown to me."

Ware stared at her, conscious of a mounting exasperation and anger at the situation in which he found himself. "Good God!" he exclaimed impatiently, "How is it possible that you can be such a green girl? If you had not been so absurdly ignorant of the world none of this would have happened!"

Stung by his contempt, Emma blurted out fiercely, "If you had not accepted Richard's wicked wager, my lord, I should not be here! I may have been foolish and ignorant but your conduct was most shockingly improper!"

She saw the spark of anger in his eyes and shrank back against the cushions, but he only said in biting tones, "I believe we can dispense with your opinion of my actions, Miss Stanton! The fact of the matter is, Richard has made dupes of both of us! Why, God only knows! But he has clearly intended to bring about *your* ruin for, if the events of this night become known, your honour and reputation will be gone forever! You see, my dear Miss Stanton," he drawled, "not one person in the whole of London would believe that a personable young female could pass the night in my house and yet remain virtuous!"

"Lord Ware, I cannot stay *here*!" Somehow she contrived to keep her voice calm and to conceal her mounting panic; bewildered, ashamed and, above all else, afraid, Emma was determined that no hint of this should be made apparent to the tall, grim-faced man standing staring down at her. She had read, enthralled, some of the gothic novels from the circulating library, now the fashion, and admired their ruthless, dark-visaged heroes; to be in the power of such a one in real life was a very different matter.

Ware crossed the room, poured some brandy into a glass and brought it to her. She shook her head, eyeing him nervously, but he put the glass to her lips, saying roughly, "Don't be a little fool, this will make you feel better." Emma found herself forced to swallow a few mouthfuls and choked a little as she felt the fiery liquid burn her throat.

Ware drank off the rest of the glass and sat down opposite to her, staring into the fire, a black frown on his face. Emma, watching him with an uncertain expression in her eyes, lay still and felt an immense lassitude stealing over her.

His lordship, now bitterly regretting his part in the affair, saw a disagreeable series of events and decisions before him. One thing was certain, in her present condition this wretched girl could not travel further that night. Tomorrow he would have to come to some conclusion about her future and, he thought viciously, her half-brother must be brought to account for his actions!

He looked up and said brusquely, "You must go to bed at once and in the morning we will decide what had best be done – the blow to your head was severe and it is essential that you should now have rest and quiet." and, without waiting for any reply, he tugged the bell-pull by the fireplace and instructed the young footman, who appeared in answer to his summons, to send for his valet.

Emma, starting to protest, found herself ruthlessly interrupted.

"You have no alternative but to remain here tonight, Miss Stanton. If you have any notion where you could go at two o'clock in the morning, without causing the very stir I wish to avoid, I should be obliged if you would inform me of it!"

Struck forcibly by the truth of these words, Emma was silent and within a few minutes a discreet-looking, elderly man, with greying hair and a dour expression, entered the room.

"You called me, my lord?" Not by the flicker of an eyelid did Willis betray the least sign of surprise; by his impassive demeanour it would appear that the sight of a very young girl lying on a sofa and holding one of my lord's fine linen handkerchiefs to her forehead was quite a commonplace occurrence.

"Yes, Willis. Miss Stanton has had a slight accident and will be staying here tonight. I wish you to light a fire in one of the bed-chambers and then escort Miss Stanton to the room yourself and see that she has everything that she requires."

It passed rapidly through Willis' mind that this menial task was one more fitting for one of the innumerable housemaids sleeping soundly upstairs in the attics than for a gentleman's gentleman, but he merely bowed slightly, saying, "Certainly, my lord." and withdrew.

A silence followed his departure. Ware, conscious that his reluctant guest was eyeing him warily, picked up her cloak from the chair where she had laid it, saying sarcastically, "You may lock your door, Miss Stanton, but I assure you that whatever may be believed to the contrary, I am not in the habit of ravishing young ladies of your age and quality!"

He saw some of the tension go from her face. She put her feet to the ground and rose shakily, painfully aware now of the indecency of her dress, and turned for him to lay the cloak about her shoulders. As he did so, his gaze rested for a moment on the tumbled curls at the back of her head, several of which had escaped from the pins that held them and lay upon the curve of her slender neck and shoulders. There was something touchingly vulnerable in the sight but, whatever his lordship's thoughts may have been, his expression remained inscrutable. When Willis returned shortly afterwards, Ware gravely bade her goodnight and remained standing for some time by the fire gazing abstractedly before him.

Escorted up the grand staircase by the silent Willis, Emma found herself in the most sumptuous bedroom that she had ever beheld, where a newly lit fire was burning brightly. Acutely aware of the equivocal nature of her situation, she was unconsciously reassured by the elderly man-servant's polite demeanour. Most welcome of all was the sight of the huge bed, for by now her head was aching furiously.

Able to observe more closely his master's young guest, Willis had recognised at once, in spite of her dishevelled appearance, that Miss Stanton was not in the usual style of his lordship's amours. Twenty-five years with the Earl's family, of which ten had been spent as my lord's personal servant, had inured him to his master's dealings with the opposite sex; but that evening, as he helped to ease Ware out of his coat, his disapproval was obvious.

After Emma's departure from the library, Ware had sat drinking a glass of brandy and brooding morosely over the evening's events. A strong sense of ill-usage had grown within him. Far from gratifying his desires, he had found himself cast in the role of villain by one who was little more than a school-girl. The female that he had so light-heartedly won at Hazard promised to be more trouble to him than any temperamental mistress. It was therefore in a black mood, having finally ascended to his dressing-room, that he submitted to Willis' ministrations.

Ware was pulling off his neckcloth when he broke the silence that had existed since he had entered the room.

"It must be understood by my household that I returned *alone* from my engagement this evening." There was subdued anger in his voice as he lifted an interrogatory eyebrow at Willis. "Do I make myself clear?"

"Quite clear, my lord!"

"You will bring Miss Stanton her breakfast yourself in the morning."

"Yes, my lord."

Glancing in the looking-glass, Ware caught sight of his valet's compressed lips, his disapproval very evident, and enquired sarcastically, "What the devil are you wearing that damned Friday-face for? Have I shocked you at last?"

Wooden-faced, the reply came, "It's not in my place to make comments upon your lordship's actions."

Ware said savagely, "It may not be in your place but I've no doubt I shall hear your opinion sooner or later, so you may as well come out with it!"

Willis smoothed the creases from his lordship's coat and said repressively, "Miss Stanton seems to be a very *young* lady, my lord."

"By God, she certainly is!" Ware murmured under his breath.

His man-servant looked up from the garment in his hands and met my lord's eyes in the looking-glass, their hard stare challenging him to continue.

"Miss Stanton appeared very *frightened,* if I may say so, my lord." he added gently and turned away to place the coat upon a hanger.

"Damn your eyes, man, do you believe that I ravished the wretched girl?" Ware demanded wrathfully.

"No, my lord, – but your manner can be ...." he paused, then continued, "shall we say, a trifle 'overbearing' at times." As he knelt to remove his master's shoes and stockings, he added reflectively, with the familiarity of an old servant who has known his employer since he was a child, "I've never known you to tamper with young ladies of that quality afore – that's dangerous work, my lord!"

Goaded beyond endurance, Ware exclaimed, "You fool, had I had the least idea ....!" he broke off and gazed morosely into the looking-glass, scowling at his reflection and wishing Miss Stanton to the devil.

Willis shook his head gloomily and forbore further comment. A nice scandal-broth his lordship had in the making, he thought to himself, not that his lordship had hitherto shown any sign of caring overmuch for society's opinion of him.

It was quite late when Emma awoke the next morning. Outside she could hear the sound of carriage wheels and horses' hooves in the square and the cries of the street vendors calling out their wares. In the house, occasional soft footsteps were faintly audible passing outside her bedroom door as she lay, warm and comfortable behind the drawn curtains of the bed, listening drowsily, half-asleep.

Suddenly all the events of the previous night flooded back and an over-powering sense of shame swept over her. What a fool she had been to have believed Richard! Too late she saw that now. But having been brought up in a house where truth prevailed, she had never doubted Richard's words nor suspected him, nor anyone, of dishonourable intentions. She flushed angrily to think how she had allowed herself to appear as a woman of loose morals, who invited the kind of treatment she had received. What an idiot, or worse, his lordship must think her!

However, before she had had time to consider how she could extricate herself from a situation which filled her with alarm, she was startled by a gentle knock at her door. Her heart beating wildly she slipped out of bed, clutching her cloak around her and opened the door nervously to find Willis waiting outside.

Entering the room he laid the tray, bearing a jug of hot chocolate and a plate of bread-and-butter, on a table and opened the shutters, saying in a colourless voice, "A fine morning, Miss. 'Tis just striking ten on the clock."

Emma thanked him in a timid voice, which made him add in a fatherly manner, "Your luggage has arrived by carrier, Miss. I will bring it up to your room shortly."

Her eyes opened wide with surprise at this news, but she thanked him gravely, striving to preserve an air of normality.

"At any rate," she thought, when he had left the room, "At least I shall now be able to wear some respectable clothes." Beyond that, try as she might, she could not perceive what she must do, for without money, or a friend or even acquaintance in London, to whom could she turn?

Long before Emma woke, the Earl had risen that morning, casting his household into disorder by a demand for breakfast at an hour considerably earlier than was his custom.

He had been in the process of tying his starched, white muslin neckcloth, one of several that Willis had been holding in readiness, when the news of the carrier's arrival had been brought to him by a footman. Ware's frown had deepened as he regarded his reflection in the looking-glass. He thought savagely that the sooner he could rid himself of this wretched girl and all her belongings the better it would be for him. But how to accomplish it? He had remained silent and thoughtful as Willis helped him to complete his dressing. It had only been as he stood up, a dashing figure in biscuit-coloured pantaloons and glossy Hessians, for Willis to assist him into his coat, that his expression had lightened; clearly some solution had presented itself, for as soon as he had eaten a hearty breakfast in the little saloon, he had ordered his curricle to be brought round to the door and had left the house.

CHAPTER 3

Lady Sophia Ancaster, sister of the Earl of Ware, was still in her wrapper, her lady's-maid engaged in dressing her blonde curls, when a servant announced that his lordship had called and wished to see her.

She was eight years older than her brother and having married Sir Peter in her early twenties, was now the devoted mother of four hopeful children. A tall, good-looking girl at her come-out, she had allowed herself, through a natural indolence, to gain more weight than she cared for and ill-natured acquaintances might have been tempted to describe her appearance as matronly. Her chief concern was the health and happiness of her children and was the only subject known to disturb her habitual calm and legendary good-nature.

Her marriage had not been a love-match, but between man and wife there existed a great deal of respect and affection. Sir Peter was a kind husband and father, a man of sober views and a reputation for sound political judgment.

When Ware was shown up to her room she embraced him warmly, for although disapproving with disarming frankness of his way of life, she was an affectionate sister.

Having dismissed her maid, she turned to Ware, asking with a smile, "To what do I owe the honour of this early call, Robert? I understood that you seldom rose before midday unless you had some sporting engagement!"

"Well, I do have a favour to ask of you, Sophie," he admitted, "but first – tell me – are you and the children in good health? And Sir Peter? I have not seen you for an age."

"Oh, we go on very well. Peter is away in the country for a few days but he will be back soon. "Her face clouded over," Only – little Miles has the measles and I am worried lest the baby should catch it. The girls I am not concerned about, for they contracted it when they were younger."

She looked at him quizzically, her blue eyes full of mischief, "But tell me – I'm all agog! What is this favour that you would ask of me? I wish with all my heart it were to receive your future wife! You know it is more than high time that you were married and setting up your own nursery!"

He was frowning as he sat down near her and said dismissively, "Time enough for that!" Then his brow cleared and he turned to her with a rueful smile.

"I will tell you what I would ask of you, Sophie. It is an odd request!" He seemed to hesitate and then said, "I had an urgent and unexpected message this morning from my man of business, old Pettigrew, whom you know. It appears that our Rector at Millford had arranged for the orphan daughter of a fellow clergyman to take up a post as governess with a family called Seaton, living in Brook Street. The girl left Berkshire on the stage-coach this morning and Pettigrew was asked to arrange for her to be met in Holborn and conveyed to her future employers. He has, just now, discovered that the Seatons have had to leave town at a moment's notice owing to illness. He sent me a note this morning asking me if I thought, knowing your great kindness, you might take in this girl, a Miss Stanton, for a few days until other plans can be made." He saw her surprise and added, "He is a fussy old bachelor, set in his ways and is clearly greatly concerned as to how to resolve the matter. I am astonished that he asked *me*, but no doubt he was too diffident to ask you directly. What do you think, Sophie? Do you think you could manage it?"

She looked very surprised and amused. "Well, this *is* a new role for you, Robert! I would not have expected *you* to exert yourself person-ally on Mr Pettigrew's account. Nor that he should have applied to you! Especially as his protégée is a young girl – I should have thought that you were the last person on earth to approach for assistance in such a case! However …. I expect that I can contrive something."

She looked at him pensively, then said, "She can assist Miss Embery, our children's governess, while she is here and, if she has had the measles, she can help to entertain little Miles. He is sadly fretful."

"I was sure I could count on you, Sophie!" Ware rose and gave his sister a warm hug. "I must be off now, for I go to Millford this morning and must send a note round to Pettigrew to set his mind at rest before I leave. I will instruct him to send the girl here when she arrives – I hope she will be of use to you. She should certainly be grateful!"

Even such a hardened cynic as my Lord Ware felt a twinge of conscience as he left his sister's house and drove home. Nevertheless, he was certain that if he had told her the whole bizarre truth her loyalty to her husband would have prevented her, whatever her own inclinations might have been, from committing herself to an action of which Sir Peter would undoubtedly disapprove. He eased his conscience by reflecting that in a few days he would have settled the affair and Sophie would be none the wiser.

In spite of his appearance of calm, he was still raging inwardly, furious at having been tricked into his present situation. He could not, in honour, turn a girl of Miss Stanton's age and upbringing out into the streets and now found himself her sole protector, her entire future dependent upon him. Unaccustomed to considering others apart from a few intimate friends, he felt a profound sense of injustice. Already, in order to preserve her reputation, he had been obliged to mount various subterfuges. For one moment he had been tempted to return Miss Stanton forthwith to her brother's house, but a man who could put his innocent sister into the hands of a known rake was not fit to be her guardian. He thought wryly, he could scarcely be considered a fit person himself to fulfil that role.

Returning home in a grim mood, he determined to call upon Richard Harding as soon as he had spoken to Miss Stanton.

It was a very different looking Miss Stanton who came down to the library at Ware's request. She wore a sombre, grey dress with a high neckline and long sleeves, shabby and old-fashioned, her hair plainly dressed, and looked pale and nervous. She was clearly ill at ease in his presence, for there was too much in her surroundings, reminding her of the previous night's events, to make her comfortable.

"Good God!" Amazed at the transformation in his unwilling guest, there was amusement in Ware's voice. Could this dowdy little school-girl really be one and the same as the seductively dressed female of last night!

Emma, her colour heightened, felt indignation rising within her. How hateful of this man to remind her of how she had looked when he had last seen her. She clasped her hands tightly together and regarded him fiercely.

"You look exceedingly, one might say *excessively* respectable this morning, Miss Stanton!"

His tone was sardonic but Emma saw the laughter in his eyes. She looked down at her dress and suddenly the humour of the situation overcame her, she tried to keep a straight face then gave a little chuckle, quickly suppressed, "It is certainly a dress of awe-inspiring dowdiness, my lord!"

Unconsciously impressed by her spirit, Ware said, "Pray sit down, Miss Stanton." and had the forethought to indicate a chair far removed from the sofa where she had lain the previous night.

He went to stand before the window and, after a short pause, said in a matter-of-fact way, "It is quite unthinkable that you should return to your half-brother's house after what has passed, since he has betrayed your trust in him." He glanced at her face and saw that she was following his words with anxious attention. "I have therefore made some temporary plans for you."

In a few short sentences he told her of the arrangements he had made and of the story that he had been obliged to fabricate in order to conceal her presence in his house and the events that had led up to it.

"You will have to remember the details of the story and abide by it absolutely. Your own personal history before you came to Richard's house need not be concealed and you will be known as Miss Stanton." He added reassuringly, "In a few days time I hope to be able to contrive, with my sister's help, some more permanent arrangement for you that will be to your liking."

She said quietly, "Yes, my lord." and sat silent a moment, looking down at her hands clasped on her lap. When she looked up and spoke again it was with a dignity strangely at odds with her youthful appearance.

"Lord Ware, I sincerely regret that my ignorance of the world and my brother's incomprehensible behaviour have involved you in my affairs. I hope and trust that I can soon establish my independence."

37

she paused, then continued awkwardly, "But I must always remain grateful to you for your kindness and consideration."

He was watching her face, surprised at this formal little speech but when, in a burst of youthful candour, she stammered, "And for n-not taking advantage of my s-situation!" he laughed harshly.

"My 'kindness' and my 'forbearance', Miss Stanton! That is indeed over-stepping the mark. You owe me no gratitude – I would expect your dislike rather than that."

There was an uncomfortable silence, then Ware said grimly, "I shall call upon Richard this morning and make quite certain that he does not dare to breathe one word of the events of last night. After that I am going out of town for a few days to my place in the country." He left the window and came towards Emma, saying, "Willis will arrange for a hackney carriage to take you to my sister's house. You will be quite safe there."

He stood a moment staring down at her, his eyes searching her face; she felt her heart beat a little faster but managed to return his gaze gravely, then rose, gave a little formal curtsy and left the room.

The next two days were the happiest that Emma had spent for a long time.

She was received most kindly by Lady Sophia, who, after a few sympathetic words about her unfortunate plight, conducted her to the school-room. There the governess was endeavouring to instil some knowledge of history into the unwilling heads of Miss Serena Ancaster, aged twelve and her sister, Mary, a stout little girl of ten. She was introduced to that stern disciplinarian, Miss Embury, who took her hand in a firm clasp and said in a gruff voice that she was happy to make Emma's acquaintance.

Miss Embury, despite her stiff manner, was much loved by her pupils. She soon made Emma feel quite at her ease and the girls were delighted to have a new companion; almost at once they were treating her rather as an elder sister and, when it was found that Emma had had measles, she was permitted to make the acquaintance of Master Miles. This young gentleman was making a good recovery but was still obliged to keep to his bed; a state of affairs considered extremely irksome by Miles whose preferred activities were normally of a energetic and boisterous nature.

Her time was pleasantly occupied in reading to the little invalid such old favourites as 'The Comic Adventures of old Mother Hubbard and her Dog' and other like rhymes and tales and telling him stories of her own childhood as well as accompanying the girls on walks in the Park or assisting them with their needlework. Nurse and the baby were confined to the nursery department for fear of infection, but the former, a stout, kindly body, looked with favour upon the new arrival, who seemed to have such a calming effect upon the young boy when he was cross and peevish.

Lady Sophia, coming upon Emma and Serena sitting side by side on the sofa in the school-room, their heads close together, poring over the pages of 'The Ladies Monthly Museum', was moved to say, "I'm sure I don't wish further misfortune to fall upon the Seaton family, but I can't help thinking how agreeable it would be if your visit to us could be prolonged, Miss Stanton!"

Emma, guiltily aware of her false position, flushed and thanked her ladyship in a subdued voice.

On the Wednesday evening Sir Peter Ancaster returned home from his country seat. He soon paid a visit to the school-room where Miss Stanton was introduced to him and made upon him a favourable impression. He raised his eyebrows when he learnt from Lady Sophia how her introduction to the household had come about, saying caustically, "You astonish me, my love, I should have thought that Robert was too deucedly selfish to exert himself in that fashion!"

It was on the following evening that Emma's happiness came to a shattering conclusion.

Sir Peter had paid a visit after dinner to White's club and there had found that the sole topic of conversation was the latest scandal caused by his brother-in-law, the Earl of Ware. The tale went that Ware had seduced Sir Richard Harding's half sister, his ward, a Miss Emma Stanton; that the girl, lost to shame although the daughter of a clergyman, had willingly left her half-brother's house at night and accompanied the Earl to his house in Grosvenor Square, where she was now living. It was reported that the information came from Sir

39

Richard himself and had been confirmed by Sir James Kent, who had been at Sir Richard's house when these disgraceful events had taken place. Polite Society, which had grown used to Ware's affairs and his succession of mistresses, was saying that he had gone too far this time; as for the girl, she was spoken of with the utmost contempt.

Sir Peter, hearing this tale on all sides, listening tight-lipped to the prurient speculation it had aroused, was in no doubt that this Miss Stanton, whose name was being bandied about so freely, was none other than the latest addition to his household. His fury grew with every second. How dare his brother-in-law have the effrontery to install his mistress in Sir Peter's house, to say nothing of his having concocted a plausible and totally untrue story in order to gull Lady Sophia and gain her assent to this scandalous arrangement! To what end Ware had done this defied imagination.

Sir Peter did not linger long. He returned home at once, determined that this degraded creature should not stay another moment under his roof.

When he burst into the drawing-room Lady Sophia was taken aback by the sight of her normally staid husband. His face suffused with rage, he paced up and down the room, recounting to her in a furious voice all that he had just heard.

At first completely bewildered, she had listened with rising amazement and indignation.

"Good God, Sir Peter, that girl is a very monster of duplicity! There is no understanding it at all. And that such an abandoned creature should be the close companion of our girls!" she shuddered, "I never would have believed that Robert would trick me in such a fashion!"

When Emma, summoned from the school-room, entered the drawing-room she could see at once that something was dreadfully amiss and her heart sank.

Sir Peter was standing by his wife's chair with a face as black as thunder, while her ladyship, sitting up very straight, looked at Emma with horrified disgust. It was Sir Peter who spoke in a voice of ice.

"Are you Sir Richard Harding's half-sister, Miss Stanton?"

Her low reply of "Yes, sir." was barely audible.

"Did you willingly accompany the Earl of Ware to his house and stay with him there?"

By now Emma was as white as a sheet. She faltered, "Yes, sir, but...."

She was interrupted before she could finish. Sir Peter made no attempt to conceal his anger, "Be silent, Miss Stanton! I have no wish for my wife's ears to be sullied by any further revelations! You have wickedly betrayed her kindness to you by coming here under false pretences and I will not tolerate your presence here another hour! You will pack your belongings at once and I will have you conveyed back to Lord Ware's house tonight!"

Seeing the horrified expression on Emma's face and how she trembled, her ladyship at last spoke, "I think in Christian charity she should delay leaving until tomorrow morning, Sir Peter. She can keep to her room tonight and her supper be brought to her." To Emma, she said with an hauteur and a severity so cruelly different to her former kindly manner, "I had thought so well of you, Miss Stanton! It makes me shudder to think of my dear innocent little daughters in the company of one who has sunk so low in depravity! May God forgive you, for I fear I cannot!"

Emma found herself unable to speak. She hardly knew how she left the room. Stricken with despair, she went to her bed-chamber and, as soon as the door was closed, sank down on a chair and gazed blindly before her.

An hour later, Miss Embery, missing Emma from her usual place in the school-room, came and knocked gently on her door and went in. She found Emma, pale and distracted, trying to collect together her few possessions and cram them into a valise.

"Heavens, child, what has occurred? Have you had bad news?"

The tragic expression in the girl's eyes, as she looked up at her, filled Miss Embery with dismay. Emma said slowly, "When I tell you what has happened to me, you will not believe me! No-one will ever believe me! Indeed, it would be better if I were dead!"

Miss Embery, putting an arm around her shoulders, gently guided her to sit down beside her on the bed and said in a bracing voice, "Dear child, it is wicked to speak so! Come now, much better to tell me what is troubling you. Then we shall see whether I believe you or not!"

41

It was difficult for Miss Embery to follow the distraught girl's story, for Emma was too upset to explain matters clearly. Twisting her handkerchief between nervous fingers, she stumbled through an account of Richard's treachery: coming to Lord Ware's part in the affair, her confusion and embarrassment were painfully evident.

Miss Embery was profoundly shocked. She had, however, no difficulty in believing Emma's story for her opinion of men was not high. Two things had rapidly become plain to her: one, that Emma was as innocent as on the day she was born, the other, that she must on no account be allowed to return to Lord Ware's protection. Even Miss Embery knew of his lordship's reputation. If he had been so unlike himself as to respect her innocence once, he was not likely to do so again in Miss Embery's opinion.

She said grimly, "My poor child, what contemptible creatures men are! To make an innocent girl the subject of a wager and such a wager! How infamous!"

In a low voice, as if honesty compelled her, Emma faltered, "Richard's conduct was indeed indefensible, but Lord Ware, one must allow, behaved honourably when he discovered who I was." She hesitated, then said with a shiver, "Nevertheless, Miss Embery, I must confess that I am afraid of him! Whatever happens, I am determined not to return there!"

Miss Embery's mouth tightened," Have you no acquaintances in London to whom you might go, Miss Stanton?"

Emma shook her head, "I know not one person in London." She added wistfully, "If only I could go back to Hinton St. Anne where I was brought up, surely someone there would take pity on me.... but I have no means to get there .... if I were able to sell my mother's pearls .... but there is no time!"

Miss Embery sat silent, frowning; then, after a moment, her brow cleared. She said resolutely, "Tomorrow morning, you must leave the house early, before anyone is stirring. I have some money saved from my wages – it is, alas, only a few guineas – but I will willingly lend it to you. With that you will be able to buy yourself a ticket on the Accommodation coach for Bath. I know that it leaves the 'Angel', by St. Clements in the Strand, then you can alight at the Marlborough stage

and from there you would not have far to travel to Hinton St. Anne."
She looked at Emma with satisfaction, "No-one will know where you
have gone and I shall disclaim all knowledge of your whereabouts!"

Overcome at such kindness and the excellence of the plan, Emma's
expression changed to one of delight. "Oh, Miss Embery! How can I
ever thank you sufficiently!" With unaffected gratitude she hugged that
stern preceptress of the young; then, taking a string of pearls from the
open valise, she pressed them into Miss Embery's unwilling hand,
saying earnestly, "You must keep these until I can repay you."

Miss Embery, her thin features a little flushed, found herself obliged
to blow her nose vigorously and apply her handkerchief to her eyes,
murmuring as she did so, "Dear child! *Quite* unnecessary! Only too
happy to help you!" however upon Emma's insistence, she was forced
to comply, and added reluctantly, "Very well, dear child – I will take the
greatest care of them until I receive your instructions."

Miss Embery's plan having been decided upon, Emma packed a few
necessities into a band-box and went to bed with a lighter heart.

She slept fitfully, afraid that she might not wake on time, but it was
well before six o'clock in the morning that she was up and dressed and
ready to leave and having embraced Miss Embery most fervently and
thanked her a thousand times for her kindness, she slipped out of the
house unobserved and made her way through the streets to the Strand,
clutching her cloak around her.

CHAPTER 4

Seated at his breakfast table that same morning, the Earl of Ware, having returned late the previous night from Wiltshire, was surprised to receive a letter delivered by hand in his sister's hand-writing. With growing uneasiness he broke the seal and read -

"Dear Robert, Sir Peter discovered at White's yesterday evening the shameful deception that you have played upon me concerning Miss Stanton. I would not have believed that you could be so lost to all sense of propriety as to foist your discarded paramour onto your own sister's family. As for her behaviour, no words can describe the disgust that I feel for her conduct, particularly as I had treated her with great kindness and even affection.

Sir Peter wished her to leave the house last night but I felt the hour was too late and it would only cause the kind of talk in our household which we wish to avoid – though, God knows, the servants will doubtless learn of it soon enough, for no scandal ever escapes them. This shockingly double-faced creature will be conveyed to your house this morning.

It will be a long time before I can bring myself to forgive you!"

The letter was signed, *"your horrified sister, Sophia."* and had clearly been written in great haste and agitation.

Ware's face grew grim as he read. When he had finished, he sat for a moment, scowling down at the scrawled lines, lost in thought; then, crushing the letter in his hand, he rose from the table and ordered his carriage to be brought round immediately.

At Sir Peter's house the news of Miss Stanton's disappearance had spread throughout the household and rumour was rife in the servant's hall. Her ladyship's maid, Trotter, gave as her considered opinion that there were sinister doings afoot and added, with a sniff and a toss of her well-groomed head, that she'd never trusted that Miss Stanton with her meek, encroaching ways," Fair got round her ladyship, she did – and my lady thinking the world of her!"

But the butler declared with authority that Miss Stanton was a true lady and a nice little thing besides and that *he* wouldn't like any misfortune to happen to her. He had hoped, therefore, that there was no connection between her disappearance and the sudden arrival of the Earl of Ware at a little after ten o'clock. My lord, thrusting his hat and gloves into Harper's hands and learning that her ladyship was not yet down, had mounted the stairs without waiting to be announced, a forbidding expression upon his face.

He found Lady Sophia sitting up in bed, a becoming night-cap tied with strings under her chin, listlessly opening the letters and invitations spread out before her. She was both worried and upset, for when the news had been brought to her by Trotter that Miss Stanton was not in her bedroom, nor could be found anywhere in the house, she had had an uncomfortable feeling that she had acted wrongly and that she should have insisted on being allowed to hear what Miss Stanton had to say in her own defence.

When Ware strode into her bedroom, instead of upbraiding him for his disgraceful conduct, she burst out at him, "Oh, Robert, she's gone without a word or a note – and no-one knows where!"

Ware stared at her, a growing anger in his face, "What the devil do you mean, Sophie?"

"She must have slipped out of the house this morning before the servants were up! She has left her valise." She looked at him hopefully, "Perhaps she has friends in London ...." Her voice died away as she saw his expression. "Good God, Robert, surely she cannot be so afraid of you that she runs away rather than return to your house?"

Ware gave a short laugh, "Would you not be afraid, Sophie, if you were young and innocent and had found yourself alone with me, at night, in my house?"

She shuddered and looked horrified. He said sarcastically, "Never fear! I have no inclination for forcing myself upon unwilling girls scarce out of the school-room! You have a very unflattering opinion of my character, I must say, sister!"

45

"But how came an innocent girl to consent to be in your house? So improper! Even at her age she must be aware that such conduct is indefensible!" There was bewilderment in Lady Sophia's voice.

Ware replied grimly, "Miss Stanton believed me to be a respectably married man!"

"Good God!" His sister stared at him.

"You may well exclaim!"

He continued, after a moment's hesitation, "I should have told you the truth from the beginning but I had hoped, in order to preserve her reputation, that no-one need know of her presence in my house that night; I wanted to place her under your protection. You see her half-brother, Richard Harding, has vilely plotted to ruin her, and I fear he has succeeded!"

He turned away from her and crossed to the window where he stood looking out. There was a moment of silence.

Lady Sophia said crossly, "I cannot conceive why you saw fit to conceal the truth from me! Such a fine Banbury story you told me! Be careful you, yourself, are not taken in!"

"You would not have received Miss Stanton," he retorted, "without Peter's approval and that I am confident he would not have given."

She said ruefully, "You are right – he would not have consented. But I cannot, for the life of me, understand how she came to be at your house!" She added thoughtfully, "It seems to me that you are well rid of her."

Ware turned back to her and she was surprised to see the look of anxiety in his eyes. He said abruptly, "She must be found at once! She has no acquaintance in London and no money. This is not the time for explanations! Think, Sophie! Who in your household might have befriended her?"

"I thought that Miss Embery, the governess, might have known where she had gone, but she says that she knows nothing."

"I should like to question her myself if I may – I believe I could persuade her to tell me if she has helped Miss Stanton." He spoke with impatience.

Lady Sophia felt a sense of mis-giving steal over her; she said doubt-fully, "Are you wise to pursue the matter yourself? Surely it can only harm Miss Stanton if *you* institute enquiries for her yourself! Whatever your intentions may be ...."

She was rudely interrupted, "Good God, Do you expect me to abandon her? Let us waste no more time! Send for this governess so that I can speak to her myself!"

Miss Embery, summoned to my lady's boudoir, where she found the tall, forbidding figure of Lord Ware awaiting her alone, at first resolutely denied all knowledge of Emma's departure. However when, in a few terse words, his lordship informed her that the scandal now attached to Emma's name was known, not only in Polite circles in London, but in the very village in which she had been brought up, she began to have inner doubts.

She stood a moment, stiff-backed, looking searchingly into Ware's face, striving to read the expression in his hard eyes. Then she said uncompromisingly, "If, my lord, Miss Stanton *had* confided in me, and I do not for one instant admit that she did, can you give me any good reason why I should tell *you* of her plans?"

She saw the relief in his expression. He said, "Miss Embery, I will take you, and you alone, into my confidence!"

As Miss Embery listened with growing amazement, she found all her powers of judgment called into question. Could she trust this man despite his reputation? Was she allowing herself to be influenced by his undoubted charm? But years of studying the characters of her pupils had given Miss Embery confidence in her own ability to form a correct assessment of intentions and motives. After a brief hesitation, and with certain mis-givings as to Emma's future happiness, she gave him all the information he required.

Ware listened intently. When he heard that Emma had had the intention of travelling on the Bath coach he swore under his breath and glanced at the gilded French clock on the mantel-shelf. As Miss Embery's story came to an end, Ware said warmly, "Miss Embery, you have, indeed, been a good friend to Miss Stanton! But I must in some sort repay you." He laid some guineas on the table and added, "If you would consign Miss Stanton's pearls to my care, I will undertake to restore them to her."

There was something so compelling in Ware's manner, such assurance in his voice, that Miss Embery found herself complying with his request, accepting without question his right to act upon Emma's behalf and never doubting that he would be successful in his search for her. It was only after she had parted from his lordship that she began to wonder if she had acted wisely. Lord Ware's reputation rose up before her and filled her with misgivings concerning the fate of her young acquaintance.

Miss Embery was not the only one to be left ill at ease after Lord Ware's departure. He had said a brief farewell to Lady Sophia and, with no further word of explanation, had announced his intention of following and finding Miss Stanton, saying in an exasperated voice, "She has taken the stage-coach to Marlborough. There is no time to be lost!"

To Lady Sophia's way of thinking, the determination displayed upon his countenance and a certain glint in his eyes did not bode well for Miss Stanton, and although she could not acquit the girl of deceitful behaviour, she thought she would not care to be in her shoes when Ware caught up with her. As to his motives, she was quite at a loss, for it was inconceivable that he could have formed an attachment to the youthful, dowdy Miss Stanton.

When Ware strode into his house in Grosvenor Square, it was apparent to every member of his household that his lordship was in a tearing hurry and in no mood to be crossed. He demanded writing materials to be set out in the library, ordered his racing curricle and his team of chestnuts to be brought to the door, and dashed off two letters without pausing for thought. Before putting on his many-caped driving coat, he handed them, sealed, to Willis, saying, "You will travel to Millford at once and give these letters to Mr Capel. I expect to arrive at Millford this evening and to remain there for a week or so."

Within a few minutes Ware had left the house, mounted into his curricle, taken up the reins and, with Jackson, his head-groom up behind him, was threading his way, at what his old servant considered to be an alarming pace, through the crowded West End streets.

Emma had managed to reach the Strand in plenty of time to secure an inside seat on the Bath Accommodation Coach from the ticket office at

48

the 'Angel'. Enquiring where she might find some refreshment, she was directed to the inn parlour, where she was able to breakfast on some ham and eggs washed down with tepid coffee; she felt that it might be a long time before she had the chance to eat again and she was hungry after her long, dusty walk. In her shabby cloak and bonnet and with her quiet manner, she attracted little notice in the inn, which was all abustle with hurried comings and goings, shouts for attention and all the sounds heralding the imminent departure of the stage-coach.

At last, shortly before nine o'clock, she took her seat inside the coach and found herself squashed between a large, middle-aged woman with a shawl round her shoulders and a capacious basket of food on her lap and a young man with protruding teeth wearing a thick frieze coat, his hat crammed well down on his head.

When all the passengers were aboard, the luggage strapped on and the outside passengers attempting to wrap themselves up against the freshness of the morning air, the coachman and the guard strolled out and mounted to their seats with an air of being well aware of their own importance. The stable boys were ordered to stand away from the horses' heads and, with much jingling of harness, rattle of wheels on the cobbles and snorting and stamping of hooves, the coach rolled forward, out of the inn yard, and began its long journey to the West country.

At first Emma sat contentedly wedged in her seat, her only feeling being one of relief that she had accomplished her objective; in her hitherto sheltered life, she had never before had to take such a journey unassisted. But as the coach left behind the busy London streets and the out-lying villages, her thoughts flew uneasily to and fro: to the uncertain future before her and to the past few days.

She thought of her half-brother, Richard, the man her father had appointed to be her guardian. What hatred for her he must have concealed under a politely aloof manner! She had been unable to conceive of any motive for his actions other than calculated malice. Never, never could she contemplate returning to live under his roof.

She thought of the Earl of Ware, in whose power Richard had placed her, and felt her cheeks grow hot at the memory of that evening in his house. Many times in her imagination she had seen again his dark, handsome face with its harsh aquiline features as he towered over her and seen again the look of contempt mingled with desire in his eyes as he bent down to kiss her. She had been very shocked; no man, other than her father, had ever kissed her before and such a kiss as this – so frighteningly intimate. There had been moreover a callous ruthlessness about his action which had terrified and humiliated her. At least, since discovering her true identity, he had treated her with indifferent civility.

Emma was thankful that, with each succeeding hour, the distance increased between her and the man who had won her brother's infamous wager. She imagined that his lordship would breathe a sigh of relief when he learned of her precipitate departure from his sister's house. How glad he would be to be absolved from any further involvement in her future.

That future she could only view with uncertainty and trepidation. The possibility that one of her father's parishioners might help her to obtain a post as a governess or companion seemed to Emma to be her only hope. She resolved, on her arrival in Hinton St. Anne, to make her way to the Manor House, where the Squire and Mrs Littleton lived and with whose daughters she was acquainted.

The difficulty of explaining her presence there, of giving reasons for seeking such employment, struck her with increasing force as the coach journeyed on. Her sombre thoughts were fortunately distracted by the other occupants of the coach. Opposite to her, next to a man who appeared to be his uncle, sat a rosy-cheeked schoolboy who, catching her eye, began to tell her eagerly about his recent visit to London and all the sights and wonders that he had seen. Discovering that the young Miss had not had the same good fortune, he spent the next hour regaling her with a detailed account of 'Astley's Amphitheatre', of the 'Museum of Living Animals' over Exeter 'change in the Strand and the famous panorama of Mr Barker in Leicester Square. Emma listened, only too happy to be diverted from her cares, to his descriptions of the wild animals, freaks and clowns and all the marvels that he had seen, until his uncle gruffly bade him stop his chatter.

Having accepted gratefully and eaten a piece of cake given her by the stout woman next to her, Emma began to feel drowsy and, in spite of the jolting of the coach over the rutted surface of the roads, soon fell asleep.

She slept for a long time, exhausted after her restless night and early rise and only vaguely conscious of the frequent stopping of the coach at the various stages.

It was well on into the afternoon when she finally woke. The boy and his uncle had left the coach and their places had been taken by a middle-aged couple. The stout woman was in the middle of a vivid description of the birth of twins to her younger daughter, an event which had evidently made a strong impression on her mind, and the more intimate details of which she was recounting in a hushed voice to the middle-aged lady opposite, while the other occupants of the coach strained their ears to hear.

There had been a considerable amount of traffic on the road and now and then they would pass a slow moving wagon or be overtaken by a post-chaise or some gentleman's carriage. Such a vehicle had just been heard to pass them at a reckless speed, when the final stage of the stout woman's anecdote was interrupted by the slowing down and, finally, the stopping of the coach on a straight stretch of road between fields and apparently miles from anywhere.

In the sudden silence that followed the cessation of movement, a chorus of voices could be heard outside: protests from the outside passengers and the stentorian voice of the coachman demanding that some unseen driver should instantly move his vehicle and cease to block the highroad in what the coachman declared to be an unlawful manner.

The rabbity-faced man leaned out of the window, then turned back to announce to an interested audience that a bang-up sporting curricle was drawn across the road ahead of the coach. Having constituted himself official commentator, he went on to describe the proceedings outside, saying in an awed voice, "Lord, there's a regular out-and-outer getting down from that there curricle! He's coming across to speak to the coachman. As fine as ninepence, he is!"

Scarcely were these words out of his mouth than a new voice could be heard outside, an autocratic, cultured voice, demanding in no uncertain terms the return of his sister, whom he declared had run away from her boarding school and was a passenger on the coach.

At this, all eyes were turned to Emma, who went very white and sat silent, shrinking back against the seat cushions. The door of the coach was suddenly wrenched open and a voice said grimly, "Come out at once, wretched child! You have caused us a great deal of anxiety!"

Emma, looking up in alarm, saw the tall figure of the Earl of Ware in a dusty driving coat, a whip in one hand, the other stretched out peremptorily towards her.

She shrank away from him, saying in a stifled voice, "No, no! It's not true! He's not my brother! I won't go with him!"

The stout woman, her eyes round with astonishment, spoke up resolutely, "No call to be frightening the young lady, sir! And whose to say whether you be her brother or no! Like as not you may be some villain as is a'trying to abduct her!" She looked around her for approval, to murmurs of assent from her fellow-passengers.

His lordship cast her a look of scorn, saying sarcastically, "My good woman, do you think that I would wish to abduct a school-girl with neither face, figure nor fortune to recommend her to my notice!"

The stout lady reddened, looking doubtfully at Emma, and murmured, "Well, I'm sure, Miss *is* very young ...."

Ware caught a look of furious indignation in Emma's eye. Now he capped his advantage by producing her string of pearls from his pocket and holding them up before her.

"Do you deny that these are your mother's pearls?" he asked sternly," Do you deny that you disposed of them in order to buy your ticket on this coach?"

Emma, looking flustered, hesitated, incorrigibly truthful, and was lost.

Ware, without waiting for her reply, announced in a voice that brooked no argument, that his sister had run away from school in order to elope with a young ensign, both of them being under age. This intelligence, coupled with my lord's air of authority, successfully put an end to any further opposition to Emma's removal from the coach.

The stout woman looked indignantly at Emma and said in a loud voice, "Well, who would have thought it!" and, as Ware's strong hand grasped Emma's arm and almost hauled her from her seat and down onto the road, the other passengers burst into speech, exclaiming,

"The quiet ones are the worst!" and, "I was never so taken in by anybody! Such an innocent air ....!"

The door of the coach was closed. The groom moved the curricle to the side of the road and the coach got slowly under way again and disappeared, swaying and jolting, top-heavy with passengers and luggage, the former all turning to look back and stare at the ill-assorted couple left standing at the side of the road.

Emma, clutching in one hand her band-box, the other arm still held in a painful grip, realised with a sinking heart that she was in the company of a very angry man.

Ware had felt considerable unease since he had learned of Miss Stanton's disappearance. Now, tired after a gruelling journey, throughout which he had been haunted by the notion that the governess might have intentionally misdirected him, he was experiencing all the fury that follows relief; fury which inevitably directs itself at the very object of that anxiety.

He said wrathfully, "By God, you have caused me a great deal of vexation, Miss Stanton! Why the devil didn't you let my sister return you to my house? You are, without doubt, the most troublesome female I have ever encountered!"

Stung by the injustice of his remarks, Emma retorted fiercely, "You had no right to follow me, my lord!" She wrenched her arm away from his grasp and added, struggling to hide the tremor in her voice, "I intend to return to Hinton St. Anne and find shelter with old friends there. I believe that they will be able to help me to find a post as a governess. So, you see, my lord, it would have been a great deal better if you had not forced me to leave the coach! I can scarcely arrive at the Manor in your company! If you will kindly set me down within walking distance, I will *trouble* you no longer."

Ware, staring down into her defiant face, which, though pale, was full of resolution, felt some of his anger evaporate.

"I fear I have some unpalatable news for you, Miss Stanton! But this is neither the time nor the place." He put his hand under her elbow and began to draw her towards the curricle where Jackson was waiting.

Feeling as if her legs could barely support her, Emma said nervously, "Where are you taking me, my lord?" She looked anxiously around her, but there was not a person in sight other than his lordship's servant.

He said impatiently, "We are going to an inn in Marlborough. *I'm* devilishly hungry and I have no doubt that you are too! We cannot talk here and we shall both feel better when we have eaten."

Jackson, a thin wiry man with a grizzled head of hair, looked with interest at his master's companion as they approached, and suffered a severe shock. Was this the reason for their headlong journey? He wondered with amazement if his lordship had taken leave of his senses!

Standing at the horses' heads, he watched Ware assist the young lady up onto the high box seat and mount up beside her. His lordship took up the reins and, ordering him to stand aside, gave the horses the office to start; as Jackson swung up behind, he hoped gloomily that his master knew what he was about!

The journey to Marlborough was accomplished in almost total silence, broken only by an enquiry from Ware as to whether Miss Stanton was sufficiently warm. She sat very upright on the seat staring ahead of her. Ware could see little of her face, which was partially concealed by the brim of her old-fashioned bonnet.

Having passed through the outskirts of Savernake Forest, it was not long before the broad High Street of Marlborough lay before them. Beyond the fine town-hall stood the ' Castle and Ball' inn and, driving into the inn yard, they found themselves in a scene of bustling activity. Jackson jumped down and went to the horses' heads and, as Ware assisted Emma to alight, the landlord, who had recognised my lord's curricle, came hurrying forward from the doorway of the inn, bowing obsequiously and enquiring how he might serve his lordship.

Having ordered Jackson to procure the best horses available to replace his weary team, Ware bespoke a private parlour and a meal for himself and his companion, adding, "Ask your wife, Rowley, to show Miss Stanton to a room where she may wash her hands and tidy herself."

As Emma was escorted up the twisting oak staircase to a little low-ceilinged room above, she thought for one moment of appealing to this comfortable-looking country woman for assistance in escaping from the Earl, but the difficulty of explaining the situation and the knowledge that his lordship was clearly an old and valued customer kept her silent. A can of water was brought for her and, having thankfully washed her face and hands and tidied her hair, she descended again to the parlour.

There she found Ware in conversation with the landlord who was supervising the laying of the table on which there were already several dishes.

"I apologise to your lordship for not having better victuals to set before you, but the ham is home-cured and my wife makes an excellent rabbit pie and has a wonderfully light hand with pastry!"

As he spoke, the inn-keeper kept glancing with astonishment at Ware's companion. As he told his wife later, "Lord knows, I was never more surprised in my life! There's his lordship, as grand as ever, if a trifle dusty and travel-worn, and that drab little mouse of a girl! We've seen him with some pretty high-flyers afore in our time, you and I, but this beats all!"

He took Emma's cloak and held a chair for her to take a seat at the table and then one for my lord. A bottle of the best claret from the 'Castle and Ball's' wine cellars was placed on the table and the landlord remained in the room to wait upon his distinguished guests himself.

Emma was surprised to discover how very hungry she was and, being young and with a healthy appetite, she managed to make a tolerably good meal in spite of her nervousness. Her glass was filled but she scarcely touched it; his lordship drank thirstily and was complimentary about the wine.

In the presence of the landlord it was impossible to say anything other than the merest commonplace. Ware, casting a glance at her wan face from under his dark brows, enquired after his sister's children and, although at first she replied mechanically, under his deft questioning, she soon became more animated, and told him several stories about Miles, who had clearly captured her affection. A little colour crept back into her cheeks and a sparkle to her eyes as she remembered some of that young gentleman's escapades, but when the meal was over, the table cleared and they were left alone, it was evident, in spite of her efforts to conceal her unease beneath a calm exterior, that she was both anxious and afraid.

Ware poured himself a glass of brandy and, pushing his chair away from the table, sat leaning back, looking at Emma thoughtfully. He said at length, "When I left you in London, I went to Richmond to see Richard and to call him to account – but he had already left home. I was told that he had travelled north and would be away for several weeks – no doubt he preferred not to meet me! We know now that before he left he must have taken great pains to spread the scandal about you in London through his friends, but he did more than that!"

He saw Emma's eyes fixed anxiously upon his face and continued in a gentler tone, "When I reached Millford, I had some enquiries made on your behalf. I sent my land-steward to Hinton St. Anne the day before yesterday," her eyes widened apprehensively as he said, "I regret to tell you that Richard has been there before you! I do not know exactly what tale he has told, but you are believed by all, from the highest to the lowest, to have run off from your brother's house in Richmond and formed a liaison with a noted libertine! It doesn't take long for such news to spread throughout a village, especially when it concerns the daughter of a former rector! There is not, Miss Stanton, a respectable household there nor in the surrounding countryside where you would be invited over the doorstep!"

There was a stunned silence. Emma stared before her, a stricken expression in her eyes, her whole mind taken up with the realisation that in all the world she was utterly alone and without any means of support. She said softly, as if to herself, "Whatever shall I do? Where can I go?"

After a moment without moving or speaking, she turned doubtfully to Ware, who sat watching her closely, and said in a diffident voice, "Clearly I must now earn my living, my lord, and I believe that I am considered to be a tolerable needle-woman – do you think it possible that I might find employment in the sewing-room in your household?"

Struck by the humour of the situation, he laughed and said provocatively, "That is not precisely the position that I had thought of offering you, Miss Stanton!"

She saw his amusement and flushed vividly at what she took to be his meaning and unconsciously put up her hand in a defensive gesture, as if to ward off the shameful proposal that she believed him about to utter, saying fiercely, "Oh, no, my lord – pray don't ....!"

However he continued in the same amused tone, "There is but one course open to you, Miss Stanton!" He paused, then added in a voice that brooked no opposition, "You must marry me immediately!"

CHAPTER 5

It had been two days earlier that the idea of marrying Miss Stanton had first occurred to Ware.

During dinner that evening Henry Capel, his land-agent, had recounted all that he had discovered during his visit at Ware's request to Hinton St. Anne. After Capel had left, Ware had sat drinking brandy and brooding over the future of this girl whose entry into his life had disrupted it so effectively.

He was indifferent to Society's opinion of his morals but of his family's name and traditions he was fiercely proud. For it to be universally believed that he had seduced and then abandoned a girl of Miss Stanton's age and quality would by no means redound to the honour of his House.

The idea of marrying Miss Stanton having entered his mind, he had begun to see in it not only the solution to the problem of her future but other advantages as well.

He was already fully aware of his obligation to marry and provide an heir to his title and lands; his relations had left him in no doubts of that. Why should not this girl fulfil this role as well as another? At her age and in her situation she was less likely to demand any alteration in his present mode of life than some spoilt beauty; yet she was gently bred and there was nothing to deplore in her ancestry. That such a marriage would shock and infuriate both his family and Society had only served to amuse him. It was, however, in letting his thoughts dwell on Miss Stanton herself that his mind had been made up. He had thought cynically that there were not many men who had been vouchsafed such a revealing glimpse of the charms of their intended brides before the wedding night! Moreover there was a stoicism about Miss Stanton which appealed to him: she had enacted him no tragedies and, he had remembered with a wry smile, had even thanked him for his *kindness* with exemplary politeness.

His mind made up, and with no thought as to his future bride's wishes, he had procured a special licence the next day, signing Richard's name, as Miss Stanton was a minor, without the slightest compunction. He did not believe that Richard would dare to raise objections to such an advantageous marriage for his ward. With the licence in his pocket, he had returned to London and had been furious to discover that the girl whom he intended to make his wife had run away.

The Earl of Ware was not a man who was excessively conscious of his own consequence, but he could scarcely be unaware that, despite his reputation as a rake, he was generally considered to be a great matrimonial prize. When, therefore, he made his offer of marriage he did not anticipate a refusal from Miss Stanton; though a little maidenly diffidence was to be expected. Miss Stanton, however, surprised him once again.

Ware's proposal was so unexpected that Emma could hardly believe that she had heard aright. She repeated in a dumb-founded voice, "Marry you!" a look of incomprehension in her eyes.

Ware watching her, repeated helpfully, "I intend to make you my wife!"

As the full meaning of his words penetrated to her, Emma stood up hastily, almost over-turning her chair and exclaiming in horror, "Impossible, my lord!"

He laughed involuntarily. If he had offered Miss Stanton the carte-blanche which she had so clearly anticipated she could not have appeared more shocked.

Emma, misinterpreting his amusement, flushed indignantly and protested, "Oh, you are only joking me! It is not civil of you to amuse yourself at my expense!"

"I am not jesting, Miss Stanton, I am perfectly serious." Ware continued to regard her with some amusement in his eyes, "I was not perhaps entirely prepared for such a violent reaction to the one honourable proposal that I have ever made!"

"You must know, my lord, that such a marriage is impossible!" She was still looking at him suspiciously.

He said, frowning a little, "I know of no reason why it should be impossible. Perhaps you can enlighten me, Miss Stanton?"

She paused, flustered and nervous. She could still hardly believe that he was serious. She said awkwardly, "You must be aware, my lord, that our backgrounds and up-bringing are utterly dissimilar, moreover we are quite unacquainted. Without respect, without trust ...." she hesitated, then added in a low voice, "without love or even affection, how could such a marriage prosper?"

For a moment Ware stared at her from under frowning brows, recollecting his own parents' marriage; the atmosphere more redolent of hostility than affection, each partner leading his or her own separate life. His mother, like a pretty butterfly, surrounded by lovers and admirers, had flitted from one amusement to another; she had had nothing in common with the late Earl, a sombre man who loved the country and all its pursuits.

He said cynically, "Fine sentiments indeed, Miss Stanton! But I fear that they are a luxury that you can ill afford! Only marriage can save your reputation and, as I must one day take a wife to provide me with an heir, this will be a satisfactory solution for both parties."

He tossed off the remains of the brandy in his glass and said softly, "Would you not care to be a Countess, Miss Stanton, and occupy a high position in Society, have untold wealth and a multitude of servants at your command?"

"No, my lord, I should *not* care for it!" Emma wondered whether his lordship could be a little out of his mind. She said earnestly, "And it is impossible that *you* could have the least desire to marry me, my lord!"

He raised his eyebrows and said sarcastically, "It was not originally my intention to *marry* you exactly, Miss Stanton, but, I assure you, with every moment that passes I dwell with more pleasure upon the prospect."

She felt herself begin to tremble and clutched the back of the chair to steady herself. Ware was still seated at the table, leaning back indolently and regarding her with some amusement. She brushed back a wisp of hair from her forehead with a hand that shook a little and holding herself very erect said, in as firm a voice as she could command, "I am indeed conscious of the honour that you do me, my lord, but I cannot possibly accept your offer of marriage!"

If she had acquiesced, even reluctantly, he might have been inclined to question the rightness of his decision to marry her; as it was, her categorical refusal only served to strengthen Ware's determination. He stood up abruptly, all trace of amusement banished from his countenance, and said harshly, "I'm afraid that you are labouring under a misapprehension, Miss Stanton! I am not *asking* for your consent but rather *informing* you of my intention to marry you! I have already obtained a special licence – we shall be married at Millford this very evening!"

He came round the table to stand beside her and added grimly, "Do you not realise, my girl, that it is well within my power to make you, for very shame, *beg* me to marry you!"

She could not fail to understand him. She gripped the back of the chair so tightly that her knuckles showed white in an effort to hide her fear of him and said resolutely "You cannot force me to come with you, my lord!"

He gave her a contemptuous look. "If you protest, the tale that I told to the coach passengers will do very well again! You must forgive me, Miss Stanton, if I offend you, but you do not remotely resemble the kind of female that I should be expected to abduct! You are far more credible in the role of miscreant school-girl! Not a soul will believe you – least of all old Rowley, who knows me well."

At this moment, as if conjured up by the pronouncement of his name, the landlord knocked on the door and, entering the room, announced that my lord's carriage was ready and waiting. "The best team that I have, my lord, though not up to your lordship's standards by a long chalk." As he spoke, his round, blue eyes were taking in the scene before him and noting the grim look upon his lord-ship's face. The girl seemed about to speak but before she could do so, Lord Ware had taken up her cloak and bonnet and, wrapping the former around her shoulders, said abruptly to Rowley, "We leave at once – my young cousin has to return to her seminary this evening and we are already late. You may send the reckoning to Millford."

Emma, clutching her shabby bonnet in one hand and feeling the eyes of the landlord fixed curiously upon her, found herself unable to speak.

As if addressing a child, Ware said "Put your bonnet on, cousin, for we must leave now."

She looked quickly up at him as he towered over her and saw the implacable expression in his eyes. As she tied the strings, with trembling fingers, under her chin, his hand was already at her elbow, grasping her none too gently. She was taken quickly out of the room and across the busy stable-yard to the waiting curricle where Jackson was standing ready.

Their arrival attracted little attention. One or two onlookers turned to stare at the tall figure of his lordship, but the London coach was shortly to depart and, in the hustle and bustle, Miss Stanton's presence was scarcely noticed.

As Ware handed her up into the high seat, Emma said in a low voice, "I think you are mad, my lord! You force me to come with you .... but you will soon regret it!"

He looked at her with a strange glint in his eyes and said ominously, "I do not believe that *I* shall regret it, Miss Stanton!"

The curricle was driven at a brisk pace along the country lanes bearing its unwilling passenger. Emma hardly noticed the countryside and the gradual change from the rolling, open downland to the wooded hills and hedged fields that succeeded them. Here, ironically indeed, the hedgerows seemed decked for a bridal: beneath the chestnut trees bearing their white, candle-like blossoms, the hawthorn flowers and cow-parsley formed a veil of white lace along the roadside. Her strongest sensation was one of being borne along upon an irresistible tide of events over which she no longer had any control.

Since she had left Richard's house, her life had been dominated by this stranger who sat beside her driving his new team of horses with such ease and skill and apparently indifferent to the feelings of his passenger; a stranger who was now determined to make her his wife! It was an astounding proposal and had been offered in such an unconciliating manner, with so little effort to be pleasing, that, if any chivalrous motives underlay it, they were effectively concealed. He was clearly determined to have his own way in everything.

There passed through Emma's mind the romantic day-dreams she had used to indulge in when she lived so peacefully at the Rectory: of some handsome young man who would fall in love with her and whom she would one day marry. Reality was proving to be very different and, despite the May sunshine and her warm cloak, she shivered and cast an anxious glance at the stern, forbidding profile next to her.

Ware must have noticed the slight movement of her head for he turned and looked down at her, his eyes searching her face for a moment, before he turned his gaze back onto the roadway stretching ahead of them, without uttering a word.

The shadows were beginning to lengthen when at last they turned off the road and drew up before some imposing wrought-iron gates, their pillars surmounted by strange, heraldic beasts of stone. The lodge-keeper must have been on the watch for his lordship's arrival, for as the horses came to a standstill, he came quickly out of his house, bowing and touching his forehead respectfully, and opened the gates wide for them to pass.

Ahead of them lay a long avenue of lime trees leading through rising ground to the house. They were approaching it from the western side, through a park where deer grazed, and the evening sunshine lit up the facade. It was indeed a magnificent sight: built originally in the seventeenth century, it had had further wings added in the Palladian style in the eighteenth century. As they drove into the forecourt, two footmen came down from the grand entrance with its double staircase to hold the horses and help them to alight. Emma thought ruefully that, after seeing his lordship's house in Grosvenor Square, she should not be surprised at the size of his country residence. The sight of it added to the sensation of unreality which now encompassed her.

When they entered the hall, there seemed to Emma to be a formidable number of servants. Several footmen with powdered hair, resplendent in their red and green uniforms and gold shoulder-knots, stood around the walls and a stately butler greeted them in a dignified manner, bowing low in his soberly coloured blue-grey coat, and betraying no surprise at the appearance of his master's companion. A footman took Ware's hat and gloves and the housekeeper, Mrs Huxstable, a thin, upright person with an imposing cap upon her head and the keys of her office at her waist, stepped forward and curtsied, asking in an expressionless voice if she could show Miss Stanton to her room. It was all very grand and intimidating to a young country girl.

Emma was conducted up a resplendent staircase, the walls and ceiling of which were decorated with painted deities disporting themselves with abandon amongst the clouds, and from thence along a corridor to a large bedroom with dark, imposing furniture and a huge four-poster bed with heavy, crimson draperies. From the three tall windows, she glimpsed a beautiful garden; formal beds were laid out around an ornamental pond, at whose centre a fountain was playing.

Mrs Huxstable, seeing the direction of her gaze, informed Emma that the gardens of Millford were famous for their beauty. Adding, in a colourless voice, "They were laid out by his lordship's grandfather, Miss Stanton. The late Earl, his lordship's father, was very attached to this house and spent many months here."

Emma could not help wondering whether the present owner of that title was equally fond of his country estate.

Mrs Huxstable showed her into the adjoining dressing-room and indicated a further door which, she informed Emma, led to my lord's own dressing-room. She spoke quietly and with respect and hid successfully her astonishment at the appearance of the young lady who was to become the new Countess of Ware.

When the Earl's letters to Henry Capel and to his housekeeper had arrived earlier that day, announcing his forthcoming marriage, the whole household had been thrown into a turmoil of excitement and speculation. Certainly not one of that vast household of servants had imagined that his lordship would take as his wife such an insignificant slip of a girl, with her unfashionable clothes and shy manner. Mrs Huxstable thought that she looked no more than a school-girl and a scared one at that.

"I will send for one of the maids to assist you, Miss Stanton." she said, "Your luggage will be brought up at once ...." As she spoke, a wooden-faced footman knocked, and carried in the band-box which contained all Emma's possessions. Mrs Huxstable removed her startled gaze from this battered object and managed courageously to finish her sentence by requesting Emma to inform her whether there was anything further that she required. She then retired from the room, more shaken than she would have cared to admit.

Although horrified to find herself once more in Lord Ware's power, Emma could not but be thankful to change out of her dusty, crumpled dress. A pleasant fresh-faced girl, with a soft west-country accent, unpacked her few belongings and helped her to put on a grey sprig-muslin dress with a modest neckline and puffed sleeves.

Sitting before the looking-glass, combing her hair before pinning it up again, Emma's thoughts flew desperately from one expedient to another to avoid this marriage. Her only hope lay, she decided, in the clergyman who was to perform the ceremony. Surely, when she explained the situation to him, he would assist her to remove from the Earl's house; for she felt certain that a man in Holy Orders could not in conscience conduct such a marriage once he became aware that the bride was an unwilling partner to it.

The maid was just laying an old, but much treasured, Kashmir shawl, that had once belonged to her mother, around her shoulders, and she had in some measure regained her confidence, when a servant knocked at the door with a polite message from his lordship, requesting her company in the Yellow saloon.

There were three men standing before the windows at the far end of the drawing-room to which she was conducted. She had an impression of grandeur, of a high ceiling with elaborate cornices, many huge oil-paintings hanging against the yellow, damask-covered walls and of ornate furniture in the French style of the previous century. The Earl, resplendent in evening dress, was standing by a table, with his back towards her, showing a book to an elderly gentleman. Watching them, standing a little apart, was a man of middle-height, plainly dressed, with a sober expression upon his face, who, looking up and seeing that Emma had entered the room, said quietly, "Here is Miss Stanton, my lord!"

As the other two men turned towards her, Emma felt her heart miss a beat, for she saw from his appearance that the elderly gentleman was a clergyman.

The Earl came forward to meet her and, offering her his arm with a gravity which seemed to conceal some other emotion, led her up to the clergyman, saying, "Mr Barnard, may I present to you my future wife, Miss Stanton." To Emma, he said in a firm voice, "Mr Barnard has kindly come here this evening – at great inconvenience, I fear, to himself – to conduct the marriage service for us in the chapel. I believe we must both be profoundly grateful to him."

Emma looked nervously from one face to the other. Clearly his lordship did not intend to allow her any opportunity to speak alone with the clergyman. The latter was looking benevolently at her in a short-sighted way and murmuring gently that it was "a great honour and privilege ...." She drew her arm away from Lord Ware and said in a low voice, "Mr Barnard, may I have a few moments private conversation alone with you?"

The old man, though continuing to regard her benignly, shook his head regretfully and patted her arm, saying in a quavering voice, "Alas, child, I am unable to hear a word that you say – for I have the misfortune of being extremely deaf!" and turning to Ware added deferentially, "If your lordship would be good enough to repeat the young lady's words to me?"

Before Emma could utter another syllable, Ware shot a glance of amusement and triumph at her horrified face as he said in ringing tones into Mr Barnard's ear, "Miss Stanton only desires to convey to you her distress at having caused you the inconvenience of coming here at such a late hour." Then, without allowing Emma time to recover from her dismay, he turned to her and said, "I wish to present to you Henry Capel, my land-agent, Miss Stanton – who has consented to give you away in the absence of any member of your family."

Emma found herself looking at a rugged-faced man in his middle-thirties who bowed politely over her hand but who, she realised, was regarding her with a good deal of curiosity. The colour rose in her cheeks as she remembered that Lord Ware had sent his land-agent to Hinton St. Anne to make enquiries on her behalf. This, then, must be the man who had reported to him and who had discovered that her reputation there was irredeemably lost; useless to appeal to one who must inevitably believe all that he had heard, and must consequently hold her in contempt. A feeling of hopelessness came over her. She looked up at Ware and saw nothing but a ruthless determination on his face.

"We must not keep you waiting, my dear sir!" he now said politely to Mr Barnard and, taking Emma's arm firmly in his, added, "Let us go at once to the chapel where Mrs Huxstable is awaiting us and who will be our second witness." With these words he led the way out of the room with Emma on his arm, followed by the stooping figure of the old clergyman and a perplexed Henry Capel.

CHAPTER 6

The only part of the Vane's medieval manor to have survived, the chapel, with its barrel-vaulted ceiling and dark seventeenth century panelling, seemed gloomy after the sunlit rooms of the great house. Its sole window, east-facing behind the altar, displayed the arms of Vane ancestors and allowed little light to enter. Only the tall, silver candlesticks on the altar lit up the faces of the couple standing before the old clergyman, and glittered on the gilded wings of the cherubs on the carved reredos.

Mrs Huxstable, standing alone in one of the side-facing pews, thought she had never seen a stranger ceremony. The Earl stood head and shoulders taller than his bride, in profile his fine-drawn, aristocratic features had a hawklike look; his expression was serious but beneath it Mrs Huxstable sensed an unmistakable gleam of triumph. Miss Stanton's face was very pale, her eyes downcast and she was plainly apprehensive. In her simple muslin dress, which served to emphasize her extreme youth, she presented a marked contrast to his lordship's fashionable appearance, and Mrs Huxstable experienced a disquieting renewal of the misgivings she had felt when she had first set eyes upon the Earl's bride.

Emma was never able afterwards to recollect fully the details of their marriage service. That any impediment might exist to the marriage did not seem to occur to Mr Barnard, who, having formally posed this question to the witnesses and to the bridal couple, moved quickly on to the marriage vows. As one in a dream, unable to alter the course of events as they unfold, Emma stumbled through the words of the ceremony in a voice so soft that even those standing around her could barely hear her. Lord Ware, however, spoke in even tones that were clearly audible; there was no hesitation in his voice as he repeated the sentences prescribed for the solemnisation of matrimony; Emma's hand, given by Henry Capel to the old clergyman, was taken in a firm grasp by his lordship, who removed the heavy gold signet ring from his own hand to place it on her finger. He felt her hand tremble in his and looked down into her face with an expression that was hard to read.

The solemn vows having been exchanged, the bridal couple knelt before the altar and Mr Barnard, in a raised voice, pronounced them to be man and wife together and said the final prayers and blessing. As Emma rose from her knees, Mrs Huxstable saw that she swayed slightly; Ware's hand was quickly at her elbow and the house-keeper was relieved to observe a softening in his expression as he looked down at her, though it was certainly not the look of a man deeply in love. Emma, struck by the alarming realisation that this strange, reckless man was now her husband, cast him one quick glance from under her eyelashes as he took her arm to escort her from the chapel. Although the marriage was not of her choice, indeed, had been against her wishes, she believed that the life-long vows that she had made before God must be honoured and shivered inwardly to think of the rights that she had now bestowed upon him as her husband.

Walking beside him out of the chapel, she looked up and saw above her the family pew, surmounted by an arch, above which carved angels supported the Earl's coronet and arms; with a sinking heart, she realised that beyond the terrifying prospect of her private life lay a whole world of public duties for which she was quite untrained and felt herself to be utterly unsuited.

Outside the chapel, Mrs Huxstable curtsied to the bridal couple and, declaring herself honoured to have been a witness to the cere-mony, wished them both long life and future happiness before return-ing to attend to her domestic duties. Henry Capel shook hands with Ware, congratulating him, and, bowing low over Emma's hand, wished her ladyship every happiness. She smiled mechanically and thanked him in a soft voice, her expression so grave that he felt a stirring of pity for her: the stories that he had heard at Hinton St. Anne hardly seemed credible when confronted by her air of youthful innocence.

Emma learned with relief that Mr Barnard and Henry Capel were to take supper with them. She was thankful for the presence of the two guests when they entered what, she was later to learn, was known as the Little Dining-room, though it was considerably larger than any dining-room she had ever seen before. She dreaded being left alone with her husband and every now and then glanced at him nervously. It was astonishing to hear herself being addressed as 'your ladyship' and lent an added dimension of unreality to the proceedings.

Ware had spoken to his guests of 'a simple meal'; Emma's startled gaze beheld an immense array of dishes set out amidst gleaming silver and flowers. She did not know that Gaston, the culinary wizard who presided over my lord's kitchens at Millford, had uttered a Gallic cry of despair when informed that morning that he was to provide a wedding feast for his noble master that very evening. Exclaiming "*Nom de Dieu! Ce n'est pas possible!* How can such a thing be done in one day!" he had, nevertheless, performed what he, himself, had termed a miracle.

They were to be waited upon by what seemed to Emma to be a positive army of servants; the elderly butler, in a dignified manner, requested my lord and her ladyship to accept his good wishes and those of the staff. Lord Ware, with a sudden smile which transformed his face, said lightly, "Thank you, Marchant! Wine for the servant's hall! See to it, please. Her ladyship's health must be duly pledged!"

Mr Barnard, who was seated beside Emma, was an ardent, amateur botanist and, having enquired from her if she had any interest in the subject and without waiting for any reply, was soon launched upon a dissertation on his life-long hobby so that she was only required to nod or smile or look grave according to his discourse. He told her that the Earl had many rare botanical books in his library, including the famous 'Anatomy of Plants' by Nehemiah Grew, and was kind enough to allow him to borrow them to further his studies and assist him with the treatise that he was endeavouring to write upon British ferns and mosses. Looking up once during this disquisition, Emma caught Ware watching her, amusement lurking in his eyes. He, himself, was deep in discussion with Henry Capel upon some estate matter. The latter, feeling perhaps that her ladyship was in need of a change of subject, broke off his conversation with Ware to ask Emma politely if she was fond of riding.

At once her face lit up as she replied, "Indeed, yes! I like it above all things – but to tell the truth, I have had little opportunity. You see, we had only an old cob belonging to my father which I sometimes rode."

Looking at her face turned towards him, her large, expressive eyes shining, Henry Capel wondered suddenly if there was not more behind this sudden marriage of the Earl than he had imagined.

"We must find a suitable mount for you, my lady." and turning to Ware, he added, "Dysart might do, but he is hardly a lady's mount."

Ware looked reflectively at Emma, who was regarding him hopefully, and said, "As soon as I have seen how well you can manage a horse, I shall buy you one for your own use."

She flushed with pleasure and replied, "Thank you, my lord!" Ware was irresistibly reminded of a child that has been promised a treat and thought wryly that his newly-wed wife seemed not to have grasped that she was now married to an extremely wealthy man, who could well afford to buy not one but several mounts for his bride.

For a while horses were the main topic of conversation, while Mr Barnard sat smiling benignly upon the company. At last Emma, feeling that he was being excluded by his deafness from participating in the discussion, endeavoured to explain to him the subject upon which so much animated talk was being expended, but was obliged to give up in despair after several attempts. Mr Barnard, mistaking 'horses' for 'houses', spoke learnedly and at length to her upon the history of Millford and she found herself listening with interest, though fully conscious that Ware was deriving considerable amusement from her failure to communicate with the old clergyman.

Supper ended, after a quick glance at her husband, who nodded his approval, Emma rose from the table, feeling horribly awkward in her strange new role as the lady of the house, and retired to the Yellow saloon. She had only a short time for reflection before the gentleman joined her and the tea-tray was brought in and set before Emma to pour the tea; a ceremony which she managed to perform without mishap, in spite of her nervousness.

At ten o'clock Mr Barnard announced that he must take his leave of them. The carriage was ordered to carry him back to the Rectory in the village and soon after he departed, bestowing further blessings on the newly-wed couple and quite unconscious that the bride had been an unwilling partner to the marriage.

71

Henry Capel was not slow to take his leave of them after the old clergyman had gone. The marriage that he had just witnessed had left him perplexed and concerned, for the bride was not at all the kind of female that he had been led to expect. Sent by the Earl to enquire about Miss Stanton's father and to find out who might be her friends in Hinton St. Anne, he had been astonished to find such a degree of animosity displayed towards her in the village. The inhabitants had evidently been deeply shocked to learn from her brother of her abandoned behaviour and the depths to which she had sunk so soon after her father's death, for the Reverend William Stanton had been loved and respected by his parishioners.

Seeing and speaking to the young Countess, he found it difficult to believe that her innocence was a sham. His lordship's motives and behaviour he found quite incomprehensible. As he walked across the park to his own house, after Ware had escorted him to the hall and there thanked him and shaken him by the hand, he thought grimly that his lordship would have much to answer for if he destroyed the happiness of such a young girl.

Left alone in the drawing-room, Emma felt a mounting panic. To distract herself from her thoughts she rose and crossed the room to examine a collection of enamelled boxes displayed upon a table.

She was standing with one in her hand when the Earl returned; she saw him in the doorway and, seeing the expression of triumph upon his face as he stood regarding her, she replaced the box nervously and turned to face him. He came straight across the room to her and standing close, put a careless hand under her chin and forced her to look up into his eyes, saying quizzically, "Well, madam-wife?"

Looking up into his face, she could not but be reminded of the passionate embrace that she had been subjected to at his house in London and seeing the gleam in his eyes, unconsciously stiffened, her heart beating wildly, forcing herself not to shrink away from him.

Ware felt her involuntary stiffening and saw the growing panic in the wide eyes that looked up at him from a pale, weary face. For a moment he stood, arrested, staring down at her frowningly, then, taking his hand away from her chin, he said abruptly, "You look worn to a thread, my girl – you had best go straight to your bed. For my part, I have some papers which I must read and which will occupy me for some time." and turning away from her, he walked out of the room.

There was a bright fire burning in the marble fire-place in Emma's bedroom and many candles alight. The same maid was waiting for her, who, when Emma entered the room, made her a curtsy and expressed her good wishes to her ladyship.

As Emma allowed herself to be prepared for bed it was with the utmost difficulty that she managed to sustain the appearance of a kindly interest in the cheerful conversation of the country-girl, for with every moment that passed she knew that the consummation of this hateful marriage was drawing nearer.

Dora had been one of the upper-housemaids until she had been ordered to wait upon the Earl's bride. "It's a great honour, my lady, to be acting as lady's-maid to your ladyship." she confided ingenuously to Emma, "And I don't rightly knows how to set about it." She added wistfully in her soft Wiltshire accent, "Doubtless your ladyship will be a'getting one of those fine London dressers to wait upon you – one who knows all about fashion and suchlike."

As she chattered away, folding clothes, helping Emma into her nightshift and wrapper and brushing her hair, Dora could not help a feeling of pity for her new mistress. She seemed so young. Like many of the junior members of the staff at Millford, she stood in considerable awe of his lordship, whom they seldom saw. They had been told in the servant's hall, that morning, of the marriage that was to take place; it's suddenness and lack of ceremony accounted for by the bride's mourning for her father. There had been general disappointment that there was not to be a grand society wedding, and a few malicious voices had been raised, questioning whether there might not be some other, and less laudable reason, for such a hasty marriage.

At last Emma was ready and Dora, bidding her goodnight, left her lying between the lavender-scented sheets. In that vast room with only the bedside candles burning, the fire cast deep shadows into the corners, conveying an overall impression of gloom; looking back as she closed the door, Dora thought how young and small her mistress

73

looked beneath the canopy of the great bed and hoped that his lordship would be kind to his bride.

Left alone, Emma struggled to subdue her rising terror. Dear God – why had she not called out for help long before – made her plight known to others? Yet ever since the Earl had forced her to leave the stage-coach it had seemed as if she had had no alternative but to comply with his wishes.

Should she perhaps have challenged his threat, made at the inn, that, if she would not consent, he would make her in the end beg him to marry her?

She sat up in bed and looked desperately around the room – could she bar the door – move some piece of furniture to prevent his entry? But there was not one piece that she was capable of moving other than a chair – a useless barricade. She thought in a panic about the moment when eventually he would come in – should she scream – should she plead with him or struggle against him? With a thudding heart, she realised that none of this could avail. She was now Ware's wife – he had a legal right to her person and could, in any case, force her to submit by reason of his greater strength.

A terrible cold feeling of hopelessness swept over her. She lay back against the pillows and tried to summon up her courage. At least, she thought, let her keep her own dignity – let there be no pleading, no tears, no useless struggles. All must be endured without her fear being visible to this strange, frightening man. She closed her eyes and began to pray with all her heart that she would be able to conceal that fear.

When Ware came into her room she had at last fallen asleep, exhausted by a day which, for her, had started with her departure from Lady Sophia's house in the early hours of the morning. His lordship was ready for bed and wearing a long, elegant, brocade dressing-gown. He came to the side of the bed and stood in silence gazing down at her.

How very different she looked from the girl whom he had laid unconscious upon the sofa in his London house. Her prim linen nightshift, with it's high neck and long sleeves, bore no resemblance to the blatantly seductive dress that she had been wearing that night. He studied her face, framed by a profusion of softly curling hair spread out upon the pillow, observed her delicate features and the appealing curve of her mouth: dark lines of fatigue lay under her eyes and there was little colour in her cheeks.

It was impossible to read the expression in his lordship's eyes as he stood looking down at his bride from under dark, frowning brows.

It was this enigmatic look which first met Emma's gaze when, her sleep disturbed, she opened her eyes and found herself looking up into his face. She stared at him wide-eyed, still only half-awake, then, her heart beating wildly, realised that the figure standing beside her bed was that of her husband. She could not take her eyes from his face as she struggled to subdue the panic that was threatening to overcome her.

He said, and there seemed to be a touch of irony in his voice, "Are you prepared to fulfil your duties to your husband?"

Now was her chance to plead, to throw herself upon his mercy but a strange defiance – a refusal to admit to her terror – forced her to reply, "Yes, m-my lord." in a voice that shook a little in spite of all her efforts.

He sat down on the side of the bed, facing her, and now there was no mistaking his expression; in his eyes there was a frightening glitter and there was a ruthless set to his mouth as he bent towards her. Murmuring under his breath, "My God, you little beauty!" he began, with assured fingers, to undo the buttons at the neck of her night-shift. She saw no pity in that dark face above her. Ware remembered only that this was the girl whom he had made his wife and whose slim figure had been so beguilingly revealed to him that night at his house. His passions aroused by the sight of this young creature, so appealing in her youth and innocence, it was only as he felt her shrink back involuntarily against the pillows at his touch and the wild beating of her heart beneath his hands that he looked again into her face. She was lying motionless, silent, and the look in her eyes reminded him forcibly of some wild creature caught in a trap that knows itself doomed.

She saw his expression harden. He drew back, frowning, and demanded roughly, "Good God – are you so afraid of me?"

She swallowed convulsively and managed to say in a low voice, "No, no, m-my lord, indeed I am not afraid ...." determined that she would not be so craven as to admit to her terror.

For a moment the hard grey eyes studied her face, then he said slowly, "You lie, my little wife, do you not?"

Silently she nodded, biting her lip, and looking at him hopelessly, feeling her self-control slipping away.

He sat staring at her, one hand still upon her breast, then, withdrawing it, he took her hand in his and, looking down at the heavy, gold ring on her finger, seemed lost in thought.

At length he looked up and now there was a softening in those arrogant eyes. He said, and there was perhaps a note of surprise in his voice, "I believe, my dear girl, that I cannot be satisfied with a frightened wife who merely submits to her husband!" and beginning to re-button her night-shift as if she was a child, he continued sardonically, "I am conceited enough to believe, my dear Emma, that I can teach you to desire my love-making, and prefer to wait until my embraces are willingly and eagerly received!"

She was staring at him, wide-eyed, trembling, as if she could not comprehend his meaning. He said gently, "Our marriage shall be in name only until we are better acquainted!"

At his words, Emma felt relief flood through her and the tears start to her eyes. She brushed them away and turned her face to the pillow, determined to regain control of herself and unconsciously presenting to his lordship an enchanting view of her profile. After a moment she turned back to Ware and said in a gruff, little voice that was not quite steady, "You are all that is g-generous, my lord and I-I thank you!"

He thought of his treatment of her that day and eyed her with astonishment. Her honesty was both disconcerting and disarming, her manners those of a well brought up child.

Raising her hand to his lips, he kissed it, saying with a wry smile, "I believe, my love, that you come off with all the honours tonight!"

He stood up then, and bending down, kissed her gently and lingeringly on the mouth. As he drew back he saw in her startled eyes a surprised, wondering look. It was so appealing that he felt an urgent re-kindling of his desire and, being determined not to arouse her fears again, bade her an abrupt goodnight and swiftly left the room.

Left alone, Emma lay very still, worn out by that night's terrors and all the conflicting emotions of the day. She found herself unable to marshal her thoughts in any order: everything seemed unreal and the future menacing. Cut off from all that was familiar, in a strange house and with, no doubt, responsibilities of which she was ignorant, she wondered how she could endure the future. She did not dare to think of her husband. Intensely grateful to him for his forbearance that night, she recognised that she was still his wife and must, some day soon, share her bed with him. Despite her fear, his gentle kiss had disturbed her strangely; she had to remind herself that he had no thought of love or even of liking for her and, as she drifted off to sleep, she thought drowsily that it was impossible to believe his lordship capable of such tender emotions.

Ware, upon returning to his own bedroom, threw himself down onto a chair by the fire and thought savagely that Emma had been right when she had said to him, earlier that day, that he must be mad to wish to marry her. He had not yet reached the point of regretting it, as she had foretold, but it was certainly ironic that a man famous in Society for his many conquests should be spending his wedding-night alone. As he considered the events of that day and the situation in which he now found himself, his sense of humour overcame his black mood and a sardonic grin spread over his handsome face.

A ruthless man, he had not anticipated feeling any qualms in possessing his young wife; after all, had he not saved her reputation by giving her his name; but when he had comprehended how overwhelming was her fear of him and seen her valiant efforts to deny that fear and to fulfil her duty to him, he had felt it to be infinitely repugnant to him to take advantage of her submission.

The sight of her lying asleep in the great crimson-draped bed had touched him profoundly. He wondered with a frown what it was about this girl whom he had married that affected him so disturbingly.

It would, he mused cynically, be a delightful challenge to overcome her fear and make her long for her husband's caresses. Meanwhile he would have to restrain his ardour and, if his enforced monastic existence should prove intolerable, he could always, on his return to London, console himself by resuming his former ways. There were plenty of women there who would welcome him eagerly with open arms.

CHAPTER 7

Outside there was brilliant sunshine and the birds were singing as Emma sat up in bed the next morning. She had woken late and, propped up against a vast number of pillows and sipping her chocolate, she could not help enjoying the unaccustomed luxury of her surroundings. How pleasant it would be to explore that beautiful garden that she had glimpsed from her bedroom windows.

Manfully striving to set aside her fears for the future, she had just decided that she should ring for Dora as soon as she had finished her chocolate, when she heard the sound of footsteps in her dressing-room and Ware came in.

He was dressed for riding and had some papers in his hand. He came straight to the side of the bed and, bending down, kissed her upon the forehead, enquiring whether she had slept well. Emma found her face suffused with blushes. How strange that a man should be so at home in her bedroom. Ware sat down on a chair beside her bed as if his presence was the most natural thing in the world and looked at her with amusement.

"You look as guilty as if you were receiving a lover instead of a husband!" he remarked mockingly, leaning back in the chair and watching her face. She looked so delightfully confused that he forbore to tease her further but, after a moment's silence, informed her that he wished to consult her about the announcement of their marriage, which he proposed to send to the 'Gazette'.

Emma read the paper that was handed to her with mounting disquiet. Ware put into words her misgivings by declaring indifferently, "It will be a nine-days wonder! I would that I could be there when my uncle reads his copy!"

She looked up at him with troubled eyes and said sadly, "Everyone will believe that I trapped you into this marriage."

To her indignation, he laughed and said teasingly, "And did you not? That wanton's dress, my dear wife! To behold you in that dress was to be enslaved!"

She looked flustered, not caring to be reminded of the night when he had believed her to be a woman of easy virtue, and retorted with spirit, "I cannot conceive, my lord, how you can say something so outrageous when you are perfectly aware that I did my utmost to escape from you!"

He replied with mock gravity, "Indeed, I am at fault! I am scarcely likely to forget that journey!"

Emma regarded him doubtfully, uncertain whether he was serious or not, and he, amused at the expression upon her face, laughed softly and asked again, "Well, do you approve the wording? I shall send it to London today and at the same time send a letter to Sophie informing her of our marriage."

Emma, assenting to the announcement, thought miserably what distress the letter would bring to Lady Sophia and to Sir Peter. Their opinion of her, and of her behaviour, expressed so unequivocally, was still vivid in her memory.

Ware rose, saying as he did so, "I am to ride out now with Henry Capel to visit some out-lying farms – he has been plaguing me to do so for months." At the door he turned and enquired pleasantly, "If you would care to drive with me this afternoon, I should like to show you some part of the estate."

Her instant acceptance and obvious pleasure pleased him and he was surprised to find himself looking forward to the afternoon's expedition: an expedition which he had only suggested from an unaccustomed sense of duty, feeling that he should at least provide her with some form of entertainment.

After Ware's departure, Emma had just finished dressing, and was wondering how she was going to occupy herself until the afternoon, when a servant brought her a politely worded message from the house-keeper. Mrs Huxstable, through her intermediary, pronounced herself to be at her ladyship's disposal that morning and would wait upon her, at my lady's convenience, to receive any instructions that she might have for her.

Having no knowledge of the lay-out of this vast house, nor in which room it would be customary to interview such an important personage in the household, Emma requested that Mrs. Huxstable should attend upon her in her dressing-room and there awaited her apprehensively.

Her entrance did nothing to allay Emma's misgivings: poker-stiff in the back, the frills of her mob-cap starched to perfection and her whole appearance considerably more fashionable than that of her mistress, the housekeeper wore a face that was rigidly expressionless.

Emma had been well taught by her father of the folly of pretending to a knowledge that one does not possess and, in spite of her nervousness, her natural honesty assisted her to inform Mrs. Huxstable that she knew nothing about the organisation of a great household. Seeing a slight softening in this formidable female's countenance, she confided to her her wish to be instructed in such matters, ".... for I was raised in a country rectory where we had only two servants living in, and I do hope, Mrs. Huxstable, that you will help me, for I should like everything to continue just as his lordship wishes."

Mrs. Huxstable had come to her ladyship's room prepared for, indeed, expecting difficulties: either the complete disinterest of one so young, or high-handed, ignorant interference in the smooth running of the household. She found herself disarmed by such candour and, unbending a little, said in a stately manner, "It will be a great pleasure and privilege to help your ladyship in any way that I can."

How his lordship could have taken as his wife this dowdy young girl was past the housekeeper's comprehension but, she thought, there was no understanding gentlemen like his lordship; she only hoped it was not some distempered-freak of his and one of which he would readily tire.

Conscious of the awkwardness of her new mistress's position, Mrs Huxstable then proposed that she should show Emma over the whole establishment that morning. This exactly coincided with Emma's wishes, for nothing could be more uncomfortable than to find oneself living in a house and yet unable to tell in which direction one should go, even if one's only desire was to walk in the garden.

They traversed, what seemed to Emma, endless rooms, including a magnificent series of State Apartments suitable for a sovereign's visit, leading, one from another, across the front of the main block of the house and overlooking the park. Even the family rooms were astonishingly numerous. They visited bedrooms, dressing-rooms and closets, as well as another drawing-room with its own ante-room, my lord's study, a vast library, a breakfast parlour and a long gallery which ran the full length of one wing of the house. The latter was of particular interest to Emma for upon its panelled walls hung portraits of Vane ancestors. Mrs. Huxstable was knowledgeable about the history of the house and of the family, and pointed out to Emma various personages who had been famous in their day, although in some cases, *notorious* might have been a more appropriate term. Here, Emma observed the portraits of Ware's parents; she recognised, in the likeness of the late Earl, the same dark hair, grey eyes set under frowning brows and aquiline features of her husband, but the latter's mouth resembled his mother's; the late countess being an ethereally beautiful woman with fair hair and blue eyes and a lively expression, a smile lurking in the corners of her mouth.

Emma had asked Mrs Huxstable to tell her the names of the servants as they encountered them about the house, for she felt that she should know the people who were to wait upon her; there was evidently an equal desire amongst the staff to become acquainted with at least the appearance of their new mistress, for as they passed through the rooms and corridors they witnessed a vast deal of activity, some of which appeared to be of an unnecessary nature.

Finally, at Emma's request, Mrs Huxstable conducted her through the domestic offices, including the kitchen, with all its attendant labyrinth of sculleries and storerooms; there, Gaston, who ruled with a rod of iron the innumerable kitchen staff, was presented to her.

Marchant, who was supervising the polishing of silver in the butler's pantry, wished my lady a dignified good-morning, having been one of the few to have met her ladyship the previous night.

With so much to interest her, Emma had, for the moment, almost forgotten the circumstances which accounted for her presence in that teeming household. It was a shock, therefore, when they encountered Willis, who was putting a final gloss to his lordship's boots – no other hand being permitted to lay a finger upon them. She felt her colour rise at the recollection of their previous encounter at the house in Grosvenor Square upon the ill-fated night of her brother's card-party; however, Willis's impassive countenance betrayed no sign of recognition and, bowing politely, he contented himself with asking her ladyship to accept his best wishes for her future happiness.

The general opinion in the servant's hall, following their first sight of the young Countess, had been decidedly mixed. Some of the women declaring themselves sadly disappointed that their new mistress was so plainly and unfashionably dressed. Of the younger men, many were astonished at my lord's choice. However, she had her champions. Her natural dignity, the unaffected and pleasant manner in which she had addressed them and a thankful realisation that, whatever else she might or might not be, she was undoubtedly a lady of good-breeding, had been strong recommendations in her favour. Indeed the great Gaston, who, like many of his fellow-countrymen, considered himself to be a connoisseur of the female sex, pronounced her ladyship to be, "of a beauty which is ravishing!" and predicted that when she went to London, "*bien habillée et bien coiffée*," she would create "a sensation the most astonishing!"

It was beneath Marchant's dignity to offer any opinion on the subject in public, but, in private conversation with Mrs. Huxstable, he declared himself to be tolerably satisfied with his master's choice. "I had my fears, Mrs Huxstable!" he had said, shaking his head solemnly, "Such a sudden marriage! Could it be possible, I thought, that my lord had taken leave of his senses and intended to make one of those painted doxies his wife!"

Only her ladyship's extreme youth gave him cause for concern, and he opined that such a very young lady might have some difficulty in dealing with his lordship's wild ways. "Although we must hope that marriage will make him aware of his responsibilities, Mrs. Huxstable, and that he will now settle down!"

If Marchant had been present during the afternoon drive that his lordship took with his young bride he would have felt that his hopes were on their way to be fulfilled. They had set off in the early afternoon in a park phaeton drawn by a splendid pair of greys whose pace was perfectly matched. Emma admired both the horses and Ware's skill with the reins, unaware that he was a noted whip. Impressed by the ease with which he handled the spirited pair, she was enchanted when he offered to teach her to drive upon some future occasion, quite unconscious of the rare honour that he was bestowing upon her.

Their excursion was a lengthy one. First they made a tour of the park, one of Capability Brown's masterpieces, which had been landscaped some seventy years before. The great sweep of parkland away from the house towards the lake, the perfectly balanced clumps of trees, made a prospect immeasurably pleasing to the eye; at every turn there were vistas of trees and lake: glimpses of a Doric temple built on rising ground, and on the northern slopes of the wood, a Gothic ruin perfectly placed to add perspective to a distant view across the park. Ware drove out through the lodge gates to the village of Millford, where the tower of the ancient church rose above the stone cottages and the inn, then on through the narrow, cobbled streets, and out into the countryside.

Emma asked many questions and soon, in her interest in her new surroundings, quite forgot the unease which she had previously felt in Ware's presence. When they visited several farms belonging to the estate, she desired him to tell her all about the tenants and their families, until Ware was obliged to admit ruefully that he was unfamiliar with those details.

"You will have to ask Henry, I'm afraid!" he confessed, and was amused to observe that Emma looked quite shocked at such ignorance. She sat quietly for a while before she said, as if excusing him to herself, "Of course, you are a great deal in London, and, I collect, you do not spend much time *here*."

If my lord was not greatly concerned about his tenants, they, for their part, were keenly interested in him and in his affairs. Seeing the phaeton pass by, the farm workers and their families looked up curiously, the women bobbing polite curtsies, the men touching their foreheads. As in all small communities, the word had spread quickly that the Earl had taken a wife and that she was very young. There had been eager interest in every household when the news had reached them that morning; rumours of my lord's disreputable life in London and the occasional scandalous house-party at the great house were familiar to them, and they wondered at the identity of the girl his lordship had made his bride.

For Ware, their expedition had been a revelation. He had not before encountered a girl who was genuinely interested in country affairs, and he could not help contrasting their conversation very favourably with the polite exchanges and flirtatious remarks, customary with the very young ladies of his acquaintance in London, which, for the most part, he had found an intolerable bore. The fresh air and gentle warmth of the late spring sunshine had brought the colour to Emma's cheeks and, glancing at her from time to time, seeing her eager, bright face beneath her old-fashioned bonnet, he began, to his surprise, to feel that perhaps fortune had indeed favoured him.

Emma was quite unaware of his lordship's rising admiration for her and when he suggested that they might alight from the carriage at a particularly pretty viewpoint, by a gate on a deserted stretch of road, she agreed most willingly and, helped by Ware, jumped eagerly down. He, having her in his arms as she alighted, found himself strongly tempted to kiss the delightful, smiling face turned up towards him, but something of his intention must have shown in his expression, for at once the happy, confident look vanished from her face, and she looked at him with large, uncertain eyes as he released her.

Annoyed with himself for his maladroitness, Ware endeavoured to overcome the constraint that had fallen upon her, pointing out the view of Millford House and the park, which could be seen in all its magnificence from that spot. But, although Emma regained her composure, she was very silent during their return journey and her manner lacked the charming spontaneity which had characterised it before.

It was about five o'clock that evening when an unexpected visitor arrived. They were in the library, Emma, seated upon a window-seat, reading a book, Ware writing at his desk across the room from her, when they heard sounds in the hall and a man's voice saying, "It's all right, Marchant, no need to announce me!" then the door burst open and a fair-haired, slimly built man strode into the room.

84

Edward Wyndham was still wearing his long, drab driving-coat and looked tired and dusty. Seeing Ware, he crossed to the desk and said urgently, "I left town the instant that I heard the rumour, and drove down here to prevent you committing this damnable folly! All London talks of it, y'know!"

Ware raised his eyebrows and said sarcastically, "It must be a rumour *quite* out of the ordinary to make you undertake such a journey on my behalf, cousin!"

"Don't jest, Robert! It's all over London that you intend to make that jade, whom you won at Hazard, your wife!" He rushed on impetuously, "Good God, Robert, she may be Richard Harding's sister, but she knew dashed well what she was about! I'll be damned if I can see why you should give your name to a woman of her stamp!" He stopped, for Ware had risen from his chair, a heavy frown upon his face.

"I do not permit anyone to interfere in my affairs, Cousin! No doubt your intentions were admirable but you could have saved yourself a long journey." He turned towards the far end of the room and said in a cold voice, "May I present you to my wife, the new Countess of Ware!"

Edward Wyndham, turning in dismay, saw for the first time the young girl sitting by the window.

"The devil, ma'am! What can I say?" There was astonishment as well as mortification upon his countenance. He had only had a glimpse of the young female who had left Richard's house that night in Ware's company, but the girl who was now regarding him shyly bore no resemblance to the brazenly-dressed, painted creature whom he remembered.

It had been a painful reminder to Emma of her situation to overhear Edward's words. Towards him, she was too honest to feel any animosity, believing, as she did herself, that the marriage should never have taken place. She rose and came across the room towards the two men: her husband, tall dark and wrathful and the slim figure of his cousin, his fair skin flushed with embarrassment.

Holding out her hand to Edward, she said quietly, "Lord Ware should not be angry with you, for you have only said what all the world will think and say!"

With a startled glance at his cousin, Edward took her hand and bowing low over it, said awkwardly, "You are magnanimous indeed, ma'am! I believe I may have quite mistaken the matter, and trust that you will forgive me." It seemed inconceivable to his mind that this girl standing before him could be the wanton that he had believed her to be.

She smiled a little sadly at him and, turning to Ware, said, "I will leave you gentlemen together, my lord. You must perforce have much to say to each other which could be more easily done in my absence."

The Earl, who had been regarding her with interest during this exchange, took her hand and kissed it, saying with a note of amused wonder in his voice, "My compliments, my lady, you are ever a delightful surprise!" However, as the door closed behind Emma, his expression changed and he stood regarding Edward with frowning eyes.

There was consternation upon Edward's face, "By Jupiter, I hope I have not sunk myself irredeemably in her sight by my ill-timed remarks, Robert! Could anything be more unfortunate!"

Ware said reflectively, "I believe that Emma is not the kind of female to harbour a grudge against you. If she doesn't bear me any ill-will for marrying her, I cannot think that she will long hold *your* remarks against you!"

A look of incredulity came over Edward's countenance, "Good God, do you mean to say that she did not look with favour on the match? Dash it, dear boy .... it ain't possible! All the matrons in London have been after you for their daughters for years!"

Ware gave a short laugh, "My dear Edward, I perceive that some explanations are called for. You had better take off your coat and sit down."

It did not take long for Ware to put Edward in possession of all the facts concerning Richard's deception of his sister, and how, in all innocence, she had consented to leave Richard's house with the Earl. "And so, cousin," he concluded, "she found herself alone in my house in the small hours of the morning!"

Edward had been sitting staring at Ware in round-eyed amazement. At these words, some very uncomfortable thoughts passed through his mind, but he only said softly, "What a devilish unpleasant situation for the poor girl!"

Ware replied shortly, "You may well say so!" He offered his snuff-box to Edward, then took a pinch himself and continued pensively, "Fortunately for Emma, I discovered a hitherto unsuspected streak of chivalry in my nature, Cousin!" He looked up at Edward and said very deliberately, "*That*, and the fact that, before I became aware of her innocence, she fell and knocked herself unconscious while striving to avoid my attentions, caused her to leave my house the next morning with her virtue intact!"

Edward looked his horror but he said nothing, his eyes upon Ware's face. At that moment he pitied Emma with all his heart.

"I told Sophie some tale sufficiently plausible for her to take Emma into her household and came down here to find out where in her father's former parish she might find a friend and a home." Ware's eyes hardened, "It was useless! Richard had already spread the scandal there and, as I later discovered, in London!"

To Edward's growing astonishment, Ware swiftly recounted his decision to marry Emma by special licence, her sudden flight and his pursuit of her, and how, finally, he had married her out of hand the previous evening.

"Good God!" Edward was almost bereft of words, "Richard Harding is an unutterable villain! Has he taken leave of his senses? Dammit, Robert, he deserves to be horse-whipped or worse!" He thought of Emma's plight and added softly, "Poor girl! What an appalling situation in which to find herself!"

Ware looked amused, "Not very complimentary to me, dear boy!" he paused, then continued with a frown, "Now I have to discover what Richard hoped to achieve. My reputation can hardly have led him to believe that I would *marry* his sister!" He added grimly, "It will be a pleasure to call him to account for his actions!"

As he heard these words, Edward thought to himself that he would not care to be in Richard's shoes when that meeting took place. The whole story, not least its final outcome, seemed incredible. Richard appeared to have run mad; moreover, his own cousin's behaviour was so totally out of character that he found himself at a loss to under-stand his motives. He looked at Ware curiously. There could be no doubt that his cousin was fond of women. The succession of expensive high-flyers that he had had in keeping bore witness to that, but his attitude towards them had seemed to be one of amused contempt. He was not consciously unkind, but there had appeared to be little of tenderness in his dealings with them. He could not help thinking that, if Ware had wanted to, he could have found some way other than marriage to save this girl's reputation. The mystery intrigued him and, when Ware broke into his thoughts by asking him abruptly if he would care to dine with them and stay for a night or two, he accepted at once.

When Emma came down before dinner, she found the two cousins awaiting her. Edward had changed from his travel-stained garments and was now resplendent in a corbeau-coloured coat and pantaloons of a modish yellow; his slim legs encased in a pair of gleaming hessians. Famous for his impeccable taste, there was a touch of artistry in the elegant folds of his cravat, and the carefully arranged disorder of his curls made the Earl look almost careless in his dress.

Whilst admiring Edward's fashionable appearance, Emma thought subconsciously that her husband, with his broad shoulders and tall, commanding figure, was the more impressive of the two.

At first she felt a little uncomfortable with Edward for by now he must have been made aware of all that had happened since the night of the card-party. However, he was so easy in his manner and so obviously anxious to make amends for his initial remarks about her, that Emma soon found that her constraint had vanished.

Gaston had excelled himself in the preparation of a magnificent dinner in honour of the bride; doubtless he had felt that he had not been able, the previous day, to do justice to the occasion and to his culinary skills. The bride, for her part, was thankful to have company for the second evening of her married life, rather than to dine tête-à-tête with her husband.

The conversation was lively. Edward had mentioned a play that he had recently seen and soon found himself being eagerly interrogated about the plays and operas being performed at that time on the London stage. Questions followed about Almack's and the sights and amusements of the Great Metropolis. With Emma's animated face turned towards him, Edward became sensible of an attraction that owed something, not only to her delicate features and large eyes, but also to a certain disarming candour in her manner, for she made not the least attempt to conceal her ignorance of the Polite World as was so often the case with young ladies of his acquaintance.

Ware interposed a remark now and then but for the most part he was silent, watching Emma's face as she listened with round-eyed wonder to Edward.

"When are you going to take my new cousin to London, Robert?" Edward asked him as the succession of courses drew to a close. He saw Emma glance hopefully at Ware from under her eyelashes. Her husband was leaning back in his chair, idly twisting the stem of his wineglass and replied carelessly, "Perhaps in a week or two. I must go to London myself first, to put in train some alterations in the house." He looked up at Emma and added, with a gleam of amusement in his eye, "Preparations for the arrival of the bride!"

Emma blushed, and Edward said kindly to her, "When Robert is too busy, it would give me great pleasure to escort you in London and to show you some of the sights."

"You are fortunate, indeed, my girl," Ware said dryly, "Edward is considered one of the arbiters of fashion! It will add considerably to your consequence to be seen about with *him*! If he takes you up – he will make you all the rage!"

She put her head a little on one side, looking at Edward with a new interest in so droll way that both men laughed, then replied with a chuckle, "I cannot believe that even your good offices could make me admired in the fashionable world – of that there can be no doubt – but I should be most happy if you would bear me company!"

Soon after she left the gentlemen to their wine but it was not long before they rejoined her in the drawing-room. Edward had, by now, quite recovered his good spirits after the shock of discovering his cousin to be already married and was, indeed, well on the way to considering it to be an excellent thing.

"Well, Robert, what are you going to provide for my entertainment this evening?" he asked, "Shall it be cards? What games does your wife favour?"

Ware looked at Emma provocatively, "I fear she may have taken games of *chance* in aversion, Cousin!"

Emma, returning his look with indignation, retorted, "Indeed, I do not care to play high, my lord, and certainly some *stakes* are not just what I like!"

Perceiving her vexation, Edward offered to teach her to play piquet, saying tactfully, "Dash it, Robert! No use gambling with you – too confoundedly lucky! What we need is a game of skill!"

So the table was set up and Emma was initiated into the intricacies of piquet and was soon pronounced by Edward to be an apt pupil. She found the time passed delightfully quickly and was surprised to hear the clock striking eleven. Thanking Edward warmly for his tuition, she bade him good night, but before leaving the room, said diffidently to Ware, "If I may, I should like to attend Morning Service tomorrow, my lord?"

He replied at once, "Certainly – I will accompany you." then, seeing Edward's astonished face, added with a faint smile, "Edward, too! High time, dear boy, you had your mind lifted to higher things!"

After Emma had left them, there was silence in the room for a few moments. Ware's face wore a stern look, his easy manner quite vanished at her departure. Edward glanced at him, then said warmly, "Well, I offer you my congratulations, Robert! You have a charming wife." He continued enthusiastically, "I believe she will be all the rage in London, y'know – she is so refreshingly different."

Ware said slowly, "Yes, she is different. I hope to God she stays so! But have you thought of the ordeal that she will have to face? Society can be damnably cruel and, after this scandal, she will find many cold-shoulders offered to her."

Edward frowned, "Be happy to stand by you both – goes without saying, Cousin! Only too glad to do anything I can! Dear little thing – it's a damned shame!" He flushed, thinking he might have said too much, and, eyeing Ware's grim face, wondered with surprise that his rakish cousin should be so uncharacteristically concerned for his young wife.

After he had retired to bed, Edward lay awake for some time thinking about their strange marriage. Even in the short time that he had seen them together, it was clear to him that matters were not all that they should be. The young bride was patently nervous of her husband. His attitude to her seemed to be more complicated: on the surface he seemed to treat her with polite good humour but beneath his courteous manner, Edward was conscious of stronger feelings held in check. He hoped his cousin would show consideration to his young wife. Regarding himself as a man of the world, not easily shocked by the manners and morals of the circle in which he moved, even he felt a certain unease in contemplating the union of this young girl with a man of Ware's reputation.

For Emma, Edward felt unqualified admiration. Most women would have bitterly resented his remarks and found it hard to forgive him; she had shown a sympathetic understanding far beyond her years. There was something particularly captivating in this combination of sensitivity with a lively, open manner. His last thought, before sleep over came him, was that Ware was a deucedly lucky man who was, as yet, unaware of his good fortune.

CHAPTER 8

Jackson had returned from London late on Saturday night with Emma's luggage. Sir Peter and Lady Sophia had not been at home when he had called at the house, so there had been, to his heartfelt relief, no possibility of being questioned about the contents of his master's letter and the events at Millford.

The trunk and valise having been safely bestowed in the carriage, he had been offered refreshment before starting his return journey. It was then that he had learned to his surprise of the young Countess's stay in the Ancaster household and of her flight from it in the early hours of Friday morning. The Earl's subsequent visit to his sister and his hasty departure had given rise to intense speculation. The local tavern, much frequented by the footmen of the neighbouring great houses, had provided some salacious rumours concerning Miss Stanton, connecting her with the Earl of Ware in a manner that cast grave doubts upon that young lady's virtue and morals and there had even been talk of a hasty marriage.

Plied with questions by the Ancaster staff and deeply shocked by what he had heard, Jackson had simply stated that it was true that the Earl and Miss Stanton had been married at Millford the previous evening. Great had been the amazement following this confirmation of the rumours, and it had been generally agreed that Sir Peter and her ladyship would not be best pleased. Being a naturally taciturn man, Jackson had said nothing of his part in the removal of Miss Stanton from the Bath coach, but had remembered unhappily the uneasiness he had felt at that time.

Upon his return home he had wasted not a moment in finding an opportunity to exchange a few words with Willis. Both members of the late Earl's household since they were young men, he and Willis had seen his heir grow up from an infant in his nurse's arms, through a mischievous boyhood, to become the handsome man who was now their master; though deploring his present erratic way of life, they remained devoted to him, remembering the many times when they had assisted him to avoid the worst consequences of his schoolboy pranks.

"Lookee, Tom," Jackson had confided, "I'm proper set about by what I've heard up in London. It seems like there were some pretty dark goings-on afore his lordship's marriage took place – I could have sworn my bible oath that her young ladyship was an innocent!" He shook his head in perplexity and looked appealingly at Willis.

The reply, given with a certain grim satisfaction, had gone a long way to reassure him.

"What's in his lordship's mind, Heaven alone knows!" Willis told him, "I knew he had gone about things in such away as to bring a hornet's nest about his ears! Howsoever, this I will say – her ladyship is as proper and virtuous a young lady as you could hope to find." he paused, then added impressively, "That's the sober truth, and if anyone tries to say different, he's a liar, and you may say, Tom Willis says so!"

Jackson, greatly relieved by these words, had returned to his duties with a lighter heart, his fears allayed that his master had been ensnared by some female unworthy to be his wife. It was one thing for his lordship to amuse himself with the muslin company, but to make of such a one the Countess of Ware, would have been shocking indeed. It would not be long, he reckoned, before rumour from London reached Millford and he was thankful to be now in a position to deny with authority anything that was said to discredit his young mistress.

It was relief to Emma to have the rest of her meagre wardrobe to choose from on Sunday morning. The day had dawned bright and sunny, with only a few small clouds in the sky, but the breeze was fresh and she was thankful to be wearing her brown merino pelisse which, although a little shabby, was comfortably warm. With her matching straw bonnet framing her face and with her bright, hazel eyes, Edward thought that she resembled a little brown sparrow. She certainly made a strange contrast to her companions' elegance and any observer must have thought it curious that two fashionable gentlemen should care to be seen in the company of such a dowdily dressed female.

The bells were still ringing as they drove the short distance to the village. It had been a long time since his lordship had attended Morning Service in the parish church and as they entered the family pew there was a flutter of interest around the church: a low murmur was heard amongst the well-filled pews, heads came together in whispered conversation, and necks were craned to obtain a better view.

As Emma knelt in her place before the service began, she was too intent upon her prayers to be conscious of the intense interest that their arrival had aroused. The familiar words of the service and the well-known hymns that followed brought a measure of peace to her anxious thoughts ; perhaps after all something good could be made out of the strange marriage that had been forced upon her.

The Earl was well aware of the excitement that their presence had occasioned and was inwardly amused. He knew that by now all the village would have heard of his marriage but rather hoped, for the sake of his bride, that the scandalous rumours from London had not yet reached it.

Unfortunately his hopes were not to be realised. Mr Barnard's sermon, a gentle, erudite homily, expressed in terms that Emma considered to be well above the heads of the majority of his auditors, came to an end; the final hymn was sung and the congregation emerged into the bright sunlight outside. It was soon clear to his lordship that several of the ladies with whom he was slightly acquainted, members of families of standing in the neighbourhood, were hastening their steps towards their carriages, shepherding their daughters before them and taking care that they should not be presented to the young countess.

The villagers were fortunately not so nice in their ideas, or else rumour had not yet reached them. The pathway through the churchyard was lined with groups of families and friends, the men raising their hats as the party from Millford House passed down it to the waiting carriage, the women dropping respectful curtsies, eager to take a closer look at her ladyship.

It was as they were crossing the churchyard that they heard a voice behind them saying, "I bid you good-morning, Robert!"

Ware, recognising the voice, stopped and turning, eyebrows raised, said with surprise, "Elizabeth! Good God, what the devil has caused you to quit London so early in the season?"

Emma saw one of the most strikingly elegant creatures that she had ever beheld; tall for a woman, the Honourable Mrs. Freddie Tremayne was dressed in a sapphire-blue pelisse with a high collar and wearing a modish straw bonnet, trimmed with ribbons and feathers, over her golden curls.

This splendidly fashionable vision replied carelessly, "Sir William Knighton prescribed country air for George – he has been sadly pulled down since he had the mumps – so yesterday, upon Freddie's insistance, I brought him down to Horton." Eyeing Emma with interest, she added, "So this is the bride about whom I have heard so much!"

Emma, glancing nervously at Ware, thought that she detected a note of chagrin in his expression as the introductions were made; he said to her brusquely, "Elizabeth is an old friend of mine, she and her husband are our neighbours here, indeed part of Freddie's land marches with mine."

Emma, her hand clasped lightly by a slim hand encased in a soft kid glove, found herself the object of a very searching look from a pair of vivid, blue eyes. Feeling horribly conscious of her shabby, old-fashioned clothes, she murmured a few polite words of greeting.

"May I offer you my felicitations, Lady Ware – we had all despaired of Robert, you know!" Mrs Tremayne was smiling, but her eyes were inquisitive, "I shall be staying down here for a few days and hope that I may call upon you one morning." Receiving Emma's shy assent, she continued in her outspoken manner, "London has been agog with some shocking rumours these past few days, Robert!" There was a malicious sparkle in her eyes as she added, "I had even heard talk of marriage, so I was not surprised when I arrived here yesterday to find our village full of the news."

She looked at Edward and said, with a wry smile, "Good gracious, I did not expect to have the pleasure of seeing *you*, Mr Wyndham! Why, it was only on Friday night that I met you at Lady Jersey's assembly and I am confident that you did not *then* have in mind a visit to the country!" The note of sarcasm was even more apparent as she suggested with a light laugh, "I suppose you have travelled down here post-haste to *congratulate* your cousin!"

Edward, who was regarding her with some irritation, replied shortly, "I *do* congratulate Robert with all my heart! He is a lucky man!"

Emma gave Edward a quick look of gratitude; Mrs Tremayne's allusion to 'shocking rumours' had made her feel very uncomfortable and she looked anxiously again at Ware: no doubt these were the same stories that Sir Peter had heard. Fortunately for her, at this moment, a small girl, clutching a bunch of flowers tightly in her hand, stepped forward from one of the groups of interested bystanders and tugged at Emma's skirt to attract her attention. Emma, turning aside from her husband, found herself being offered a posy of hedgerow flowers by a small person in a spotless pinafore and cap, who curtsied politely and smiled up at her. Bending down to receive the flowers, she thanked the child and asked for her name, remaining to question her for a few moments while Edward stood watching her.

It had been less than six months before, that Elizabeth Tremayne, conscious of Ware's admiration, had made it abundantly clear that she would be by no means averse to a discreet affair with him. Fascinated by his reckless charm, she had been in no way daunted by the knowledge that her husband was one of his best and oldest friends; but here she had misjudged his lordship, who, for all his libertine propensities, did not consider the seduction of the wife of one of his friends to be an enterprise that he could undertake with honour, and had rebuffed, in the most civil manner, the lures that she had cast in his direction. The memory rankled with her still.

She and Ware had by now walked a little way ahead and, as they drew near to her carriage, she said in a low voice, full of astonishment, "Good God, Robert – a mere child!" then, feminine intuition having gleaned something of the situation, she shot him an ill-natured glance from her fine eyes and murmured, "I declare, I cannot but pity her – I fear you have been foolish enough to have frightened your little bride – I would not have expected *you*, of all people, to be so maladroit!"

She saw the spark of anger in his eyes and knew that her words had struck home. He looked at her coldly and said contemptuously, "You waste your sympathy, my dear Elizabeth! You should curb the sharpness of your tongue – such malice does not become you!"

She coloured at this, but there was no opportunity for her to reply for at that moment Emma and Edward were drawing near. Emma, her eyes alight with pleasure, showed the bunch of flowers to Ware, saying, "Look at my charming gift! The child's name is Mary Price and she lives in one of your cottages near the Home Farm – such a dear, friendly little girl!"

Ware's expression, as he looked down at his wife, came as a shock to Elizabeth Tremayne; she had never seen him with quite that look before. Thinking cynically that he would soon grow bored with youthful simplicity and look for satisfaction elsewhere, she re-affirmed her intention of calling upon Emma and, having made her farewells, departed, conscious of a feeling of acute irritation at this unexpected marriage.

As they drove back to Millford House, Emma could not help remarking wistfully that she had never before seen anyone as lovely or as elegant as Mrs Tremayne. Ware made no comment but Edward told her that Elizabeth Tremayne was an acknowledged beauty and universally admired. Her husband's silence made Emma wonder uncomfortably if he was contemplating the marked contrast between his bride and this fashionable female and discovered, to her surprise, that she found the notion profoundly disagreeable. As if in answer to her thoughts, Ware looked at her appraisingly and said with a hint of amusement in his voice, "Charmingly as you look, my dear Emma, I believe we must buy you a whole new wardrobe when we get to London – after all, you *should* have some bride-clothes."

She looked down at herself ruefully and nodded, saying, "Quite out of the present mode and shabby into the bargain!" then, smiling up at him, added, "How delightful it would be to be fashionably dressed!"

A brief, thoughtful silence followed, then she continued in a troubled voice, "I fear that it will put you to a great deal of expense, my lord, for I have no funds to draw upon, you know, so that it must all fall upon you!"

Ware looked down at her worried face, an expression of amused surprise in his eyes but, before he could say anything further, Edward interposed with a shout of laughter, "Good God, Emma, Robert is as rich as Croesus! He dashed well won't even notice the expense!" He looked at her consideringly, "I believe you may well set a new fashion, cousin, for your looks are quite out of the ordinary and your manner is certainly not in the usual style."

Overcome by this unexpected encomium from one who she had been informed was a leader of fashion, Emma looked delightfully confused and sat quietly in a happy day-dream contemplating this agreeable prospect. Watching her, Edward thought wryly of the lavish cartes-blanches bestowed, in the past, upon Ware's mistresses. They had certainly not worried their pretty little heads about abusing his generosity! It would be odd, he mused, if the same thought had not struck his cousin.

That afternoon they had decided to ride in the Home Park so that Ware could judge how experienced a horsewoman his wife was before buying her a suitable mount. The Earl rode a raking, black horse, a fine animal, full of spirit and one of his favourites; he had mounted Edward on a chestnut, a thorough-bred which he had recently acquired; for Emma, Jackson had brought round a pretty bay mare with a soft mouth and a quiet disposition.

It was one of the happiest afternoons that Emma had spent for many months. Edward's presence relieved her of any awkwardness that she might have felt in being alone with her husband; her mount, although quiet and well-behaved, was an agreeable change from her father's sedate old cob, and she thoroughly enjoyed the fresh air and exercise in such beautiful surroundings. She could not help admiring the Earl's skill as a horseman and the ease with which he handled his lively mount. He looked a fine figure in the saddle and seemed to have shed his stern manner, his indifference and his cynicism. Emma thought, with surprise, that he looked both younger and less formidable.

Edward, now upon excellent terms with his new cousin, enjoyed some lively exchanges with her and clearly viewed her with ever increasing admiration. So much so that, unknown to Emma, his lordship became aware of a growing sense of irritation at the attention that Edward was receiving and at the happy laughter that greeted his sallies and, by the time that they returned to the house, found himself, to his surprise, regretting his cousin's presence.

As they passed through the hall, Ware observed that one of the footmen on duty displayed a fine black-eye. "What the devil have you been doing, Thomas?" he enquired with amusement, "Been in a mill?"

The tall young man, looking acutely embarrassed, glanced uncomfortably at Emma and replied stiffly, "Yes, my lord."

Ware looked at him curiously and seemed about to speak, then, changing his mind, mounted the stairs with the others in thoughtful mood. There was still a slight frown upon his face as Willis assisted him to change his garments. His valet, after one discreet glance at his sombre expression, busied himself about his duties in silence and wondered what had cast his lordship into such gloom.

At length Ware said abruptly, "I do not usually concern myself with the affairs of the servant's hall, but I should be interested to know how Thomas came to acquire his black-eye?"

"I understand, my lord, that the young footman in question became involved in a brawl down at the 'King's Head' last night."

Ware raised his eyebrows, "Can you tell me the reason for this deplorable incident?"

Willis hesitated, "I believe," he said at length, "Thomas took exception to some unfortunate remarks made in his hearing, my lord."

His lordship's eyes narrowed, "You're being devilish discreet, Willis! What were these remarks?"

"You ain't going to like it, my lord!" Willis said frankly.

"The devil take it – out with it, man!"

"One of the Tremayne grooms insulted her ladyship, my lord."

"I see!" There was an ominous expression upon Ware's face, "And what exactly did he say?"

Willis looked uncomfortable, then, striving to use terms which would give least offence, replied gently, "He said as her ladyship was no innocent when you married her, my lord."

There was a moment's silence. Willis thought that he had seldom seen his master look so grim.

"It seems that I am indebted to Thomas." He looked sharply at Willis, "Is there much gossip in the servant's hall?"

An expression of scorn appeared upon Willis's face, "*Talk*, my lord, there's always *talk*!" He assisted his master into his close-fitting coat, murmuring, "But this I will say – very taking ways, her ladyship has – made quite an impression, my lord." He added carefully, "Having met her ladyship in London before your marriage, my lord, I am in a position to refute personally any scandal that foolish persons may care to repeat." He hoped that he had not gone too far and looked anxiously at the Earl, but Ware only crossed to the window and stood looking out.

'Proper blue-devilled he is', Willis thought to himself, 'I knew that there would be trouble right from the moment that I set eyes upon her ladyship! It's wonderful to see how my lord's notions of propriety have changed since he met her!'

Dora had lost no time in regaling Emma with a colourful description of the fight at the 'King's Head'. Full of indignation at the insult to her mistress and having a soft spot for Thomas, who, like her, was Wiltshire-born, she poured scorn upon the veracity and courage of the Tremayne's cockney groom as she helped Emma to prepare for bed that evening. She had already grown fond of her young mistress and had, herself, no doubts about her virtue.

Emma's heart sank. Coming so soon after Mrs Tremayne's reference to 'shocking rumours' in London, the incident at the village inn had made her realise how thoroughly Richard had done his work to ruin her; she had not expected the evil talk about her to have spread so widely and so fast. As Dora brushed her hair and chattered on as she worked, she wondered what would have become of her without Ware's protection; when the little money from Miss Embery had run out she might even have had to return, disgraced, to Richard's house.

These thoughts were uppermost in Emma's mind when Ware came into her bedroom that night. She was in bed, reading, with only a part of her mind upon her book, and, as soon as she saw him, she laid it down and said impetuously, "I am beginning to realise more and more how deeply I am indebted to you, my lord, for rescuing me from the consequences of Richard's malice! These shocking rumours about me are known even *here*! I had not believed it possible that he could be so successful in spreading his wicked lies." She looked up at Ware with consternation upon her face, so filled with indignation that, for that instant, her fear of his presence in her room was quite forgotten.

He stood regarding her quizzically, one eyebrow raised and said, "I came to tell you that I must return to London tomorrow and shall be away for about a week." There was laughter lurking in his eyes as he added, "I am happy to learn that you believe yourself to be in my debt – I shall now look forward to my return with eager anticipation – what could be more agreeable than to be awaited by a grateful wife!"

She felt her colour rise. He spoke teasingly but she could not avoid wondering how long his patience with her would last and wished she had not spoken so heedlessly. Vividly aware of the restraint that he had chosen to exercise, she said with sudden candour, "I fear that you have made a bad bargain, my lord, in marrying me!"

There was a moment's silence. He continued to stare at her but now the laughter had gone from his face. He said abruptly, "The devil of it is you're so young!" and turned away, murmuring under his breath, "And too honest!" as he went to stand before the fireplace. The change of mood was disconcerting.

"It is perhaps as well that I am leaving tomorrow." The tone of his voice was cold. He came back to the side of her bed and stood looking down at her with a strange expression upon his face. Suddenly he said savagely, "God, what a damnable situation!" and, turning on his heel, left her without another word.

CHAPTER 9

The next morning Ware left early to drive to London. He paid a brief visit to Emma before leaving but his manner held no overtones of the previous night's conversation. He came in while she was still in bed, sitting propped up against the pillows, eating her breakfast, and was already dressed for the journey in a long driving coat, his hat and gloves in his hand. She put down her cup, startled; he seemed to be in a hurry to be gone.

"I am leaving now and expect to be away for the rest of the week. You must ask Henry for anything you may need – he will be only too happy to show you whatever you may wish to see, here or in the neighbourhood." He stood by the side of the bed, observing, as he spoke, the pretty disorder of her curls and her wide, solemn eyes. "I hope that you will ride if the weather is fine. Edward returns to London today, so you will be bereft of company." He added, frowning, "I trust that it will not be too tedious for you."

She shook her head, "There is such a vast deal to see and do here, my lord, I could not be bored."

He bent down and kissed her lightly upon the forehead, saying softly, "Farewell then – at least you will have a few days of rest with no fears to trouble you!" Then he was gone.

Emma lay back against her pillows with the strangest of feeling. The house suddenly seemed very quiet. In the distance she could hear faintly sounds of domestic activities and outside in the garden someone was clipping a hedge. How could it be, that in the absence of this man, of whom at times she was so afraid, she now felt unprotected and unsure? Was it possible that she was going to miss the presence of her autocratic husband?

Later, downstairs in the morning-room, Edward came to say goodbye to her. He took her hand, saying with a rueful grin, "I would most willingly have stayed longer but your ogre of a husband informed me that it would not be proper for me to remain here in his absence. He has grown suddenly very gothic in his ideas!"

Emma laughed and said confidingly, "Well, I hope to see you soon in London." adding, with a twinkle in her eyes, "Please to remember, Cousin Edward, that you have promised to escort me and to bring me into fashion by so doing!"

As soon as he had arrived in London, Ware had called to Grosvenor Square one of the leading decorators of the day: the Countess's apartments, unused since his mother's death, were to be refurbished and prepared for Emma's arrival, and soon an army of upholsterers, painters and other tradesmen dedicated to the adornment of the houses of the rich, were set to work. The heavier furniture having been replaced by elegant pieces of Mr Sheraton's designs, the walls and bed were hung with pale apricot silk and, in my lady's boudoir, pretty gilded furniture in the French style was ordered to complement the Aubusson carpet and Sèvres porcelain upon the mantel-piece.

It was not the first time that his lordship had ordered the preparation of a fit setting for a member of the fair sex, for he had been a generous lover, but he had never, hitherto, lavished so much attention upon every detail nor taken such pains to achieve the effect of simple elegance which he was confident would most appeal to his young wife.

The day following his arrival, Mr Pettigrew was also summoned to wait upon his lordship. The meeting took place in the library and, as he entered the room, Mr Pettigrew gave a sharp look at his noble patron from over his gold-rimmed spectacles. All his working life he had been attending to the affairs of the family and had been hoping for some years that its present head would settle down and marry. Now, if rumour was correct, a marriage had taken place – but what a marriage! No marriage settlements arranged beforehand, a portion-less bride – not that the Earls of Ware were lacking in funds – but to Mr Pettigrew's mind such arrangements were the fitting overture to matrimony.

The lawyer could discern no difference in the Earl, no sign that marriage had softened either his character or his manner. He was polite but cool. He informed Mr Pettigrew that he had married a Miss Emma Stanton by special licence on the previous Friday; that she was a minor and had been the ward of her half-brother, Sir Richard Harding, since her father's death the previous year. He gave Mr Pettigrew the name of the Reverend William Stanton's solicitors and requested him to take whatever legal steps were necessary to terminate Sir Richard's guardianship of his wife and to prevent any further participation on his part in her affairs.

"I wish to return to Millford in a few days time, so please proceed as quickly as you can."

"I shall do my utmost, my very utmost, my lord, to expedite matters." Mr Pettigrew collected his notes together and added solemnly, "May I extend to you, my lord, my congratulations upon your recent nuptials!"

His lordship, bowing slightly, thanked him gravely and offered him a glass of sherry before he left.

Mr Pettigrew returned to his offices in Lincoln's Inn Fields shaking his head over what he considered to be a sadly ramshackle affair, lacking the dignity due to an ancient and noble family, and found himself wondering what lay behind such a strange marriage. Grave doubts as to its future arose in his mind, for even in the dusty offices of Turnbull, Pettigrew and Harley there had penetrated disturbing rumours concerning the new Countess.

The first call that the Earl made was upon his sister. He found her in her drawing-room, a fat little pug asleep upon a cushion near her feet. She was reading a letter and looked up, with surprise when he was announced.

"Good gracious, Robert, the last person that I expected to see!"

He bent down and kissed her cheek, saying, "I feel that I owe you an apology! It was quite abominable of me to make use of you as I did, but at the time there seemed no other course to take."

As he sat down beside her, he said with a teasing look, "Aren't you going to congratulate me, Sophie?"

"So it *is* true!" She turned a horrified face towards him, "Robert, you must be mad! A girl of seventeen with neither looks, nor fortune, nor position to recommend her! It is a disastrous marriage and one that I fear you will regret – why you will tire of her in a month!" She went on dolefully, "It has caused the most dreadful scandal – I suppose that you realise that not a soul will receive her, for all the world knows that she willingly left her brother's house to come to you!"

He gave a harsh laugh, "My dear Sophie, before you pass judgment, let me now acquaint you with the true facts!" For the first time he told her, in detail, how Richard Harding had deceived his sister. Lady Sophia's delicate eyebrows drew together in a frown, "The wager was, of course, altogether monstrous, but what a fool she was, Robert, to believe such an unlikely story!"

"Only a green girl, Sophie, too honest herself to suspect others of duplicity!"

There was a reminiscent look upon Ware's face as he began to describe how he had pursued Miss Stanton to Wiltshire and how, there, he had forced her to marry him. Lady Sophia, listening with ever increasing amazement, found it incredible that her handsome, eligible brother should have taken this insignificant girl as his wife. At the same time she could not help feeling, in spite of herself, a growing sensation of pity for Miss Stanton and preferred not to let her mind dwell upon what such a forced marriage would have been like for one so young and inexperienced.

"Have you brought her to London, Robert?" she asked when he had finished.

"No, she has remained at Millford. I wished first to obtain your agreement to act as her sponsor and to see that she *is* received in Society." He saw Lady Sophia's look of horror and added reproachfully, "Good God, its not like you, Sophie, to condemn someone out of hand!"

She thought of her husband and said firmly, "I am persuaded that Sir Peter will certainly forbid it – he is still enraged, you know, at your deception of me!"

"And has every right to be!" Ware said ruefully, "But when he knows the true story, I believe him to be too just a man to object." He added with a coaxing smile that his sister found hard to resist, "If *you* will receive her, others will follow. Even then it will be an ordeal for her, for she has not the least idea how to go on in Society and will badly need your help."

She looked at him doubtfully, "You must bring her to see me – I can promise you nothing!" adding in a vexed voice, "If you intended to shock and annoy your family and friends you have certainly succeeded admirably!"

Ware laughed softly, "I confess that I find a certain entertainment in the furore that my marriage has caused!" He leaned back in his chair and looked at Sophie reflectively, then, taking out his snuff-box, he flicked it open, saying as he did so, "I shall not, however, tolerate any slight to my wife - *she* has done nothing to deserve it!" It was said gently but there was such a grim look in his eyes as he spoke that Lady Sophia could be left in no doubt that he was thoroughly in earnest.

"No, indeed!" she said sharply, "It is certainly *your* fault – I am surprised that she does not hate you!"

She saw him frown. He said thoughtfully, "No, she does not hate me, her nature is too generous for that!" He inhaled a pinch of snuff and said under his breath, "But she is afraid of me .... sadly afraid!"

Lady Sophia was shocked and a little dismayed. She had always disapproved, as an elder sister will, of his hedonistic attitude to life, and had never had the least desire to enquire too closely into his amorous affairs; this was different. She had been brought up to accept that many men had their discreet liaisons, but the females who were their partners in those clandestine amours were more than willing. She looked doubtfully at Ware, filled with sudden misgivings. He, seeing her look, smiled at her warmly and said affectionately, "You are a kind-hearted woman, Sophie! I assure you, there is no reason to look just so – I am not such a monster as you seem to fear!" and with these words, rose to his feet saying, "Now I must go, but I will bring Emma to see you when we come to London next week." and having kissed her, departed, leaving Lady Sophia staring after him with a puzzled frown and a growing bewilderment.

Edward, upon his return to London, had invited Ware to dine with him and so, that evening, he made his way to Edward's lodgings in Great Ryder Street. The other guests, already assembled when he arrived, were eagerly questioning Edward about Ware's sudden and astonishing marriage when his tall figure was seen in the doorway. There was a brief silence. His lordship, surveying the scene with narrowed eyes, had a distinctly forbidding expression upon his face.

Lord Redford was the first to speak, "Well, Ware, so you are leg-shackled at last! Lord! It comes to the best of us!" He shook Ware warmly by the hand, his good-natured face betraying some degree of embarrassment.

Viscount Redford's own betrothal had been announced a month previously. He and his bride-to-be, a Miss Annabel Wantage, a girl of impeccable lineage and considerable fortune, were shortly to be married with great pomp and ceremony at St George's, Hanover Square. Ware's eyes sparkled appreciatively, "At least mine was a quiet wedding, George! I can't say that I envy you all the fuss!"

"By Jove, you're right there!" groaned the much-tried, future bridegroom, "It's enough to give one a distaste for the whole state of matrimony!"

Humphrey Featherstone then came forward, "Beg you will accept my felicitations, Robert! Wish you very happy!" He offered Ware his snuff-box, his thin face still wearing a nervous expression, "Dash it, never thought that *you* would settle down, dear boy! Great sorrow and dismay amongst the fair sex, y'know – much weeping and gnashing of teeth!"

"When are we going to meet the bride?" Sir Andrew Holt asked with interest as he joined the circle around Ware, "Edward has made us all eager to make her acquaintance."

"I shall bring her to London next week." Ware had turned to Edward, eyebrows raised questioningly.

The latter poured him a glass of wine and said easily, "An enchanting girl! You'll see – Robert's a lucky man!"

It seemed as if his lordship was re-assured, his manner relaxed and he received the congratulations of the remaining member of the party, Mr Felix Grantham, with a smile and a laughing enquiry as to the progress of that gentleman's wooing of a certain Miss Barrington, who was, by all accounts, a notable heiress.

The conversation turned to the recent purchase of a pair of match-greys from the Earl of Sefton by Sir Andrew Holt, who was a member of the exclusive "Four-in-Hand" club and a famous whip, and the heated discussion which followed put an end to any further talk of matrimony.

After dinner a move was made to continue the conviviality of the evening at one of the clubs and it was agreed to step round to Watier's in Piccadilly; Mr Grantham and Sir Andrew being obliged to decline the invitation, having made plans for an early start the next morning.

Inside Watier's, the rooms were ablaze with lights and crowded with gamblers, some sitting at the tables, others standing observing the play. The first of the gaming rooms was given over to Pharoah and Deep Basset. Several acquaintances greeted them and Ware was conscious that his arrival had caused a stir of interest. It would, however, have been impossible to read what was passing through his mind. He moved forward with Edward into an inner room where the chink of dice could be heard and the groom-porter's voice calling out the odds. The bank, held by Lord Sandwich, seemed to be doing well; the room was quieter than the one they had left, the players intent upon the throws.

Ware, glancing around the room, saw Sir James Kent, who had been present at Richard's house upon that fateful night; he was seated at the table, his neck-cloth loosened, a half-filled glass at his elbow and bore all the signs of one who had drunk deeply. Sandwich looking up and seeing Ware, greeted him in a friendly manner, saying, "Come and join us, Robert, and find out whether your luck still holds!" Before he could reply, Sir James's voice could be clearly heard during a sudden, brief lull in the general conversation.

"Damme!" he pronounced thickly, looking around him with a leer, "*Luck*! Fellow doesn't know when he's well-off! Wins a lovely, willing armful at play and then is fool enough to marry the chit!"

As he finished speaking, he felt an iron grip upon his shoulder, twisting him roughly round in his chair and found himself looking up into Ware's face. His lordship, tight-lipped was staring down at him.

"You know, Kent," he said softly, "I have been thinking for some time how unhealthy London air is for you! If you take my advice you will remove yourself to the country for a period of time. I believe it would prolong your life to absent yourself from this and other like establishments!"

There was a sudden deathly hush around the table. Edward kept his eyes fixed upon Ware's face. Sir James rose unsteadily to his feet, his mouth hanging open a little, his face suffused with colour. "Confound you, I'll be damned if I know what you are talking about, my lord!" he blustered, his hand trembling as he tugged at his neck-cloth.

"I think you understand me very well! If you open your mouth too wide, my friend, it could be fatal!" Ware turned away from him contemptuously, saying to Sandwich as he took Kent's place at the table, "What stakes do you set, my lord?"

Play re-commenced. Several knowing glances were exchanged while Sir James stood irresolute for a moment, then, with a muttered curse, he moved away and left the room.

It did not take long for news of the encounter to spread rapidly throughout the clubs and drawing-rooms of the fashionable world. Clearly the Earl of Ware did not intend to tolerate any slighting remarks made in his presence about either his wife or his marriage. Only a fool, in view of my lord's reputation in affairs of honour, would risk incurring his wrath by doing so.

Amongst the correspondence that had been awaiting him in Grosvenor Square, there had been an invitation from Lady Sheldon inviting him to join her party at the Drury Lane theatre to see a performance of Massinger's newly revived play, "A New Way to Pay Old Debts", with the great Edmond Kean in the role of Sir Giles Overreach. He had sent a note round to her house accepting the invitation and on the Thursday evening presented himself at her box shortly before the beginning of the first Act. Bowing over her hand, he excused the tardiness of his reply, saying apologetically, "I have been out of town for a week or more and have only just returned from Millford."

Lady Sheldon rapped his knuckles playfully with her fan; she had a soft spot for such a handsome rake. "Nothing namby-pamby about Ware!" she had said to her protégée, Miss Charlotte Danvers, who was enjoying her first season under the guidance of her godmother.

"Well, Ware," she said to him in her blunt way, "so you have fooled us all! Stolen off and married out of hand some girl nobody has ever heard of. Faith, I wish you joy! But where is your bride?" she added in a rallying tone, "Not weary of her already, surely?"

My lord frowned, but there was no malice in her plump, good-natured face and smiling eyes. "She comes to town next week." he replied shortly, "I am here merely to put in hand some alterations in my house." He exchanged greetings with the rest of the party and shook hands with Miss Danvers with whom he was already acquainted; a young lady of eighteen, a pretty, kittenish creature, who stood in considerable awe of this dashing Non-pareil of the Corinthian set.

It had been the cherished ambition of Lady Sheldon to make a match between her god-daughter and the Earl and, although there had been nothing distinguishing in the attentions that he had paid to her, at least he had shown no interest in any other eligible female. Now those hopes were dashed. She was, naturally, fully aware of the rumours circulating about his marriage and of the gossip which had so effectively blackened his wife's reputation; indeed, most hostesses of her acquaintance were resolute in their determination not to receive a young female so deep sunk in iniquity.

During the interval a great many eyes were turned upon Lady Sheldon's box; the tall figure of the Earl was easily distinguishable and the other occupants of the box were subjected to a close scrutiny to ascertain whether the new Countess could be discovered amongst them. Ware, who was seated beside Miss Danvers, began to question her politely about her home in the country and, soon realising that it was a subject that held little interest for her, turned the conversation to her forth-coming ball and to the pleasures of the London Season. She replied with more animation but had little to say that was not the merest commonplace. As he listened, he saw in his mind's eye Emma's eager face and remembered her interest in the people on his estates and her wide-eyed wonder at Edward's description of the social life of the great metropolis.

After the second Act, Humphrey Featherstone entered the box, having caught sight of Ware, and after saying all that was pretty to the ladies in a few well-turned phrases, suggested to his lordship in a low voice that after the final curtain they should pay a visit to the Green room, where, he said, the loveliest pair of eyes and the most neatly turned ankles were to be seen in the person of the young actress playing one of the minor parts in the production.

As it happened another member of the cast was well known to Ware. Miss Fanny Lomax, performing the role of the chambermaid, had been, some months previously and for a short time, Ware's mistress. The parting had been amicable: Miss Lomax not wishing to confine herself to one lover and my lord refusing to share her favours.

At the final curtain, when all the calls had been taken amidst fervent applause, Ware politely thanked his hostess and, with Mr Featherstone, made his way backstage to the Green room. There was already a crowd of people there, for it was customary for many of the aristocratic young bucks to seek the acquaintance of the younger actresses and Ware had been prominent amongst them. He was greeted warmly by his friends and if some were surprised to see him so soon after his marriage they evidently considered it politic to keep their thoughts to themselves.

He soon saw Fanny, a lively, dark-haired beauty. She was still attired in her stage costume, a dress cut prodigiously low, displaying her well-rounded figure to advantage, her face still rouged and painted. She came up to him at once, a surprised expression upon her animated little face and, looking up at him roguishly from under her blackened eyelashes, said, "What an unexpected pleasure, my lord!"

He kissed her hand and said lightly, "So you have missed me, Fanny?"

"Why, certainly I have missed you, my lord!" She was looking at him boldly now and there was no mistaking the invitation in her sparkling eyes. His pulses quickened as he thought, "By God, I have lived like a monk this past week!"

She saw the gleam in his eye and put her hand caressingly on his arm, saying "I feared we should not see you for a while!" There was a wicked smile upon her face as she stretched up to murmur, soft-voiced, in his ear, "I am glad, my lord, that the delights of the marriage bed have not kept you from your old friends!"

She knew at once that she had made a mistake. His whole expression and demeanour changed upon the instant; now there was a haughtiness in his eyes, a stiffness in his back. Ignoring her remark, he took her hand and gently removed it from his sleeve. Before releasing it, he raised his quizzing-glass and, looking down at the fine ring upon her finger, enquired with a note of sarcasm in his voice, "A new acquisition, Fanny? A new admirer?"

She flushed angrily and said in a low voice, "So I am not to speak of your wife!" He bowed politely, "Exactly so, my dear Fanny!"

By now other men were demanding Fanny's attention and she turned a little aside to greet them, accepting their compliments with practised ease, a smile and a flirtatious glance for each one. Ware's gaze went round the crowded, over-heated room. There were several women such as Fanny present: except for a talented few, however high their artistic aspirations may have been at the outset, the majority had been obliged to abandon their ambitions and been forced to support themselves by pleasing men like himself. Emma, as he had first seen her, had been like a parody of one of these girls. He remembered the shock he had experienced when he had looked down upon her unconscious face and, mercifully, had recognised in time the innocence and extreme youth underlying her appearance.

With this recollection of her so vivid in his mind, somehow Fanny's attractions for him had vanished. He thought sardonically 'the Rake Reformed!' and moving away from the circle surrounding her, spoke briefly to Humphrey Featherstone and left the theatre.

Dismissing his carriage, he walked home through the moon-lit streets, deserted save for the stray reveller returning to his home. As he strolled along, the watchman, calling the hour, bade him goodnight. A thousand thoughts passed through his mind; he imagined Emma asleep in her bed at Millford: why did he feel this strange tenderness for her that, so far, had over-ridden his desire to possess her? He felt as if she had bewitched him – all his past ideas of women turned upside down.

As he strolled through the empty streets, he admitted to himself, for the first time, that he desired her love and affection as well as her person and doubted whether he could be satisfied with less. He thought savagely that, as her husband, he found himself at a disadvantage! A few days before he had imagined that it would be a pleasant pastime to gain her willingness; but he had misjudged the matter entirely – he had never felt more serious in his life.

CHAPTER 10

Exploring the pleasure gardens after Edward's departure had been a delight and a wonder to Emma. Besides the formal rose-beds with their central lily-pond and fountain, there was an ancient knot-garden, laid out in an intricate design, its low box hedges enclosing small beds filled with aromatic herbs; close-clipped yew formed a background to long herbaceous borders, and the lawns, shaven and weedless, extended into the distance; there, exotic pines, brought from the former American colonies, formed a contrast to the fresh green of the native oaks and beeches.

Emma sat resting for a while upon a stone bench set in a sheltered corner, while, around her, the lilac bushes filled the air with their sweet scent. The warmth of the sun, the glowing colours, and the drone of the bees eagerly probing the flower heads, were like balm to her troubled heart and, for the first time for many days, she began to feel a sense of tranquillity.

As she sat there, she heard footsteps on the gravel path and an elderly man in breeches and gaiters, wearing a blue apron, came into view round the corner and approached her. For a moment, with fast-beating heart, Emma wondered whether he would think her to be an intruder; however, taking off his hat, he wished her good-morning and said respectfully, "I'm Upton, my lady, his lordship's head-gardener. My lord instructed me, before he left this morning, to conduct your ladyship around the gardens and to show you the Great Vine and the succession houses."

"Oh, I should like that above everything!" Emma stood up eagerly, for here was someone who could answer all the many questions that she was longing to ask.

The tour took a considerable time. There were many glass-houses and, behind mellow brick walls, against which apricot and pear trees had been trained to grow, stretched the vegetable gardens. Here the orderly rows of vegetables and soft-fruit seemed to be sufficient to feed an army.

Upton, with the habitual pessimism of the professional gardener, shook his head sadly over the recent bad weather and foretold poor results with a certain melancholy relish. He had, on first sight, viewed his new young mistress with a suspicious eye and was sceptical of her interest: in his experience, young ladies seldom knew the difference between one plant and another and certainly had no knowledge of cuttings and plant-propagation. Now he found himself impressed in spite of these forebodings and, when Emma left him to return to the house, having thanked him warmly, he stood staring after her, scratching his head, his lined, weather-beaten face expressing amazement.

In the courtyard, Emma encountered Henry Capel on horseback on his way to the stables. He dismounted at once and asked her, with a polite bow, if he could be of service to her in any way. It was the first time that they had met since the night of her marriage and Emma felt a degree of awkwardness, which she tried, not very successfully, to conceal. Nervously, she told him that she had been enjoying a tour of the gardens.

Henry, aware of her unease, wished inwardly that he could tell her how sorry he felt for her; instead, he said with a smile, "If you would care to ride this afternoon, Lady Ware, I could show you some of the outlying farms and cottages."

"Thank you, that would indeed be delightful!" Her face lit up. Until that moment, the dismal prospect of a solitary afternoon had stretched before her. Thus it was that after a light luncheon, she rode out beside Mr Capel, mounted upon the same bay mare that she had ridden on the previous day.

At first conversation was difficult but there was too much of interest to be seen for any constraint on Emma's part to endure for long. Her questions to him betrayed a knowledge of crops and animal husbandry that astonished him and, on expressing his surprise, she had informed him that her father had been interested in all aspects of farming and, from being so much alone together, had imparted his enthusiasm and knowledge to his daughter. At this point, Emma remembered the little girl, Mary Sharp, whom she had met in the churchyard, and enquired whether she might visit the family who, she recollected, lived near the Home Farm.

This proved to be less than half-a-mile away: a long, low building, surrounded by its accompanying buildings, barns and piggeries. Nearby stood a pair of thatched cottages and, outside one of these, Emma saw at once the little girl who had presented her with the bunch of flowers; she was nursing a rag-doll on her lap and alongside her a small boy, about two years old, was attempting to build up a pile of battered wooden bricks. Mary, perceiving the identity of the young lady riding beside Mr Capel, jumped up and ran into the cottage, shouting excitedly, "Mother, Mother, come quickly! Here be her lady-ship! Oh, come at once!"

Meanwhile, with Henry Capel's assistance, Emma had dismounted, and was bending down talking to the little boy when Mrs Sharp appeared in her doorway, sleeves rolled up to the elbow, wiping her hands awkwardly upon her apron, her cheeks flushed; she bobbed a curtsy to her ladyship and, bidding her a respectful good-day, asked if she would care to take some refreshment, "A glass of milk, my lady, or perhaps some home-brewed cider?"

Emma confessed that she was indeed thirsty and, having informed Mr Capel that she would not be long, stepped inside the cottage into a low-ceilinged room which clearly served as both kitchen and living-room. Mrs Sharp, who had had it in mind to bring out whatever drinks were required, followed her inside, profuse in apologies for the mess and muddle. She had obviously just finished preparing the dough for her bread and had set it to rise near the hearth, covered with a cloth. The room was rather dark but very clean: strings of onions and bunches of herbs hung from hooks in the beams and there was a pleasant smell of what appeared to be a rabbit stew cooking gently at the side of the fire. Mrs Sharp wiped a cloth over the top of a stool for her guest.

As she sat down, Emma remarked hastily, "I must not detain you long, Mrs Sharp – I can see how busy you are! I only wished to make your acquaintance and to thank Mary again for the pretty flowers that she gave me." She took the thick tumbler of milk and giving Mary, who had followed them into the room, a warm smile, asked Mrs Sharp how many children she had.

"Mary's my youngest, my lady." Mrs Sharp replied proudly, "We have Jemmy, who's out with his father just now, and our Jane has started work in the dairy up at the big house."

"Then the little, curly-haired boy with Mary is not one of yours?"

"No, no, your ladyship! He belongs to Sarah Anderson. She be stricken with the typhus, poor lamb – an' proper poorly with it – so they say! We took in little Tom when first she wus ill, for fear like that he might catch it."

"Has she someone to care for her, Mrs Sharp?" Emma enquired.

Mrs Sharp looked dubious. "Neighbours have had to keep away for fear of infection, my lady. Her husband won't let anyone next nor nigh her save the nurse." She hesitated, then added, "To tell the truth, your ladyship, I'd say that nurse ain't no use to anyone!"

Emma's face expressed her concern, "Where does this Mrs Anderson live?"

"About a half-hour's walk away, my lady, down Springly Bottom – they've a cottage there."

Emma drank her milk thoughtfully and enquired of Mary, in a friendly manner, the name of her doll, then looking around her appreciatively, asked Mrs Sharp whether she and her family were comfortable in their cottage.

"That we are, my lady!" Mrs Sharp was beginning to feel quite at ease with her ladyship and, leaning forward, added confidentially, "I might just mention again to Mr Capel that there be a bit of that thatch that'll need repairing afore long."

Emma rejoined Henry Capel, who had been holding their horses, and, while he drank the cider that Mary had brought out to him, showed him, with Mrs Sharp's assistance, where the faulty thatching was letting in the rain. As he agreed to set the work in hand, he was not sure whether to be amused or irritated at having his duties pointed out to him by his employer's young wife.

Having thanked Mrs Sharp and said goodbye to the children, they remounted and continued their ride. At first Emma was rather silent and Henry Capel noticed that she glanced at him once or twice. At length she turned to him and said diffidently, "I hope that you were not offended at my pointing out the thatch to you. Perhaps I should not have done so – but sometimes tenants are afraid of mentioning such things!"

He was aware of feeling faintly surprised; Lady Ware, inspite of her youth, was evidently conscious of the feelings of others. He smiled at her reassuringly, "You were quite right! On such a large estate one can easily overlook a small repair that needs attention."

Her brow cleared and she said with relief, "Thank you – now I can be easy – for I should not like you to think me a busybody, for ever interfering in matters that don't concern me!"

It seemed strange that evening to dine alone in the huge dining-room, waited upon by Marchant and a footman and to sit afterwards in the drawing-room. Emma tried to occupy her mind with all that she had seen that afternoon and with plans for the following day, but she found her thoughts turning again and again to her husband. She imagined him in London, thankful to be amongst his friends again, and wondered if he would forget her very existence. He had said that he would be back in a few days, but perhaps he would remain away for weeks. He had spoken so strangely to her the night before – was he perhaps already regretting his marriage? Her own feelings confused her. One thing was certain however: in spite of everything, in spite of all her fears, she missed his company and would have been thankful if he had walked into the room that minute.

The next morning Emma rose early, her head full of plans. Mrs Huxstable was summoned and was asked to put in hand the preparation of various soups and jellies and suitable sustaining foods for an invalid. The carriage was ordered for midday and, soon after twelve o'clock, Emma set forth, accompanied by Dora and several large baskets, as well as a bundle of sheets and pillowcases. Jackson was surprised to be directed to Springly Bottom: he wondered what scheme his young mistress had in mind: whatever it was it had certainly put her in a very good humour, for she was talking cheerfully to Dora as they drove along.

Their destination reached, Emma ordered the carriage to stop and announced her intention of alighting. A cottage lay a short distance off the road up a narrow path. Having instructed Dora to wait for her in the carriage, Emma walked up the path and knocked on the door. It was answered by a young man, roughly dressed in a smock and breeches and wearing leggings above his heavy boots. He had a worried expression on his face and seemed at a loss for words, looking in a bemused manner first at Emma in her plain, old-fashioned clothes and then at the gleaming carriage beyond her with its fine horses.

"Is your name Anderson?" Emma enquired; as he nodded slowly, she added reassuringly, "I have heard that your wife is ill with fever and have brought some soups and jellies for her." Receiving no reply, for the young man seemed quite dumbfounded, she continued, "I am Lady Ware, you know." She felt her colour rise as for the first time she uttered these words, as strange in her ears as they must be to his, and asked politely, "May I come in? I should like to see your wife."

He shook his head violently; there was a look of dull pain in his eyes. "Don't-ee come in here, m'lady! 'Pothecary says 'tis that typhus my Sarah has! She be terrible sick with it! Nurse has come in but she don't seem able to do nothin' to ease her – my poor Sarah be tossin' and turnin' summat awful!" The poor man's eyes had filled with tears.

Ignoring his objections, Emma put him gently aside and entered the cottage; there was no sign of an invalid but a none too clean-looking old woman was sitting by the fire in an armchair, her cap awry, her head sunk upon her chest and clearly asleep by the sound of her heavy breathing. The room was stuffy and had a faintly sickly smell.

"Is this the nurse?" Emma regarded her with astonishment and moving forward, touched her on the shoulder to arouse her; there was no response. Glancing around her, she noticed an empty bottle lying on the floor beside the woman; horrified, she turned to Anderson, saying in a shocked voice, "This dreadful old woman is drunk! *She* can be of no use to you. You must get rid of her at once – why, she may do your wife more harm than good!" Concealing her mounting dismay, she went through a low doorway which led to the adjoining room. It was lit by only a small window but Emma could distinguish in the half-light a young woman lying upon a bed in the corner, roughly covered by some blankets, her face and hair bathed in sweat, her eyes closed, as she turned and moaned pitifully.

She went at once to the side of the bed and took one of the woman's hot hands in hers, saying softly to herself, "Something must be done at once!" She stood a moment looking down at her, frantically searching her mind to recall all that she had learned about the care of such cases, then turned and said, "I will do all I can for her – but can you tell me what the apothecary has directed?"

"Left some medicine, he did." he sighed heavily, "Don't seem to do a mite of good! Said if fever don't lessen, my poor Sarah won't last more'n a day or two!"

Shocked, Emma said stoutly, "I'm sure your wife will recover – she looks as if she is a strong, young woman." but these brave words were far from reflecting her real thoughts.

Returning to the carriage, she summoned Dora to help her to carry the baskets and bundle to the cottage, instructing Jackson to walk the horses as she would be obliged to keep him waiting for some time. Meanwhile, the drunken nurse had been turned out of the cottage and came staggering down the path towards them, muttering imprecations and protests at her summary dismissal and glaring at Emma, whom she rightly conjectured to be the cause of her downfall. Ignoring her, Emma continued upon her way, pausing at the door to tell the astonished Dora to remain outside.

"But I must help your ladyship," Dora protested, "It ain't fitting for you to be waiting upon the likes of them!"

"Nonsense! I prefer to make myself useful. Besides, you have young brothers and sisters and should on no account run the risk of infection – it is typhus, you know!" Without attending further to Dora's continued protests, Emma closed the door firmly behind her and began to set about her task.

Summoning Anderson to help her, she ordered him to bring some water from the pump and soon had the poor young woman washed and in the clean shift which he had found for her. Sheets were put on the bed and Emma moistened Mrs Anderson's parched lips with a cold drink; the fever was still dangerously high and she was delirious, moaning and crying out in an alarming manner.

"You must remain beside her and bathe her frequently to cool her." Emma stood for a moment beside Anderson looking down at the pathetic figure upon the bed, "I shall send for the doctor to come and see her as soon as possible." as she spoke, she saw the painful expression of anxiety upon his face and said, with an assumption of cheerfulness that she was far from feeling, "I shall come again tomorrow – so you may be easy in your mind."

At first, during the drive back to the house, Dora attempted to remonstrate with her mistress but she encountered such a firm refusal to discuss the matter further and there was something so determined in her ladyship's manner, that Dora fell silent, eyeing her mistress uneasily from time to time.

That evening Emma's thoughts turned constantly to the sick woman. She had ordered one of the grooms to be sent to the doctor's house requesting him to call as soon as possible in Springly Bottom but she feared that there was little that he could do. Mrs Anderson's best hope lay in the possession of a strong constitution and in careful nursing and she resolved to return there the next day at an earlier hour.

It was beginning to get dark, and the candles had already been lit, when a footman came to the Small drawing-room and announced that Mr Capel had asked to be permitted to see her. Emma looked up with pleasure as Henry Capel was shown into the room; she was tired of her own company and of her thoughts and glad of some distraction.

However, when he sat down opposite her, she saw that he looked worried and asked him anxiously if anything was amiss. He sat looking at her for a moment in silence and then said in an oddly formal manner, "I hope your ladyship will forgive me for what I am about to say, but, in Lord Ware's absence, I feel that it is my duty to speak to you on this subject – I trust that you will not consider it an unwarranted interference on my part."

Her eyes opened wide with dismay. She said apprehensively, "Have I done something wrong, Mr Capel?"

"It is not exactly something wrong, Lady Ware." he hesitated, "I am referring to your visit to Mrs Anderson this afternoon."

He saw incomprehension in her face and continued awkwardly, "I am aware of the kindness of your intentions, my lady, but I fear that his lordship would not approve of your having any contact with such a dangerous disease as the typhus! Permit me, therefore, to arrange for one of the female servants to attend to Mrs Anderson in future?"

Emma frowned, "And put *their* lives at risk – to say nothing of their families! No, Mr Capel, *they* cannot refuse an order! I intend to visit Mrs Anderson myself tomorrow."

It was said with an air of finality; the interview was proving to be more difficult than he had expected. He said earnestly, "It was Jackson who informed me of your visit to the cottage; he told me that there was concern in the servant's hall – that they fear that they will be blamed when Lord Ware returns." He did not repeat Jackson's precise words, which were infinitely more explicit, "For Gawd's sake, sir, stop her ladyship going there again, Mr Capel! My lord will be as mad as fire when he finds out! There'll be the very devil to pay – mark my words – for his lordship would never permit sich a thing if he wus here!"

She raised her eyebrows, "Of course no blame shall be attached to the servants, I shall tell Lord Ware so myself." She spoke quietly but Henry Capel was impressed by the firmness in her voice. In spite of it, his own misgivings impelled him, for her own sake, to make one last attempt to dissuade her.

"Forgive me, my lady – I believe I have not made myself sufficiently clear!" He was looking at her gravely and spoke with a deliberate emphasis, "I fear that Lord Ware's displeasure will fall equally heavily upon *you* – indeed, not to put too fine a point upon it – I believe he will be extremely angry when he learns of what has occurred!"

He thought that she turned a trifle pale at his words but there was a purposeful set to her mouth as she rose and held out her hand dismissively to him, saying in a determined voice, "I am very much obliged to you, Mr Capel, for your thoughtfulness, but I do not care to discuss the matter further."

As he bowed over her hand and bade her good-night, Henry Capel felt a growing astonishment at such resolution in one so young, and quitted her company torn between admiration and regret: he had failed in his efforts to protect her but he did not believe for one moment that his autocratic employer would allow himself to be over-ruled in this affair.

For the next three days Emma continued to visit Mrs Anderson, remaining longer with her than hitherto and thus enabling her husband to leave her bedside, but she no longer took Dora with her in the carriage. His lordship's household watched events and waited uneasily for my lord's return, none of its members caring to make any further references to their mistress's visits to the cottage.

On the third day Emma found at last a definite improvement in her patient's condition. When she arrived that morning with her customary basket, she was greeted at the cottage door by Anderson and one look at his face was enough to tell her that the news was better.

"Oh, my lady! I do believe as her fever be abating!" the poor man said, taking the basket from her, his face wreathed in smiles.

The news was true. For the first time Sarah was no longer delirious; she was lying quietly in her bed, very pale and weak, and when Emma laid her hand upon her forehead it was cool to her touch; the crisis that the doctor had foretold had been passed and now rest and good food should complete the cure. Emma's relief was scarcely less than that of the young husband; she had done some nursing in her father's parish but never before had she held the sole responsibility for the care of a sick person. She sat down beside the bed and was obliged to take a strong hold upon herself not to betray her emotion.

Seeing that Mrs Anderson's eyes were open and fixed upon her, she leaned forward and said gently, "You must rest quietly now – no need to concern yourself with anything. Little Tom is well and soon you will be fully recovered." The young woman, too weak to reply, reached out a thin hand towards her and held Emma's hand in a feeble grasp, her eyes full of tears of gratitude. It was with a much lighter heart that Emma attended to her needs and, having left Anderson with further instructions, was driven home, intending to return the next day to make certain that her patient's condition continued to improve.

CHAPTER 11

Elizabeth Tremayne had several times found herself thinking of the Countess of Ware; Lady Ware had been so different to the style of young female that she had expected, and the contrast between this ill-assorted couple intrigued and provoked her; Lady Ware's features were well-enough and she had a delightfully slender figure, but she looked so absurdly young. Mrs Tremayne could see nothing about her which would interest a man of Ware's known tastes. Her clothes, moreover, were positively shabby and old-fashioned; he, by contrast, was always well dressed in his own careless fashion, affecting the plain style of Mr Brummel. She found Lord Ware's preference for this dowdy girl, as opposed to her own exquisite person, to be a new and, she thought angrily, provoking blow to her pride.

It was on the Saturday morning following their meeting that Mrs Tremayne determined to fulfil her promise and pay a morning call upon the Countess. Emma was seated in the yellow saloon, striving to compose a letter to Miss Embery, when Mrs Tremayne's name was announced and the footman ushered her into the room. Rising hastily in confusion, Emma wished with all her heart that she were not alone.

Mrs Tremayne swept in, a vision of fashionable loveliness; as the day was fine and warm she needed no more than a light shawl over her Polonese robe and petticoat of fine cambric, and wore a bonnet-cap composed of jonquil satin to match gloves of yellow kid. Emma greeted her shyly and bade her sit down beside her upon a sofa near the tall windows, which were open-wide to the terrace allowing the pleasantly warm air to fill the room with the scent of newly cut grass and the murmuring of a pair of doves strutting upon the path outside.

At first conversation was strained: commonplaces about the weather were exchanged and the beauties of Millford House extolled. Her hostess being, by now, more at ease, Mrs Tremayne began to question her adroitly about her life before her marriage. Emma, lost in recollection of the past, told her without reserve about her happy life at the Rectory and of her sorrow at her father's sudden death.

Mrs Tremayne, watching her eager, animated face, enquired softly where and when she and Lord Ware had first met and was interested to observe an immediate change in Emma's manner. With heightened colour, she replied in a guarded voice, "We met at my half-brother's house in Richmond, ma'am, two weeks ago."

"A whirlwind courtship indeed!" Mrs Tremayne gave a little trill of laughter and patted Emma's hand, "You must have made a prodigious impression upon Robert in so short a space of time!" She saw Emma blush vividly and asked lightly, "Where is he this morning? I hope that I am to have the pleasure of seeing him."

"Alas, he is not here, ma'am, he left for London on Monday." It was clear from Emma's expression as she replied that she found nothing strange or shameful in the absence of her bridegroom.

Mrs Tremayne was intrigued and saw her opportunity. In accents of feigned pity, she exclaimed, "My poor child! Gone already – and so soon after your marriage! Upon my word, what brutes men are!" and shaking her head sadly, added pensively as she cast a sly glance at Emma's discomforted face, "But, good gracious, one cannot expect a man to reform his way of life all at once! You may console yourself with the reflection, my dear, that you are prettier by far than Robert's latest mistress – I can assure you of that – a young actress of no more than passable looks!"

Her words came as a profound shock to Emma. She had no reason to doubt Mrs Tremayne's sincerity and, aware that she, herself, had little knowledge of the ways of the fashionable world, believed her, and was sensible of a feeling of distress that took her by surprise. Later she would reflect upon this unwelcome information but now she knew instinctively that she must hide her feelings and replied at once with a tolerable assumption of calm, "I believe you are under a misapprehension, ma'am. My lord has matters to attend to in his house in London before we go there." then, hastily searching for some means to change the subject of conversation, she offered her guest some refreshment and, in the subsequent arrival and dispensation of ratafia and macaroon biscuits, the talk turned, to her relief, to local affairs.

Setting down her glass, Mrs Tremayne remarked smilingly, "I daresay that you have had a constant stream of morning-callers, Lady Ware, to offer you their good wishes – I am fortunate to find you alone!"

"Oh, no, ma'am. Not one person has called." Emma thought that she detected a glimmer of satisfaction in her visitor's face and added cheerfully, "I have been more than occupied in going about the estate and acquainting myself with my lord's tenants."

"Heavens, Lady Ware, you will put us all to shame! I had thought at your age your head would be full of balls and routs and excursions of pleasure!" Mrs Tremayne eyed her hostess with surprise, "We have a large circle of friends in the neighbourhood, you know." and she began to enumerate for Emma's benefit the notable families living in the vicinity, finishing her discourse by saying, "The Priestleys, my dear, are a charming family, their daughter, Jane, is about your age I should say. My brother, Hartley, is quite taken up with her." She paused, then added thoughtfully, "You and Robert must dine with us – Freddie will be coming down to Millford tomorrow, so might I suggest perhaps Monday? And I will invite the Priestleys too – for I am confident that you will find them agreeable." She did not reveal to Emma that they were probably the only family in the neighbourhood, or for many miles around for that matter, who would consent to meet the now notorious young Countess of Ware.

Surprised, Emma hesitated, uncertain what her husband's wishes might be upon the subject, then murmured her thanks, adding, ".... if my lord is returned – it would give us great pleasure ...."

Mrs Tremayne seemed content with this reply and rose to take her leave, inwardly vexed by her apparent failure to disturb the young bride's innocent trust in her husband. As she took Emma's hand, she said in a low voice, with every appearance of friendliness, "You must forgive my frankness! I feel deeply for you, you know – to be married to a man who, with so vast an experience of women, is doubtless cruelly demanding in his attentions!"

Emma withdrew her hand quickly, her eyes sparkling with indignation; she was not conscious of the sound of footsteps outside, approaching the open window, as she retorted emphatically, "I do not wish to appear discourteous, but it is quite unthinkable that my marriage should be a subject of discussion between us. I can, however assure you, ma'am, that your pity is misplaced – Lord Ware has always displayed towards me the utmost consideration!"

In the brief silence that followed this announcement, a deep, male voice spoke from the open window behind them, "My dear Emma," Ware declared softly, as he stepped into the room, raising his quizzing glass to survey the startled faces turned towards him, "such an encomium has me almost unmanned! I can scarcely believe that I deserve such praise!"

He saw the surprise and embarrassment on Emma's flushed, angry face and turned to her companion; for one brief moment Mrs Tremayne's countenance displayed her discomposure before a mask of polite indifference concealed her feelings.

"Good gracious, Robert, how you startled us! You come upon us just as I am taking leave of your charming wife! You see – I kept my promise to wait upon her."

He raised an eyebrow and said meaningfully, "I only regret that I did not arrive earlier so that I, too, might have had the pleasure of your company and conversation!"

"I was commiserating with Lady Ware upon her solitude." Mrs Tremayne looked from one to the other, her sharp eyes absorbing every nuance in their respective attitudes. "You are to dine with us on Monday, Robert – Freddie will be there and is eager, I am sure, to meet your bride – as will be all Society to behold her!" She inclined her head graciously to Emma, saying, "Goodbye, Lady Ware — 'till Monday then!" and swept out of the room.

As the Earl escorted her to her carriage, he said to her in a fierce undertone that quite startled her, "If you injure that girl with your tongue, Elizabeth, you will live to regret it! God only knows what you have been telling her!"

She turned back to him as she mounted the carriage step and replied sarcastically, with a toss of her elegant head, "Only the truth, Ware! No more than the truth!"

He came back into the saloon frowning heavily but his brow cleared when he saw Emma sitting forlornly upon the sofa, gazing ahead of her with unseeing eyes. He sat down beside her and taking her hand in his, kissed it, saying, "I did not know that I possessed such a worthy advocate!"

He was smiling at her, but one glance into his face showed her the serious expression in his eyes. She said impulsively, "I am sorry to say it since she is a friend of yours, my lord, but I find that I do not care overmuch for Mrs Tremayne!"

Watching her face curiously, he asked, "What has she said to vex you?"

There was a pause; eyes downcast, Emma said in a low voice, "Matters that I should not care to repeat to you, my lord ...." then, with a sigh, she looked up at him and tried to smile, adding shyly, "I am glad to see you home again – I had not expected your return so soon."

"And you are truly pleased to see me? Or is it that your impeccable manners prompted you to say so?" There was a teasing note of incredulity in his voice.

Her candid reply to this raillery touched and amused him as she said thoughtfully, "I was surprised to discover that I missed your company, my lord!"

The Earl's business having been completed on Friday morning, he had found himself unexpectedly eager to return to Millford and had set off almost immediately, passing the night at Christ Church, where his student days at Oxford had been spent, and leaving there early in the morning. Requested to visit the stables upon his arrival at Millford and cast a knowledgeable eye over his new hunter, he had walked back to the house across the garden, wondering ruefully what his wife's response would be to his return.

Leaning back against the sofa cushions and observing the grave look in her brown eyes, the droop of her shoulders, he felt a strong impulse to take her in his arms. Instead, he said in a matter-of-fact voice, "I have some surprising news to communicate to you, Emma! Whilst informing your father's lawyers of our marriage, my man, Pettigrew, has discovered the motive for Richard's conduct!" He saw her start at the mention of her half-brother's name, her big eyes anxious.

"It's a long story. Your father had an aunt, a wealthy widow named Harriet Randall, who died barely a week before your father's fatal accident. This Mrs Randall, being childless and having quarrelled irrevocably with her husband's relations, made a will leaving all her money to your father. His death, following so closely upon hers, prevented him from making any alterations to the provisions that he had made for you. Indeed, it is not certain whether he even knew that he was the heir to a considerable fortune."

She was following his words intently, a puzzled frown upon her face.

"Mrs Randall's will was disputed by her husband's family and it was only in the last two weeks that your father's lawyers wrote to Richard to inform him that *you* had inherited no less a sum than eighty thousand pounds from your father!"

Emma said slowly, her eyes wide with amazement, "Richard said nothing to me! Not a single word!"

Ware said cynically, "We now come to the shocking part of the affair! As your guardian, he had control of your money *until you married*. His own affairs are in a disastrous state, his creditors growing ever more demanding – he evidently decided to take what steps he could to ensure that you would *never* marry and by keeping you in ignorance of the fortune that you had inherited, intended to use the money entrusted to him to extricate himself from his present difficulties and to enable him to continue in his present way of life."

She sat motionless, staring at him in bewilderment.

"I believe his plan to ruin you was made upon the spur of the moment when he received that letter. Knowing that I was dining with him that night, he staked everything upon the chance that I would accept his disgraceful wager."

His dark brows were drawn together in a frown now, a grim expression upon his face. "One night spent in my company would be sufficient to destroy your reputation for ever, and Richard took great pains to ensure that that fact should be widely known. After that, it would be highly unlikely that *any* man would offer for you."

Emma gazed at him in horrified silence. He said self-mockingly, "My role was the seducer! I was to have taken my pleasure of you and then abandoned you to your fate." he gave a harsh laugh, "To have cast you out penniless or, perhaps, to have recompensed you generously for the loss of your virtue! It was not, shall we say, a particularly flattering estimate of my character!"

He took her left hand in his and gently turned the heavy gold ring upon her finger. "It gives me great satisfaction to learn that our marriage has defeated his ends."

"It was abominable of him to think so ill of you!" she said with strong indignation, "When *your* conduct has indeed been most honourable!"

He raised an eyebrow at that, momentarily diverted by her championship and said reflectively, "But if I had not accepted the wager ...."

Suddenly the recollection came to her of a fleeting glimpse she had had that night: a figure in the doorway of the book room at Richard's house, an older man, rather stout, with a flushed face and a lewd look in his blood-shot eyes as he had stared at her. Suppose he had wagered and won her! She shuddered and her hand trembled in Ware's grasp. He, misunderstanding her involuntary movement, released it and, standing up, crossed to the open window and stood looking out, his back turned to her.

"You have nothing more to fear from Richard," he said evenly, "and such a sum of money will give you a measure of independence which I am sure will be most welcome to you."

Emma was silent for a moment; it was hard to grasp that she was now the possessor of what was by any standards a very large fortune. She said thoughtfully, "Now at least I shall be able to pay for all my purchases when we go to London."

She was surprised when Ware turned round quickly and said in a decided voice, "You will do nothing of the kind, my girl! Your own fortune shall be entirely at your disposal, to use in any way that you think fit, but I have already arranged an allowance for you which I trust will be sufficiently generous to cover all your requirements."

He was regarding her so frowningly that, after one look at his face, she did not dare to argue. Instead she asked him whether he had passed an agreeable time in London. The news that, amongst other engagements, he had visited the theatre reminded Emma uncomfortably of her conversation with Mrs Tremayne; was this the confirmation of her visitor's remarks?

Clearly he had not, however, been so distracted by other company as to forget his wife's present dilemma. At that moment one of the footmen entered the saloon bearing a large dress-box and several other packages and, upon Ware's instructions, laid them upon the sofa-table behind them.

Ware's expression softened, "Open them, Emma, I have made some advance purchases for you – the rest can be done when we go to London."

As her husband watched her with some amusement, Emma, like an excited child, lifted the lid of the box and unfolded a delightful chemise dress of Indian muslin, simple, but unmistakably the product of a fashionable dressmaker.

She held it up against herself and, looking at him with shining eyes, exclaimed joyfully, "Oh, thank you, my lord – it is exquisite – how clever of you to have chosen so well!"

There followed an evening gown, gloves and two pairs of slippers and, in a sealed package, a case containing a gold bracelet set with pearls and turquoise which Ware told her he had had sent from the bank, adding, with a smile, "The rest can await our arrival in Grosvenor Square."

Her pleasure was obvious, the slippers were tried on, the bracelet clasped upon her arm and she turned to him with amazement, "My lord – all a perfect fit! What a lucky chance!"

Amused and thankful that, in her innocence, she had not realised that this was by no means the first time that he had made such purchases for a young female, Ware found himself surprised by the extent of the inner satisfaction that her delight had given to him.

After luncheon, as Ware had declared himself to be obliged to spend the afternoon closeted with Henry Capel upon estate matters, Emma had ordered the carriage, intending to pay her customary visit to Sarah Anderson. She was on her way downstairs, ready to depart upon her errand, when Ware came out of the library, a grim look upon his face, and asked her if she could spare him a few moment's private conversation.

In the library she found Mr Capel collecting together some papers and wishing him good afternoon, looked enquiringly at her husband. Ware said abruptly, "That will be all for now, Henry." He stood in silence as his agent, after a polite bow to Emma, left the room; as Capel closed the door behind him, she was vaguely conscious that he cast an uneasy glance in her direction.

"Pray be seated, Emma – there is something of importance that I have to say to you." Ware was standing before the fireplace looking extremely forbidding. "Henry has told me – it was his duty to do so – that in my absence you have been visiting a woman who has typhus."

Emma, who had been regarding him apprehensively, started to say, "That is true, my lord, but I thought ...." and found herself at once interrupted.

"I do not doubt that your intentions were admirable but I must ask you to discontinue your visits." There was a set look about his mouth as he added, "It is an extremely infectious disease and I do not care for you to run the risk of catching it. If it is your intention to go there this afternoon, I must request you to change your plans."

She looked up at him, an earnest expression upon her face, "The nurse who was supposed to be caring for Mrs Anderson was quite unfit for her work – I truly believe if I had not been there Mrs Anderson would have died!" She hesitated then continued ruefully, "I am sorry, my lord, to disregard your wishes, but I *must* visit her again – I cannot in conscience abandon her now!"

His face hardened as he replied sarcastically, "Then your conscience must be silenced! Good God, you have already put yourself in grave danger by your foolhardy actions – I am surprised that none of my servants thought it proper to perform such tasks for you!" he added scornfully, "It was hardly fit work for my wife!"

She rose from the sofa and came towards him, saying emphatically, "It was not their fault, believe me! My maid pleaded with me to allow her to accompany me and Mr Capel told me that the servants were anxious – but I did not wish to expose members of your household to such a risk."

He looked down at her and said impatiently, "I believe that they are amply rewarded for their services!"

"But not for putting their lives in jeopardy!" she retorted, "I should never forgive myself ...." she broke off, her eyes searching his face for some sign of relenting as she added, "Surely it is my duty to care for your people?"

He was still frowning, and if her words had touched him he showed no sign of it, "Fine sentiments, no doubt! Perhaps there are *other* wifely duties that I might consider of greater importance!" He saw her wince, but continued in the same implacable tone, "I regret that you do not see fit to comply with my *request*. I have, therefore, no alternative than to *forbid* you to continue your visits! You will not enter that young woman's cottage again – I shall make other arrangements for her care."

This uncompromising statement did not have its desired effect; if Ware had anticipated a docile acceptance of his edict he was to suffer a disappointment. Forgetting, perhaps for the first time, the awe in which she held her husband, and incensed by his autocratic manner, Emma felt a mounting indignation, certain in her own mind that what she had done was right and just what, as papa's daughter, she should do. The colour rose in her cheeks as she said fiercely, "I *shall* certainly go to see Mrs Anderson again, my lord, and nothing on earth that you can say will stop me!"

Her husband, regarding the flushed face turned up towards him, her eyes sparkling with defiance, said infuriatingly in a scornful voice, "My dear Lady Ware, you look magnificent in such a rage – what a pity that so much emotion should be wasted! Don't you realise, my girl, that I have only to give orders, forbidding your use of the carriage and horses, to stop you!"

For a moment she stared at him, suffering all the pain and frustration of impotent fury, then, moving quickly to the door to the hall, said in the voice of one goaded beyond endurance, "Even if I have to walk every inch of the way, I shall still go!"

Ware's face softened a little, as he called after her, "Believe me, Emma, it is only of your own health and safety that I am thinking."

At the door, she turned, forgetful of all else but her bitter disappointment and anger, and, prompted by some hidden hurt of which she was barely conscious, retorted, "Why should *you* care, my lord? Perhaps it would be better for both of us if I were dead!"

In an instant, before she could leave the room, he had crossed it in a few quick strides and had seized her wrist in a most ungentle grip, saying furiously, "What the devil do you mean by that?"

She was too upset to consider what she was saying; the words tumbled out, passionately and illogically, "Then I should no longer be a burden to you – you could return to your fashionable friends – and to your mistresses – and – and then marry some female who understands such arrangements!"

She had barely finished speaking when she found herself grasped painfully tightly by the shoulders; there was a look in his lordship's eyes that made her heart beat faster as he said in an icy voice, "Don't ever dare to say such a thing to me again, my girl! Are you so lost to every vestige of propriety that you don't realise how improper it is in you to even mention such a subject?" Still holding her tightly, he continued in a furious voice, "Unless you give me your word that your visits to that woman will cease, I shall lock you in your room myself!"

By now thoroughly ashamed of her outburst and more than a little scared of such an adversary, who she was conscious would not scruple to carry out his threat, Emma said stiffly, "You force me to promise and .... and I do so!"

As he released her and turned abruptly away, she felt as if her legs would barely support her. She managed to stammer out, "S-someone must see Mrs Anderson – she is expecting me ...." then finding her voice choked with emotion, she broke off and fumbling blindly for the door-handle, left the room.

Back in her bedroom, Emma, threw herself onto her bed, her mind in a turmoil; indignation and shame alternating in her thoughts. Aware that her care of Mrs Anderson had certainly saved that young woman's life, she had been happy in the knowledge that she had achieved something worthwhile in the unfamiliar position that she now occupied. Ware's anger seemed unreasonable and, besides, a bitter disappointment to her. She thought crossly that she supposed she should have realised that he was too proud and too conscious of his own consequence to concern himself with the welfare of those whom he must consider to be of the lower orders of society. No doubt, in his eyes, she had acted in a manner unfitting for the Countess of Ware.

But how could she have flung in his face his liaisons with other women? What possible justification had she had – a wife in name only? Her cheeks burned at the thought. Doubtless, he would find it hard, perhaps impossible, to forgive her; with a lowering sensation she realised that she must have sunk herself irredeemable in his estimation. Mrs Tremayne had indeed much to answer for.

It was all the more humiliating, following on, as it did, upon her genuine pleasure at his return; something she would not have believed possible a week ago. How kindly he had spoken to her of Richard's betrayal and of the fortune that she had inherited, how generous his gifts to her had been; at that moment, that very morning, she had never felt more in charity with him.

Meanwhile downstairs, Ware, an angry man, felt at the same time disturbed by their quarrel. When Henry Capel had informed him of Emma's contact with typhoid fever he had experienced a degree of perturbation that had surprised him; furious with Emma for taking such risks upon herself, her obstinacy had increased his wrath, for he was not accustomed to having his wishes thwarted. To have his amorous affairs cast up in his face, and in such a way, had been more than he could support; having for once in his life foregone the gratification of his desires for the sake of his young wife, and forborne while in London from finding compensation in another woman's arms, her remarks had broken the tight rein that he had held upon his temper.

He paced up and down the room, a black scowl disfiguring his handsome face, torn between the conflicting desire to beat her soundly and to make passionate love to her, and knowing that he could do neither.

Gradually, as his temper cooled, he realised that it was most probable that her recent visitor was responsible for putting such ideas in her head. Were there not some grounds for believing that Emma was not entirely indifferent to him if she resented so profoundly the thought of other women in his life? He ceased his restless pacing and stood a moment gazing out of the window, seeing in his mind's eye Emma standing before him, looking up into his face, her eyes full of fire, unaware of the delightful picture that she presented; certainly she had not been afraid of him then! Now he would have to be even more patient and find a way to recover what had been fast becoming an increasingly easy relationship between them.

In Springly Bottom, Anderson was utterly astounded when, on opening the door in response to a peremptory knocking, he discovered the Earl of Ware standing upon his doorstep and, behind him, a maid carrying a large basket. Flustered and ill-at-ease, he was reassured by the kind way in which his lordship spoke to him, asking after his wife and telling him that Lady Ware would not be able to come any more but sent her good wishes.

"She has sent her maid instead, who will see to your wife's needs."

"Thank'ee, thank'ee my lord," the words tumbled out incoherently, "Please to step inside, my lord!" He ushered his lordship into the kitchen, Ware having to stoop low to pass through the doorway and, once inside the cottage, seeming to fill the room.

Dora went through into the bedroom and Ware took the seat offered to him. Anderson, his honest face flushed at the unexpected honour, said earnestly, "My Sarah, she be a fair bit stronger today, and 'tis all on account of her ladyship, my lord! I ain't never seen anything like it in all my born days!" He paused dramatically, "Changed the bed linen – washed my poor Sarah, she did! Every mortal thing that could be done for her, my lady did – never a thought for her own safety!" His face reflected all the wonder and gratitude that he clearly felt.

His lordship nodded gravely and, bidding him take a seat also, began to question him as to the nature of his work. On learning that he was employed on the estate as a gamekeeper, Ware was soon engrossed in a long discussion upon the problem of poachers and the keeping down of the vermin who jeopardised the lives of the pheasant chicks. On familiar ground, it was not long before Anderson was quite at his ease and, forgetting their relative status, was soon setting his noble employer to rights as to the best methods of dealing with stoats and weasels and suchlike matters which occupied his daily life.

When Dora's work had been completed and the sick woman made comfortable, she returned to the kitchen where she found her master being most agreeably entertained. Her re-appearance must have recalled to Anderson the relationship in which he stood to his companion, for he reddened and rose to his feet, saying awkwardly, "I begs your lordship's pardon if I've been too free! My Sarah do say I gets to talkin' over much at times, my lord." But his lordship only smiled at his confusion and declared that he had enjoyed their conversation and had learned a vast deal that had interested him.

On their journey back to the house, Dora told him that Mrs Anderson's fever had left her but that she was still very weak. "Oh, your lordship, it touches your heart to see how grateful she is to my lady," she marvelled, "says it over and over again!"

Ware found his respect for his young wife had increased considerably. He had experienced an over-powering wish to see for himself these people, with whom she had involved herself with so little regard for the danger to her own person. He could not but be affected by what he had seen and heard and was better able to understand her determination not to abandon them.

Later that day at dinner conversation was kept strictly to generalities: Emma, thankful for the presence of the servants, was composed but quiet; her husband said nothing to her of his visit to Anderson's cottage. As soon as the meal was ended, Emma excused herself, saying that she had a headache, and returned to her bedroom. It was there, as Dora helped her to undress, that she learned to her astonishment that Ware had driven out to Springly Bottom. "You should have seen his lordship sitting there in that little bit of a kitchen, my lady, and young Jem Anderson chattering away to him as if they wus the best of friends! Sarah Anderson, she's ever so much better, my lady, though terrible thin and pale. I told her as I would be back tomorrow if that's what your ladyship would wish."

CHAPTER 12

Ware did not visit his wife's bedroom that evening; he was finding it increasingly difficult to sustain his self-imposed role of forbearing husband, and they did not meet again until they drove to the parish church to attend Morning Service.

As they came out when Matins was ended, many smiling faces were turned towards them amongst the villagers and it was borne most forcibly upon his lordship how considerable was the impression that his young countess had made in one short week. To Mrs Sharp and her family, Emma stopped to speak briefly and to tell the Anderson's little boy how well his mother was progressing; vastly to her relief, Mrs Tremayne had not attended divine service that morning.

After luncheon, Ware returned to the library to work with Henry Capel and it was there that Emma found him before dinner. She came in diffidently: Henry had gone and Ware was seated at his desk writing. He stood up when he saw her and looked at her questioningly with raised brows.

She said hurriedly, "Forgive me for disturbing you!" and crossing the room to his desk, stood before it, straight-backed, her eyes fixed upon his face. Taking a deep breath, she said in a rush, "I wish to apologise for what I said yesterday!" a little colour rose to her cheeks as she added frankly, "It was unforgivable of me – I had no right – no right whatsoever – and the remembrance of it has troubled me all day."

As her eyes met his she could not help wondering what thoughts were passing behind the saturnine countenance above her as he regarded her gravely. She would have been amazed and confused if she had been able to read his mind.

He looked down at the slight figure before him, her face lifted up to his and thought involuntarily, "By God, she is enchanting!" then, noticing the dark circles beneath her eyes, felt ashamed that he had treated her so roughly. Giving her a sudden smile of surprising sweetness, he said gently, "My dear girl, you must forget about it – as I shall do – we were both angry yesterday!"

Her expression lightened, "Thank you, my lord – and I must thank you also for visiting the Andersons – I was relieved to hear that Mrs Anderson makes good progress."

There was a gleam of humour in Ware's eyes as he remembered his conversation in the cottage, "Thanks to you, Emma, I had the most instructive half-hour! I am now so well-informed upon the subject of vermin that, if ever I should be obliged to quit my present position in society, I believe that I could make a tolerable success as a gamekeeper!"

She chuckled appreciatively at the notion and felt considerably relieved as, with a smile, he continued, "Now that you are here, I must tell you some news which I believe will please you. Edward is to visit us again. I am astonished that he quits London so readily at this time of year, however, we may expect him tomorrow."

There was something in his voice which conveyed to Emma the notion that he was not best pleased at the forthcoming visit; to her, it was indeed welcome news and her face must have displayed her delight as she said warmly, "I like your cousin, my lord – I shall look forward to seeing him here again."

Edward arrived the following morning, and strode into the house wearing the look of one who anticipates the pleasure of several days spent in agreeable company.

He found Ware and Emma in the garden, the latter coming forward, both hands outstretched, to greet him, saying happily, "Cousin Edward, this is a delightful surprise – I was so pleased when my lord told me that you were coming to visit us."

As he straightened from bending to kiss the glowing cheek offered to him, he caught a glimpse of Ware's face behind her, displaying an expression of obvious disapproval and thought to himself as he shook him by the hand, "By Jupiter, he don't like her showing her pleasure at my company!" and mischievously vowed to himself to do all in his power to further provoke his cousin. "Do him good to be shaken out of his damnable arrogance! Besides – she's a charming girl!"

His first duty, however, was to convey to Ware the news of the death of an old friend of the late Earl.

"Old Alexander Kempton's gone at last, Robert – I heard the news this morning. He died yesterday."

Ware looked grave, "Poor old fellow, he has been ill for months. I must send my condolences to Lady Kempton and find out when and where the funeral is to be."

He found Emma eyeing him sympathetically and said briefly, "An old friend of my father's – and incidentally, a keen follower of the new agricultural methods: from what you tell me, your father would have approved of him. A regular martinet as well – I must confess that I stood in considerable awe of him as a boy!"

It was hard to imagine her husband in awe of anyone, Emma reflected, as she turned to Edward and began to tell him of their invitation to dine with the Tremayne's the following day.

It was a relief to Emma to be able, thanks to her husband's forethought, to present a fashionable appearance to dine at Horton.

As she clasped the pretty bracelet about her wrist – so fortunate that it looked so well with her mother's pearls – she wondered what kind of reception would be accorded to her by her host. That her hostess had taken her in aversion was clear to her, in spite of her professions of friendship; but, after all, she told herself stoutly – what was that to her? There was nothing to be gained by being so poor-spirited as to let herself be cast down by so trivial a matter and she determined to enjoy the evening to the best of her abilities.

The other guests were already assembled and, when their names were announced, Emma's heart sank a little as she saw before her a group of strangers, apart from her hostess, all of whom seemed to have their eyes fixed only upon her.

It was the Honourable Freddie Tremayne who came forward to greet them, a broad-shouldered, thick-set man, whose fashionably cut garments seemed too tight and too constricting for their owner's ease. "My dear Robert, this is a great pleasure! Your servant, ma'am!" His honest face was incapable of concealing his astonishment as he gazed at his friend's bride. His wife's description of Emma he had discounted – setting it down to some form of feminine jealousy. Could this slip of a girl, so insignificant apart from the huge eyes that were regarding him with faint amusement as if she comprehended his surprise, be the wanton whom all the Polite world condemned?

Elizabeth Tremayne was now beside them, and taking Emma's arm in the most friendly fashion, drew her forward to present to her the rest of the company, feeling some degree of irritation that her guest now presented a fashionably elegant appearance. So Ware had been at work here – there was no doubt that his taste was impeccable.

Mr and Mrs Priestley were the first to be introduced: he, an older man with a lined face and the dark complexion of one who has spent many years enduring the rigours of a tropical climate, and his wife, a woman with fine, dark eyes and heavy features, who wore her hair in an elaborate style, festooned with ribbons and feathers. Mr Priestley was obsequiously polite; Emma had never seen a deeper bow, as he raised her hand to his lips – she could not but be amused, and smiled gently at both these strange people who seemed so amazingly pleased to make her acquaintance. A cool greeting from the Earl seemed not to depress their spirits and Mrs Priestley eagerly presented her son and daughter.

"Jane has been longing to meet you, my lady, for I believe that you are much of an age. She is to make her come-out this year – indeed we travel to London next week. Mr Priestley 'as taken a house in London for the season – in the best part of town, you know!" she added complacently.

It was hard to understand how Mr and Mrs Priestley could be the parents of such a daughter. Miss Jane Priestley was a pretty, gentle-looking girl with soft, dark hair, her delicate features in strong contrast to her mother's bold looks. She said a few soft words in greeting and seemed genuinely pleased to meet Emma. Her brother, George, resembled his father in looks but lacked the air of vigour and resolution that emanated from his parent. This was not, Emma decided, a man who was likely to set the Thames on fire.

At this moment the arrival of the old Rector and his wife and daughter took Mrs Tremayne from Emma's side and her place was taken by a young man of middle height, whose features and fair hair proclaimed him to be, without doubt, a close relation of her hostess. Introducing himself in lofty tones as being brother to that lady, he spoke to Emma with a condescension that surprised and disgusted her.

Fortunately she was not obliged to endure his impertinent conversation for long, nor his unwelcome eyeing of her person, for his attention was diverted to Miss Priestley who asked softly whether he would be returning to London shortly and whose eyes and smiling face clearly indicated her hopes that his answer would be in the affirmative.

To Emma's faint surprise, his pale, dissolute countenance took upon it a look of eager anticipation, "My dear Miss Priestley, if you are to be there, wild horses could not keep me away!" and turning his back upon Emma, he whispered something in Miss Priestley's ear which made her blush and hide her face with her fan.

The Earl, who had been drawn into conversation by George Priestley, was looking exceedingly bored, Emma thought, as she now glanced around her. Edward, coming to her side, murmured in her ear, "Where on earth did Elizabeth find these incredible people? A regular set of jumped up mushrooms! I've heard the father's a nabob – owns a plantation, they say!"

Horrified to think that his remarks might be over-heard, Emma whispered back indignantly, "Be quiet, Edward, you will offend their feelings! And Miss Priestley looks to be a charming girl!"

"It seems to me that she's besotted with that ass, Hartley – and he, no doubt, is after the money-bags!"

Their whispered conversation seemed to stir Ware to action; excusing himself from enduring further a long and boring recital of the movement of shares on 'Change, he took Emma's arm and led her across the room to renew her acquaintance with Mr Barnard and to meet his wife and his daughter, Miss Alice Barnard, a lady no longer in her first youth and, as yet, unmarried.

Emma took an immediate liking to Miss Barnard, whose friendly smile and agreeable voice appealed to her.

"I suppose that you are intimately acquainted with the present company, Miss Barnard." There was a trace of envy in Emma's voice, "I confess I find it odd to be amongst strangers for, you know, I was used to living in my father's parish – where, of course, I knew everyone!"

"So you are a clergyman's daughter too!" Miss Barnard's eyes twinkled, "I wonder whether life went on there much as it does here – we are a quiet, sober, one might say a boring group of persons for most of the year – then, all at once, our lords and masters descend upon us from London and we are set in a turmoil of dinner-parties and gossip! They go together so often, do you not think!" She looked from Emma to Ware, then said quietly, with a hint of laughter in her voice, "So our wild, wicked Earl has been tamed at last! I congratulate you, my lady, I am sure that he will make an excellent husband!" She saw Emma's embarrassment and added, "You must forgive my outspokenness – it is my one claim to fame in this neighbourhood!"

It was said so pleasantly that Emma found it impossible to take offence at such frankness. She glanced quickly at her husband, hoping that he had not overheard Miss Barnard's comments, and said soberly, "He has been good to *me* – that is all I know!"

Miss Barnard must have sensed that here was dangerous ground, for she changed the subject and began at once to speak of Sarah Anderson and to congratulate Emma upon her successful nursing of that unfortunate woman.

The dinner that followed, with its succession of courses, bore witness to the skill of the Tremayne's cook and to the excellent viands provided by the Wiltshire countryside. Emma, seated on the right of her host, as befitted both her new station in life and her due as a newly wed bride, was thankful for his friendly conversation. Upon her other side, Hartley Tremayne barely deigned to address more than a remark or two to her during the meal, his whole attention being centred upon Miss Priestley, who sat upon his right. It was not, she felt with some amusement, a great loss. He seemed intent upon depressing any pretensions that Emma might be supposed to have acquired in her new role as countess, and, at the same time, puffing off his own conse- quence. She found him faintly ridiculous and infinitely preferred his brother-in-law.

At the other end of the table, Mrs Tremayne divided her attention equally between Ware, in the place of honour on her right, and Mr Priestley on her left. She was all smiles and pleasantness – listening gravely to Mr Priestley's dissertations upon the slave trade and the iniquities of the present system of taxation and amusing Ware with her accounts of the latest scandals, concealing tactfully the fact that his own marriage was at that very moment providing the most prurient speculation of all.

Opposite Emma, Mrs Priestley regaled them with an account of their forthcoming stay in London. The number of their servants, the excellence of their carriages and the magnificence of the Ball to be given in honour of her daughter all featured prominently in her conversation. Her unfortunate propensity for occasionally misplacing her aspirates added to the bizarre nature of her conversation. Addressing Emma across the table, she said obsequiously, "I hope your ladyship will h'attend, ma'am, your presence would add the h'ultimate distinction to our little gathering!"

Replying kindly that she was not certain as yet of their future plans for the coming months, Emma could not help being surprised that Mrs Tremayne should be encouraging her brother to bestow his attentions upon the daughter of such a parent.

Edward, from his position at the table between Miss Barnard and her father, for the numbers precluded a perfect distribution of the sexes, found time to observe with detached interest, Hartley's determined pursuit of the charming Miss Priestley, coupled with his barely concealed incivility to Emma. It was a foretaste of what lay before her, if and when Ware should take her to London, and as his gaze turned to Emma, now deep in conversation with her host – they having discovered a mutual interest in gardens, he wondered how she would deal with this kind of hostility.

Ware, fortunately for Hartley, too far removed from Emma to be conscious of his cavalier treatment of her, felt increasingly bored as the evening progressed. He had had enough of George Priestley to last him a lifetime and the Priestley parents were both vulgar and pushing. Miss Jane Priestley was certainly a beauty but he wondered cynically whether she had any sense in her pretty little head. For a moment his gaze moved up the length of the table to rest pensively upon his wife, there was no question but that *she* possessed a formidable strength of character, quite remarkable in one of her age. For a moment he frowned

– how difficult it was proving to be to gain her confidence after such a bizarre beginning to their relationship.

It was at that precise instant that Emma, happening to glance in his direction, saw the frown and wondered anxiously what lay behind her husband's displeasure, hoping fervently that she was not the cause.

Her host, who had observed the exchange of glances, leaned towards her and said suddenly in a low voice, with a rare flash of insight that would have surprised his friends, "Best thing Robert ever did – marrying you, ma'am! Clear as daylight that he's mad about you! I hope you care for him too, my lady!"

She felt herself blush, hardly knowing how to answer him. He must have understood her confusion, for, before she could make any reply, he added, "Don't answer me, ma'am – dashed well impertinent of me to say such a thing! Always was an impetuous fellow but I'm deuced fond of Robert, you know!" and he turned again to Mrs Priestley with a polite enquiry about the duration of their stay in London.

As Mrs Tremayne dispensed cups of tea after the ladies of the party had withdrawn from the dining room, Emma found herself, to her surprise, being complimented by Mrs Barnard upon her successful nursing of a case of typhus.

Mrs Barnard's faded prettiness was ill-served by her unbecoming gown with its drab colour and superfluity of trimmings, but there was genuine admiration in her eyes as she drew Emma to sit beside her upon the sofa, saying, "We were all astonishment, my lady – and you so young! So brave!" she added inconsequentially, "Of course, Lord Ware has seldom stayed here long and then only to entertain his London friends …. such shockingly wild parties ….!" she sighed, then suddenly recollecting whom she was addressing, she stopped, hand to mouth, horrified with herself for her lack of tact.

Emma smiled at her sympathetically, inwardly amused at her indiscretion, and wondering whether she might be able to share her amusement with her husband or would he disapprove of her levity? She realised with surprise that she had no idea. For someone who by all accounts had led such an improper life, he seemed to have amazingly strict ideas where she was concerned.

144

Miss Jane Priestley next claimed her attention, asking her whether she was familiar with the surrounding country. "We have only been here for a year, you know – quite newcomers – and there is still so much that I have not yet seen." She looked very conscious as she added, "Mr Hartley Tremayne has suggested that we might form a party later this week to visit Avebury – the circle there is famous – massive stones – so picturesque and romantic! What do you think, Lady Ware?"

Inwardly considering that Hartley Tremayne's presence would certainly not add to her own enjoyment of such an outing, she realised that Miss Priestley saw the matter in a very different light, and said cheerfully, "A charming idea, Miss Priestley, and would, I think, provide an agreeable entertainment for my husband's cousin. Let us consult the gentlemen when they rejoin us."

Miss Priestley, her pretty face wreathed in smiles, continued ingenuously, "If you and your husband will join us, Lady Ware, I am certain that my mother will give her consent to the expedition, for unfortunately Mr and Mrs Tremayne return to London tomorrow."

It amused Emma to discover herself cast in the new role of chaperone, and to a girl of her own age at that. It sounded to be, nevertheless, a delightful project and as soon as the gentlemen entered the drawing-room, for they had not lingered long over their wine, she approached her husband, telling him of Hartley Tremayne's proposal and asking him, with a sparkle in her eyes, if it would be agreeable to him and to Edward to accompany her.

Ware looked enquiringly at Edward, who stood beside him, and seeing his agreement, smilingly gave his assent to Emma and crossed the room to Hartley's side to confirm the arrangement.

The latter, now seated close to Miss Priestley and deep in conversation, rose to his feet, saying hopefully, "I hope that you will consent, Robert – if this weather holds, it should make a pleasant outing – a picnic is always a jolly affair."

The following Wednesday was chosen as being convenient for all concerned. Only George Priestley, in an excessively wordy speech, pronounced himself regrettably unable to form one of the party and it was finally arranged that the two young ladies should be conveyed in the Earl's carriage, the gentlemen to accompany them on horseback.

Emma could not help noticing that, whereas Mrs Priestley seemed fulsomely in favour of the projected expedition, her husband was looking far from pleased and his sharp eyes were regarding young Mr Tremayne with considerable disfavour.

CHAPTER 13

Afterwards Emma wondered whether she should not have foreseen the astonishing events of the following Wednesday.

On the Tuesday morning following the Tremayne's dinner party, Mrs Priestley and her daughter had called upon Emma and had found her alone in the drawing-room: Edward and her husband having gone out earlier to shoot pigeon. They had hardly been seated for more than a few minutes than Hartley Tremayne had been announced and had strolled into the room, conveying to Emma the strong impression that he believed himself to be conferring a notable favour upon her by his presence.

She had been obliged to bestow her attention principally upon Mrs Priestly during the visit: compliments had streamed from her visitor's lips, no part of Emma's person and surroundings being exempt from Mrs Priestley's praises. It had all been rather uncomfortable.

Meanwhile Hartley Tremayne, having seated himself beside Jane, had engaged her in a low voiced conversation. There had been no doubt in Emma's mind, as she glanced at them from time to time, that Jane Priestley was thoroughly in love with him.

This had been confirmed later that day by no less a person than the young lady herself. Before the visitors had departed, having been plied with glasses of ratafia and macaroon biscuits, Emma had been invited to accompany Miss Priestley on a drive to Marlborough that afternoon to make some minor purchases.

It was during the course of this expedition that Jane had confided to Emma her love for Hartley and the unhappy situation in which they found themselves. It had appeared that, upon applying to Mr Priestley for his daughter's hand, Hartley Tremayne's suit had been dismissed out of hand, and in such a fashion that any hopes of a change in the future in the father's opinion of her suitor's character and prospects were destroyed.

"My father is cruelly unfeeling!" Jane had told Emma, with tears in her lovely eyes, "But I won't give Hartley up!"

Finding herself inwardly in agreement with Mr Priestley in his estimate of the young man, Emma had confined herself to expressions of sympathy and had counselled patience, "No doubt, when your father sees that you affections are unchanged, he will reconsider his decision, and after all," she had added hopefully, "You are only seventeen, which is overly young to be thinking of marrying!"

On being reminded by her tearful companion that that was precisely Emma's own age, she had been obliged to withdraw this remark, thinking wryly as she did so that she, herself, had not had even an opportunity of exercising *any* choice in the matter of her marriage.

Before they had parted company that afternoon, Emma had been pledged to secrecy and had been uncomfortably aware that she had failed to convey her own disapproval of Hartley Tremayne to the unhappy girl.

When Ware and Edward had returned, she had, as a consequence of her promise, said nothing to them of Miss Priestley's confidences, merely saying that she had enjoyed her afternoon and that she was looking forward to the following day's expedition.

When Ware told her that he would be unable to form one of the party after all, she had had to acknowledge to herself that she had been profoundly disappointed, for she found him to be a most agreeable companion. However she could not argue with the reason for his absence: Lord Kempton was to be buried near Abingdon and it was only civil that the son of his father's old friend should attend the funeral.

"I received the message this afternoon." Ware had told her, "I am sorry, but there is no help for it." He had seemed irritated, she had thought, though he had added, "Of course you and Edward must go to Avebury – I know that you look forward to it."

Wednesday dawned fine and bright, with every prospect of remaining so for the rest of the day. Ware departed early, after a hurried breakfast, and as he bade his sleepy wife farewell, thought ruefully how infinitely he would have preferred to have accompanied her upon the picnic party.

It was nearing mid-day, and Emma, having attired herself in her new Indian muslin, was regarding herself in the looking glass with some satisfaction, when a note was brought to her room. Opening it, she read the scrawled lines with growing astonishment and horror, then jumped to her feet and went at once to find Edward, a shocked expression upon her face.

She found him in the hall, in conversation with Marchant and looking his usual elegant self, and rushed into hurried speech.

"Cousin Edward – a word with you, please!"

He turned and regarded her anxious face with surprise, saying reassuringly, "You look delightful, cousin – and a charming bonnet, if I may say so."

"Never mind that now!" Emma almost dragged him into the library and closed the door, "I have just received a note with the most shocking news, Edward! I can hardly believe it to be possible." She was looking at him with wide, unhappy eyes.

"Perhaps you will tell me what has occurred ....?" What in Heaven's name was afflicting his young cousin? Edward stared at her with astonishment, instantly hoping that her news had no connection with her husband's lurid past.

"It's Jane Priestley, Edward – she writes that she is eloping with that wretch, Hartley Tremayne! Her parents expect her to be accompanying us on the picnic and instead Hartley has sent their chaise early to collect her and intends to drive her to his aunt's house near Oxford – then they will travel to Scotland to be married, for she is still under age, you know! She seems to think that I will approve, and that I will remain silent!"

"Good God!" Edward looked stunned. "I would not trust that scoundrel an inch!"

"Edward, we must stop them – I cannot bear to be a party to such a shocking folly, but for Heaven's sake let us do so without allowing her parents to become aware of their intentions!"

"My dear Emma, we have not the slightest notion where his aunt lives."

"No matter, if we leave at once, we may overtake them on the way – there is really only one route to Oxford I believe."

He stared at her for a moment, nonplussed, but the thought of the gentle, innocent Miss Priestley in the clutches of an unprincipled scoundrel such as Hartley Tremayne was not an agreeable one.

"Come, Edward, we must leave immediately!" Emma was all impatience.

He grinned at her suddenly, "Very well – but I hope you know what you are about! What in Heaven's name will Robert say?"

"Of course he would approve – I wish he were here." Emma seemed blithely confident, "Let us not delay another moment."

Ware's curricle was ordered to be brought round immediately instead of the carriage, and in a remarkably short space of time they had departed, both in an optimistic mood, believing that the runaways would soon be overtaken and congratulating themselves upon their foresight in having, as a precaution, sent back the groom to the stables, hoping thereby to avoid any public knowledge of the elopement.

Blithe optimism, however, soon began to give way to doubt and they were beginning to feel tired and cross when their enquiry, at the third inn at which they had halted, gave news of a couple who answered to their description of the fugitives and who had not long since obtained a change of horses.

Their confidence miraculously restored, they continued on their way, Edward striving to obtain the best possible speed from their new horses, whom he roundly condemned as a pair of slugs, but when several hours had passed and the day was well advanced, Emma began to fear that their quarry had already turned off the Oxford road. All at once, a mile or so short of Wantage, she saw a familiar-looking chaise drawn up in the yard of the "Queen's Head" and seizing her companion's arm, cried triumphantly, "Look, Edward! I believe we have found them! Is not that the Tremayne's carriage?"

The despised bays being hastily reined in, the curricle was turned and driven briskly into the yard. Emma had been correct, there was no mistaking the new chaise, its paintwork glistening. Jubilant that their objective had been achieved, they scarcely gave a thought as to their next move as they entered the inn.

Jane's departure from her parent's house had been accomplished without the least difficulty. Under Hartley's instructions to her in a private note, she had informed her parents that Lady Ware had that morning sent word that she had been delayed and had therefore sent her carriage to collect Jane to transport her to Millford House, where Lady Ware and the gentlemen would join her for their expedition. If her farewell of her mother and father had been of a more affectionate nature than might have been deemed appropriate for one leaving merely upon a day's outing of pleasure, her parents were not conscious of anything untoward. Mr Priestley had merely grunted his acknowledgement of her kiss; only the participation of the Earl and Countess of Ware in the proposed expedition had persuaded him to give his consent.

Neither parent had noticed that the smartly painted carriage did not bear the Earl's coat of arms and had happily seen their daughter depart with light hearts and hopeful thoughts of her future. They were certainly not aware that the departing carriage had stopped outside the entrance to their property, nor that Hartley had there mounted up beside their daughter and taking her hand in his had kissed it tenderly. As he did so, nothing, Jane thought, could ever equal her happiness at that moment. He was so chivalrous, so careful of her honour that she knew, without a doubt, that she could entrust herself into his hands.

They drove steadily all day, with only the briefest stop for some refreshments. Harley, at first so gentle and loving, soon seemed to be more pre-occupied with their progress and their speed – or lack of it – than with his lovely companion and her happy chatter. Even Jane fell silent and became aware of her companion's frequent nervous glances behind them, as he urged the postilion's to make greater speed.

She was thankful to descend from the carriage and to enter the inn when they pulled up at the "Queen's Head". It was by now late afternoon and a great part of her early excitement had worn off – she hung upon Hartley's arm and looked up at him lovingly, saying in a low voice, "My dearest, how I long to reach your aunt's house and to rest! I must confess to being shockingly tired." She noted that his face lit up at her words: he had seemed very thoughtful and silent for the past few miles.

"My poor sweet!" All his tenderness was returned, "Listen, my love – I shall ask the landlord if you may have a bed-chamber to rest yourself for a while. We had best eat here – there is still some distance to travel and I must confess to being deucedly sharp-set."

Shown upstairs to a large bedchamber and supplied with a can of hot water by a smiling maid, Jane was thankful to wash her face and hands and to lie down upon the bed. She lay thinking dreamily of her future husband and hoping that her parents would not be too distressed when they learned of her marriage.

She had almost dropped off to sleep when she heard a soft tap upon her door and before she had had time to make any response, Hartley had entered the room and stood by the bed looking down at her.

"Why, how you startled me!" She felt the colour mount to her cheeks as she sat up; his presence in the room and the look in his eyes making her suddenly feel shy and awkward.

Hartley, his face flushed, for he had tossed off several large brandies since arriving at the inn, thought with be-fuddled satisfaction how deucedly lucky he was that this heiress to a large fortune was at the same time such a lovely creature. His pulses racing, as she came to her feet he seized her in his arms and began to smother her face and neck with passionate kisses.

With a little cry of alarm, Jane struggled to release herself – this was not the gentle, deferential lover who had attracted her so strongly with his fair good looks and charming manners.

He, aware of her fright, and finding that it only served to increase his rising passion, held her a little away from him and said in a thickened voice, "Damn it, Jane – you are to be my wife after all! No harm in pre-empting the marriage ceremony!" With a coarse laugh, he added, before his lips closed again upon hers, "No question *then*, that your father will have to agree to our union – better to make certain of that tonight, lest we should be overtaken!"

It had been decided by Edward that once they had found the young couple, Emma should claim to be Miss Priestley's sister, thus facilitating their enquiries. Entering the inn in high good spirits and rejoicing that their exhausting journey seemed to be at an end, they were informed by the landlord that a young couple had arrived a short time before who answered to their description. As they were, thankfully, about to enter the inn-parlour, he stopped them, saying with a meaningful smile and a roguish look, "Taken one of the bed-chambers, 'e 'as, sir! I 'opes as you don't mean to disturb them – proper little love-birds, I'd say!"

Exchanging a horrified glance with Edward, Emma improvised quickly, "A case of serious illness in the family, I fear! And no time to be lost!" and seizing Edward by the arm, she began to ascend the stairs.

"Good God! My dear Emma, I don't know that we ought ...." Edward hung back, consternation upon his face, "Not at all the thing ....!"

Before Emma could reply, a faint cry of distress came from above and, with an oath, Edward pushed her roughly aside and, hurriedly mounting the stairs, burst open the door of the nearest room.

The sight that greeted him was indeed a shocking one: Miss Priestley, her dress torn at one shoulder, was struggling ineffectually to prevent Hartley from forcing her back upon the bed, while his hand clamped over her mouth muffled her cries. As Emma entered the room behind him, Edward strode forward with an exclamation of angry disgust and pulling him away from the terrified girl, turned him around and planted a well-directed blow to his chin, knocking him senseless to the ground.

Subconsciously registering her surprise that the willowy Edward should prove himself to be such an excellent performer with his fists, Emma went swiftly to Jane's side, and taking the weeping girl in her arms, whispered, over her head, to Edward, admiration for him glowing in her eyes, "What a detestable creature – but you were magnificent, cousin!"

By this time inquisitive faces had appeared at the bedroom door and Edward, anxious to prevent any further notoriety attaching itself to these events, requested in peremptory tones that assistance be brought to remove 'this gentleman' to another bedchamber, adding mendaciously that there had been a most unfortunate accident.

It was not in mine host's interest that any scandal should besmirch the reputation of his premises and he was only too willing that the whole incident should be terminated as quickly and as quietly as possible, so it was only with a sly grin at Edward and the remark, "Werry unfortunate, sir! An' by chance you seems, to 'ave 'urt your knuckles too, sir!" that he summoned the boot-boy and, with his assistance, carried the unconscious Hartley from the room.

It would have been in every one's best interests for Edward and Emma to have departed instantly with Miss Priestley but the shock proved to be too much for her. To Emma's inner disgust, upon Jane rising to her feet, all colour had fled from her cheeks and she had sunk fainting to the ground. There was nothing to be done but to wait until she had recovered from her ordeal, and with this end in view, Edward laid her gently upon the bed, while Emma drew the curtains half around her and they prepared themselves to wait.

CHAPTER 14

The obsequies for the late Sir Alexander Kempton having been completed and his condolences proffered to the sorrowing widow and her family, Ware set out upon his return journey with the agreeable sensation of having performed his duties in a fitting manner and found himself looking forward to finding his wife and cousin awaiting him at Millford.

As he travelled homewards, with as much speed as was consistent with the shocking state of the roads, he could not help reflecting wryly that Emma's entrance into his life had changed his views to a degree that he would not have, hitherto, believed possible.

An unhappy childhood, a beautiful mother whose sole aim in life seemed to be the pursuit of pleasure, and the ample means at his own disposal for the gratification of his every desire, had thrust him into the company of a section of society whose selfishness was only exceeded by its greed and snobbishness. Certainly he had friends from school and from Oxford, men, some of whom inwardly deplored his life-style, whose company he enjoyed; but in the main his experiences with women had only strengthened his opinions: from the young girls making their debut in Society to the members of the Petticoat Company, all, he was conscious, were more in love with his fortune than with his person, and his cynical awareness of this fact added a bitter note to his amorous adventures, leaving his heart untouched.

Emma was as different as it was possible to be: the extraordinary honesty that pervaded her every word and action, her determination to do what she believed to be right, contrasted sharply with the self-absorption and false words of Society and the demi-monde that flourished around it. Whether their imminent return to London would change her present attitude to his vast wealth, time would tell, but, he thought to himself with a reminiscent smile, he would be surprised if that were to occur. That this resolute character should own such an outwardly beguiling form made him doubly fortunate.

He believed that he was slowly gaining her confidence, no easy task when so-called friends such as Elizabeth Tremayne took it upon themselves to enlighten her about his past life. That, he was convinced was what had occurred in his absence. He was frowningly considering this event and viewing Elizabeth's apparent friendliness to Emma with suspicion, when the coach slowed momentarily to a walking pace in order to pass a lumbering farm-wagon upon a wider stretch of the highway and the change of pace caused Ware to glance idly out of the window. To his utter astonishment he beheld, drawn up in an inn yard, his own curricle, unmistakably bearing his own coronet and coat of arms.

Rapidly ordering Jackson to turn the carriage at the first opportunity, as soon as they drew into the yard, he jumped down, a heavy frown upon his face and, striding across to the bowing landlord, indicated his curricle and peremptorily demanded the identity and whereabouts of its driver.

"Drove up 'ere not long since, m'lord! Some strange goings-on 'ere today!" Mine host appeared anxious to distance himself from any future trouble. "A young gentleman, fair-haired like – your lordship – with a young lady – big brown eyes – insisted I show 'em up to the bed-chamber ...."

Before he could finish, he found himself thrust roughly aside, "Never," the innkeeper told his wife later, "never 'ave I seen a cove with sich a nasty look in 'is eye – my Gawd, I wouldn't care to 'ave been in those young 'uns shoes, I tells you straight!"

Ware, striding white-faced into the inn, glanced around him and, seeing the stairs, mounted them two at a time and hearing familiar voices, burst into the first room before him.

Emma, seated in a chair by the window, had been engaged in a spirited argument with Edward as to how they were to bring to a close Miss Priestley's elopement. Edward firmly maintaining that her parents must be informed; no other course, he insisted, being possible. Emma, sympathetic to the poor girl's plight was anxious to avoid such a betrayal of her folly, and willing to provide an alibi despite the neces-

156

sary prevarications which that would entail. As the door flew open, two startled faces were turned towards the intruder.

Before them, Ware's tall frame filled the doorway, and one glance at his face caused Edward, instinctively, to take a step forward to hide the seated girl – for there was murder gleaming in those hard grey eyes set beneath fiercely frowning brows.

White-faced, Ware whispered softly, between clenched teeth, "You shall die for this, cousin! My God, that it should be *you* of all people!"

Before Edward could stammer out a word of explanation, Emma had jumped to her feet; Ware's words had not been audible to her but there was no mistaking his anger, "My lord, pray do not blame Edward! It was I who suggested we use your curricle – you see, we had no other means of getting here!" As she spoke, she had come quickly forward and now stood between them, looking up at Ware with wide, candid eyes that held no fear in them, only some degree of anxiety.

His furious eyes rested for a moment upon her up-turned face and for a terrible moment Edward believed that he would strike her; then she added coaxingly, "I am so thankful that you are come, my lord, though goodness knows how you found us! *You* will know just what we should do – I said to Edward earlier that I wished you were here!"

At last something in her words penetrated his all-consuming rage, the fire in his eyes died down and he stared at her, utterly taken aback, then said slowly, in a mystified voice, "You wished I was here....?"

"Oh yes, my lord, for what are we to do with Miss Priestley? It is such a puzzle – Edward says we must tell her parents! And then there is Hartley ...."

Now Ware was looking from her eager face to Edward's in total incomprehension. "Miss Priestley? Hartley? What the devil have they to say to anything?"

Edward, thankful that the moment of danger seemed past, and only too well aware of the construction that his furious cousin had put upon their presence in a bedchamber of the "Queen's Head", took up the story, saying briefly, "Hartley Tremayne persuaded Miss Priestley to elope with him – Emma learned of it, so we followed them in order to stop him."

"And you expect me to believe that? So where *are* this eloping couple?" There was still a grim note in Ware's voice.

Emma moved away from him to the bed and quietly drew back the curtains, saying in a low voice, "Here is Miss Priestley, my lord!" and to Ware's astonished gaze, the slight form of a girl was revealed lying beneath the covers: her face pale, her eyes closed, and breathing softly. It was certainly Miss Jane Priestley! She was equally certainly asleep....

For a moment Ware stood staring at the sleeping girl, then he turned to survey the two guilty faces regarding him anxiously. Edward, in the act of opening his elegant snuff-box with a hand that shook imperceptibly, met his eyes squarely; it was evident that he had had a bad fright but intended to carry it off with a nonchalant air. It was more difficult to read Emma's thoughts.

She said again apologetically, "I did not think that you would be so shockingly angry, my lord."

"What was I expected to believe, finding you and Edward alone at the inn and in one of its bed-chambers? Good God, Emma, have you no thought of your good name? Of your reputation?"

For a moment she stared at him, her brown eyes wide with amazement, then a crimson tide of colour mounted to her cheeks, "You mean .... you thought that I had run off with Edward ....!" She looked from one stern masculine face to the other, then, suddenly, burst out laughing, her eyes sparkling with merriment.

A slow smile lightened Ware's face. Edward said disgustedly, "No need to think it such a joke, Emma – plenty of young women would jump at the chance of being asked to elope with me ....!" but his face broke into a grin as he added to Ware, "Thought my last hour had come, dear boy! You want to watch that nasty temper of yours – get you into serious trouble one day!"

The sensation of profound relief that had swept through Ware bore with it an added dimension: Emma, conscious of no wrongdoing on her part had shown no fear of him! Indeed, she appeared to credit him with the ability to solve all problems. His good humour quite restored, and agreeably surprised to find that his wife evidently considered the notion of Edward as a lover as something to be laughed at, he said cheerfully "My dear fellow, I believe I can scarcely be blamed for jumping to the wrong conclusion – what would you have thought in my place?" then, turning to Emma with a smile and a look that for an instant made her heart beat a little faster, he murmured teasingly, "Why, madam wife, you have a touching faith in me! Could that mean that you applaud all my past actions and decisions where you are concerned?"

She looked at him consideringly, her head a little on one side; his meaning was clear, and she had to confess to herself that, upon reflection, it was odd that she should place so much confidence in him.

"My lord," she said at last with a chuckle, "someone who is capable of riding rough-shod over all opposition is certainly not going to be daunted by the prospect of irate parents, and in any case," she added mischievously, "Mr and Mrs Priestley would regard any kind word that fell from your lordship's lips as a nugget of pure gold! So you see, you are the very person that we need to end this wretched business satisfactorily."

It was almost twilight by the time the Earl's carriage drew up before the Priestley's residence. Ware, handing down his wife and Miss Priestley, could not help reflecting with a certain sardonic amusement, that if anyone had told him a week ago that he would be associating with such odiously commonplace people, he would have refused to believe it.

Miss Priestley, having been comforted by Emma to the best of her ability and even more effectively by Edward's kindness, had been instructed grimly by Ware in the tale that she was to tell: the picnic had taken place, the Earl and Countess had been present and it had been unfortunate that too long an exposure to the sun had caused her to faint and thereby necessitating a period of rest at a local hostelry. Mr Hartley Tremayne had, of course, returned home independently.

Upon their arrival, Miss Priestley, whose awe of Ware greatly exceeded her respect for her parents, had managed to carry off her part in this subterfuge without causing any suspicions to be aroused. Indeed, so great were their feelings of the honour done to them by the presence of Lord and Lady Ware in their home, that Mr and Mrs Priestley scarcely bestowed more than a few words of sympathy upon their daughter and, following Emma's recommendation, that much chastened young lady was allowed to retire to her bed-chamber.

Returning home alone together, Emma felt herself impelled to thank Ware again for his assistance, but, at the same time, she had a horrid feeling that some kind of apology was due to his lordship. That he had misinterpreted her presence with Edward at the inn still filled her with astonishment and something of this must have been betrayed in her voice as she said, "My lord, I am so grateful to you for your assistance." then, looking down at her clasped hands, continued hesitantly, "I know that I have angered you and for that I am sorry, but I thought .... as a married woman, you know .... and Edward is your cousin ...." she looked up at him hopefully and found hard eyes regarding her.

"My dear Emma, you will find when we go to London that it is not by any means unusual for a dissatisfied wife to take a lover! I fear that you would not find *me* a complaisant husband!"

Emma, wishing heartily that she had not once more aroused his wrath, thought quickly that he must regard her as his property, along with all his magnificent possessions and, as such, to be fiercely protected. She could not, however, allow such an imputation to her honour to pass unremarked. With a straight look from a resolute countenance, she said, "You may rest assured that, whatever may be the habits of Society, I, for one, intend to keep all *my* marriage vows."

He regarded her intently, now barely visible in the gathering gloom, then, eyebrows raised quizzically, replied, "You relieve me profoundly, my love – and we shall soon have ample opportunity to put such worthy resolutions to the test – for I have decided that we shall leave for London tomorrow."

"Tomorrow, my lord! Good gracious, how sudden!" Emma's face expressed surprise and delight. She added hastily, "It is so lovely here that I could never tire of it, but I own that I shall look forward to seeing London."

He saw then that, after a moment, a shadow of doubt seemed to cloud those shining eyes and believing her to be thinking of her previous stay in the Ancaster household and of the rumours concerning her, said with a grim smile, "Believe me, Emma, you will be received in the manner that your position as my wife demands."

She was startled by his ability to read her thoughts and found herself, once again, marvelling at their growing friendship and at her newfound dependence upon this often over-bearing and arrogant man.

CHAPTER 15

The next morning, very early, all was bustle and confusion in the household. The day dawned grey and misty, but Dora declared, as she assisted Emma to dress, that there was every sign that the sun would break through as the day advanced. She was to accompany her mistress and wait upon her until such time as a fashionable lady's-maid could be engaged. Filled with excitement at the prospect of a visit to London, she was moreover, to have the honour of travelling in the carriage with her ladyship, Lord Ware intending to drive his curricle himself; the only cloud upon her horizon was the thought of leaving Thomas, who was to remain at Millford.

They all assembled in the hall before their departure save Edward, who had bidden them a regretful farewell the night before, having decided to visit friends in Devizes while he was in Wiltshire and to return to London later in the week. Ware, observing Emma wrapped once more in her grey cloak, was reminded nostalgically of the last time that he had seen her wearing it; the recollection of that day when he had abducted her from the coach and forced her to come to Millford, determined him to make up to her some day soon all that she had suffered at his hands.

It was plain, however, that she had stoically set aside any thoughts of the difficulties that might lie ahead and greeting him with shining eyes, she asked at what hour they might arrive in London.

"We shall dine in Reading and should be in Grosvenor Square by nine o'clock or thereabouts. I have my own horses at the post-houses on the way so we are not dependent upon hired cattle."

The time for departure having arrived he helped her up into the chaise and turned away to mount the curricle, where a magnificent team of greys were being held with difficulty by a groom and a diminutive tiger.

It was a relief to arrive in Reading and to stretch their legs. A private room was bespoken and the landlord and his servants bustled about to ensure their every comfort: it was not every day that the Earl of Ware honoured them with his custom. No attention having been spared and an ample repast set before them, Emma soon discovered how agreeable it was to travel in his lordship's company.

They did not linger long for Ware wished to reach London before nightfall and a considerable distance still lay before them. Emma found that she became tired of looking out of the carriage window and slept for a while. When she awoke they had gained the outskirts of London, there were houses and gardens, and soon they were in the thick of the traffic; even at that hour the streets were crowded, and noisy with the rattle of wheels on the cobbles, the cries of the street traders and the general turmoil of busy streets. It was nearing nine o'clock in the evening when they reached Grosvenor Square. The windows of the house were ablaze with lights, the curtains not yet drawn.

It was a strange moment for Emma as she entered that house for the second time in her life. Ware had drawn her arm through his as they mounted the steps: the vast hall seemed full of lights and people; an elderly housekeeper stepped forward and curtsied, and Emma, smiling automatically at her greeting, felt her heart beat faster. How much had happened in the brief time since she had arrived here late at night, alone with the Earl! In her excitement at the thought of seeing London and all its wonders, she had subconsciously preferred to overlook the fact that her return to this house must re-awaken memories of that terrible night.

She found herself being conducted upstairs by Mrs Plummer, a comfortable, motherly-looking woman, and shown into the most delightful set of rooms that she had ever seen. The decorators had done their work well – the bed-chamber was charming: apricot silk glowed upon the walls in the candlelight, the bed was hung with curtains bearing a Chinese pattern of birds and flowers, and in the adjoining room, upon the dressing-table, lay a set of silver brushes and other articles of toilet for a woman of fashion. Through a further door, lay her boudoir with windows looking onto the square: here the delicate blues and greens of the carpet were repeated in the decorations. Emma exclaimed with delight, looking around her with amazement, her gaze passing from one elegant object to another.

Mrs Plummer had left her and she was standing alone in the bedchamber, admiring her surroundings, when Ware came into the room from the adjoining dressing-room. One look at her face should have rewarded him for all the efforts he had made to please her. Emma came across the room to him at once, her eyes alight with pleasure, and said impetuously, "How can I ever thank you enough, my lord, for providing me with these beautiful apartments?"

The quizzical expression upon his face – one eyebrow raised – was sufficient to bring home to her the foolish ingenuousness of her question. Her cheeks burned and she drew back a step. Was all this planned to gain her acquiescence? Did her strange husband mean to assert his marital rights that very night now that they had returned to the scene of their first encounter?

For one instance Ware was tempted – how delightfully simple to make this delicious creature repay his generosity with her own self. It was the kind of exchange that had until now been a commonplace in his life – but was this what he truly desired? He believed not.

The increasingly saturnine expression upon his face filled Emma with alarm but she need not have been so fearful. He merely took her hand in his and kissed it lightly, saying, "If you are pleased, my love, I am more than repaid. Tomorrow we will visit the dressmaker – a milliner too – so that you will feel fit to move in the first circles!" then, seeing that she was still regarding him warily, he went to the door through which he had entered, and added gently, "I know that you are tired after our long journey – I wish you a good night's sleep and sincerely hope that London will be equal to your expectations." and immediately withdrew from her presence.

The next morning Emma came down the grand staircase ready to go out, her shawl over her arm. In the hall a porter was sitting near the front door in his high-backed chair and two footmen stood stiffly to attention when they saw her.

She looked around her, realising with a hint of amusement that she had no knowledge of her surroundings, the apartments behind the

163

many tall double doors a mystery to her. The only room that she had ever entered before was the library – hardly a room with which she was impatient to be re-acquainted. Perhaps to see the outside world, the square that had looked so enchanting from her windows, was the simplest and most enjoyable course she could pursue.

The massive front door was swung open for her and she stood on the top step regarding the square before her. It was a scene of much activity: a maid-servant was passing tugging along a fat and reluctant pug for its morning constitutional, a young footman strode by with a letter in his hand and many street vendors were crying their wares; even quite near her a young girl with a tray filled with bunches of herbs was calling softly, "Lavender, sweet lavender, who'll buy my lavender?"

Emma was near enough to her to be struck by her shabby clothes and the extreme pallor of her thin, grimy little face and it was with distress rather than surprise that, in the next moment, she saw her falter, take another uncertain step forward, then, with a faint cry, fall to her knees and collapse at the foot of the steps.

In a moment, casting aside her shawl, she was kneeling beside her and was shocked to perceive upon closer examination that the unconscious girl was more emaciated than any human being she had ever before beheld.

It was useless to attempt to lift the poor creature herself but help was needed urgently and those persons in the square who were near enough to have perceived the girl fall seemed to be in no way anxious to render assistance.

Covering the poor creature with her shawl, Emma regained the hall and addressing the nearest of the footman, requested him in urgent tones to accompany her outside to where, she said, "A poor girl is in need of help and must be carried into the house!"

Reporting afterwards to his deeply interested fellow servants, Andrews had expressed to them his absolute astonishment, not only at the nature of the command but at her young ladyship's air of authority. It was common knowledge in the servants' hall that their new mistress was of humble, though respectable, origins and the shocking gossip that had accompanied their marriage was as well known to Lord Ware's household in Grosvenor Square as it was to London Society.

"Could 'ave knocked me down with a feather!" he exclaimed to an interested audience, "Not so much as batted a bloomin' eyelid, 'Carry her into the library, if you please, and lay her on the sofa.' she sez to me, as cool as you please! Which I done, smart like, for she gave me such a look I wouldn't 'ave dared to h'argue with 'er, and a poor, wretched little bit of a thing the girl was!"

Emma was quite unaware of the footman's reactions – she was far too concerned with the young girl's plight to even consider how the incident might appear to others. She sent at once for Dora and for hartshorn and was kneeling beside the sofa trying to arrange the cushions behind the girl's head – the poor creature was still unconscious – when she heard a masculine voice exclaim, "Good God, Emma! What the devil are you about?" and turned to find her husband standing in the doorway regarding the scene before him with a notable lack of pleasure, indeed his lordship was frowning quite horribly, wondering in Heaven's name in what new escapade his wife had now embroiled herself.

The Earl of Ware was not a cruel man but his way of life precluded all but the most fleeting contact with the lower orders and if at times some incident occurred which drew his attention to the desperate conditions existing in parts of London and in the countryside, he would conclude regretfully that that was the way things were; it was no part of his duty to ameliorate the situation save to direct his own land-agents to do their duty by his tenants and workers.

"Oh, my lord, what shall we do? I've never seen anyone so thin! The poor girl has collapsed – no doubt it is days since she has eaten!" Without a moment's hesitation, Emma included her husband in her dilemma.

By now Ware had approached the sofa and was regarding the poor girl with a kinder eye; perhaps because her rescuer was looking so hopefully at him as if he held the solution to her problem in his hands.

It was a sight ironically similar in one respect to that which had met his eyes barely a month ago in this very room: a young girl lying unconscious upon that selfsame sofa – yet there all likeness ended, not for this poor creature the soft curves and smooth, delicate skin of youth, this girl was pitifully thin – almost a skeleton – he could not help thinking that if he had turned Emma out of his house that night, as in a moment of rage he had been tempted to do – would she now resemble this pathetic scrap of humanity? Recoiling from the thought, he turned his eyes upon his wife.

"Explain, my dear Emma, if you please – to what do we owe the sudden appearance in my house of one of nature's unfortunates?"

It was hardly an encouraging speech but Emma was too engaged with the immediate problem to be aware of Ware's displeasure; quickly she described what had happened and, as she held the girl's hand in her own, added with perfect confidence, "I know, my lord, that you will be as eager as I am to help the poor child."

His lordship's most pressing wish was to have this pathetic creature removed forthwith from his library and from his sight and it was fortunate, at least for Emma's opinion of him, that at that moment Dora should have appeared before he had had time to express this desire. Seeing help at hand, he said resignedly, "Let your maid find a more suitable place for the girl to recover, then she can be fed and re-clothed and her address discovered so that she can be conveyed to her home."

Dora was only too anxious to bestow the poor unfortunate elsewhere and quite in agreement with his lordship; she was inexpressibly shocked to find such a person in his lordship's library – verminous perhaps, certainly disgracefully dirty; moreover, she could see at once her employer's displeasure and was sorry that her mistress should have involved herself in another adventure that might cause her high-handed husband's wrath to fall upon her again.

Her mistress, however, was too bound up in her concern for the girl to be conscious that her husband, though his advice was all that it should be, did not enter into her feeling upon the matter. Rising to her feet, she looked gratefully at him saying, "Of course, that will be best – some warm food and a comfortable bed …. but I am confident that you will agree, my lord, that she should remain in this house until more can be discovered about her circumstances – she must indeed be destitute and friendless to have been reduced to such a state."

His lordship regarded her eager face with a mixture of resignation and a growing and unexpected sensation of amusement, his expression softened and he said politely, "By all means, my dear Emma, but I

166

sincerely hope that we shall not be obliged to give board and lodging to *all* the unfortunates in London – though, to be sure, this house is reasonably spacious after all!"

She looked at him suspiciously, then laughed, saying, "Not quite *all*, my lord, only *one*!" and was about to turn her attention to the safe bestowal of her patient when at that moment the girl stirred, her eyelids fluttered and opening her eyes she looked fearfully up into Emma's anxious face.

At once Emma knelt down beside her, saying gently, "You are quite safe, my poor child, – rest quietly and in a moment you shall be given food and drink – you fainted, you know, upon Lord Ware's doorstep." The girl seemed partially reassured, more perhaps by the tone of her rescuer's voice than by her words, and, with a murmured expression of gratitude, closed her eyes again wearily.

Now Andrews was summoned again and the girl carefully carried away, with Dora in attendance and many instructions from their mistress to take the greatest possible care of their charge.

Ware had moved to stand before the window while this procedure was completed, wondering with a surprising lightness of heart what further revelations of his young wife's character lay before him. How startled Society would be if this were to be typical of her behaviour when confronted by the ugly side of London life. Watching her, he was struck again by her astonishing faith in her fellow-men's good nature – how his sister would laugh to hear how he had been made an accomplice in the rescue of a destitute girl – God knows what the child's history would turn out to be – not an edifying one, of that he was certain.

The door having closed upon the departing procession, Emma turned back towards him and, now that this minor crisis was passed, for the first time aware of her surroundings – the oil-painting above the fireplace – the walls lined with books – the fender upon which she had struck her head. It was all quite apparent to Ware as he watched her that she was remembering the last time she had been in that room and he wondered sardonically what she must now be thinking. How ill-prepared she was for her future life – married to a man whose uncle, even, had proclaimed him a libertine. Well, at least he could put to good use now his past experience in pleasing the fair sex!

As Ware came towards her, Emma could not help contrasting this smiling, handsome man with the harsh, frowning rake whom, in terror, she had confronted that night and when he said, "It is a perfect summer's day. Shall we drive out at once? I believe my curricle must now be at the door." it was impossible not to smile in response. She laughed when he added, "There is nothing like the purchasing of an elegant wardrobe to distract the mind in the most delightful way!".

The Earl skilfully threaded his way through the traffic, controlling with ease the pair of horses who, being fresh, were ready to take exception to every barking dog and every passing cart. Emma sat silent for a while, lost in thought, then said confidingly to her companion, "I fear, my lord, that I am sadly ignorant in matters of dress, and sincerely hope that you will advise me, for *you* must be fully conversant with all the latest fashion for females and will be able to tell me precisely what I should wear."

Ware looked sharply down at her, but she was clearly quite unaware that she had said anything improper and appeared to believe it to be perfectly natural that he should be so knowledgeable about female attire. It was going to be, he thought with amusement, an entertaining expedition.

When Emma entered the portals of Madame Celestine's smart establishment in Bond Street on the Earl's arm, she was more than thankful for her husband's presence. Madame came forward in a rustle of silk, her sharp eyes, in a thin pointed face, taking in at a glance the whole situation; not for one moment did she betray in look or word that his lordship was a familiar figure in her showrooms, many the pretty ladybirds who had benefited from his generosity and been indulged to their heart's content with feminine fripperies.

She curtsied low to Emma, asking in what way she could serve her ladyship and declaring herself honoured by a visit from Madame la Comtesse; inwardly she was triumphant at acquiring so wealthy and distinguished a client as the Countess of Ware. Indeed, her experienced eye saw at once that this very young girl had a style and an air quite out of the ordinary; her slight, youthful figure would, more-over, show off Madame's exquisite creations to the utmost advantage.

The next hour or more passed like a dream for Emma. Ware having explained that a complete wardrobe was required for his wife, Madame summoned her minions and commanded them to bring before her illustrious clients all the latest creations from Paris. A profusion of morning dresses, walking dresses, carriage costumes, riding-habits, opera dresses and ball gowns were shown to them. Emma, completely bewildered by the number, the beauty and the complexity of this array, had little to say; his lordship dismissed one or two outfits as unsuitable and Madame angrily sent away a very *outré* evening dress, more suited to the Earl's previous companions, which one of the showroom staff had been rash enough to display.

As Emma was still in half-mourning for her father, it was decided that most of her evening dresses should be white and those for the daytime, besides white, to be of a soft dove grey or palest lavender; for the moment she would confine herself to a limited number of dresses until the mourning period was past, and in the meantime Madame would be preparing further outfits in colours which she could not at present wear with propriety.

She was sent to try on several models, including an elegant pale grey riding-habit in a military style with a dashing hat to match, and a carriage dress consisting of a Russian mantle of lavender sarsenet lined with satin and trimmed with a rich frog fringe, worn over a white jaconet muslin dress; it felt very odd and uncomfortable to be standing before Ware as he looked her over critically, all his attention seriously engaged.

"For the *grande toilette*, I believe that I have just the model that will suit Madame's youthfulness and show off her figure to perfection." With an air of triumph, the astute Frenchwoman produced an enchanting dress of delicate white gauze embroidered with seed pearls and silver thread, worn over an ivory satin petticoat, the sleeves puffed and the neckline cut low and square.

Emma exclaimed with delight; it was the prettiest dress that she had ever seen, but, when she tried it on and appeared before her husband, she felt horribly conscious of the lowness of the neckline and asked rather anxiously whether it could not be cut a little higher. However Madame Celestine at once declared it to be quite '*comme il faut*' for a *'jeune mariée'*, "It is not, after all," she said, with a meaningful smile, "as if Madame la Comtesse was an unmarried girl. It is perfectly *convenable* to show off Madame's delightful figure!"

Ware, highly amused at this exchange, perfectly understood Emma's diffidence, but, although the bodice was cut low, it was by no means indecorous as had been one or two of the dresses that had been discarded. There was no doubt that he had enjoyed seeing the transformation of his young wife into this elegant, fashionable creature and thanks to Madame Celestine's skill and his own good taste, this had been achieved without any sacrifice of the simplicity which suited her youthfulness and the engaging candour of her manner.

What seemed to Emma to be an astounding number of outfits were ordered, and among them the carriage dress which was to be quickly altered and sent round to Grosvenor Square that day, so that Emma could wear it to call on Lady Ancaster in the afternoon. They left Madame Celestine's with all parties eminently satisfied, not least the owner of the establishment, who declared herself afterwards, to her chief saleswoman, to be *'aux anges avec cette jeune fille ravissante'*, whom she shrewdly foretold would be the sensation of the Season.

By the time they had returned to Grosvenor Square, they had made several further calls in Bond Street and Emma was the proud possessor of several pairs of shoes, sandals and half-boots, of gloves and silk stockings and an adorable cottage bonnet, trimmed with curled ostrich feathers, to wear with her new carriage-dress, the price of which had made her gasp with amazement.

She had been rather silent on the way home and several times Ware had looked down at her serious expression and wondered what thoughts were passing through her head; with a groom up behind them, it had not been practicable to have a private conversation and Ware had forborne from questioning her, confident that what he had come to realise was her habitual honesty, would soon impel her to tell him whatever it was that was troubling her. Could it be the problem of the destitute waif that awaited her?

However it seemed that her preoccupation must have some other cause. As soon as they had entered the house Emma had excused herself and after a short time had returned to take luncheon with him with the happy news that the girl, now found to be called Abigail Hunt, though still painfully weak, had recovered sufficiently to be fed and was resting for the moment in Dora's bed-chamber until her rescuer had time to discuss with her her future.

This information imparted to Ware, Emma's manner throughout luncheon was distant; she answered Ware's remarks mechanically and ate very little. As soon as the meal was over and they had gone into the little saloon, she went across to the window and stood looking out onto the square. He sat down, took up a book and began to read, fully aware that every now and then Emma turned to look at him and then turned back again to continue her contemplation of what was after all a very unremarkable scene outside.

For Emma was finding herself confronted by a dilemma. As she covertly regarded the figure of her husband, leaning back, his long legs stretched out before him, his book held in strong, elegant hands, and representing the very epitome of all that a young girl might desire in a lover and a husband, she wondered at her own fearful reluctance to fulfil her wifely duties. Now, above all, when his generosity had been so magnificent. And yet .... and yet he did not – could not *love* her; how hateful it was to her to find herself simply an object of his passions, another possession. Moreover, in her heart, she was still afraid, afraid of those very passions which had been so frighteningly revealed to her at their first encounter.

Inwardly, she rebuked herself – to take all and to give nothing in return – how ungenerous was her behaviour .... something must be said, and at once, before her courage failed her: her conscience would not allow the moment to pass.

The decision made, she came across to him and, sitting down beside him, said in a low voice, "Pray forgive me, my lord, for inter-rupting your reading, but there is something troubling me and I cannot be easy until I have spoken of it to you!"

He closed his book, his eyes upon her worried face and said gently, "I am all attention, my love!"

She began to speak haltingly, "You have given me everything! The beautiful clothes that you bought for me this morning – my apartments newly decorated and furnished – and you will not permit me to use my own money to pay for anything! *You* have given me far, far more than I could possibly deserve – such generosity – and *I*...." She swallowed nervously and then continued, speaking quickly and in so low a voice as to be almost inaudible, looking down as if unable to meet his gaze, "*I - I* have given you *nothing*, not even that which is yours by right as my husband, and I am ashamed! You have been so good to me and yet.... you see...."

He interrupted her and, if Emma had felt able to raise her downcast eyes, she would have seen the amusement in his expression as, in rallying tones, he said, "My dearest girl, let me hear no more of this nonsense! Nothing could exceed the pleasure that it has given me to provide a setting worthy of your delightful self, and," he added, with a wicked grin, "think how it will add to my consequence when all the world beholds the fashionable elegance of my wife! So, you see, it is myself that I have been indulging, for, you know, I have my reputation as a connoisseur of beauty to consider!"

She looked up at him at this, considerably relieved, but he could see that she was still not entirely easy and was not, therefore, surprised when she said to him, with the frankness and simplicity that he had come to expect from her, this time regarding him directly, "You are all that is kind, my lord! If you will but be generous enough to allow me a little more time .... I-I promise you that I will fulfil my d-duties to you as your wife!"

It was a moment that Ware would not easily forget. He had vowed to himself never again to arouse her fears, and that nothing should tempt him to break that resolution; but, by God, here was temptation indeed.... the one whom he most desired to possess, a desire that grew stronger with every day spent in her company, seated so confidingly close beside him! It was the hardest task in the world not to take her that instant in his arms, to smother that trusting face with ardent kisses.... a bitter temptation, without doubt – for was he not after all her husband?

To conceal his feelings, he stood up abruptly and moved away to the bookshelf, saying lightly, "You shall have all the time you need, my dear Emma, for your happiness must be my first object."

Fortunately at that moment the tension in the room was broken by the door opening and a footman announced the arrival of several large dress-boxes. It came as a welcome relief to both of them: Emma had felt such a confusion of emotions that she had found herself unable to answer him. Ware came back to her side and suggested that, as soon as she had changed her apparel, they should venture forth again and call upon his sister: an ordeal which, for Emma's sake, he thought should be got over as soon as possible.

CHAPTER 16

It was Harper, the butler, who opened the door to Lord and Lady Ware and he was too well-trained in his profession to show any sign of recognition when his eyes alighted upon the young Countess. Nothing could have been more proper than his dignified bow nor the manner in which he announced to her ladyship, "The Earl and Countess of Ware!" as he ushered them into the drawing-room.

Looking up from her needlework, Lady Sophia saw before her, across the room, such a startlingly handsome couple that for a moment she was lost for words. His lordship was always a striking figure. Now, in his coat of dark blue superfine, tight-fitting pantaloons and glossy Hessians, he presented the very model for any fashionably aspiring youth; but it was his excellent figure and commanding height, coupled with his darkly handsome looks that first attracted the eye. It was, however, the very young lady at his side, her head barely reaching his shoulder, who held most interest for Lady Sophia; the girl approaching her upon the arm of her husband was dressed in the first style of elegance, her beautiful face framed by a becoming bonnet. Could this really be the former Miss Stanton whom she remembered as a plain, dowdily dressed young person?

"Well, Sophie, do you not greet us? I have brought Emma to see you again." There was amusement in Ware's voice.

She stood up hastily, scattering skeins of silk in all directions and came forward. As she did so, she noticed Emma's anxious glance upwards at her husband, his reassuring smile to her and the way that he gently guided her forward. A sudden, startling thought came into Lady Sophia's head, 'He has fallen in love with her!' and, in her own mind, she added to herself with surprise, 'I believe it will be the making of him!'

It was impossible to greet this shyly smiling girl with the hauteur and reserve that Lady Sophia had been prepared to receive her. She took both Emma's hands in hers, a kindly expression upon her soft, plump face and said, "So we are sisters now! I hope we shall come to be firm friends – though, to be sure, I am a great deal older than you!"

"You are all kindness, my lady," Lady Sophia found a pair of large, candid hazel eyes regarding her as Emma said straightly, "I did not expect to be received so generously after the wicked deception that was played upon you, my lady – and I do beg your pardon with all my heart!"

Lady Sophia, turning to Ware, said wryly, "We shall blame it all upon Robert, my dear!" and leading the way to a sofa, sat down, saying inconsequentially as she invited Emma to take a seat beside her, "Such a headstrong man – you must not let him have his own way in everything – such a mistake, you know!" No sooner were the words out of her mouth than she realised regretfully that they were sadly lacking in tact in view of the circumstances of the marriage and observing Emma to blush and look adorably confused, she hastily changed the subject.

"The children were in the greatest excitement when they learned that their new aunt was none other than the very same Miss Stanton of whom they had grown so fond! They will certainly wish to see you before you leave." She admired Emma's elegant outfit and heard of their morning's shopping expedition with secret amusement.

Ware said, "Do you think you could accompany Emma tomorrow, Sophie? She could have no better guide than you to explore all the shops that your sex delight in."

"My dear, with pleasure! What could be more delightful?" She smiled in friendly fashion at Emma, who was by now feeling considerably more comfortable and beginning to esteem her sister-in-law the kindest person in the world.

"We hope," he added, "that you and Peter will dine with us in Grosvenor Square today and accompany us to the opera. 'The Magic Flute' is to be performed and I believe that Emma will enjoy it."

His sister, having signified her pleasure and their acceptance, enquired whether he had the intention of attending Lady Challenor's ball, "I hear that it will be a shocking squeeze – four hundred invited – they say the Prince Regent may look in during the course of the evening!" Ware nodded, with a smile directed to his wife's eager face,

175

"It will be an excellent opportunity for Emma to make her first appearance in Polite Society."

At that moment children's voices could be heard, there was a stir and a bustle outside the door, and, upon going into the hall, they met the nursery party returning from their afternoon walk in the park.

They were a sight to gladden any mother's heart: Serena and Mary, one dark, one fair, looked charmingly in their bonnets and muslin dresses. Mary was clutching a wooden hoop and stick and the young son and heir, his little face aglow above the collar of his frilled shirt, was astride his hobby-horse; beyond them were Miss Embery and Nurse, the latter with Baby Charlotte in her arms, and surprise and pleasure lit up the children's faces as they perceived their new aunt.

Miss Embery, looking above and beyond her young friend's modish bonnet, saw the dark face of the Earl of Ware, a softer expression than she recollected having seen before in his eyes, and thought thankfully that her judgment had not been at fault. Amidst the explanations of delight, Emma stepped forward impulsively and shook Miss Embery warmly by the hand, saying softly, "Dear Miss Embery, how good you were to me!"

She found Miles, his hobby-horse abandoned, tugging at her skirt, saying proudly, "I know you are my aunt now, 'cos Serena told me so! Are you going to come and read to me? Please come up to the nursery *now* – I do so much want to show you my new soldiers!" The girls, more shyly, added their entreaties, and Emma, rosy with pleasure, turned diffidently to Lady Sophia who gave her assent with a warm smile.

The junior party mounted the stairs in a group, Miles clutching Emma's hand and telling her eagerly about the new puppy that he had been promised by his papa. Watching them go, Ware said, "You have a charming family, Sophie!" but she observed that his eyes were following the pretty, animated figure of his wife.

Leading him back into the drawing-room, Lady Sophia remarked as she did so, "I am glad to have the opportunity of speaking to you alone." and, once the door was closed, looked at him with a troubled expression upon her kindly face, saying earnestly, "I believe you should warn Emma that she will certainly meet with many rebuffs – I know of several dowagers of my acquaintance who say they will not receive her – there is a great deal of prejudice against her, you know – Richard Harding did his wicked work well and I fear that she will be cruelly hurt."

Ware was frowning thoughtfully, "I believe her own innocence to be her best defence against such malice, Sophie. If I warn her, she will be the more conscious of it." He added, with a wry smile, "I have discovered since our marriage that Emma is a considerable heiress – perhaps, when that is known, it will go some way to restore her in the eyes of the world: she could not then be accused of conspiring to entrap a rich husband."

Lady Sophia listened with growing astonishment and indignation as Ware told her all that he had learned from the lawyers and of the motive behind Richard's evil plan.

"What an abominable story – if people only knew the truth!" she exclaimed when he had finished, "But I suppose that Emma would not care for it to be spoken of – he is her half-brother after all – a near relation."

"I believe we shall brush through without any further revelations – and, with your kind support, all will soon be forgotten." He laughed cynically, "Depend upon it, there will soon be some other scandal to set all the tongues wagging!" He paused, then continued with a grin, "One thing I must tell you, Sophie, that will surprise and amuse you – Emma has already seen fit to rescue a poor girl who collapsed outside my house this morning – and we only arrived in London yesterday evening! Had her carried into the library – you can picture my astonishment when I discovered her there, and," he added ruefully, "my initial annoyance! Ironic, is it not – the wicked Earl of Ware become a philanthropist!"

It seemed as if surprise predominated in Lady Sophia's mind – she laughed appreciatively but clearly her amazement was great. There was, she thought swiftly, a great deal more to this pretty young creature than she had realised. Some in Society would approve but many would regard Emma with derision if they knew of the incident.

At this moment the subject of their conversation returned from the nursery and Ware having requested his sister's help in seeking out an experienced lady's-maid to wait upon his wife, they took their leave of

Lady Sophia – she, for her part, offering to send round her own hair-dresser that evening so that Emma's appearance might be further enhanced by a fashionable hair-style for her first evening at the opera.

After they had departed, Lady Sophia sat a long time pondering upon the future of her brother's marriage: such a strange beginning to married life could not fail to present manifold problems; she found it hard to reconcile what she knew of her brother's past life with the obvious concern that he now displayed for his young wife, above all – how did Emma regard her husband?

Monsieur Henri was only too happy to dress the hair of *Madame la Comtesse*; quite apart from his desire to please Lady Sophia and to gain the future patronage of a valuable client, he saw at once that the young Countess would be a credit to his skills. As his deft fingers arranged Emma's curls into a delightful style '*a la greque*', with artfully contrived ringlets confined by a filet of satin ribbon, he complimented her upon the colour of her hair, surprising Emma, who had long regretted that she was neither a blonde nor truly raven-haired, as was the fashion, but possessed locks of an indeterminate brown.

It was almost time for the arrival of their guests when she came down to the drawing-room; she was wearing a dress of pale oyster-grey satin with a scalloped hem and long sleeves: the stiffened lace collar emphasizing her slender neck around which she wore her mother's pearls. When Ware saw her, he was irresistibly reminded of moonlight on water and seeing the admiration in his eyes, Emma blushed and, as he kissed her fingers, asked softly, "Do you approve, my lord?"

He nodded, saying teasingly, "You look so charmingly, my dear wife, I am confident that my brother-in-law will be captivated instantly!"

Sir Peter Ancaster was undoubtedly impressed and amazed by Emma's appearance. Lady Sophia had wisely said very little to him about the astonishing transformation of their erstwhile guest and when she had informed him that the notion had come to her that Ware's affections were engaged, he had found it impossible to believe; now he was not so sure. Emma spoke to him with a charming frankness, "Your wife has forgiven me, Sir Peter, and it is my earnest hope that you will pardon me too!"

Seeing her grave expression and the absence of artifice in her manner, Sir Peter found himself unbending; it was not possible to resist such an appeal. Soon he had entered upon a most agreeable conversation with her, her interest in country matters having encouraged him to describe to her his handsome estates in Norfolk and the new farming methods which he was seeking to introduce there.

Dinner passed off most pleasantly; Emma, eager to learn all that she might about the opera that they were to hear that evening, hardly noticed the succession of delicious and elaborate dishes that were set before them, and wore an air of suppressed excitement.

Her first view of the interior of the theatre quite equalled, even excelled, all her expectations. From his lordship's box the whole auditorium was visible and she was astonished at the vast size of the great proscenium arch and at the sight of hundreds of glittering candles that lit up the crimson walls, the elaborate gilded decorations and the painted ceiling.

At first it was the theatre itself that occupied Emma's attention but, as she began to regard the fashionable throng of people before her, she became aware that a disconcertingly large number of faces were turned towards their box where she was seated next to Lady Sophia. Those interested persons near enough to see unaided were staring openly at her, others, further off, had their opera glasses trained upon the Earl's box, and there were several gentlemen who had raised their quizzing-glasses and were regarding her in a very uncomfortable manner.

She turned to Ware, who was seated behind her, but before she could speak, he indicated to her that the orchestra was about to commence the overture and she was silent. In the period that followed she soon forgot both her surroundings and her unease; never before had she heard such glorious sounds: the music seemed to fill the air, obliterating all else and she sat enthralled by all she saw and heard. At the end of the first Act she turned again with shining eyes to Ware, saying, "How splendid it is! I had no idea...."

He looked at her radiant face saying with a smile, "I am glad that it pleases you – I did not think that *you* would be bored, as would be many young ladies of my acquaintance."

Around the theatre now there was a burst of conversation, a general movement: the ladies fanning themselves, the gentlemen rising to stretch their legs, to visit the boxes or to promenade in the corridors. Sir Peter left them to speak to a friend, and Lady Sophia, anxious to divert Emma's attention from the very obvious interest that was again being taken in their party, immediately began to discuss with her the artists who were singing the principal roles.

She was assisted in her endeavours by the arrival of Edward Wyndham, who had come to pay his respects to his new cousin and who, bowing in his graceful fashion over Emma's hand and eyeing her with obvious admiration, felicitated her upon her appearance. She replied laughingly, without any sign of coquetry, "How very pleased I am to be sure, that you approve! You see, I have not forgotten that you are said to be an arbiter of fashion – if I have *your* approval I must be modish indeed!"

Lady Sophia was looking her surprise at this exchange and at the good terms upon which they stood, and enquired curiously of Emma when and where she and Edward had met.

"Poor Edward came hastening to Millford to prevent my lord from making a shocking misalliance!" was the reply, given without any sign of embarrassment, "But he arrived too late – and has since been good enough to accept me as a cousin and, I hope, as a friend."

Edward looked stunned at these forthright words; his expression drew a chuckle from Ware and led Lady Sophia to declare with amusement that she had never before seen Cousin Edward deprived of speech.

At this moment they were joined by Mr Humphrey Featherstone and Sir Andrew Holt who, consumed with curiosity to meet Ware's bride, entered their box and were presented to Emma, who greeted them with a shy smile, saying, "I am indeed happy to meet my lord's friends – it adds greatly to my pleasure in what is a most delightful evening for, you see, I have never attended an opera before!"

Sir Andrew, drawing up a chair beside her, began to talk of the rival pleasures of the legitimate theatre and an operatic production, and found himself charmed by Emma's eager interest. Mr Featherstone, standing behind them, took a delicate pinch of snuff from Ware's proffered snuff-box and said in an undertone, "By God, Robert, you're a d-devilish lucky man! Never told us that you had married a beauty!"

Ware regarded him thoughtfully and it was a moment before he replied, saying with unmistakeable emphasis, "Twice lucky, my dear fellow, for my wife is as virtuous as she is beautiful!"

Mr Featherstone looked justifiably startled: nothing in his lordship's past would have led one to suppose that he set any great value upon such an attribute, rather the reverse in fact; nor did the rumours circulating about his bride encourage the belief that she was a young lady of high moral principles.

Observing his open-mouthed astonishment with a frown, Ware said austerely, "You find it surprising, dear boy?"

Mr Featherstone made a quick recovery, "I call it a d-dashed miracle, Robert, that such a paragon consented to marry you!"

Ware's frown vanished; re-assured, and confident that Emma was in good hands, after a moment he left the box, saying that he wished to pay his respects to Lady Sheldon whom he had seen in the audience.

While continuing her conversation, Emma found herself scanning the tiers of boxes to observe whither his lordship had gone and was surprised at her own feeling of relief to behold his fine, tall person in one of the boxes opposite, bowing over the be-ringed hand of a stout, and by no means young, lady wearing a startlingly bright crimson toque trimmed with feather plumes.

Mr Featherstone and Sir Andrew having made their bows and quitted the box, they were succeeded by a foppishly dressed young man, who greeted Edward and, bowing low, kissed Lady Sophia's hand in an extravagant manner. As her sister-in-law presented Mr Horace Brownlow, Emma observed with surprise the exaggerated padded shoulders and over-tight waist of his black evening coat and the profusion of fobs and rings adorning his person. Although unaware that he had been one of those present at the card-party at her half-brother's house, she found that she did not at all care for the manner in which he was regarding her, nor, when he spoke, for the words with which he addressed her.

"Honoured, I'm sure, to meet your ladyship," he said, his whole manner expressive of contempt, "We men are all eager to become acquainted with the dazzling '*prize*' that Robert has won!" His sharp little eyes were looking her up and down in a frankly appraising manner as he added, "What delight to behold the charms that have *captured* one who has conquered so many!"

It was perfectly clear to Emma, by his emphasis upon the word 'prize' and by his attitude towards her, that a great deal more than a flowery politeness was intended; she felt herself blushing, but retorted with strong indignation, "Sir, if you were a friend of Lord Ware, as your familiarity would suggest, you would not refer, however indirectly, to an event which can only cause embarrassment to his wife and would, I am confident, be excessively displeasing to him!"

Such devastating candour quite overset Mr Brownlow, who changed colour and stammered, "Your ladyship quite mistakes my meaning.... not for the world would I offend you.... beg you will not suggest to your husband that any offence was intended...." and with many polite bows to the company, took himself off, looking considerably affrighted and not a little incensed.

"Well said, cousin!" Edward was frowning, "He is a contemptible creature – but I fear that you have made an enemy – he will not care to have such a set-down witnessed by others and he has a spiteful tongue."

Lady Sophia, half amused, half distressed at her sister-in-law's directness, said gently to Emma, "You know, dear child, it will not do to set up people's backs! It may be wiser to ignore such foolishness."

"Dear Lady Sophia, I should find it hard to do so." Her expression of indignation lightened and she gave a chuckle, "What an odd looking man he was, to be sure, I could hardly keep my countenance when I saw him!"

"Oh, he is one of the dandy set." Edward grinned as he stood up to leave them, "A regular popinjay!" Bowing over their hands in farewell, he added in an undertone to Emma, "I hear that the Priestleys are come to town. One cannot help wondering what Society will make of them. I fear that they will not be well-received."

In Lady Sheldon's box, Ware was greeted by the words, "So you have brought her to London at last! And a diamond of the first water, as one might expect of you!"

Thanking the dowager for the compliment with a smile, he took a seat beside her and said, "I am come to make a demand upon that kindness for which you are so justly famous, ma'am. I should be greatly indebted to you if you would consent to call upon my wife. There is, I am only too well aware, a vast deal of prejudice against her – of which, mercifully, she is at present barely conscious – for the rumours circulated so assiduously by her half-brother are known everywhere." He added emphatically, "It is doubly unfair, I assure you, for her *virtue* equals her *beauty* – indeed, she is utterly blameless!"

Lady Sheldon gave a crow of laughter, "Come, Ware, surely you are not setting yourself up as a judge of virtue! *You*, of all men!"

"On the contrary, ma'am," he replied swiftly, "I am precisely the person to recognise and appreciate such a rare quality as goodness – for I have already sampled all the bad ones and found them surprisingly little to my taste!"

This was said to her with a sardonic grin that made her chuckle the more and say "I could never resist a handsome rascal! Very well – I will call upon Lady Ware – I can hardly wait to meet such a pattern of perfection!"

Ware remained with the ladies during the second interval which preceded the end-piece; a succession of gentlemen appeared in their box and were duly presented to Emma, but there was no repetition of the kind of remark favoured by Mr Brownlow: no-one was fool enough to incur the wrath of his lordship, who stood beside her, outwardly agreeable but with a steely-look lurking behind his smile. Emma appeared to be quite equal to all the flowery compliments lavished upon her, for in spite of her youth and inexperience, she had no difficulty in recognising them for what they were worth and, although agreeably surprised to hear such delightful things said of her, was clearly not in any way likely to have her head turned. She said afterwards to Ware, with laughter in her eyes, "These gentlemen would be quite at a stand if they had not had a classical education, for I believe that I have been likened to every goddess that I have ever heard of and to some of whose existence until now I was quite ignorant!"

CHAPTER 17

It was perhaps fortunate for Jane Priestley that their departure from London was to take place so soon after her ill-fated elopement.

Entirely engrossed in all the preparation necessary for so momentous an event as the launching of her only daughter into Society, Mrs Priestley failed to observe Jane's subdued manner and pale cheeks. If she had done so, no doubt she would have set it down to the absence of Mr Hartley Tremayne, news of whose unexpected departure from Norton had reached her ears.

Her husband had greeted this intelligence with relief. He had not the least desire that his pretty daughter should throw herself away upon a mere commoner. He had, moreover, a shrewd idea that young Mr Tremayne's pockets were to let and that it was rather love for her father's fortune than for Jane's person that motivated the young man's courtship.

While trunks were packed and the whole household thrown into a turmoil around her, Jane found her thoughts often turning to the events at the 'Queen's Head'. How horrible had been the transformation of the man whom she had believed that she loved! She trembled at the recollection; was that what all men were like beneath their courteous manners? There had been something so repulsive, so animal-like in Hartley's assault upon her. All the pleasurable sensations aroused by his respectful wooing of her had vanished in that moment when she had discovered his intent and had struggled frantically to save herself.

Pleasanter, by far, to let her mind dwell upon the young man who had come to her rescue. She thought of Edward Wyndham with a shy wonder. How kind he had been, how considerate of her feelings! So different to the Earl of Ware. She thought with a shudder that she would not care to cross his lordship .... True, he had succeeded in extricating her from any scandal and, thanks to his presence, her return home had been accomplished without her parents learning of her folly and of her narrow escape from shame; but there had been precious little sympathy in his hard, grey eyes and she wondered fleetingly what it would be like to be married to such a man.

At last the great day arrived and, in a positive procession of carriages, laden with members of the family, possessions and servants, the Priestleys set out for the great Metropolis.

That evening, after Jane had retired for the night, even *her* crushed spirits revived by the sights and sounds of London, Mrs Priestley expressed her contentment and her future plans to her husband.

"Well, Mr Priestley, I must say you've done us proud, my dear!" she looked around the vast salon complaisantly, "Everything of the best and in the latest fashion!"

Her husband nodded his head, "Aye, lass, none of your old style furnishings – all spanking new!" He recollected the faded walnut and mahogany furniture, the soft-hued chintzes and damasks now relegated to the attics, and regarded with satisfaction the dark, heavy Egyptian-influenced pieces, the plethora of brilliant colours, of stripes and satins that surrounded them.

"Jane and I will have a vast deal of shopping to do, William, before we'll be fit to h'appear in society, for I've no doubt we should look to be a couple of real country dowds until we do. What's good enough for Wiltshire won't do for London, you know!"

Mr Priestley looked at his wife's eager face and smiled benignly, "That ain't no more than I expected, my dear. All I says is – pay as you go – that's my motto! I ain't short of the blunt but I won't stand for bills being run up. Nothing wrong with *my* credit – but that's one department where I ain't wishing to ape my betters!"

Mrs Priestley continued complacently, "Alicia Foster is to call upon us tomorrow – she'll set me right as to how to go on. A good friend, she's been to me, since Sir Ralph died...."

Her spouse appeared to view Lady Foster's friendship with less enthusiasm. With a sour smile, he rejoined bluntly, "That's as maybe, Mary – seems to me she's changed her tune mightily since she discovered her husband left her without a penny! Thought herself too grand before that to be bothering with us plain folks!"

However Mrs Priestley's mind had flown on to weightier matters. "We'll 'ave to give a grand ball for our Jane's come-out, Mr Priestley. Though it will be best if we get to know our way around before we start issuing h'invitations. If we could get Lord and Lady Ware to attend...." her dark eyes sparkled, "Why, that would be the making of us!"

Upon the following morning, Lady Foster duly called and having bestowed an affectionate greeting upon 'her dear Mary', prepared to enter with enthusiasm into all Mrs Priestley's plans. After a swift, incredulous glance at her sumptuous surroundings, she felicitated her hostess, tongue in cheek, upon the new furnishings and enquired whether an invitation had been received for Lady Challenor's ball.

"She's such a dear friend of mine, you know, Mary! It will be one of the events of the Season. And I believe that your husband is acquainted with Lord Challenor?"

Mrs Priestley replied in the affirmative, looking with satisfaction at the engraved invitation upon the mantel-shelf. " 'E and William are as thick as thieves ever since William put him in the way of making a fortune in some h'enterprise or other!"

Lady Foster, suppressing a smile at this description of the relationship between his lordship and Mr Priestley, added, "I hope that you and your family will dine with me on Wednesday, my dear, for we must see that you and Jane have the opportunity of making some acquaintances amongst the Ton before the ball."

It had been planned to be Mrs Priestley's moment of triumph. "Well, my dear, we have good friends in *that* quarter! The Earl and Countess of Ware, you know! Neighbours of ours in Wiltshire – we met them at the Tremayne's and our Jane struck up quite a friendship with Lady Ware." she prattled on, unconscious of the change in her friends expression, "A charming young girl, Lady Ware – no height in her manner at all. Of course, his lordship's a trifle top-lofty, but, nevertheless, he called at our house! The young ones all went on a picnic party together...."

Suddenly becoming aware of Lady Foster's compressed lips and pitying expression, she faltered, her pleasure spoiled and added anxiously, "No doubt you are acquainted with Lord Ware?"

"My dear!" Lady Foster's pale eyes gleamed with malice, "On no account must you acknowledge a friendship with *that* couple! Lord Ware is quite in disgrace – of course he has always been known as a shocking rake – but his wife ....!"

She paused dramatically, her thin cheeks flushed with prurient satisfaction. "*She*, my dear Mary, is no better than a light-skirt – a wanton who left her brother's protection to live with Lord Ware! The marriage came later and no-one can conceive why on earth he took such a creature as his wife!"

Mrs Priestley looked appalled and, at the same time, thoroughly perplexed, "Are you sure, Alicia? I can hardly credit it...." she thought with astonishment of the sweet-faced girl whom she had been so proud to know.

"My dear, not one person will receive her, believe me!" Lady Foster spoke emphatically, "I have been told upon the best authority that she will be shunned by Society. For your own sake, and for Jane's, you must not, upon any account, permit her to set foot in your house – that is – if she should have the temerity to call upon you!"

Mrs Priestley's hopes were sadly dashed. Inwardly thanking Heaven that she had been warned in time to prevent her committing an error that would have, perhaps, ruined Jane's chances, she wondered resentfully how Mrs Tremayne could have introduced her to such a disreputable couple – young Mr Wyndham, too, was upon good terms with his lordship. Was he also not a desirable acquaintance? It was all horribly confusing! Setting aside these perplexing problems, she accepted her friend's invitation with pleasure and thought how thankful she was to have Lady Foster's guidance through the coming weeks.

For her part, Lady Foster left the Priestley's house with a feeling of satisfaction. She had already secured the presence of an old friend of hers amongst her guests for Wednesday evening. George, Marquis of Frant, had been seeking a wealthy young heiress to take as his wife for some little time in order to relieve his acute financial situation. Here was a golden opportunity to promote an alliance, which, if successfully achieved, would undoubtedly be useful to her in the future. George would be grateful and in his gratitude would, no doubt, not forget his old friend. That the marquis was a man ruined both physically and financially worried her not one jot: the Priestleys desired a title and the marquisate was indeed an ancient one. To Jane's feelings upon the matter she gave little or no thought.

The day following their visit to the opera being Sunday, the Earl and Countess of Ware attended Divine Service at the Chapel Royal and, after the service was ended, encountered Sir Peter and Lady Sophia and exchanged greetings with them. Somewhat to Emma's surprise, Lord Ware did not linger long outside. She had become aware during the service that their presence had caused quite a stir amongst the fashionable congregation and had expected to be presented to at least one or two of the elegantly dressed couples who were, without doubt, acquainted with his lordship. She decided, however, upon their return home, to keep her thoughts to herself; after all, it was more than likely that, despite his determined words, her husband might well be ashamed of a bride so far below him in rank and fortune. It was a lowering thought but one that must be stoically endured. He had certainly been very silent since they had re-entered the house.

A most welcome diversion was provided by the arrival of Edward and perhaps on account of her previous gloomy thoughts, Emma greeted him with unconcealed pleasure. Ware's reception of his cousin was rather less welcoming; saying coldly, "Good-morning, Edward, I did not expect to see you so early upon a Sunday morning!" he continued to peruse the papers that he held in his hand.

Edward grinned, and, unable to resist further exasperating his relation, replied instantly, "It ain't you that I've come to see, Robert! You flatter yourself!" then, turning again to Emma, perfectly conscious that Ware was listening to every word inspite of his apparent pre-occupation with his reading, said softly, "It seems that your husband ain't best pleased to see me – does he mean to keep you entirely to himself?"

Oblivious of the constraint in the atmosphere, Emma chuckled, "By no means! Rather, I fear, he may be anxious how to avoid having me entirely upon his hands – for, as you know, I have not a single acquaintance in London."

By now, Edward had led her to a sofa at some distance from Ware, and, sitting down beside her, leaned forward and said confidentially in a low voice, "I wondered, Emma, if you might consider calling upon Mrs Priestley now that they are arrived in London?"

She regarded him with astonishment, "Mrs Priestley? Why, how you do surprise me! I seem to remember you describing her and her husband to me in the most unflattering terms...."

An amused expression in Edward's eyes, a certain consciousness in his manner, made Emma open her eyes wide; her lips close to his ear, she whispered, "Is it Miss Jane Priestley who has captured your interest?"

He nodded, "I confess there is something about her – a charming innocence .... and it is quite clear that her parents are ambitious; no doubt they intend her to make a brilliant match and will not be too particular how they achieve that end. So, you see, she will have need of a good friend."

Emma, all seriousness now, was only too pleased to do something for Edward and if she wondered at his liking for a girl who, to her mind, had displayed an astonishing lack of judgment, she nevertheless replied at once, "I will call upon Mrs Priestley tomorrow. Perhaps Jane would care to drive out with me one day; that is, if my lord is agreeable."

Lord Ware was, at that moment, looking very far from agreeable. The subject of his wife's conversation with Edward was unknown to him, for the distance across the salon that now divided them precluded his over-hearing their words, but their attitude, heads close together, and their lowered tones, gave to him a most disagreeable impression of intimacy.

He put aside his papers and came across the room to them and at once embarked upon a conversation with Edward about a mutual acquaintance, coldly ignoring Emma, and making her feel sadly that her husband must indeed be beginning to regret ever having brought her to London. She had, she reflected ruefully, only encountered, so far, Ware's male friends – doubtless they had accepted her, being less nice in their ideas of rank and propriety. How was she to fare at the hands of the females in Society?

Later that day she was to discover that she was not the only one to feel a shadow lay over the pleasure of being in London.

She had gone with Dora to speak to poor Abigail Hunt, for whom a truckle-bed had been placed in Dora's bed-chamber; the girl's gratitude had known no bounds and, gently questioned by Emma, she had revealed that an elderly nobleman had brought her from Yorkshire to serve as a sewing-maid in his London house. A man who had then forcibly seduced her – it was a vile tale – and who, upon discovering that she was to bear his child, had turned her out of his house with neither reference, money nor even her own few pathetic possessions. Becoming desperate with hunger she had been forced to steal some bread. In a trembling voice she described to Emma how she had been caught and arrested and thrown into prison. "Oh, my lady it were a place not fit for animals!" Here, amid the filth, squalor and wretchedness, she had been befriended by another woman prisoner, and, upon being released a few days ago, she had gone to live with her in some pathetic lodgings near Covent Garden. The day before had been her first attempt to earn herself some money.

"But the baby, Abigail?" Emma asked her softly.

"Miscarried, my lady – how could it be otherwise! *And*," she added bitterly, "I ain't sorry neither – for it would have been *his*!"

"And your family? Do they know what has happened?"

"Why, no, your ladyship, for how could I send to them?" Tears sprang to Abigail's eyes, "I can't write, my lady – nor had I the means nor the money – and what they must think of me ....."

Overwhelming pity rose in Emma's heart and with it hatred of equal strength for the man who had ruined this poor girl's life. Now, however, practical steps must be taken. She said reassuringly, "I will write at once to your parents and send them money so that your mother can come to London, for clearly you are too weak to travel yourself. In the meantime, once you are stronger, you can assist in the sewing-room here. I am sure that you are an excellent worker."

Nothing could equal Abigail's gratitude – to her it seemed as if an angel from Heaven had come to her rescue; Dora, too, was infinitely touched by the scene that she had witnessed.

It was perhaps for this reason that, when she and her mistress had regained Emma's bedchamber, she suddenly burst into tears. A sympathetic enquiry as to the cause of her distress had brought forth a sad recital of woe, punctuated by heart-rending sobs.

"I know it ain't nothing compared to what that poor child has suffered – but it's Thomas, your ladyship! I misses him so, my lady – an' me thinkin' it would be so wunnerful to be in London! If only he was here, my lady ....." She pulled a pocket-handkerchief from her apron and blew her nose vigorously, striving to continue more calmly, "I knows as we can't be married, ma'am, while we're in service together like, but, oh, my lady, Wiltshire do seem to be a powerful long way away! An' that Betty, down at Millford...." her voice rose to a wail, "A proper designing cat, she be, an' she's got her eye on him, too, ma'am!"

Emma, her ready sympathy aroused, attempted to comfort Dora as best as she might and lost no time in endeavouring to ameliorate the situation. That evening, when the tea-tray had been brought in after dinner and it seemed that her husband, as he sat beside her, was in a more affable mood, she broached the subject diffidently.

"My lord, would you find it objectionable if I ordered that Thomas be sent for from Millford to join the staff here?"

Her husband, eyebrows raised, regarded her earnest face with surprise, "Thomas! Good God, whatever puts you in mind of him? Haven't we servants enough here?"

She shook her head, her face a little flushed; surely he did not think that she was complaining about poor service; for certainly she had never in her whole life been waited upon, hand and foot, as she had been since her marriage. "Oh, no, my lord – it's Dora, my maid! She's in love with him, you know." She could see that he was beginning to look amused and regarded him hopefully.

He said pensively, "And you think we should arrange our household to suit the *amours* of our staff?"

"I believe that we should consider their well-being where possible, my lord."

It was clearly a novel idea to her husband, who, though attached to the older members of his household, had never given a thought to their private lives nor to their feelings. Dora, he thought, could not have chosen a more apt ambassadress for her cause – how could he resist that trusting face turned towards him, the clear, brown eyes searching his countenance for signs of approval of her scheme. There flashed through his mind the thought that Thomas was separated by scarcely a greater distance from his love than he was, metaphorically speaking, from his own wife! No doubt, one day soon, she would reward his patience – but was that what he desired – the dutiful submission of this charming girl? Here, at any rate, was an opportunity to raise himself in her esteem! And at precious little cost to himself, he thought wryly.

Emma had already remarked a softening in his expression and her face lit up as he said teasingly, "By all means, my dear girl, let us make smooth the path of true love. You may send for Thomas at once – it was wretchedly unobservant of me not to have noticed this romance burgeoning before my very eyes!"

With a happy smile, she responded at once, "I was sure that you would agree when you knew of the circumstances, my lord." adding guilelessly, "I have been told so much about your wicked way of life but I believe that a great deal more could be said of your kindness and consideration!"

He regarded her face, his eyebrows a little raised in surprise. Doubtless, Emma meant every word that she had said and clearly had no idea how wide she was of the mark, "A singularly misguided notion, my love, you really must not place such astonishing faith in my good nature!" A little roughness entered his voice as he added cynically, "Surely you must have been aware that my actions are largely motivated by self-interest."

She shook her head, a little smile playing about her mouth, "I do not believe so, my lord."

For a sudden, startling moment he thought that she was about to put out her hand to him, so softened was the expression in the eyes that gazed into his, then she drew back, her colour heightened and said shyly, "I will tell Dora at once of her good fortune, my lord." and rose from her place beside him and left the room.

CHAPTER 18

Emma's first action the following morning was to write to Abigail's parents and to obtain from his lordship some money for the mother's journey from Yorkshire.

As he franked the package before it was committed to the post, Ware wondered cynically to what lengths his wife's charitableness was to lead him in the future. The world would certainly be a very different place if Emma had her way.

These tasks completed, Emma decided to pay the morning call upon Mrs Priestley that she had promised to Edward and as my lord's elegant barouche conveyed her to the Priestley's residence, she was thankful to think that, upon this occasion at least, she could be confident of a warm reception of her call. There had been no doubt that Mrs Priestley had been immensely flattered by their attention in Wiltshire, and although she quite realised that it was her present rank that made her so welcome an acquaintance, it was at any rate a relief to know that she need fear no coldness from that quarter.

Having descended from the carriage, she glanced up at the imposing facade and observed with some amusement that, in an upper window, Mrs Priestley's startled face was visible for a moment before the curtain was allowed to fall back into place.

It came, therefore, as a shock to be informed by the stately butler, who opened the door to her and received with an expressionless countenance her name and her request to see Mrs Priestley or her daughter, that neither his mistress nor Miss Priestley were at home.

For a moment Emma stared at him in disbelief, then, striving to preserve her dignity, she handed him the cards with which his lordship had kindly provided her, and turned away, crushed by a hateful sensation of rejection.

The journey home seemed scarcely long enough to compose her thoughts. Was it possible that Mrs Priestley, perhaps unsuitably attired to receive so noble a caller and being flustered, had ordered her butler to deny her visitor? Emma did not believe so. There had been no time for such an order to have been received; instructions had clearly already been issued that Mrs Priestley was not at home to the Countess of Ware.

Ware was in the hall, having just returned from a visit to his boot-maker in St James's Street, when Emma re-entered the house and he at once expressed his surprise that she should have returned so soon.

"I didn't think that Mrs Priestley would allow you to escape so quickly!" he said smilingly, then, observing that something had upset her composure, continued easily, "Come into the library, my love, for you look as if you could well do with some refreshment."

As he handed her a glass of wine, he said brusquely, "What has happened, Emma? I can see that you are distressed."

"Is it so apparent, my lord?" She sighed, "It is only that it seems that I am not worthy to be received by the Priestleys of this world!"

"Good God – what damnable impudence!" Ware's face was black as thunder as he took a seat beside her.

Regarding anxiously his scowling countenance, Emma said placatingly, "Poor Mrs Priestley – no doubt someone has taken the trouble to inform her of the scandal concerning me – and I am sure that she would not feel her position in Society sufficiently secure to run counter to popular opinion."

There was a brief silence.

Ware seemed to be making some effort to control his anger; the black look vanished to be replaced by a rueful grin. He said, "And to think how old Priestley was bowing and scraping to us when we returned his daughter to him!" He took Emma's hand, "For God's sake, my love, don't look so stricken – it will all be forgotten in a trice. One need scarcely mourn the loss of the Priestleys' acquaintance!"

Fortunately there was soon to be a diversion. Before Emma could make any reply, the doors were thrown open and, following swiftly upon the footman's announcement of "Lord Rupert Vane, my lady!"

she beheld a stout gentleman advancing towards her, both hands outstretched, who kissed her heartily upon both cheeks, then stood back to survey her from head to foot, an expression of the greatest curiosity upon his face: a face, Emma swiftly realised, that bore ample evidence of the triumph of art over nature.

"Well, dear boy, I must own that you lost no time in following my advice!" Lord Rupert transferred his gaze to Ware who, having risen to his feet, was regarding him with some suspicion, and added, with not the least attempt to lower his voice, "An' a charming little filly, too, by Jove – but you always had impeccable taste, Robert!"

"Emma, my love, may I present my Uncle Rupert! His manners, alas, leave a great deal to be desired but no doubt with your usual graciousness you will forgive him." There was tightness about Ware's mouth, a steely look in the eyes that regarded his kinsman.

Lord Rupert appeared unabashed. "No need to get on your high horse, my boy – met young Edward in Brook's and heard all about it from him!" He turned back to Emma, "Devilish situation for you, my dear – thing is – take my advice – don't let him bully you! Deucedly forceful fellow, Robert!" He paused, then added with a twinkle in his eyes, "Present him with a son and heir, my girl, and you'll soon have him eating out of your hand!"

Emma, her face scarlet with embarrassment, cast a swift, uneasy glance at her husband and ignoring these outspoken remarks, said gravely, "It is good of you to accept me, Lord Rupert, for ours cannot be the marriage for which you and the rest of your family must have hoped – I am only too well aware of that!" and requested her visitor to take a seat beside her.

He looked considerably taken aback at this frank admission; the little eyes in his plump, painted face opening wide with surprise, his mouth falling open and, as he sat down beside her with an audible creaking of the corset that confined his ample form, he said disarmingly, "By Jove, I can tell you, my dear, you ain't at all the kind of girl I was expectin'! Thought you'd be some regular bread-and-butter Miss!" His sharp eyes flew again to Ware, who was by now regarding the pair of them with some amusement, and rested there a moment before he spoke again.

"You're a deep one, Robert – but, by Jupiter, I'll swear that you've got more than you bargained for here! An' I never did think it was good for you to have all those gels doting upon you!"

Ware laughed suddenly, "You're a shrewd old rascal, Uncle! Ain't much that escapes you!" He looked reassuringly at Emma and said to her lightly, "Lord Rupert prides himself upon his address with women, my dear wife – you must beware of his blandishments!"

She smiled in friendly fashion at their visitor, reflecting inwardly that there could scarcely be a greater contrast in appearance than that which lay between uncle and nephew, and said politely, "Will you dine with us, sir? It would afford us great pleasure if you would do so."

Lord Rupert was more than willing. Conscious of the strange relationship that he had speedily discerned to exist between this disparate couple, his curiosity was aroused; there was, he gradually became aware during the course of the meal, an odd mixture of trust and some underlying fear in his hostess's feelings for her husband. For his part, upon the surface Ware displayed towards her the attitude of a good friend rather than a husband, but there were moments when, caught off guard as he regarded his wife's face as she addressed her conversation towards her guest, Lord Rupert had caught a glimpse of inner strain in those handsome, aquiline features, of desire held under iron control. His interest further aroused, he employed every art in his not inconsiderable power of pleasing women to draw Emma out and noted with amusement that flattery was not the way to obtain her favour but that she enjoyed with artless delight his stories of the droll behaviour of various prominent members of Society, and of their odd fashions and fancies.

For her part it was a relief to discover that her husband's kinsman was prepared to accept her and compensated her in some measure for her experiences of that morning.

Emma was up early the day after her introduction to Lord Rupert, and when Lady Sophia was driven up to the door, she was ready and waiting to be handed up into the carriage and take her seat beside her ladyship. They drove first to the premises of Messrs Harding, Howell and Company in Pall Mall, for Emma had told Lady Sophia, in a discreetly lowered voice and to her sister-in-law's secret amusement, that she wished to purchase materials for the making up at home of new undergarments and nightshifts, adding in a confidential whisper in Lady Sophia's ear, "I have only those which I wore as a schoolgirl and they are sadly worn and old-fashioned."

Lengths of the finest and softest white lawns and cambrics were cut off and parcelled up for them, and proceeding to the Pantheon Bazaar in Oxford Street, they were able to purchase the delicate lace and ribbons for trimmings that were required. Emma's eyes sparkled at the sight of the multitude of tempting articles offered for sale and she acquired several pairs of kid gloves and a length of silver gauze. She much admired a handsome shawl of Norwich silk and when they had returned to the carriage, discovered that it had been surreptitiously purchased for her by Lady Sophia whilst her attention had been diverted elsewhere; her sister-in-law, presenting it to her, said with a smile, "You will look very well in it, dear child, and I wish you will call me 'Sophie', for you must know, it is the most agreeable thing in the world for me to have such a charming sister and to know that my brother's future happiness is assured!"

An uneasy expression came over Emma's face as she thanked her warmly for such a generous gift and for some time afterwards she sat silent, lost in her own thoughts. To distract her, Lady Sophia began to recount her recollections of Ware as a little boy: being eight years his senior, she remembered him clearly as a small child and described to Emma his love of horses and dogs and his affectionate nature. "Our mother was not a very maternal woman, you know, she did her duty in providing her husband with an heir but she had no real love for children. I believe Robert was often hurt by her indifference and we saw very little of our father."

This revelation shed a new and strange light upon her husband and one that roused Emma's pity; she said softly, "Poor little boy!" Her own childhood, inspite of her mother's death, had been a happy one and her relationship with her father had been close and affectionate.

As they drove down Brook Street on their way home, their carriage was held up in the press of traffic and a landaulet approaching them was halted momentarily beside them. The occupants, two modishly

197

dressed ladies, seemed to be deep in conversation but, looking up as their progress was arrested, the elder of the two, a handsome matron in a bonnet profusely trimmed with ribbons and feathers, smiled and bowed graciously to Lady Sophia. However, when her eyes, moving past her ladyship, lighted upon the young girl sitting beside her, the smile vanished from her face, she looked stonily at Emma as if she had no existence, then, turning to her companion, she said in a voice that was clearly audible, "How I feel for dear Lady Sophia! To have to *recognise* that jade that Ware has taken to wife! It is beyond anything – quite abominable!"

Her companion's reply was lost to them, for at that moment the line of vehicles began to move forward again. Lady Sophia, her face angrily flushed, turned to Emma, almost speechless with indignation; the latter had become very pale as she said, conscience-stricken, "I should never have come to London! I am so grieved to have imposed upon your kindness ...."

She was interrupted by Lady Sophia, who took her hand, saying vehemently, "I never cared for that Lady Knaresborough, a most disagreeable woman!" She added inconsequentially, "I am sorry for her daughter, a very plain girl but clever and agreeable; her mother has been trying to get her off her hands for the past year or more. No wonder that she is displeased to find that you have captured the most sought after prize on the Marriage Mart!"

Emma shook her head, she was sitting up very straight but there was an expression of dismay in her soft brown eyes as she said in a resolute voice, "You are all kindness, my lady, but we both know that that is not true – however unjustly, I am believed to be an abandoned female – to have acted without shame! This is not the first time that I have been made aware of my reputation. Perhaps in the end it will be forgotten, in the meantime, I must learn to endure it."

By now they had reached Grosvenor Square and Lady Sophia, ordering the carriage to wait for her, accompanied Emma into the house to take some refreshment. They were together in the little saloon, examining their purchases, when a footman announced that Lady Sheldon had called to see her ladyship. Emma, with a startled glance at Lady Sophia, bade him admit her and stepped forward to greet her visitor. Recognising at once the stout, fashionably dressed figure as the friend whose box at the Opera House her husband had visited, she curtsied and, bidding her welcome, desired her to take a seat beside her.

Having bestowed a brief greeting upon Lady Sophia, Lady Sheldon fixed her bright, enquiring eyes upon Emma and said bluntly, "I have been eager to meet you, Lady Ware, for my curiosity has been aroused! You have upset all the young ladies in the Metropolis!"

The charming, youthful face beside her clouded over, "Alas, ma'am, it is not only the *young* ladies that I have offended! I believe that my reputation at present is such that I can only marvel at your kindness in waiting upon me."

"Like that, is it?" she patted Emma's hand, "Well, I must be honest and admit that if Ware had not asked me to call, I might not have done so!" She looked at Emma consideringly and murmured, as if addressing herself, "Quite a beauty, but not at all in his usual style – and such eyes!" she paused, then added, "Lady Ware, may I give you a piece of advice? I am an old woman and perhaps you may think it an impertinence, but I have a fondness for Robert and, indeed, I wish you well."

"I believe that I stand in great need of good advice, ma'am!"

"You have nothing to fear from the men, you can trust to Ware for that: a few sly remarks, perhaps a warmer manner towards you than you may care for, but no-one will dare more than that!" Lady Sheldon gave a wry smile, "It is the gentler sex that will cause you most pain! You must ignore them, Lady Ware! Remain true to yourself and do not show the least concern for their opinion, for, if you know *yourself* that you have nothing to be ashamed of, *they* cannot harm you! And above all," Lady Sheldon added emphatically, "always be in the forefront of fashion – set a new style in simplicity and you will make all others appear over-dressed!"

Emma, thanking her warmly, looked doubtfully towards Lady Sophia, who exclaimed at once, with a crow of laughter, "Most excellent advice, Emma! I confess I wish that I had thought of it myself! You shall do for the women what poor Mr Brummel has done for the men – simplicity is just in your style, and nothing can give one greater confidence than to know that one looks one's best."

She began to discuss with Lady Sheldon Lady Challenor's forth-coming ball, which was expected to be one of the most dazzling events of the Season. Lady Sheldon was to be present with Miss Danvers; she said reassuringly to Emma, "I shall be sure to see some of my acquaintances before the ball and shall let it be known that you have been sadly maligned and that, moreover, Ware has displayed unexpected discernment in his choice of a bride!"

At that moment Ware, himself, came into the room and, bowing over Lady Sheldon's hand, said warmly, "I knew that you would approve! How good of you to call at once." He looked enquiringly towards Emma, who by now had quite recovered from her dismay at the rebuff that she had received during her drive, and who smiled back at him, saying cheerfully, "Lady Sheldon thinks that I should bring simplicity into fashion, my lord! If that were possible, it would be the most delightful idea – I hope that you agree!"

By the time the visitors had left, Lady Sophia having offered to take Lady Sheldon up in her carriage, Emma was upon the best of terms with her new acquaintance and feeling considerably re-assured and, upon Ware's suggestion, decided to return Lady Sheldon's call upon the following day.

CHAPTER 19

There could be no doubt of the warmth of her hostess's welcome the next morning when, her name having been announced, the butler ushered Emma into Lady Sheldon's stately drawing-room. An additional pleasure was to find no less a person than Lord Rupert Vane bearing Lady Sheldon company.

"Charming, my dear child!" Lady Sheldon rose from her seat extending both hands and, clasping Emma's in her own, held her at arm's length as she surveyed her from head to foot, nodding her head vehemently and causing the numerous ribbons adorning her cap to bob violently. "Simple muslin – no trimmings and a delightful figure! Well done, indeed – you have taken my advice!" She turned to Lord Rupert, "May I present Lady Ware – Robert's bride! Who would have ever thought, my dear, that he would have shown so much sense!"

Lord Rupert, bowing over Emma's hand, smiled at her embarrassed face, "We've met, my dear Fanny. Had the pleasure of making her acquaintance a day or so ago. So you've been giving Emma the benefit of your advice ...." He looked from the slim, plainly dressed girl to her exuberantly attired hostess, eyebrows raised, plainly puzzled.

Lady Sheldon chuckled, "My dear Rupert, if I didn't dress myself in some outlandish fashion no-one would spare me so much as a glance!"

His lordship grinned as he regarded her affectionately, "If you have taken Emma under your wing, my dear, she is fortunate indeed." He turned to the young girl, "It ain't going to be easy for you, child. There's too many prepared to believe the worst. Why, only last night I heard ...." he was about to expatiate upon the subject when the door was opened again and the butler announced, "Lady Foster, my lady!" as a tall, thin lady in her early fifties entered the room, casting a swift appraising glance around the present company.

"Alicia! How delightful to see you!" Lady Sheldon stepped forward, "You know Rupert, of course, and this, my dear – this is a charming new acquaintance of mine – Ware's bride." She observed Lady Foster's startled expression as she became aware of Emma's identity, and continued quickly, "Rupert and I were just remarking how lucky his rascal of a nephew has been to secure such a wife for himself!"

Emma, meeting the new arrival's cold, penetrating glance with a grave expression, said quietly, "Lady Sheldon is too kind, my lady. I am the one who has had the good fortune to have gained such a friend and in so short a time."

So this was the disgraced female of whom she had heard so much and so little to her advantage; Lady Foster made a quick inner decision. It had been amusing to depress Mary Priestley's pretensions regarding her acquaintance with the Countess of Ware: useful too – for she wished to retain her position as social-arbiter over her friend – but, if Lady Sheldon and Lord Rupert were prepared to acknowledge the bride as worthy of their friendship .... far wiser to range herself upon the young Countess' side; it would please Mary too, for it had been clear that she had been greatly taken with the girl.

"Lady Ware, a great pleasure to meet you! May I offer you my felicitations upon your marriage." A smile had reached Lady Foster's lips, but failed to be reflected in her eyes. "I believe you to be acquainted with friends of mine who have, a day or so ago, arrived in London – the Priestleys – who live near Millford. Mary Priestley has told me that she recently had the pleasure of making your acquaintance there."

It was difficult to conceal the astonishment that her words had aroused in Emma. Had she wrongly interpreted her reception at the Priestley's house? It seemed as if that must be so and she felt a warm tide of relief flood through her, causing her response to Lady Foster to be more forthcoming than it might otherwise have been.

"Oh, yes, my lady, I know the Priestleys – and their daughter, Jane, is a charming girl." She turned to Lady Sheldon, "You would like her, ma'am – such a pretty, gentle creature. I believe she is to make her come-out this season and I am sure she will be all the rage if such qualities are as admired here as they should be!"

Lady Sheldon, glancing quickly at Lord Rupert's face, where an expression of sardonic amusement reigned, patted Emma's hand and said with a chuckle, "I'm sure Miss Priestley is all that you say, my dear – but for my part, y'know, I like a girl with a bit of spirit – no milk-and-water misses for me!" She turned to Lady Foster, "Now, tell me, Alicia, what's the latest 'on-dit'? I hear that Greenwich has fallen out with his wife – what a strange marriage that has turned out to be!"

The two ladies fell to an earnest exchange of gossip while ratafia and biscuits were offered and Lord Rupert, who prided himself upon being a connoisseur of the decorative arts, showed Emma a delightful display of snuff-boxes collected by the late Sir Henry Sheldon.

During the following half-hour, several friends and acquaintances of Lady Sheldon called; to all of whom Emma was duly presented and, upon each occasion, became conscious that their smiling faces and cordial words were greatly at variance with the uncharitable thoughts that were, doubtless, occupying their minds. She could not, however, be anything but heartily grateful to her kind new friend and hoped that Lady Sheldon's influence would in some degree restore her reputation.

All that had transpired was reported eagerly to Ware upon her return home. To his pleasure in hearing of Lady Sheldon's success in improving Emma's reputation in society was added his amusement at her lively description of the persons concerned. Lady Foster, he knew – his father had been acquainted with her late husband – and Emma's portrayal of her as 'a heron-like female with cold eyes' was so exact that he burst out laughing. To hear Emma's present report upon the Priestleys gave him less pleasure. He considered them to be a tedious couple and their daughter a foolish girl destined to become the prey of some penniless fortune-hunter.

Emma looked shocked when he gave this opinion. "Oh, I trust not, my lord! Surely her parents ...."

His eyebrows shot up in amused incredulity, "My dear wife, what trusting faith you have in human nature! The Priestleys, I fear, are out to make a great match for their daughter – a title, at least – a Duke, if possible or a Marquis perhaps! And I don't doubt for one moment that Miss Priestley will happily accede to their plans."

Emma shook her head obstinately. She had a better opinion than that of the Priestley's daughter; besides, she was aware, too, that Jane Priestley had attracted Edward's notice. Ware seemed oblivious of his cousin's interest and she feared that, when he did learn of it, he would not approve.

Upon leaving Lady Sheldon, Lady Foster hastened to the Priestley's house to report upon her changed opinion of Lady Ware. She found her friend sitting with her daughter in her grand drawing-room looking wretchedly bored and at once addressed her with every appearance of contrition.

"My dear Mary, I find I am *quite* at fault – quite wrongly informed! Really, one should not believe all one hears!"

Mrs Priestley looked her surprise and waited for her friend to continue.

"The Countess of Ware, you know .... I have just this moment come from Lady Sheldon, quite an eccentric character but mixes in the highest circles – a friend of the Prince, no less – Lady Ware was actually *there*, Lord Ware's uncle, too, Lord Rupert Vane – so you see, my dear, there's no question but that you *can* acknowledge her acquaintance – Lady Ware's, I mean!"

Mrs Priestley's eyes opened wide and Jane uttered an exclamation of delight. "There, Mama, I knew it was all a hum! Anyone who knew her could not possibly believe such tales about her."

Though finding some difficulty in following Lady Foster's logic, Mrs Priestley's satisfaction was great. Here was her fashionable friend, a member of the circle to which she aspired, admitting her mistake. Her handsome face glowed with pleasure, "Gracious, Alicia, quite a turnabout! Well, I shall certainly call upon Lady Ware tomorrow."

A delightful conversation now followed, delightful at least for Mrs Priestley and her daughter, and they were just repeating for the third or fourth time how certain they had been in their minds that Lady Ware was a paragon of all the virtues when the door opened and the footman announced that Mr Edward Wyndham had called to see Mrs Priestley.

"Show him in, Roberts." Mrs Priestley's cup was full. "My dears, what an agreeable surprise! 'E's a very pleasant young gentleman,

Alicia – no doubt, you are already h'acquainted with 'im." So great was her excitement that her mindfulness of her aspirates fell into confusion.

Before Lady Foster had time to reply, Edward had entered the room, observing with satisfaction as he did so that the daughter of the house was present and bore upon her countenance unmistakeable signs of being pleased to see him.

"Your servant, Mrs Priestley! Lady Foster, how do you do? Miss Priestley, a great pleasure!" Edward's bow was perfection itself. Nor could any fault be found in his appearance. If Emma had been present she would have been forced to acknowledge that Ware's description of his cousin as an arbiter of fashion was richly deserved; the fit of his coat was immaculate, his cravat tied to a nicety, nor did he betray by the least sign the startling impression made upon him by Mrs Priestley's opulent furnishings.

Mrs Priestley was all graciousness and was so much taken up with the new arrival that she failed to notice the signs of displeasure evinced by her old friend. Lady Foster soon took her leave, reminding her hostess as she departed that she would see them again that same evening.

Mrs Priestley confided, "Such an old friend of ours, y'know, Mr Wyndham. We dine there tonight. Lady Foster is anxious to extend our acquaintance in London."

Edward would not have been so gratified to receive this information if he had had any knowledge of the persons to whom Miss Priestley was to be introduced. As it was he spent a delightful half-hour with the two ladies and although nothing could have been more proper than his conversation and manner, Jane received the agreeable impression that she might count Mr Wyndham amongst her admirers. In the first moment of seeing him she had been painfully reminded of the last time that they had met, an occasion which she remembered now with a mixture of shame at her own folly and pleasure at her rescuer's kindness and tact.

Lady Foster's dinner-party that evening was not an unmixed success. She had given a great deal of thought as to her guests and, besides the Marquis, had invited Sir John and Lady Bruce, a couple of about her own age, to whom entertaining and being entertained was the very breath of life and who could be counted upon with some degree of certainty to invite the Priestleys to one of their numerous receptions or breakfasts. There were also present Mr Sherston, an eminent banker and figure of substance in the City, and the lady he had married, the daughter of an aristocratic family who had guaranteed him his place in society and then had quietly faded into the background. Their son, Mathew, was also present; Lady Foster had no fears that he would outshine the Marquis in Jane's eyes: he was an excessively dull young man, totally eclipsed by his brilliant father and with neither conversation nor address.

There was no doubt that the Priestley parents enjoyed their evening. Mr Priestley in particular was delighted to make Mr Sherston's acquaintance: a man of whom he had long heard the highest reports and acclaimed by those who knew him as one of the shrewdest investors in the City. To Mrs Priestley, the presence of a Marquis and the delightful schemes for her daughter's entertainment that were proposed to her by Lady Bruce made it an occasion of real pleasure.

For Jane Priestley, however, the dinner-party had been a sad disappointment. Seated between the Marquis of Frant and Mr Mathew Sherston, she had spent an evening that had tried her good nature to the limit. Young Mr Sherston had been more devoted to the excellent food set before him than to the young lady at his side – he had applied himself to his viands with enthusiasm and only spared her the occasional remark such as, "Do you care for London, Miss Priestley?" whilst barely attending to the reply. Far worse was her companion upon the other side.

When Lady Foster had first introduced the Marquis to her, Jane had experienced a feeling of some surprise and disappointment. The Earl of Ware, though a forbidding figure in Jane's eyes, had been all that she had imagined an earl should be. George Helford, Marquis of Frant was below average height, thin to the point of emaciation, with scanty hair and a poor complexion and looked to be far older than his forty-eight years. Disappointment had turned to disgust at his efforts to ingratiate himself with her, which took the form of a series of fulsome compliments accompanied by many warm looks. He seemed to believe that his title was sufficient recommendation to render him attractive in her eyes. It was very far from the case; even if she could have over-looked from pity his unprepossessing appearance, nothing could have reconciled her to his manner, and beneath the praises lavished upon her in a low voice, she had the wit to recognise a note of condescension that provoked her beyond words.

Returning home in their carriage when the evening had ended, Jane was disturbed to learn of her parents' opinion of the Marquis.

"Such a charming man, every inch the h'aristocrat! 'E was very taken with *you*, Jane, dear!" Mrs Priestley's delight knew no bounds.

Even Mr Priestley had been impressed. Jane was the apple of his eye, his ambitions for her boundless. For once his native shrewdness was overborne by visions of his young daughter mixing upon equal terms with the cream of society and he was easily able to discount to himself any impression he might have received of an under-lying contempt beneath the affable words addressed to him during the evening by this high-born member of the aristocracy.

CHAPTER 20

Jane would have been even more dismayed if she could have over-heard the conversation that took place between her parents that night.

Before the candles in their bed-chamber were extinguished and following a mutually satisfactory revue of the evening's entertainment and their new acquaintances, Mrs Priestley pronounced reflectively, "She took 'is lordship's fancy, Samuel, no doubt about it!" she paused, then continued meaningfully, "That Mr Wyndham, my dear, I don't think that 'e should be h'encouraged!"

"Mr Wyndham, my love? What has he to say to anything?" Mr Priestley looked perplexed.

"I know my girl, Samuel! She likes 'im and 'e's got a pleasant way with him. 'E called this morning and there's no doubt in my mind that it was Jane 'e hoped to see again. Now, love – he's a nice enough young man but 'e ain't got a handle to his name nor likely to get one, as Alicia 'as h'informed me, and it's a title our Jane deserves." She added tactfully, "You were quite right about Mr Tremayne, my love, she can do better than a mere commoner for a husband."

Mr Priestley nodded his head and gave her an appreciative grin, "With her looks and my money, the sky's the limit, my dear! You do as you think best." He gave her a resounding kiss and turned upon his side to dream of a golden future for his lovely daughter and, through her, for his family.

As a result of this conversation, when Edward called the following morning to request the pleasure of driving Miss Priestley in the Park that afternoon, permission was denied. Received by Mrs Priestley in the small saloon, he was disappointed to be told that Miss Priestley had other engagements that afternoon and it was evident from her manner that, for some reason that was not apparent to him, he had fallen beneath Mrs Priestley's displeasure.

Mrs Priestley wasted no time in making a morning call upon the Countess of Ware, bringing her daughter with her.

"So regrettable that I was not at home when you called, your ladyship!" Mrs Priestley brazenly announced once she was seated, "For nothing could give me greater pleasure than to renew our acquaintance."

Emma smiled inwardly, clearly Mrs Priestley was unaware that her presence in her own home had been perfectly apparent to her caller. She turned to Jane, who to Emma's surprise looked to be a trifle downcast, "And how are you enjoying your visit to London, Miss Priestley? Have you already made many new acquaintances and encountered old friends?"

Miss Priestley cast a swift glance at her mother's face before replying, "Why, yes, my lady, Lady Foster has been most kind in inviting us to dine and ...." her face brightened, "Mr Edward Wyndham called yesterday."

Mrs Priestley broke in eagerly, "Our Jane has met the Marquis of Frant, no less, your ladyship! He dined at Lady Foster's last night!" Her satisfaction was obvious and she leaned forward towards Emma to continue in a confidential voice, " 'E sat next to her, my lady, and there's no question about it, 'e took a shine to our little girl! What do you think of that, my lady?"

One look at Jane's unhappy face made clear *her* thoughts upon that subject; Emma thought of Ware's comments upon the Priestley family and felt her sympathy rise for the young girl. "I am not acquainted with the Marquis, ma'am, but I am not at all surprised – I am sure that Miss Priestley, with her delightful looks and sweetness of manner, will attract many admirers."

Her reply was swept aside by her guest in a lengthy encomium upon the Marquis of Frant. In Mrs Priestley's opinion he was, indeed, a god among men, although she did have the honesty to admit that he was a trifle older than her daughter. "But that's all for the best in *my* eyes, your ladyship – a man of his age is past the follies of youth."

At luncheon, later that day, Emma recounted to Ware how horribly his predictions seemed to be about to be fulfilled. She asked him thoughtfully what kind of man was the Marquis of Frant and was horrified by his reply.

"An elderly degenerate who has lost his entire fortune at play!" was Ware's succinct rejoinder. He looked at his wife's face that mirrored her distress and said gently, "My love, I fear it is the way of the world. Frant is a ruined man in health and fortune and the only way he can find out of his difficulties is to marry an heiress. The Priestley's have a daughter and are anxious to purchase a title for her! These things happen every day in society."

It was not a view that could find favour with Emma. She said indignantly, "Why that is wicked, my lord! To sacrifice a young girl's happiness for a title! Indeed, I had thought and hoped that the Marquis might be ...." she hesitated, then continued in a lower tone, "Might be like you, my lord, for you are the only member of the aristocracy with whom I am acquainted." She caught sight of her husband's raised eyebrows and quizzical look of amusement and rushed on with a heightened colour, "But if he is elderly and sick and does not even care for her ...."

"If she does marry him, my dear Emma, no doubt she will, in time, take a lover and so he will be paid back in his own coin." For the moment Ware seemed to have little interest in Miss Priestley's future. Too often he had observed the same events taking place in the circles in which he had been reared. It had been a pleasant surprise, however, to hear his wife express the hope that Frant might resemble *him*! How little, he thought wryly, did he know of Emma's present feelings for him.

It was this uncertainty and the increasing difficulty that he was experiencing in living in close proximity to the object of all his desires that made him view almost with relief the neccessity of being absent for a few days in Leicestershire, where the agent who attended to his property in that county had requested his presence and opinions. The increasing fear that at some moment he might find himself unable to control his passion and, thereby, lose forever her regard and with it any hope that he might have of gaining her love, made a few days absence seem positively desirable.

"My love, setting aside this distasteful subject, I must tell you that I have to leave you for a few days. My presence is asked for at my estates in Leicestershire – some decisions to be made for which my agent seeks my advice." He could not avoid studying Emma's expression as he spoke – would she show relief or disappointment?

At first he had the pleasure of descrying a look of anxiety in her eyes, as if his presence was neccessary to her but, as she replied, he was disturbed to observe, with the added sensitivity of a lover, that some other thought had gained ascendancy in her mind – some plan as yet not formulated.

"I am sorry, my lord, that you have such a tedious journey ahead of you. Are they matters of some importance?"

It was a surprise to Ware to find that her first thought was to the nature of the business involved. How utterly unlike her contemporaries she was! He shook his head, "Not of any great significance – but Sherston needs to review some outgoings. There are big changes now in agricultural methods, you know." As he spoke, he inwardly acknowledged that matters that a few weeks ago he would have dismissed as tedious and unimportant, had, since his marriage, gained new interest in his eyes.

Emma nodded her head sympathetically, "I shall miss you, my lord, but thanks to Sophie and Lady Sheldon I shall not feel quite without friends and then there is Edward ...."

Ware looked at her consideringly, but his words did not truthfully reflect his thoughts as he replied, "For that I can say that I am thankful, my love!"

Disturbed by his lack of success with Mrs Priestley, which had only served to increase his wish to renew his acquaintance with her daughter, Edward decided to call in Grosvenor Square and seek Emma's advice, confident that he would find in her a sympathetic listener.

He found his cousin and his wife in the library and soon learned of Ware's imminent departure.

"I leave tomorrow morning – it is a nusiance but it cannot be helped and I shall be back before Lady Challenor's ball."

Edward was faintly amused, "By Jove, cousin, who would have thought that *you* would be attending so conscientiously to your estates!" He turned to Emma, saying with a disarming grin, "So, thus is the rake reformed and becomes a model land-owner – you have a deal to answer for, my girl!"

For some reason that was not clear to him, Ware found this remark both irritating and unflattering. Claiming austerely to have letters to write, he returned to his desk at the far end of the room, leaving Emma to entertain his cousin.

It was a perfect opportunity for the latter to raise the subject that was uppermost in his mind. As he took his seat beside Emma on the sofa, he said in a low voice, "I am glad of the opportunity of consulting you, Emma – and it is on a matter upon which I have no desire to involve Robert...."

She looked her surprise, "Why, of course, I shall be only too happy – but surely my lord's advice would be of more value to you?"

He shook his head impatiently, "You have heard perhaps that I have called upon the Priestleys." His eyes lit up as he added inconsequently, his voice rising, "So lovely, Emma – perfection itself – so gentle...."

"I presume that you refer to Miss Priestley and not to her mother!" Emma whispered, eyes dancing; she could not resist to tease but Edward was too engrossed in his subject to be amused, nor did either of them notice that Ware had looked up from his writing, a heavy frown upon his face, as the few words, "so lovely, Emma, perfection itself....", had been audible to him and it was with a grim look that he returned to his task while his ears strained to catch the remainder of the conversation.

Edward now leaned forward and said confidentially, "This morning I called to invite Miss Priestley to drive out with me in the Park, only to be told by her mother that she had other engagements – and in such a manner, Emma, that I could see at once that I was no longer a welcome caller. Can you imagine what I could have done to merit such a reception? I was received most kindly when I first called upon them"

No trace now remained of Emma's amusement, she said thoughtfully, "I believe that I know the reason and I am truly sorry for it. You must know that Mrs Priestley and her daughter called here this morning – it must have been after you had been to their house – and I was told by Mrs Priestley that they had met the Marquis of Frant yesterday evening, at Lady Foster's, and that, to Mrs Priestley's delight, the Marquis was greatly taken with her daughter!"

"Good God, Emma, that old roué! Surely they cannot consider him to be an eligible suitor!" Edward's horror and disgust were very evident.

Emma regarded him earnestly, choosing her next words carefully, then, in a whisper, she said, "I fear that they do, cousin, and, moreover, Miss Priestley seemed sadly downcast!"

Edward's youthful face grew suddenly stern. For a moment he was silent, staring at Emma, and to Ware, who had raised his eyes again from the page, though their conversation was inaudible, it was a look that he could not remember having seen before upon Edward's face.

"For God's sake, Emma, it can't be true!" The words burst from him, "What's to be done?"

She looked at him worriedly and said softly in a sad voice, "My lord believes that the Priestley parents have set their heart upon a title. He tells me that such arrangements are commonplace. You must know that he has no regard for the parents."

"But you'll help me, dear Emma? Better not to tell Robert – he's such a stickler for the proprieties these days – there's no knowing him!" His face brightened," If *you* could ask Jane to drive in the Park – then I might contrive to meet you there and have the opportunity to speak to her."

Emma nodded, casting a swift glance in her husband's direction, "I will send a note round tomorrow to the Priestley's house – my lord leaves for Leicestershire in the morning so there is no need for him to know our plans." She smiled conspiratorially at Edward, then, with a change of manner, asked him in her normal voice whether he approved of her morning gown, reminding him once again with a chuckle that he had been recommended to her as a leader of fashion.

"Is that not so, my lord?" she laughingly addressed Ware and was considerably taken aback when he replied sarcastically, without even looking up, "There is doubtless more to Edward than I had dreamed of, my dear wife!"

When the noble Marquis of Frant condescended to pay a call upon Mrs Priestley he received a very different reception from that which had been accorded to Mr Wyndham. While Emma was listening sympathetically to Edward's tale in the library in Grosvenor Square, Mrs Priestley was pressing her hospitality upon her aristocratic visitor and it could not but be abundantly clear to him that she was overjoyed at his presence in her drawing-room.

"Such a delightful occasion yesterday evening, your lordship – Lady Foster is a friend of ours of long standing, you know! So regrettable that Mr Priestley is not at 'ome!" Her handsome face a trifle flushed, she nevertheless felt herself to be fully in command of the situation and, fortified by the opulence of her surroundings, quite equal to entertaining her guest single-handed.

The Marquis was at his most agreeable. Too much was at stake to permit any sign of his distaste, indeed dislike, to appear in his manner. Here, around him, were clear indications of great affluence and, if he played his cards aright, the little heiress could be his before the Polite World had had the chance to set eyes upon her and before others could rival him for her hand. Once the settlements had been agreed and the marriage knot tied there would be no necessity to associate in any way with his wife's parents. How such a mother could have produced that charming child was to him a source of astonishment.

"My dear Mrs Priestley," he surveyed her drawing-room through his quizzing glass, "May I congratulate you! A delightful room – quite puts one in mind of his royal Highness' furnishings in Brighton – in the very latest mode.... excellent, excellent!"

Mrs Priestley's cup was full and in her eyes her visitor's unprepossessing appearance, his pale dissipated countenance and languid air, took upon them a Jove-like aspect.

"No expense spared, my lord, that's Mr Priestley's way." She looked around her complacently and added with a knowing look, "But I don't doubt, your lordship, that it ain't nothing compared to your lordship's fine 'ouses!"

The Marquis was obliged to take a firm grip upon himself. That this jumped-up mushroom of a woman should take it upon herself to suggest a comparison between her vulgar surroundings and his ancient estates was almost unsupportable; he had not even the grace to admit to himself that through his own fault these same possessions were now in imminent danger of crumbling away into ruins, or even of falling into other hands.

"Cullhampton is, indeed, thought to be something quite out of the ordinary." Frant sipped his wine, at least that was of excellent quality, and sought for an opportunity to reveal the purpose of his visit and thereby bring to a speedy conclusion this disagreeable encounter.

At that moment Jane, having been informed that her mother was entertaining a visitor and required her presence, entered the room with the barely recognised hope that the caller might prove to be Mr Wyndham.

Even the Marquis, whose opinion of himself and of his own conse-quence was astonishingly high, could not fail to observe her disap-pointment when her eyes alighted upon his person. She came forward slowly, curtsied in response as he bowed over her hand, and seated herself as far away from him as good manners permitted.

"My dear Miss Priestley, how quite charmingly you look!" There was already something almost of condescending possessiveness in Frant's tone. He turned to her mother, upon whose countenance maternal pride was mixed with a degree of vexation – what in the world was Jane about, seating herself so far from his lordship? "It was with the express purpose, ma'am, of inviting Miss Priestley to drive with me in the Park tomorrow that I have called this afternoon."

An expression of extreme gratification appeared upon Mrs Priestley's face.

"Well, my lord, I'm sure Jane would be h'onoured by sich con-descension."

Miss Priestley was looking very far from being pleased at the prospect of such an outing. She cast a swift glance of appeal to her mother, saw that the appeal was unavailing and murmured some words of compliance.

In the exchange of civilities that followed Jane took little part; the bright prospect of a London Season dimmed by the realisation of the extent of her parents ambitions.

When the Marquis had departed, having achieved his objective and in the consciousness of his own worth quite heedless of Miss Priestley's feelings of antipathy, Jane declared her objections in round terms, "Why, mama, the Marquis is old enough to be my father and...." she shuddered, ".... and the hateful way he looks at me!"

"You ungrateful girl! 'Ere's your father 'as brought you to London so as that you may make a fine match." Mrs Priestley's face was scarlet and her already ample person seemed positively to swell with indignation, "Such foolishness! I never heard the like before. Not another word now, my girl – your father and I know best what's good for you!"

The only occurrence that brightened the gloom of the following morning for Jane was the arrival of a note from Lady Ware inviting her to drive with her at five o'clock the next day, an invitation which was accepted with alacrity; both mother and daughter being upon this occasion in agreement. Mrs Priestley, giving her consent, added complacently, "Just as I thought, Jane dear – the very best circles! Nothing, my love, is too good for you!"

The drive in the Park with the Marquis of Frant proved to be for Jane as disagreeable in every particular as she had anticipated. Handed up into his elegant phaeton, for his lordship would not have considered for one moment any retrenchment in his expenditure upon his *own* comforts, she felt even the touch of his hand upon hers to be repugnant.

Their conversation throughout the drive remained uniformly one-sided. The Marquis, believing that all that was required of him by any young female was to compliment her lavishly upon her appearance, quite sickened Jane with his praise. Then, wishing to satisfy himself as to the extent of her father's fortune, he made some discreet enquiries into his business activities; enquiries that proved to be of little avail, for Jane had not the least interest in or knowledge of such matters.

Upon several occasions, as they passed by other carriages, she was keenly aware of the interest that her presence in the Marquis' phaeton afforded others and wished herself, with all her heart, elsewhere. To be obliged to sit beside him, in close proximity, was quite horrible – she did not think that she had ever encountered anyone quite so repulsive and her heart sank. How could she escape from the awful fate that loomed before her?

It was at this moment, when her spirits were at their lowest ebb and the Marquis had just commenced a description of his principal country-seat in Derbyshire with the intention of further impressing his companion, that Jane perceived a familiar figure approaching.

Edward, mounted upon a fine bay horse and deep in conversation with Mr Humphrey Featherstone, looked up as the phaeton drew near and was stunned to discover the adorable Miss Priestley seated beside the Marquis; as he raised his hat as the phaeton passed him by, his eyes met Jane's and he saw the look of misery upon her face.

Mr Featherstone, unaware of the identity of the young female, exclaimed disgustedly, "Good God, Edward, who the d-devil has that satyr, Frant, got his hands on now? What kind of parents would allow a d-daughter of theirs to drive out alone with him!"

There was a grim expression upon Edward's face as he drew his mount to a walk and it was a moment or two before he could bring himself to reply.

"Name of Priestley, new neighbours of Robert's at Millford! Met them at Elizabeth Tremayne's – a delightful girl, Miss Priestley, but not up to snuff, y'know.... Damn George Frant – fellow ought to be exterminated!"

It was said so viciously that Mr Featherstone glanced at him open-mouthed, his resemblance to a startled hare even more pronounced than usual.

"Beg you'll not take the matter in hand yourself, dear boy! Devilish good shot – old George – y'know!" Then, seeing no change in his companion's ferocious expression, he added hopefully, "Enter the lists y'self, Edward. Fellow like you ought to be able to cut out that d-desiccated old rip! After all – stands to reason – girl bound to prefer a younger man and, not wishing to p-puff you up, dear boy, there's many a jealous husband who fears you, though ...." he paused and looked at Edward musingly, ".... can't for the life of me see why, considering you don't pay more attention to one female than another!"

For a moment Edward stared back at him blankly, then his expression lightened. "By George, old fellow, I believe you've got it – 'Out of the mouth of babes and sucklings'!"

Mr Featherstone gazed at his friend with alarm, "Ain't said a word about babes! For God's sake, Edward, dear boy, mind what you're about!"

But his companion had broken into a canter and, by the time that they drew up their horses again to a walk, Mr Featherstone's never very retentive mind had moved on to more important topics of which the most beguiling was the prospects for the racing at Epsom.

Ware, entering his wife's boudoir to bid her farewell before departing for Leicestershire, found her seated at her bureau writing a note, her back turned towards him. For a moment he stood in the doorway regarding her: the short curls that clustered about her head, the curve of her cheek, and felt an irresistible urge to place a kiss upon the nape of her neck. As he stood there, she turned towards the door saying as she did so, "Dora, could you ...." then broke off seeing that it was her husband and coloured faintly, her hand moving instinctively to cover the paper upon which she had been writing.

"Gracious, my lord, how you startled me!"

She was certain that he would not approve of any extension of her acquaintance with Miss Priestley, better, therefore, despite her dislike of dissembling, that he should be unaware of her intentions; then, observing that he was dressed for travel, she added quickly, "I did not realise that you must leave so early, my lord."

Ware was by now wearing his most saturnine expression. To whom was her note intended? That she did not wish him to know was clear; his pride forbade any enquiry.

As he approached her, she looked up at him, a troubled expression upon her face. He seemed angry and cold: hard, grey eyes frowned down upon her.

Hateful thoughts whirled in Ware's head, 'Good God, had it come to this? A jealous husband! Never had he thought to see himself in such a role! Had he frightened this child so grievously at the start of this crazy marriage that she would turn instinctively to someone younger, someone of a gentler nature?'

He said briefly, "Yes, I must be gone at once." and, taking her chin in his hand, stood staring down at her upturned face a moment as if, by doing so, he could read her thoughts, then adding briefly, "I shall return on Tuesday." he suddenly stooped and kissed her full upon the mouth and without another word turned on his heels and left her.

If he could have seen the brightness of her eyes, the way her fingers softly touched her lips after he had left the room his suspicions might have been lessened, as it was he found his journey profoundly disagreeable and caused his agent in Leicestershire to wonder what could have caused his employer to be so preoccupied with his own thoughts that he failed to display his usual capable grasp of the details concerning the estate that were being set before him.

CHAPTER 21

Hyde Park was looking its best as the Earl of Ware's carriage turned in at the gates: the fresh green of the trees and beyond them a cloudless blue sky gave a welcome feeling of peace after the noise and bustle of the London streets.

Emma's companion, dressed to perfection, for her mother, not trusting to her own judgment, had shrewdly put her daughter's wardrobe into the hands of the leading dressmaker of the day, felt her spirits rise imperceptibly: surely Lady Ware, who once before had come to her rescue, could help her to escape from this alliance which, it seemed, her parents were planning.

It was soon apparent to Emma that Miss Priestley was both unhappy and longing to confide in her. Their conversation upon such trivial matters as the weather, the newest fashions and the comfort of his lordship's carriage had lasted a sufficient period of time for them to have reached the centre of the park; so when Jane said softly, "Lady Ware there is something that I must tell you ...." Emma, indicating with a speaking glance the groom up behind them, called to the coachman to stop by the next pathway leading from the main carriage drive and continued cheerfully, "Let us take a little walk, Miss Priestley, I quite long for some exercise in such delightful sunshine!"

Once the two girls were at some distance from the carriage, Jane broke into a disjointed account of the intrusion of the Marquis of Frant into her life.

"He is quite hateful, Lady Ware, so old and hideous .... I would die rather than marry him!"

Her distress was so genuine and so profound that it was incredible to Emma that any parents faced with such an obvious antipathy to their choice should persist in their endeavours.

"Why, Jane are you so sure that your parents would force you into such a distasteful marriage?"

"Oh, yes, my lady – I am certain of it! It is what they have always dreamed of for me and because he has such a fine title they will not see or believe how hateful he is to me! If he proposes marriage, and I believe that he will, what is to become of me?" she shuddered, her eyes full of unshed tears.

It was very bad. Emma, wishing heartily that she could enlist her husband's support in an endeavour to frustrate the Priestley's plans, had the dismal feeling that he would not consider it a matter in which he could interfere, nor would he care for her to do so. She tried her hardest to comfort the poor girl, pointing out that once Jane attended balls and routs she would meet other and younger men of rank who might be more agreeable to her and who also might offer for her hand and receive her parents' approval.

They were on the point of regaining the carriage-way, Jane having to some extent regained her composure and feeling that she had at least one friend in London in whom she could confide, when she exclaimed suddenly, "Why, is that not Mr Wyndham?" and Emma saw that Edward, who had dismounted by their empty carriage and handed his reins to Ware's groom, was approaching.

Edward had called in Grosvenor Square shortly after Emma had left the house to drive to the Priestleys and correctly surmising that she had invited Miss Priestley to drive with her, had ridden to the Park with all speed in the hope that he might encounter them.

"Cousin Emma, how delightful! Your servant, Miss Priestley!" As Edward, hat in hand, bowed over their hands in greeting, Emma remarked with interest the faint flush of colour that rose to Miss Priestley's cheeks, the brightening of her eyes and noted that her companion's hand was held by Edward a fraction longer than mere politeness dictated.

There seemed to be a new air of purposefulness about Edward: his habitually cheerful, friendly countenance exhibiting an expression that could best be described as grave.

"Charming weather is it not, cousin? Miss Priestley, I am happy to see you today in better company! I hope you are not offended by my saying so?" Edward's bluntness was rewarded.

"Oh, Mr Wyndham," Jane's face was scarlet, her eyes downcast, "That *you* should have seen me with his lordship .... that you might have thought it was by *my* wish ...." she seemed unable to continue.

"Alas, it is all the fault of Miss Priestley's parents, Edward." Emma, seeing her companion's confusion, hastened into explanation, "In *their* eyes the Marquis would be a brilliant match and Miss Priestley is greatly distressed." She looked at Edward hopefully, "What's to be done, cousin? I am sure that you will agree with me that we must offer our assistance!"

Edward was frowning, "Can't for the life of me see what's to be done at present ...." He took Jane's hand again in his and his sincerity was obvious, "Never fear, Miss Priestley, I ain't going to let that odious fellow Frant succeed. Even if extreme measures are called for!"

This statement seemed to have the happiest effect upon Miss Priestley: she gazed upon Edward with such trustfulness that Emma felt her misgivings rise. She said with alarm, "Whatever do you mean, Edward, 'extreme measures'? I do beg you to be careful what you are about!"

His insouciant reply did little to relieve her anxiety, "Ain't sure myself yet, cousin, but leave it to me." then, not wishing to define further his pledge of assistance, he began to speak of forthcoming social events and upon discovering that Jane was to attend a recital at Lady Bonham's declared to Emma's surprise that he would honour the concert with his presence.

By now it was time for the ladies to return home and they parted from Edward in better spirits than when they had set out. It was rapidly becoming clear to Emma that there lay more than a quixotic chivalry behind Edward's offer of assistance to Miss Priestley. He seemed for once in his life to be in earnest and although she was glad upon Jane's account her heart sank a little when she thought of her husband's displeasure at this outcome. He would certainly not approve of any connection between his family and the Priestleys.

As she drove home after depositing Jane at her parents' house, she wondered anew how it could have been that Ware, a man so proud of his family's ancient name, should have allied himself with *her*, a person of merely respectable antecedents and of horribly tarnished reputation. Her heart beat a little faster at the thought that flew unbidden to her mind – could he, indeed, have felt some softer feeling for her to have acted so contrary to his convictions; for there was no doubt that she had been completely within his power; so easily could he have forced her to become his mistress. How ironic that this was what the world believed him to have done before their marriage.

Further consideration of Jane's plight prompted Emma to send at once a footman to Edward's lodgings, with a note inviting him to dine with her that evening. More thought must be given to the problem and, besides, she could not feel easy in her mind about Edward's intentions. That any impropriety might exist in dining alone with her husband's cousin never entered her head; if such an idea had occurred to her she would have dismissed it out of hand, so laughable was the notion that any tender feelings might exist between herself and Edward.

No confidences being possible before the servants, it was not until dinner was over and the tea tray had been brought to the drawing room that Emma was able to reveal her concern. What she learned was hardly calculated to decrease her anxiety.

"I don't know how it is, Emma ...." Edward crossed to the fireplace and stood looking down into the flames, "In spite of those appalling parents, in spite of that child's foolish adventure with Hartley Tremayne, there is something about her .... an innocence and ...." he turned and looked up at Emma and there was honest perplexity in his eyes, "I feel an obligation to protect her."

Emma nodded slowly. Here was a very different Edward from the one who had accompanied her reluctantly upon their bid to save Miss Priestley's honour. She had to acknowledge that her respect for him had increased but was this change in him simply a sign of an infatuation for a charming girl? She said thoughtfully, "She has great beauty, Edward, and sweetness of character I am sure, but is there – not to put too fine a point upon it – a lack of judgment – a foolishness there?"

He was at once upon the defensive, "My dear cousin, just because *you* are such a resolute creature – so fearless and – and so ...." Words seemed to fail him.

Emma laughed, "Devoid of feminine feelings, you would say! At least, Edward, I would never fall for the blandishments of a man like

Mr Tremayne! However, be that as it may, what is to be done? Her parents' ambitions are boundless: is there any way in which the Marquis could be discredited in their eyes?"

Edward looked thoughtful, "His reputation is very bad but I fear that they would set little store by mere rumours. Perhaps the best thing to be done, as you are in Miss Priestley's confidence, is for you to keep me informed at once of any immediate threat to her peace of mind and meanwhile I will set enquiries afoot as to how he may be discredited."

CHAPTER 22

Little did Emma and Edward realise that events had moved on, even before their conversation together had taken place.

Upon returning home from her drive in the Park with Emma, Jane had entered the house with a delightful feeling that the world was somehow a better place than it had appeared to her only a few hours before: the sun all at once shone more brightly, the birds singing amongst the trees in the square sounded quite charmingly and she had the pleasantest recollection of the expression in Mr Wyndham's eyes as he had bidden her farewell.

Even the message, that she received from the butler before she could ascend to her bed-chamber and remove her bonnet, to the effect that her parents desired her presence at once in the drawing-room, failed to destroy this agreeable state of mind.

"You want me. Mama?" She kissed her mother's cheek affectionately and dashed on, "Oh, I have had such a delightful afternoon – Lady Ware is so kind – I find her quite charming. We met Mr Wyndham, you know ...."

Mrs Priestley frowned slightly. 'Mr Wyndham, indeed! What had he to say to anything – they had other and more important fish to fry.' she thought brusquely.

"Never mind that now, my love – your father and I have excellent news for you!" She saw Jane's look of surprise and hurried on, "Your father received a note from the Marquis of Frant this afternoon – h'asking for an interview with 'im tomorrow – and it's all arranged, my dear – after morning service! Oh, Jane, who would have thought it! And so soon!"

Her air of triumph was unmistakeable and yet still Jane failed to realise the import of the announcement. She recollected the Marquis's enquiries about her father and asked, "An affair of business, mama?

Well, indeed I am pleased for papa that his lordship should think so highly of his advice."

Mrs Priestley's patience, never her strong point, began to wear out, "Foolish child," she cried, "where are your wits? 'E'll be coming to ask your pa's permission to pay his addresses to you – that's what it's about – about wanting to marry you, my girl!"

"Oh no!" All colour had fled from Jane's face, "It's not possible, Mama – how can you think such a thing? I can't – I won't believe it – why he scarcely knows me – has only met me a few days ago ...."

Her only hope was that it was all a mistake; it *must* be. Her mind refused to admit the possibility of a declaration so soon by the Marquis – a possibility too terrible to contemplate, especially now!

Mr Priestley, who had been regarding his daughter with surprise and disappointment, judged it best to intervene – Mrs Priestly looked as if she could barely contain herself.

"My dear Jane, no doubt modesty forbids you put the same interpretation upon this interview as your mother and I do. Time will tell which of us is right. In any case it is a most desirable connection."

He spoke soothingly and Jane, seizing upon that which she wished to believe, said again, "It will be financial matters, papa, you'll see that I am right." and, with a pathetic attempt at a laugh, added, "After all, you *are* a great man in the City!" and swiftly left the room before anything further could be said upon the subject of the Marquis's intentions.

Alone in her room, she gave herself up to a flood of tears. It must not, could not, be true that that odious person was coming tomorrow to ask for her hand! She would die rather than marry him!

Having cried herself into a state of exhaustion she began wearily to consider what means she had of avoiding such a destiny.

How providential that she had spoken to Lady Ware that very afternoon and even more fortunate that Mr Wyndham had chanced upon them. Even in her present state of misery she could not prevent a soft smile touch her lips at the thought of that meeting in the Park.

What ever happened, whatever her parents might say – whatever they might threaten – she would not, indeed *could* not accept any offer of marriage from the Marquis of Frant, and she determined that for the

226

rest of the day she would strive to avoid the subject; for as long as she refused to recognise her parents' version of tomorrow's interview, the more easily could she escape their pressure upon her.

"Well, Mr Priestley, 'ere's a fine state of affairs!"

Jane having quitted the room, Mrs Priestley, thwarted of the opportunity of haranguing her daughter, turned her fire upon her husband. "You're too soft with her, William, indeed you are. The foolish girl! Business affairs! Next thing we'll be 'aving our little madam saying 'No' to his lordship!"

Mr Priestley shook his head. "Better let her think about it quietly, my dear – it's all come sooner than we expected." But there was a steely look in his eyes as he said flatly, "She'll follow her parents' wishes in the end, you mark my words, Mary!"

At church the next morning, Mrs Priestley had been gratified to observe the stir of interest occasioned by the presence of her pretty daughter and soon after their return home the eagerly awaited interview had taken place; the Marquis having arrived punctually at midday.

While the lady of the house awaited its outcome impatiently in the splendid drawing-room and Jane stood before her bedroom window gazing out blankly at the street below, her heart beating furiously, Mr Priestley received the anticipated request for his daughter's hand in the library, where leather-bound books lined the walls and were seldom if ever disturbed by their new owner.

The Marquis, after goading his valet to the point, almost, of handing in his notice to his noble employer, was dressed to perfection, or so he believed, his sparse locks arranged with care.

So confident was he of the answer that he was to receive, so languid in his manner and so lacking in any sign of genuine feeling, that Mr Priestley felt an unexpected impulse stir within him to send this arrogant lord about his business. Even Frant, not usually sensitive to the feelings of others, and, in particular, of those that he considered beneath him, realised, from his host's expression, that he must put some semblance of ardour into his flowery sentences.

'Miss Priestley had stolen his heart in the first moment that he had set eyes upon her .... her welfare and happiness would be his first care if he should be granted the honour and privilege of becoming her husband ...!' These and other well-turned phrases were sufficient to convince Mr Priestley; for so heavily did the Marquis' coronet weigh in the balance that it only required a modicum of good feeling to be expressed on Frant's part for the scales to come down in his favour.

A few, but to the Marquis vitally important, words were spoken upon the matter of settlements, of meetings between their respective legal representatives, then Mr Priestley, his heart swelling with pride, ushered his caller into the drawing-room and presented him to his wife, saying complacently, "Well, my love, here's his lordship wishing to make our little Jane his bride and I must tell you that I have given my consent most heartily – the sentiments that he has expressed being all that they should be!"

Mrs Priestley was exultant – her dearest dreams come true – Jane to be a marchioness – and before she had even made her come-out! This would make some of those stuck-up ladies that she had met change their tune. To the Marquis she was her most gracious, "How delightful it will be, my lord, to welcome your lordship into our family!"

The Marquis, experiencing an inward shudder, kept a smile upon his face and murmured, "So kind, ma'am." with a polite bow in her direction.

Very grandly Mrs Priestley summoned a footman and desired him to request Miss Priestley to descend to the drawing-room.

The implications of this message were immediately evident to the anxious girl waiting above and as she slowly descended the stairs she experienced a sense of both desperation and, fleetingly, of uncertainty. Now that the moment had arrived she remembered how right her father had been about Hartley Tremayne – could it be possible that, in his good opinion of the Marquis of Frant, he was again correct? How terrible it would be to go against her parents' wishes for a second time – to defy them. The words 'honour thy father and mother' flew rapidly through her mind. However, upon entering the drawing-room, one sight of her noble suitor, a figure to her of repellent aspect and hateful manner, was sufficient to steel her resolve – all the obstinacy, so often apparent when driven to the wall, in those of an habitually compliant nature, rose to the surface within her – never, never would she consent to marry this man!

Her mother came forward to meet her, her face wreathed in smiles, "Jane, my dear, 'ere's his lordship wishes to speak to you privately!" and as Frant bowed low over Jane's trembling hand, a gleam of satisfaction in his eyes, she added, "Now, Mr Priestley, we'll leave 'is lordship for a few moments to settle things!" and hustled her husband out of the room.

There was a moment's silence. Jane remained standing, her eyes cast down, her whole person filled with dread.

The Marquis advanced and, taking her hand in his, began to speak, wishing impatiently that the wretched girl would look up into his face.

"My dear Miss Priestley, it must have been apparent to you that your beauty and the sweetness of your nature have quite captivated my heart!" He searched in his mind to recollect the phrases that he had rehearsed – it was really damnably hard work to speak like this to someone who appeared to be so little interested, "Will you, my lovely girl, do me the honour of becoming my wife – of being the future Marchioness of Frant?"

Now she did look him in the face and even he, thick-skinned and self-confident as he was, felt a shock of astonishment and affront at the expression of dislike in her eyes.

She withdrew her hand quickly and, in a low voice that surprised even herself by its firmness, said, "No, my lord, I cannot and will not consent to be your wife!" then, backing away from him towards the door, shaken but triumphant at her own temerity, murmured disjointed words about "grateful for the great honour .... regret that she was unable to accept..." and fled from the room. The Marquis had hardly had time to recover from this, to him, astounding rebuff, when Jane's parents returned in the happy expectation of hearing the confirmation of an engagement which was already a certainty in their eyes. To find Jane gone, a visibly furious Marquis alone in the room quite took them aback.

"What's this, my lord?" Mr Priestley hurried forward, a frown upon his face, "Is something amiss?"

"Your daughter, my dear sir, has declined my offer!" Frant spat out the words venomously, "I must tell you, sir – the offer is withdrawn!"

Mrs Priestley burst forth into speech. At all costs this nobleman must be placated, and putting out of her mind for the moment the fine dressing-down she would give her ungrateful daughter, she said with an assumption of calm, "There now, didn't I say, Mr Priestley, that Jane might need a little time to adjust to the great h'onour bestowed upon her! Never fear, my lord, 'tis only a foolish modesty that's afflicted our girl. Give her a little time and she'll soon come about, after all, when all's said and done, she ain't so well acquainted with your lordship. When she knows you better, my lord, she cannot fail to change her mind."

Somewhat mollified, Frant considered his position. The father's words further encouraged him.

"Rest assured, my lord, there's no question but that the answer will become 'yes'! *I* shall make sure of that! She's young, needs guidance, your lordship, and don't rightly recognise where her interests lie."

His worldly ambitions having been aroused, no daughter of William Priestley was going to be permitted to let her foolish whims and fancies stand in the way of his family's advancement in Society.

He added shrewdly, "I'd rather a great heiress like my Jane – and that's what she is, my lord – be married to a sensible man of high position than to some no account young fortune-hunter!"

He had hit precisely the right note. The spectre of imminent ruin had been haunting his lordship for some considerable time. The words 'a great heiress' rang pleasantly in his ears. It seemed as if the father was in earnest and the daughter would be brought to heel. That there might well be an added piquancy in subduing a reluctant bride, once the knot was tied, further persuaded Frant not to withdraw his suit.

"My dear sir, I spoke hastily – forgetting the youth and inexperience of your lovely daughter – by all means let us become better acquainted. You must make allowance for the natural distress to my feelings ...."

Mr Priestley's relief knew no bounds. "Most understandable, my lord! I believe that Jane may already be regretting her foolishness."

Mrs Priestley eagerly added her endorsement of these sentiments and, with a swift stroke of diplomacy, invited the Marquis to accompany them to the theatre upon the Tuesday evening.

"Just a family party, your lordship. We've tickets for the Drury Lane Theatre and you'd be most welcome."

Upon this happier note the Marquis departed, and so conscious was he of his own worth that he had no difficulty in accepting the Priestley's reasoning. In any case it seemed that the chit would be made to obey her parents; *their* wishes in the matter were crystal clear. His spirits rose and he decided to take himself, in celebration, to one of the discreet establishments that enjoyed his patronage, where the girls could be counted upon to be happy, or at least willing, to accommodate his depraved desires and passions.

In the confrontation that followed his departure, Jane was left in no doubt of her parents' views. Summoned to the drawing-room, with no account taken of her red eyes and wan looks, a tide of reproaches and furious directions for the future swept over her bowed head. Both parents in their several ways made their opinions clear; no disobedience to their wishes would be tolerated; they would allow her more time but the outcome must be clear: she was to marry the Marquis of Frant and that was to be the end of the matter.

Once she tried to speak, to demur, but her words were cast aside impatiently as of no consequence. If she had not so recently spoken to Emma, all resistance might have been destroyed for by nature she was pliable and obedient. As it was, she left the room pale and tearful but fully resolved not to consent nor to lose a moment in sending a message to the Countess of Ware.

That same morning, while Jane was confronting the Marquis, Emma had received some startling information.

While she was dressing and wondering how she should best employ her time in the absence of her husband, Dora had informed her that Abigail's mother had arrived that morning in London and, having come immediately to Grosvenor Square to see her daughter, was most anxious to thank her rescuer.

It was agreeable news. For now the girl's future could be settled and Emma sincerely hoped that Mrs Hunt would take her daughter back to Yorkshire, where the poor child could start a new life again and, in time, forget the terrible events that had been forced upon her through the wickedness of her employer.

Mrs Hunt proved to be a tall, respectably dressed woman, a little in awe of her surroundings but with a downright manner of which Emma heartily approved.

Bobbing a curtsy, she took the seat which Emma indicated, and leaning forward, poured out her gratitude in heartfelt terms, finishing by exclaiming in wonder at the youthfulness of her benefactor. "Eh, your ladyship, I mun' say I never 'spected thee wus just a slip of a lass, if thee'll pardon the liberty, m'lady!"

"Probably the same age as Abigail," Emma replied soberly, "so I am fully able to understand her terrible situation! How on earth, Mrs Hunt, did it come about that you permitted her to take employment with such a monster?"

"T'weren't him we saw, my lady, t'was the housekeeper .... I'll never forgive her, ma'am, as long as the Lord gives me breath – it would'na be *him* as folks like us would meet! Eh, if I'd had the least inkling what he wus like, I'd never have permitted any lass of mine to set foot in his accursed house! A'course, we knew him by sight, my lady, livin' as we do in Yorkshire an' nearby to the great house and a reet miserable lookin' creetur he be too – old enough to be my girl's father!" She shook her head sadly and added, as she rose to her feet, "Eh, lass .... your ladyship, I should say – I prays as God will punish that wicked man – indeed I do – 'the Marquis of Frant'," she almost spat out the name, "I curses him, with a mother's curse, for what he has done to my little lass!"

The name came as a shock. The sudden coincidence quite taking Emma's breath away. She stared at Mrs Hunt aghast, repeating slowly, "The Marquis of Frant?"

A stern look came over Mrs Hunt's face, "Does tha' know him, my lady?"

"No, no, thank God! But I've heard of him recently .... a young friend of mine ...." she paused – she must think, she must speak to Edward. Then she continued quickly, "I may wish to see you again, Mrs Hunt, before you return to Yorkshire. In any case it would be best if Abigail had a few more days rest before your long journey home."

"That Dora of yourn, my lady, a reet nice lass she be, she's found me a place nearby where I can get lodgings for a day or so, 'till my Abby's fit to leave." the mother looked anxiously at Emma, "Can my lass bide here a while longer, my lady? Eh – how can I ever repay your ladyship!"

Still stunned by the astounding information that Mrs Hunt had so unwittingly placed in her hands, Emma willingly agreed that the young girl should remain in Grosvenor Square for a few days longer and bade her grateful visitor farewell.

After Mrs Hunt had left her, Emma sat a moment, horrified at what she had just learned. That the man who had destroyed this poor girl should prove to be the very same man whom the Priestleys were encouraging as a future husband for their daughter was shocking news indeed and, by turning the poor child, penniless, out of his house, the Marquis of Frant had gone beyond even the deplorably low standards that she had come to recognise existed in the Polite World.

It was mid-afternoon when Emma received Jane's note and as she read it her determination was further strengthened. Ever since Mrs Hunt's revelations she had been puzzling as to how she could forestall any possibility of an alliance between her young acquaintance and such a man; now to learn that Frant had that very day proposed and that her parents were exerting their utmost pressure upon their daughter to accept him made urgent steps necessary.

The hastily scrawled lines betrayed the degree of agitation and despair experienced by their author and Emma pitied her with all her heart. Something must be done and at once and, after a little consideration, she seated herself at her bureau and wrote a polite invitation to Jane, requesting the pleasure of her company to a picnic in Richmond Park upon the following day: a note which could perfectly properly be shown to Mrs Priestley and an expedition which would give the two girls a greater opportunity than a short drive in Hyde Park to form a plan to circumvent the Priestley's ambitions for their daughter's future.

Having despatched this missive, Emma wrote an urgent note to be delivered to Edward, requesting him to call upon her as soon as possible that evening and to hold himself in readiness to join Miss Priestley and herself in Richmond Park the next day.

It was late when Edward eventually called in Grosvenor Square; the tea-tray had already been removed and Emma had been anxiously turning over in her mind how much longer she should wait before retiring to bed when Edward was announced. Before the footman had even closed the door, she exclaimed in heartfelt tones, "Thank Heavens, Edward – I thought that you would never come and I need you badly!" and felt relief flood through her.

Edward looked his amusement at this fervent welcome; he had dined out, and dined well, that evening and had only received her message upon his return home. Now, in an expansive mood, he approached Emma, an appreciative look in his eyes and said provocatively, "Don't think Robert would care to hear you welcome me in such flattering terms, coz! Am *I* to solace your loneliness?"

Emma, having observed during this speech his flushed face and heard the slight slurring of his words, spoke impatiently, "Oh, Edward, don't say you are partly disguised? And *now*, when I need your help!"

"My help, cousin! 'Course I'll help you!" He made a supreme effort to concentrate and said slowly and carefully as he sat down, "Meet you in Richmond Park, that's what you wrote – with that lovely girl – Miss Priestley." he frowned, "Something's wrong there, ain't it?"

"Oh, Edward, everything's wrong! The Marquis of Frant made an offer this very morning for Miss Priestley's hand! She has refused him but, in the note that I received this afternoon, she writes that her parents will force her to marry him in the end! She has appealed to me for help – desperate, poor child. But there's worse, Edward, I have heard the most terrible story this morning – it was *Frant* who forcibly seduced that poor girl whom I found upon our doorstep! Moreover, when it was found that she was carrying his child, he turned her out of his house without a penny, without a single possession – she was obliged to steal, you know, lost the baby and was in prison!"

"Good God, Emma, are you sure of this?"

"There's no doubt about it – her mother has come down from Yorkshire to take her daughter home and told me today the name of the villain who had seduced her …. that's why I have arranged this meeting with Miss Priestley – we're to picnic there and you must help me to think of some way of aiding her. It doesn't bear thinking about – to be forced to marry such a man! It was bad enough before, but now – when we have learned what he is capable of ...."

How clearly she remembered her own wild terror when marriage had been forced upon her by a stranger, but here disgust and revulsion must be added, there could be no comparison between the handsome Earl of Ware and this elderly degenerate – Jane Priestley *must* be saved from such a fate.

Her words had sobered Edward, "No, by God, Emma! What an appalling tale! I'll put my mind to it, never fear." he added slowly, "Ain't felt like this about any young female before!" and stared at her as if astonished at his own reactions. "Curst unfortunate that I ain't in prime twig tonight – think better tomorrow, dear girl – everlastingly grateful to you ...."

Thankful that some sense of the urgency of the matter had penetrated Edward's fuddled brain, Emma described carefully to him their meeting place in that part of Richmond Park, near Richard's house, with which she was familiar. "Meet us there at mid-day, Edward – we must and shall find a solution!"

She escorted him to the front-door, where he stood a moment looking down at her with amused admiration in his eyes, "Ain't anyone quite like you, cousin! And, by Jove, you know well enough Robert wouldn't approve of this escapade!"

As she laughed and thrust him out into the night saying, "Don't tell me that *you* will squeak beef on me!" she heard sounds behind her and turned to find Marchant had entered the hall and was standing by the table, a disapproving expression upon his face.

"Mr Wyndham's gloves, my lady! He's left them behind!"

Emma's mind was too full of problems of a more serious nature to attend, "Never mind, Marchant – he can collect them next time he calls." and, moving from the door, she ascended the stairs to her bedchamber, leaving the butler standing in the hall dismayed and thoughtful.

CHAPTER 23

The drive to Richmond Park seemed long and tedious. Being obliged by the presence of Ware's servants to avoid any discussion of Jane's predicament, both Jane and Emma found it hard to fill the time with idle chatter. However at least Emma was able to inform Jane during the course of the journey that Edward was to meet them in the park. She could not but be amused to observe her companion's shy smile and soft rejoinder, "Mr Wyndham! Why how agreeable!"

Once near that part of the park that Emma had proposed as their destination they soon saw Edward. He rode up to the carriage and greeted them, hat in hand, his words merely the currency of polite exchange but the expression in his eyes revealing his concern.

They were soon agreed that the pleasantly sheltered spot that he had discovered while awaiting them would be an excellent place for a picnic. The rugs were spread and the hampers unpacked and Emma, declaring that they would wait upon themselves, instructed the grooms to withdraw with the carriage and horses to the shade of some nearby trees.

As soon as they could no longer be overheard, Jane, who had been finding it increasingly difficult to confine her conversation to mundane affairs, burst forth in an agitated manner.

"Oh, Lady Ware, the shame of it – to have to seek your help and that of ...." she glanced, blushing, at Edward, "of Mr Wyndham! Before it was *my* folly – how *could* I have been such a fool – but now .... oh, dear Lady Ware, I am desperate indeed – I would destroy myself rather than marry that man!"

The look upon the girl's haggard face, so different to her normal diffident manner was sufficient to convince Emma that these were no idle words. She stretched out her hand and clasping Jane's in hers, said warmly, "There's not a particle of shame in seeking help from friends,

Miss Priestley – both Edward and I are determined to assist you, for we are convinced that your parents are quite unaware of the kind of man that they wish you to marry."

"No, by Jove! The most damnable blackguard that ever lived! Forgive me, but there ain't no other words to describe him." Edward's face was wrathful, "You won't have to marry him, Miss Priestley, because I'm dashed well going to put an end to his existence!"

"Edward! No!" Emma looked, and was, horrified, "What can you mean?"

"Call him out, coz! Make some pretext – nothing, of course, concerning Miss Priestley – say I dislike the cut of his coat – which is true enough, by Jupiter!"

Jane was looking at Edward, round-eyed with amazement, but before she could speak, Emma, seeing in her mind's eye Edward's lifeless form upon the ground: a triumphant Marquis standing over him, and all to no avail – interposed dampeningly, "Nonsense, Edward, what good would it do to get yourself killed – no doubt Frant has more experience than you in affairs of honour – in any case, if you did succeed, you would have to fly the country! Let us have no more talk of killing, if you please!"

Edward was looking extremely offended at this summary dismissal of his heroic proposal, but the look of admiration in Jane's eyes and her soft words, "Oh, sir, I could never permit you to risk your life for my sake!" served somewhat to mollify his feelings. He rejoined crossly, "Well, what better ideas have you then, cousin?"

Emma had had plenty of time to reflect since receiving Jane's note and already a plan had been forming in her mind. She said thoughtfully, "Miss Priestley, if your parents had some proof of Frant's evil past would they then withdraw their consent to your marriage?"

"Certainly my father is very strict in his ideas, ma'am, he is a profoundly religious man – a Methodist, you see. But how could he be convinced? It seems he is blinded by titles – consumed by ambitions for me and for his family."

Emma's eyes were beginning to sparkle. "Edward, you remember what I told you about Abigail and her mother? Mrs Hunt would not hesitate, I am certain, to accuse the Marquis to his face! If it could be contrived in Mr Priestley's presence .... surely that would suffice to convince him!"

"By Jove, Emma, you've hit upon the very thing!" Edward's face lit up, "But how is it to be managed?"

Jane was looking her bewilderment at this odd exchange, "Of what do you speak, my lady? Who *is* this Mrs Hunt and what has she to say to anything?" It was all quite incomprehensible but her hopes were slowly rising.

As briefly as she could, Emma told her the history of the girl now recovering in Grosvenor Square and of her mother, and how she, herself, had discovered with horror and surprise the identity of the villain.

Jane shuddered, "Dear God, to be asked to marry a man capable of such evil deeds ...." For a moment she remained silent, then she added thoughtfully, "I know that the Marquis is to accompany us to the theatre tomorrow – could that provide some opportunity ....?"

"By Jove, Miss Priestley, it would be perfect – a public place – what could be better? That is to say ...." Edward turned to Emma, "Do you think that Mrs Hunt would agree?"

She nodded her head, "I will arrange to speak to her this evening. But we must make certain that she accuses him when he is with Miss Priestley's parents." She reflected for a moment then, eyes dancing, added, "I believe, Edward, that it would be an excellent idea if we could both also be at the performance tomorrow night – then we could manage to leave the theatre with the Priestleys – it would make it easier for Mrs Hunt."

Such is the optimism of youth that the three young people were soon agreed that they had found the perfect solution; Edward would provide tickets for Emma and himself and for Ware, who, it was expected, would by then have returned home and, once a few further details had been discussed and Jane's dress for the following evening had been decided upon, so that Emma could describe Jane's appearance to Mrs Hunt, they fell to with hearty appetites and consumed the greater part of the elegant picnic that his lordship's chef had provided. Jane and Edward in particular seemed to have quite cast aside any fears for her future; only Emma, thinking of her absent husband and wondering rather dismally how he would view their plans, had an uncomfortable feeling that he would not regard them with the same enthusiasm, and, moreover, that he would have no difficulty in determining who was the author.

As she observed her companions, she could not avoid the realisation that tender feelings clearly existed now on both sides. There could be no doubt of the hero-worship in Miss Priestley's large blue eyes and her perfect trust in Edward's abilities to rescue her once again had served to re-enforce his protective instincts. They had eyes only for each other and Emma soon realised that her presence was more than probably frustrating a delightful exchange of confidences.

Having no fear that Edward would take advantage of this innocent young creature, for he seemed suddenly to have acquired unexceptionable ideas of propriety, she rose to her feet and announced her intention of taking a short and solitary stroll beneath the trees in order to settle in her own mind just how she had best approach Mrs Hunt upon the subject of the Marquis.

In fact, her mind was fixed upon quite other matters.

As she slowly wandered along a grassy path she could not avoid a faint feeling of envy of Jane despite the girl's appalling predicament. Clearly Edward was falling in love with her and she with him, their delight in each other's presence obvious to the merest observer. How very different was her own situation.

Her footsteps had, by now, led her to that part of the park that adjoined Richard's property and she sat down upon a nearby fallen tree-trunk, her thoughts drawn back to that night, so few weeks ago, when Richard had placed her in the hands of the man whom he had planned should ruin her.

What a monster her half-brother had proved to be! She thought sadly that she would never understand men – such strange, unpredictable creatures – and Ware – Emma sighed, her lips curving in an unconscious smile as she thought of him – how amazingly handsome he was! She laughed to herself suddenly, thinking ruefully, 'Could it be that *I* am falling in love with this extraordinary man?'

Certainly he did not love *her*. Indeed, at times, when he looked at her so coldly, she wondered whether he must not now be bitterly regretting his decision to marry her – not even the pleasures of the marriage bed yet to compensate him for Richard's deception.

Sitting, lost in these thoughts, Emma was unaware that she was being observed. Mr Humphrey Featherstone, riding in the park while visiting friends in Richmond, noticed with interest the figure of a girl, fashionably-dressed, sitting alone beneath some oak trees. As she rose and walked slowly away from him, he recognised her to be Lady Ware.

Richard's house being so close at hand, his first thought was, "Must be visiting her brother!" then, recollecting recent events as they had been recounted to him by the gossips, mused, "Dash it! Surely that ain't possible ...!" and rode on with a puzzled frown upon his amiable, if vacuous countenance.

Rejoining the young couple, Emma found them seated, their heads close together, in earnest conversation – Edward sprang up as he saw her, and laughingly declared himself eminently satisfied with her as a chaperone, "Never would have believed that you could be so tactful, cousin!" while Jane, some of the strain now removed from her face, turned a blushing, happy countenance towards Emma.

The two young girls returned home in vastly better spirits than when they had set out; Edward's conversation and loving looks as they parted had given Jane the warmth and comfort that she so badly needed and Emma felt confident that, once their plans had been put into action, a successful outcome was assured. She had, as a precaution, requested Edward not to disclose their arrangements to Ware, and resolutely put out of her mind any doubts that lingered about her husband's views of their scheme. No matter what he might think, she was quite certain that Miss Priestley's marriage to the Marquis must be averted at all costs and with gritted teeth was quite prepared to endure his displeasure at her interference.

There proved to be no difficulty in obtaining Mrs Hunt's agreement to accuse the Marquis in full view of the public. Requested by means of Dora to come to Grosvenor Square, she had listened with ever increasing enthusiasm to Emma's proposals.

"Doan't thee have any doubts, your ladyship – I'll make that devil regret the day that he wus born!"

"Are you sure you will recognise him, Mrs Hunt?" Emma inquired.

Mrs Hunt laughed scornfully, "I'll know him reet enough, m'lady! Asides, I'll take my Abigail along with me, she'll not be too poorly now, thanks to thee, to stand by me. An' with thee mebbe able to leave the theatre with that Priestley family, I reckon I'll know him, never fear!"

Re-assured by this declaration, Emma described in some detail Miss Priestley's evening gown and cloak and Mrs Hunt departed, agog at the prospect of revenge upon her daughter's seducer and clearly relishing the forthcoming encounter.

That night Emma went to bed with a lighter heart. Jane Priestley would be saved from an appalling fate and it was a strong possibility that she would soon find happiness with Edward – that is to say – if her parents could be persuaded to give their consent.

Perhaps, shocked by what they were to discover about their daughter's present suitor, they might turn with relief to a young man of worth and position. As Emma turned upon her side to compose herself for sleep, she wondered drowsily if she could, by some miracle, persuade Ware to give his support to such a marriage. In any case he would be returning tomorrow as she had anticipated, for a message to that effect had been awaiting her upon her return from Richmond and he would therefore be a witness to the public revelation of Frant's iniquity.

Her last thought before sleep overcame her was to recognise how very welcome her husband's return would be – the social round of the Season was an intimidating prospect without him beside her: his protective presence a sure defence against the ill-will which she knew surrounded her.

By some strange irony of fate, while the three conspirators were eagerly discussing their plans in Richmond Park, not more than a few hundred yards away from them a very different conversation was taking place.

Sir James Kent, calling at Richard's house to ascertain whether his friend had returned from the North, had been shocked to discover him, haggard and unshaven, slumped before his writing-table in the book-room, a half-empty bottle by his elbow.

Sir Richard had departed from his home upon the day following his card-party, having instructed Mrs Steadman to expect Emma's return. Anticipating that his half-sister, seduced and ruined by Ware, would have no alternative but to return to his house, he had preferred not to be present when this event took place. Reproaches and lamentations were not at all to his taste and he had thought it advisable to allow some time to elapse before he returned home.

Having spread the scandalous news of his sister's departure with Ware, he had travelled north and it had been a week later, while staying with a friend in Scotland, enjoying some rough shooting and thankful to be out of reach of his creditors, that he had been appalled to read at breakfast a notice in the 'Gazette' announcing the marriage of the Earl of Ware to Miss Emma Stanton.

His face drained of colour, he had set down his cup with a shaking hand, the words seeming to dance before his eyes. He had been so sure of the success of his plan! Never had he imagined that a man like Ware would marry Emma: Ware's succession of mistresses, his cynical attitude towards women and his apparent lack of principle where they were concerned had led Richard to entertain that feeling of certainty, which is the hall-mark of all inveterate gamblers, that his ruse would settle all his difficulties.

Now his sister's fortune was lost to him forever and he was not fool enough to expect that any part of Ware's vast wealth would come his way. The man who had married Emma, for whatever quixotic reason, was scarcely likely to look with favour upon the villain who had plotted her ruin.

He had returned home a week later to find a pile of unpaid bills awaiting him and several letters of an unpleasantly threatening nature from his tailor and from his wine-merchants. Most terrible of all had been a politely worded note from Mr King of Clarges Street, calling his attention to bills of considerable sums of money to which he had put his name and which had now fallen due, and informing him that 'unless payment was received forthwith', he would shortly be receiving a visit from a member of that well-known firm of money-lenders.

Mrs Steadman, who was experiencing difficulty in retaining the services of the two maids, their wages sadly overdue, had spoken frankly to him upon his return, "Something has to be done, Richard! Things cannot continue as they stand – I've half the tradesmen in Richmond here demanding their money!"

Sir Richard had felt the net tightening around him, and had begun to drink heavily, sitting day after day in the book-room.

Surveying Harding's crumpled clothing, his neck-cloth awry, Sir James Kent stared at him in amazement, "Good God, Richard, what the devil ails you? You look all to pieces, man!"

Sir Richard looked up, his prominent, blood-shot eyes filled with resentment. "Money, by God, James – money! Or the lack of it! Tha's what's the matter!" He brooded heavily over the words, then burst out again, "An' there's that damned sister of mine, curse her – more money now than she'll know what to do with!"

Sir James sat down and looked at his friend with renewed interest. "Do you mean your half-sister, Ware's wife?"

"Aye, the devil take him – an' her! Who would ever have thought that he would marry her, the sly little trollop! Now all that money's gone – only thing that might have saved me!" He groaned and added, "I'm done for, James – rolled up!"

He poured himself some more wine with a trembling hand and pushed the bottle towards Sir James, who was regarding him with a mixture of pity and curiosity.

Sulkily, Richard muttered, "Must have married her for some crazy whim – damnably impulsive fellow!" then added with a coarse laugh, "No doubt he has no further use for her now!"

"You're fair and far out there, I can promise you that!" Sir James, with a reminiscent scowl, growled resentfully, "Met him at Watier's one evening a week or two ago – he came in with Wyndham and some others. I made some remark about his winning your sister at Hazard – I was a fool to do so in his hearing but I was a trifle foxed at the time – he was on his high horse at once – threatened me in that damned unpleasant way he has! I can tell you, Richard, it's all over town that he's half in love with the girl! Or, at least, that's the latest on-dit!"

Richard sat staring at him, his mouth open, astonishment written all over his face, "Half in love with her?" he repeated incredulously, "Don't believe you – damme, it's not possible! A man like Ware!"

He leaned back in his chair, too drunk to think clearly, and added argumentatively, "Tell you, he's never cared a jot for any female – discards 'em as soon as they bore him – heart of stone!"

"Well, it seems he cares this time! Surely you can turn that to advantage – he must be one of the richest men in the country."

"More likely to blow my brains out!" Richard said roughly, but he was beginning to look thoughtful. Kent's words seemed to have stirred him out of his lethargy. He made a visible effort to pull himself together and said, "Well, James, enough of myself! No knowing what may turn up! I'm damned glad to see you – done me a power of good .... Did you have any luck at Epsom?" and turned the talk to the all-absorbing topic of the Turf, no more being said upon the subject of the Earl and his wife.

Late that night, after Sir James had left, Richard sat a long time in his armchair gazing vacantly into space, an idea slowly forming in his befuddled brain. He stood up to refill his snuff-box from a jar on the bookshelf near him and, clumsy in his movements, dislodged some old newspapers. As he bent to pick them up, a headline caught his eye. He stood staring at it, reading it through several times, an arrested expression upon his face, then, laying aside the journals, he returned to his writing table, sat down and drew the standish towards him. There was now a growing excitement in his manner; he picked up the pen with a trembling hand, hesitated a moment and then, with an evil smile upon his face, he began to write.

CHAPTER 24

Ware had not found in his visit to Leicestershire any relief from the burden that his impulsive marriage had placed upon him. "Out of sight – out of mind." had not proved to be true, indeed, rather had its contrary truism been correct. "Absence makes the heart grow fonder." was, he thought grimly, far more applicable to his own state of mind. A seductive vision of Emma had never been far from his thoughts.

"Good God," he had wondered, "has it come to this! Moping like any love-sick swain!"

As he travelled homewards, he resolved to make every effort upon his return to gain her affection by exemplary kindness and good humour and hoped ruefully that not too great a strain would be placed upon him in fulfilling this resolve, saintliness not being, he was the first to admit, one of his most obvious attributes.

With these good intentions in the forefront of his mind, he strode into his house filled with the milk of human kindness and was disconcerted to find in the hall, as he handed his hat and gloves to Marchant, a pair of men's gloves lying upon the console table.

"A visitor, Marchant?" he enquired, frowning.

"No, my lord. Mr Wyndham called here late Sunday night." Marchant's face was expressionless and yet Ware had the strong impression that his butler had not approved of the visit. "I was not aware of his departure, my lord, and so was not able to hand him his gloves, before he left."

Ware nodded absently and asked, "Is her ladyship downstairs?" resolutely setting aside the vexing suspicions that had instantly arisen, unbidden, in his mind.

"Lady Ware is in the library, my lord." Marchant retired in his customary stately manner, reflecting sadly that her ladyship's arrival in the Earl's household had not proved to be an unmixed blessing. Maybe his lordship should have chosen one of his own kind!

Emma had been engrossed in a novel from the lending library, lent to her by Lady Sophia, and did not at first look up when the door opened. Ware was thus able to look upon his wife for a moment in silence, relishing the sight of her slim figure dressed in one of Madame Celestine's most beguiling morning dresses. His senses profoundly stirred, he was delighted when, upon raising her head and seeing him standing in the doorway, she jumped up and came forward, pleasure sparkling in her eyes.

"My lord, how very good to see you! How was your journey? Is all well in Leicestershire?" the questions poured out as she took his arm and led him to the sofa.

Ware was enchanted. It could not be doubted that she was truly pleased to see him. He sat down beside her and answered all her eager questions and, when they were ended, enquired how she had amused herself in his absence.

In that very moment he wished his words unsaid.

Emma was looking straight into his eyes as he spoke and he knew at once that she had something that she wished to conceal from him. It was like a blow to the face.

She said slowly, "Let me see – Oh, yes – I drove one day in the Park with Miss Priestley. Poor girl – the Marquis of Frant has proposed and she has refused him – but I fear that her parents will force her into the marriage – it is tragic, my lord!" She hesitated, her husband's expression had changed – far better to keep silent upon her and Edward's plans. She looked away from him.

"Have you seen Edward?" Ware could not restrain himself from asking – why had she not mentioned his visit?

"Why, yes, my lord, we met him in the Park, and," she added hurriedly, awkwardly, "he called here one evening, I forget when ...."

There was a brief silence. Emma was painfully aware that her husband was not best pleased. If this was the effect that the mention of Miss Priestley's problems had upon him then she must not upon any account mention Mrs Hunt and her own discovery about the Marquis' past.

The announcement of luncheon at that moment came as a relief to both of them. Ware, sternly reminding himself of his resolution, attempted to set aside his horrid suspicions; he must, after all, remember that Emma was still mistrustful of him – no doubt her lack of candour had been due to some youthful folly of which she was afraid he would disapprove.

By the time he had entertained her with diverting stories of the evening that he had spent with the local Master of Foxhounds in Leicestershire, an eccentric whom Ware declared to be the most fanatical follower of hounds in the entire country, Emma's good spirits were restored; so it was with an easy mind that he announced his intention of driving to Kensington village that afternoon.

"I am sorry to have to leave you alone so soon after my return but I have heard from Andrew Holt that there is a light-mouthed lady's hack for sale at the stables there and I am anxious to see you suitably mounted." Ware told her. "If I like the mare, we shall ride tomorrow afternoon." He added with a smile, "Perhaps you are not aware, my love, that anyone of consequence *must* be seen riding or driving in the Park at that time of day!"

"Gracious, my lord, how very agreeable that such a delightful occupation is fashionable." Emma was surprised and amused at the notion that one must be seen at a certain time of day – what a great deal she still had to learn," It is most kind of you to look for a mount for me – I shall look forward to your return."

Ware went off well-pleased with his new stratagem and vowing to himself to keep a firm hold upon his tongue and to remember that his wife was, after all, a very young and inexperienced girl who might well have quite innocent matters which she preferred not to reveal to her husband.

Some malign fate, however, seemed determined to test his resolve to the full. Arriving at Sir Andrew's lodgings to take that gentleman up in his curricle, he encountered another acquaintance upon the door-step.

Horace Featherstone seemed delighted to see him. "Ain't seen you in an age, Robert! Where the devil have you been?"

"Leicestershire – for a few days." Ware grinned, "Hardly an age, dear boy!"

"Thought of you yesterday – something brought you to mind – what the devil was it?" He looked vaguely around him as if seeking inspiration, "Only came back from Richmond m'self this morning .... by Jove – that's it! Saw Lady Ware yesterday – in Richmond Park, near Richard's house, which surprised me .... devil take it, shouldn't have said that ...." He looked anxiously at Ware's face and was not re-assured to see his friends brows contract in a frown. "Just on her own, y'know – taking a stroll, I expect .... lovely day ...."

"No doubt." Ware spoke abruptly, saw the look of anguish on his friend's face, his startled eyes regarding him with some trepidation, and laughed suddenly. Richmond Park on a summer's day was harm-less enough after all. "I'm on my way to Kensington to look over a horse – hoping to take Andrew with me."

After a few more exchanges they parted company and Ware set out with Sir Andrew with only a few remaining sensations of unease.

Ware having departed, Emma was in her boudoir light-heartedly trying the effect of a new shawl and admiring her reflection in the looking-glass, when there was a knock on her door and a footman entered bearing a letter upon a silver salver which he presented to her, inform-ing her as he did so that it had been brought round by hand. Taking it with some surprise, she noticed that the writing of the superscription was vaguely familiar and wondered, as she broke the wafer and opened it, whom her correspondent could be.

As she read, the colour fled from her cheeks, she put out a hand blindly for a chair to support herself, the shawl slipping unheeded to the floor. The letter was written in an untidy hand and was headed *"Richmond, Monday."* and read - *"Dear Emma, I am faced with utter ruin and, if I am not able to set my hands upon a large sum of money by the end of this week, I shall be declared a bankrupt and committed to prison. You are now a wealthy woman and it is well within your power to aid me. I therefore must request you to place at my disposal the sum of five thousand pounds which would for the moment relieve my situation.*

In case you are unmindful of the gratitude that you owe me for being instrumental in your attaining your present position of rank and wealth, I must inform you that unless you accede to my request I shall be obliged to take steps which would encompass you in ruin, a ruin more absolute even than that which faces me now! For if you fail me, I intend to inform your husband – and Society – that during the period in which you lived in my house you seduced me into an incestuous union with you, against the laws of God and man, and that this drove me to the desperate measure of wagering you at play to rid myself of your wickedness.

Doubtless you are aware of the recent separation of Lady Byron from her husband following the revelations of his scandalous liaison with his half-sister. As a result the latter is now ostracised by Society and Lord Byron obliged to leave the country. Lord Ware is a proud man, proud of his name and possessed of a violent temper – I warn you, if you value your own life and reputation, you must take steps immediately to bring to me the sum that I demand to ensure my silence. These are desperate measures but I am a desperate man and I will not hesitate to carry out my threat if you should fail me, even though by doing so I accomplish my own ruin!

The signature was Richard's and Emma, white-faced and sick with horror, read for a second time his terrible words, hardly able to grasp his demands and his horrifying threat, then, with pounding heart and hands that shook, she put it from her, as if even to hold it in her hand was a contamination. His wicked lies, affronting her innocence, made her feel faint and ill. She seated herself, trembling, in the chair she had clutched for support and stared ahead of her with unseeing eyes.

Having experienced already Richard's disregard for her safety and welfare, she had no doubts that he would be capable of carrying out his threat. For one brief moment she considered telling Ware, longing to lay the whole matter before him to resolve, but with sinking heart she realised that she had not the courage to do so; there was no reason upon earth to suppose that he would believe her – no means existed of proving the falseness of these terrible lies. She shuddered to think how his attitude towards her would change, and behind the fear of physical violence lay the desolating realisation that any hope of his acquiring an affection for her would be at an end. Desperately, she cast about in her mind as to what course of action she could follow. Even if she had wished to do so, it would be impossible for her to find so vast a sum of money – somehow she must gain more time – she *must* see Richard at once and beg him not to carry out his monstrous threats.

She stood up unsteadily and rang the bell, her mind in a turmoil. Thank God, Ware was out and, if Dora could be trusted, she might visit Richard without her husband's knowledge. How fortunate that it was still this simple country-girl who attended her and upon whose loyalty she believed she could depend; moreover Thomas had now arrived from Wiltshire and could perhaps assist her.

Dora was shocked and horrified when she entered the room and saw her young mistress; she was moving restlessly about the room, her face white and strained, her great, tragic eyes filled with despair.

"My lady – you are ill?" Dora, full of concern, approached her mistress.

Emma ceased her pacing and stood looking searchingly into her maid's plain, honest face, "Dora, can I trust you?" her voice shook, "I need your help but you m-must promise not to betray me!"

"I swear you can trust me, your ladyship – why, I'd do anything for you, my lady – you know's that ...."

"I have to go out – but *no-one must know that I have done so*! Ask Thomas to find me a hackney carriage and require it to wait at the corner of the Square – then you must help me to leave the house by the servant's entrance and watch for my return by the same way." She added urgently, "If *anyone,* whoever they may be, should ask for me while I am out, you are to say that I am laid down upon my bed with a sick-headache and can see no-one!"

Dora, looking alarmed and astonished at these directions, said doubtfully, "Should I not accompany you, my lady?"

Emma shook her head, "No, no, I *must* go alone! Besides, you will be needed here in case anyone calls to see me. Quickly – help me to change my clothes and then get Thomas to go at once to find me a hackney."

In haste, Emma put on her old dress and brown coat and bonnet, for in these clothes she could more easily leave the house unobserved. With trembling fingers, she fastened a veil over her face and, when Dora returned a few minutes later, followed her, descending by way of the back-stairs, into the nether regions of the house. From there, unnoticed by any of the servants, she slipped out into the area and up the steps to the street; at the corner a hackney carriage was waiting and she hastened towards it, looking nervously around her and feeling wretchedly ill-at-ease. She did not, however, observe a fair-haired, slim young man crossing the square at that moment. She gave the driver Richard's direction in Richmond, mounted up into the hackney and sank back thankfully, glad to be concealed from the sight of any passer-by.

Edward, having managed to acquire tickets for the play that the Priestleys were to attend, had come to call in Grosvenor Square with the object of inviting Ware and his bride to the theatre that evening and thus fulfilling his part in Emma's plan. As he drew near the house, he saw the slight figure of a woman, veiled and shabbily dressed in brown, slip out from the servant's entrance. For a moment he could have sworn it was his new cousin: the clothes and figure seemed familiar to him, but she was gone so quickly and, moreover, it struck him as such an unlikely event, that he came to the conclusion that his imagination must be playing him tricks.

In response to his enquiries at the house for the Earl, the porter told him that his lordship had gone out but that her ladyship was at home; the footman, despatched upstairs to inform Lady Ware that Mr Wyndham had called and was desirous of seeing her, returned to the little Saloon where Edward was waiting with the intelligence that her ladyship was laid down with a bad headache and greatly regretted that she was unable to see anyone. Accepting this information with an impassive countenance, Edward requested that his sympathies should be conveyed to her ladyship and, leaving a message for the Earl, quitted the house with a thoughtful expression. What on earth could Emma be up to?

The journey to Richmond was both slow and uncomfortable. The interior of the vehicle was none too clean, straw lay upon the floor and the springs left much to be desired: a very different mode of travel to his lordship's beautiful, well-sprung carriages; but to the solitary passenger, unmindful of these defects, the journey passed all too quickly.

Emma was struggling to compose her thoughts. She dreaded the coming interview, indeed the very nature of her errand sickened and frightened her; to be obliged to humble herself before this man who had not long since attempted to ruin her and was now prepared to make these shocking accusations, a man whose grossness of manner and person repelled her, this was an ordeal that she could hardly bear to contemplate.

When at last the driver pulled up before the door of Gresham House, her heart was beating painfully. He looked at her pityingly as she requested him to wait and to convey her back to London, wondering idly what had served to distress the poor young creature.

The front door was opened by an untidy-looking maid-servant who, casting one glance at Emma's face, exclaimed in amazement, "Miss Stanton! Well I never! .... *Your ladyship,* I should say!" She stepped back to allow Emma to enter, staring at her with barely concealed curiosity. There were footsteps on the stairs and Mrs Steadman came into the hall, her bold eyes looking Emma up and down and noting with surprise the old-fashioned clothes, the pale face with large, anxious eyes fixed upon hers.

"Gracious, Emma, fancy you coming to visit us! I must offer you my congratulations on your marriage, *my lady!*" With a sneer, she added, "Who would have thought when you left this house that *that* was to be your destiny!"

There was a grudging admiration in her manner which to Emma was particularly displeasing, as if the marriage had somehow been of Emma's own contriving. She made no reply to the housekeeper, only saying in a grave voice, "I wish to see Sir Richard, Mrs Steadman."

"Your brother is in the book-room – I will tell him that you are here." The housekeeper left Emma and, crossing to the book-room door, entered the room and closed the door behind her. A murmur of voices could be heard, then, returning, she invited Emma to enter, saying with a malicious grin, "He's not quite himself this afternoon, *if* you take my meaning! There's no doubt he's been indulging himself over freely of late, poor man!"

The sight that met Emma's eyes was not a pleasant one. Richard was sprawled in an armchair, a bottle and a glass by his side, his face flushed, his whole appearance dishevelled. The room lacked any semblance of order, the writing table piled high with papers, some strewn upon the floor, and there was dust everywhere, the air heavy with the fumes of wine.

He looked up as Emma entered but made no attempt to rise. "Well, my girl," he said thickly, "have you brought the accursed money?" He was staring at her with blood-shot eyes, striving to focus them on the slight, stiff-backed figure before him.

Emma regarded him with horror, she had seen him before a trifle fuddled but this was something far worse. She clasped her hands tightly together and began to recite, with all the resolution that she could command, the speech that she had prepared.

"Your letter forced me to come here, Richard, although after your terrible treatment of me, I should have preferred never to have set eyes upon you again ...."

She was interrupted impatiently, "Cut the moralising, sister, and come to the point!"

Taking a deep breath, Emma struggled on, "Of course I regret the situation in which you now find yourself, but it is quite impossible for me to find this large sum of money immediately without ...." She paused, swallowing painfully, and continued in a low voice, "Without my husband's knowledge – I have no access as yet to the money that I have inherited and it may well be some time still before I do."

He began to struggle to his feet, his face suffused with rage, shouting at her as he did so, "Don't try to f-fool me with those missish airs! God damn it, ain't you married to one of the richest m-men in the country? You little fool! Get Ware to advance the money – advance it against your inheritance if tha's what you wish!"

He started to come towards her, clutching at the side of the table to steady himself. Emma stood as if turned to stone.

He drew himself upright before her and almost spat in her face, "Made him make an honest woman of you, didn't you? Lord knows how!" He leered at her, the saliva running down from the corner of his slack mouth, "*Now* you can use your wiles on him again, my pretty one!" He was looking her up and down in a way that gave her the sensation of having been stripped of her clothing, "Get the money

253

from him or it will be the worse for you – for if you don't – by God, I s-swear I'll make your name infamous throughout the land. That precious husband of yours won't keep you then!"

Emma could hardly speak, her terror and disgust mounting at every second. Her half-brother, standing swaying before her, hardly seemed a rational being. How could she touch the heart of a man who seemed to be beyond reason, beyond any feeling of humanity? Forsaking all attempts at dignity, she cried desperately, "For the sake of our mother, Richard – for the sake of truth and justice – for your own honour – you must not tell these wicked lies about me! For the love of God! I beseech you not to do so!"

She knew at once that she had failed. He began to curse and swear at her, repeating again and again that he must have the money by the next day.

At last, in a trembling voice, she asked him how, if she were somehow able to find this sum, this could be accomplished, "For it would be impossible for me to repeat this journey without my lord's knowledge!"

Richard stood a moment, his brain confused with wine, struggling to put his thoughts in order; after a few seconds a cunning expression came into his eyes, "D'you go to the Challenor's Ball at Twickenham tomorrow night?" he demanded. Receiving her assent, he continued, with a sudden increase in clarity, "Bring the money with you, my girl! There's a pavilion in the grounds – by the lake – built like a damned Greek temple, pillars and so forth – you must meet me there at midnight when all the guests will be at supper." He paused, then said viciously, "But, by God, if you fail me – I shall that *very night* start the rumours about you, a word here, a word there — it's not difficult you know!" He gave a savage laugh, "All the world loves a scandal! How they will relish this one! And the next day – a letter to Ware himself!"

Emma shuddered and backed away from him. Somehow she must stop him. In a faint voice, she whispered "I will meet you there!"

He seemed content. A slow smile, horrible to see, spread across his face. No thought for her entered his head, no pity; he only saw an escape for himself from the results of his own folly and felt an immense childish satisfaction at his own cunning.

254

Trembling, Emma left him standing there; she left the house and, mounting up again into the waiting hackney carriage, began the long weary journey back to Grosvenor Square. Sitting there, exhausted by emotion, she felt only despair and as she stared blindly out of the window, tears ran unheeded down her face.

CHAPTER 25

Dora was frightened by her mistress's appearance when Emma returned to the house. Once they had reached the bedroom unseen, she helped the poor, pale, trembling girl out of her drab clothes and wrapped her in a dressing-gown, speaking to her all the while in a soft voice as she would to a child, comforting and coaxing her, then, sending for a glass of cordial, she stood beside her as she sipped it.

At last Emma said that she would lie down on her bed. "Has his lordship returned to the house yet?" she enquired anxiously.

"No, my lady, not yet. Mr Wyndham called while you were out but I sent a message down – just like you instructed, ma'am. Said as you were not well and thus unable to see him."

Left alone, Emma lay upon her bed struggling with all the will-power at her command not to weep: it could not be long before Ware returned and she must not show him a tear-stained face. When she was calmer, she must decide what she should do – but how could any moment be accounted the *right* one to ask one's husband for five thousand pounds, and that, moreover, without offering any explanation for such an extraordinary request?

She did not have long to wait for his return. He entered her bedroom with all the sense of well-being that a man feels when he has completed a satisfactory piece of business and is about to present his wife with a gift which he is confident will afford her infinite pleasure.

Ware had spent an agreeable afternoon with Sir Andrew: the mare, a pretty, well-mannered grey, with a head which proclaimed Arab blood in her breeding, had been everything that he required. She was to be delivered to the house the following morning and he was looking forward to seeing Emma's face when she beheld her new mount.

But one look at the white, strained face on the pillow put all such happy thoughts out of his head. He came to the side of the bed and took her hand, saying gently, "My poor Emma, what has happened to you? Are you not well?"

She tried to smile and, looking up at him, said ruefully, "I have the headache, my lord – so stupid of me —but I am sure that it will soon pass."

He stood, scanning her face with a worried frown, "Edward called while I was out and has left a message inviting us to accompany him to the Drury Lane theatre tonight – a musical drama by Benjamin Thompson, I believe – nonsensical stuff, though the music is by Parry – but if you are not well I will send word that we cannot come."

The cruel dilemma in which she now found herself had weighed upon her mind so heavily, to the exclusion of all else, that her plan to defeat the Marquis' marriage seemed like a far off dream. With an effort Emma forced herself to play her part.

"Depend upon it, my lord, a distraction will be the very thing for me – doubtless it will assist me to forget my headache and, besides, I must not be giving in to such a trivial complaint – you will be thinking me to be a poor creature indeed!"

He put his hand lightly on her forehead, saying teasingly, "You, my love, a poor creature! No, never!" but was relieved to find her skin cool, for his thoughts had flown to her recent contact with the typhus and for one moment he had feared that she might have a fever.

"If you are certain that you feel well enough, I will accept and will invite Edward to dine here beforehand." He left her to change his garments but still not easy in his mind, for he sensed that someone or something had disturbed her in his absence, and so, while Willis assisted him to dress, he enquired whether there had been any other callers, besides Edward, while he was out.

"I believe not, my lord. Only a letter was delivered earlier by hand for her ladyship."

Perplexed by this reply, Ware wondered whether the letter could have contained some reference to the rumours circulating about their marriage. No doubt, being alone, Emma had had too much time to dwell upon these unpleasant thoughts and had fallen into a melancholy. He hoped that he and Edward would be able to set her mind in a happier direction.

His hopes, however, were not to be realised. Edward arrived and they dined promptly in order to be in good time for the play. At first it seemed as if Emma had regained her good spirits; she enquired after Ware's expedition to Kensington and expressed her pleasure at hearing of the horse that he had bought for her, but there was a odd, wistful expression in her eyes as she thanked him for all the trouble that he had taken and she looked quite startled when Edward asked her what she was to wear to Lady Challenor's ball upon the following evening, gazing at him blankly for a moment before she replied with an attempt at a smile, "You must wait and see, Edward, for I mean to surprise you!"

She was still looking very pale and hardly touched the food that was set before her and, when the conversation turned to politics, she sat abstracted, so engrossed in her own thoughts that Ware had to speak to her twice, before she attended, to tell her that it was time that they departed for the theatre. More and more convinced that it was the fear of the rebuffs and slights that she might receive when she appeared in public which was disturbing his young wife, Ware made up his mind not to leave her side during the evening.

The third member of the party was also preoccupied with his own thoughts. Edward could not fail to notice Emma's sad, abstracted air, and Ware's solicitous attention to her precluded any idea that there had been a serious difference between them. Recollecting the brown-clad figure that he had seen slipping out of the house in Grosvenor Square, he resolved that, at the first suitable opportunity, he would endeavour to find out discreetly what was so evidently, troubling her. Could it be connected in some way with Miss Priestley's problems? He hoped most devoutly that nothing would go wrong with their plans.

Following their introduction to Sir John and Lady Bruce at Lady Foster's dinner-party, Mr and Mrs Priestley had received invitations from that hospitable couple to a breakfast to take place upon the following Monday.

Mrs Priestley was in seventh heaven, "You see, Mr Priestley, 'ow well everything 'as turned out! And once our little girl is a Marchioness....!"

Mr Priestley nodded with satisfaction. Things were progressing just as they should and, warmed by this reflection, he suggested to the wife of his bosom that she should purchase a new outfit for the occasion.

The breakfast had been most enjoyable. Lady Bruce had introduced them to a large number of her acquaintances and, fortunately for the Priestley's happiness, they had been unaware that several of her guests had excused themselves from being presented, considering the Priestleys to be tainted by too immediate a connection with Trade.

The only event that had cast a shadow over Mrs Priestley's pleasure was a conversation that she had held with Mrs Sherston, who had also been present at Lady Foster's dinner-party. That faded lady had heard that Miss Priestley had been seen driving in the Park with the Marquis of Frant and, although resigned to finding herself and her opinions considered to be of small importance in contrast to those of her husband, had felt impelled to warn Mrs Priestley that her daughter's escort was generally accounted to be a man of doubtful morals.

Unfortunately her remarks were of such a veiled nature as to be well-nigh incomprehensible to one of Mrs Priestley's forthright nature. The warning had, however, been sufficiently disturbing to warrant her calling upon Lady Foster later that day.

After a pleasant discussion of the breakfast that they had both attended, Mrs Priestley had voiced her concern in the plainest of terms.

"The Marquis, Alicia, my dear – 'e ain't an immoral man, I 'ope?"

Lady Foster was taken aback by such bluntness but quickly rallied. "Why, what tittle-tattle is this that you have been listening to, my dear?" She leaned forward and murmured confidentially, "You and I are women of the world, Mary – we know what men are ... poor, foolish creatures ... I wouldn't say that George hasn't been a touch wild in his youth – but that's all behind him now. Whatever you may have heard, my dear – you can put quite out of your head!"

This avowal was precisely what Mrs Priestley wished to hear and upon that account she had not the least difficulty in believing it to be the truth.

She was further re-assured to observe upon returning home that Jane had come back from her picnic in Richmond Park with Lady

259

Ware in better spirits than when she had set out. She was still subdued and pre-occupied in her manner but her mother sensed that beneath it lay some inner contentment.

"I reckon she's coming round to our way of thinking, Mr Priestley. Mebbe it was all too sudden for our girl." Mrs Priestley told her husband that night. "Now she's 'ad time to reflect ..." she shot a considering glance at her husband: should she or should she not repeat what she had heard about the Marquis? Better, perhaps, to tell him what Alicia had said, for there was no knowing who might recount to him some gossip about Frant.

"If you hear aught about his lordship's morals, Mr Priestley – to 'is detriment, I mean – you can disregard it. I spoke to Alicia today after hearing some such talk and she tells me that that is a thing of the past, long since behind him!"

Mr Priestley frowned, "How women's tongues do wag," he replied scornfully, "of course he's sown a few wild oats in his youth – stands to reason! Probably some old cat is jealous of the attention my lord has been paying to our Jane." He pondered for a moment upon the foolishness of the female sex, sublimely convinced of masculine superiority, but, at the same time, the thought occurred to him that it might be as well to keep an eye upon his prospective son-in law.

As soon as Edward and his guests had arrived at the theatre, he had quickly surveyed the audience and found, to his relief, that the Priestley party were already seated in their box and, better still, the box was situated not far from their own. To observe Frant seated beside Miss Priestley, whispering confidentially in her ear was painful indeed and only made bearable by the thought of this villain's coming discomfiture.

He pointed the party out to Emma and Ware. The latter looked at them with distaste and said dismissively, "A sorry sight – an alliance between over-weaning ambition and greed!"

The harshness of her husband's judgment further dismayed Emma. How little sympathy he had for the frailties of the human condition. How, in heaven's name, was she to confess to her urgent need for such a vast sum of money?

When the performance commenced, the comedy being enacted on stage seemed only to further darken Emma's thoughts. Even in the dim light of the auditorium she dared not let her real feelings show for she was conscious that her husband, sitting beside her, often had his eyes upon her face. If only she had never received Richard's letter – how different the evening would have been. Her situation, her marriage, had been difficult enough before, but now, faced by the terrifying prospect that lay before her – the deceit, the lies – it seemed as if she would have given anything to go back to the state of affairs that had existed before she had received his letter.

As it happened, during the interval, Ware was called away by an old friend of his father who was beckoning to him to join their party and found himself obliged, for politeness sake to go. Edward, finding himself for a moment alone with Emma, turned to her and said anxiously, "I cannot help noticing that something is troubling you, Emma. Has some problem arisen with our plans for tonight?"

She shook her head, "No, all is well and Mrs Hunt will be there with her daughter." She tried to smile reassuringly at him and, to her horror, found her eyes filling with tears.

Edward looked his dismay: his redoubtable little cousin, of whom he had grown so fond, in distress! He said to her softly, "I believe I saw you leave Ware's house by the servant's entrance this afternoon and take a hackney carriage. I suppose it would be improper for *me* to enquire the reason for your secrecy but I advise you most strongly to confide in Robert if you are in some difficulty – much better, my dear girl, to tell him yourself, you know!"

he hesitated, then added thoughtfully, "It would be far worse for you, Emma, if he should find out some other way."

He was utterly taken aback by the sudden look of fear in her eyes. She clutched the sleeve of his coat and whispered urgently, "You will not tell him that you saw me, Edward! Promise me that you will not tell him!"

"Certainly not! Good God, cousin, what do you take me for?" He patted her hand reassuringly, "None of my business – but be more than happy to help you if it be in my power to do so."

He was looking doubtfully at her, finding himself more uneasy than ever, when at that moment Ware returned – nothing further could be said upon the subject and, soon after, the curtain rose again and the play continued.

To Emma, the performance came all too quickly to an end – the coming interview with her husband drawing inexorably nearer.

As they joined in the audience's applause, Edward whispered in her ear, "Don't forget we must join the Priestleys, coz!"

She nodded and setting aside with an effort her own pre-occupations, said politely to Ware, "If it would not be too disagreeable to you, my lord, I should very much like to speak to Miss Priestley as we leave the theatre?"

It is doubtful if Ware would have consented to renew his acquaintance with Miss Priestley's parents in the normal course of events but his concern for Emma's state of mind, for her only partially concealed anxiety, obliged him to accept the meeting with a good grace, saying cheerfully, "If you wish it, my love, I will say no more – only for pity's sake let us not become bosom-bows with such a foolish couple as her parents appear to be!"

There was a little difficulty in making their way through the crowded corridors but Ware's unmistakable air of authority, his tall, distinguished figure made their passage easier than might have been expected and they had already joined the Priestley's party before the main entrance of the theatre had been reached.

"Lady Ware, 'ow most delightful!" Mrs Priestley, being escorted by the Marquis, was enchanted, her face glowing with pleasure. Her husband, who was behind her, bowed to the Earl – how well everything was turning out – "An excellent performance, don't your lordship think?"

His lordship, looking a little aloof, agreed politely and Emma, coming close to Miss Priestley, said softly into her ear, "Courage, dear Jane, all will be well!"

The Marquis of Frant, confident that his courtship was now proceeding on more hopeful lines, was pleasantly surprised to discover my Lord Ware acknowledging his acquaintance with the Priestleys; he was at the same time intrigued to set eyes upon this chit that Ware had married, about whose name so much scandalous talk continued to circulate amongst the Ton.

"Evenin' Ware – amusing stuff, don't yer think?" he said ingratiatingly, "Ain't had the pleasure of meeting Lady Ware – do please present me, Robert!"

The exchange of these few sentences had brought them out of the theatre onto the steps of the entrance and before Ware could reluctantly perform the requested introduction, a middle-aged woman, dragging a young girl by the hand, had darted forward from amongst the few onlookers who were standing on the pavement and seized Mrs Priestley by the arm. Mrs Priestley shrank back with astonishment at this furious vision and found herself, to her horror, being addressed.

"For God's sake, ma'am, doan't 'ee let that pretty lass of yourn have aught to do with this black-hearted villain!" the woman cried, pointing her finger at my Lord Frant, who seemed to turn pale at her words, "Got my poor Abigail with child 'ee did, ma'am – more shame to him – seduced her last year when she wus only fifteen an' working in his house....!"

The Marquis tried to push her aside, "The poor creature's mad – escaped from Bedlam, no doubt, ma'am. Good God – never set eyes on her before!"

But Mrs Hunt was not to be halted, she flung off Frant's hand on her shoulder and shouted at him, "You know my Abigail all right and tight, my lord, an' you wus the cold-hearted villain who turned her out of your house without a penny to her name when you discovered she wus carrying your child – nigh on died, she did, starving in the streets...."

Frant turned to Mr Priestley, who, all at once, was looking grim-faced beside him, and, blustering, horrified, for by now he had recognised the girl, expostulated, "Never heard such a farrago of nonsense in my life, sir! Beg you that we leave at once – most unpleasant incident.... distressing for the ladies!"

The small group of onlookers, who had been watching and listening avidly to this exchange, began now to be restive and there was a decidedly hostile atmosphere. Moreover a press of people had formed behind them, striving to leave the theatre.

The Earl of Ware, looking down at his wife's face, caught the fleeting, anxious glance that she cast at him from under her eyelashes and felt an immediate surge of relief. Was this the cause of Emma's pre-occupation? It hardly required a genius to realise that she had had some hand in the proceedings taking place before them, for he strongly suspected that this woman's daughter was the very same poor young creature whom Emma had taken off the streets into his house. With a wry smile – what in God's name would this slip of a girl do next to astonish and provoke him – he said austerely, "I believe our carriage has been called forward, my dear!" and bowing politely to the thunder-struck Priestleys and at the same time ignoring Frant, he descended the steps with Emma's hand on his arm.

Edward, obliged by politeness as their host to continue with his guests, managed to cast an expressive look in Jane's direction before he followed Ware and Emma. His spirits were high. Surely this accusation must have finished Frant in Mr Priestley's eyes.

Miss Priestley, thankful that all, it seemed, had fallen out so well, was yet a little frightened by the stir and public interest that Emma's plan had excited, and clung to her father's arm. It was not a calculated move but it could not have had a more telling effect. Mr Priestley was shocked. Genuinely attached to his daughter, he had allowed his native shrewdness to be overborne by the visions of rank and splendour that had been dangled before him; now the warning that he had received about the Marquis' morals flew to his mind – this poor woman's accusations were all too readily believable! The scales suddenly removed from his eyes, it seemed to him that the noble lord had shrunk visibly and literally into a contemptible creature.

He surreptitiously took a business card from his pocket, for he never failed to have one or two about his person – one never knew when some good business opportunity might occur – and pressed it into Mrs Hunt's hand, saying roughly, "Come and see me, my good woman!" then, taking Mrs Priestley's arm, his daughter still trembling at his side, he gave the briefest of bows to Jane's discomforted suitor and forced a way through the crowd of persons now surrounding them.

If Ware had hoped that the success of this incident, which he was confident was of his wife's contriving, would restore her spirits, he was soon to be disillusioned. Having said their farewells to an Edward who strove valiantly to conceal his delight and having mounted within their carriage, Ware asked Emma with a teasing smile whether she had observed how closely the young girl outside the theatre resembled Emma's protégée. "Quite a coincidence, my love!" he remarked placidly, watching her face.

At first she only replied absently, "Yes, my lord." then, realising what she had said, added quickly, "I mean, *no*, my lord – no coincidence – it was all *my* doing, as I see you must have guessed – are you very displeased?"

"My dear Emma, not displeased, only astonished at your infinite resourcefulness!" This, being said with a teasing look, drew no smiling response from her as he had anticipated it would, and he found himself disappointed to discover that her spirits were still so low. Concerned and puzzled he asked her gently, "Is your headache still troubling you, my love?"

"My headache?" It took her a few moments to recollect her excuse and she added hastily, "Quite gone now, I thank you, my lord." She seemed to withdraw into herself and a silence fell upon them.

As they approached the environs of Grosvenor Square, Emma found that her heart was beating so wildly, and was so loud in her ears, that she could hardly believe that it was not audible to Ware in the confined space of the carriage. She sat tense and upright, gripping her reticule tightly in both hands. Ware leaning back against the cushions, kept his eyes upon her face in the semi-darkness; from all that he had already learned of his wife's character, he was confident that she would soon acquaint him with whatever was clearly lying so heavily upon her mind.

He was not surprised, therefore, when, as soon as they had entered the hall, she turned to him and said nervously, "May I have a few moment's conversation with you, my lord, before I retire?"

They went into the library, where candles were burning and a tray had been set upon a side-table. Emma having declined his offer of some refreshment, Ware crossed to the table and was pouring himself a glass of cognac when he heard his wife say in a strained voice, "Is it possible, my lord, for you to advance to me some part of the money that I have inherited from my father?"

It was probably the last thing that he had expected to hear and he turned round swiftly, astonishment written upon his face. She was sitting on one of the sofas, looking towards him, a painfully intense expression in her eyes.

Endeavouring to hide his surprise, he came across to her and sat down beside her, saying evenly, "It is possible, of course, but if there is anything that you require, surely *I* can provide it for you – nothing, my dear girl, would give me greater pleasure!"

He could see that she was trembling and it was a moment or two before she spoke again. "You are very kind, but it is not something that I wish to purchase ...." She seemed unable to continue and sat looking down at her lap where her fingers were nervously pleating and un-pleating the edge of her shawl.

He said gently, "And what sum of money is it that you wish me to advance to you?"

She could not look up at him; she did not see the kindness and the perplexity in his eyes. She said wretchedly, "It is a l-large sum, my lord – it is ... it is f-five thousand pounds!" The words she dreaded saying spoken at last, she closed her eyes for a moment, fearing to hear his answer. There was complete silence in the room.

"I appear to be a very inadequate provider!" There was no mistaking the sarcasm underlying his words. Emma took one swift glance at his face and saw his expression had hardened; he was looking at her now with narrowed eyes as he continued, "And how soon, my dear wife, do you require this advance?"

Emma thought desperately, 'What in the world must he think of me?' but she had chosen her course and had no alternative but to continue, however distressing the consequences.

"I need to have the money tomorrow, my lord, if you please." The words were scarcely audible, as if the softness of her voice could somehow diminish the peremptoriness of her demand. But now Ware felt a growing conviction that something sinister lay behind her sudden urgent need for money; he took one of her hands in his and said earnestly, "Surely you can trust me, Emma! Good God – for heaven's sake tell me *why* you have such a pressing need for this vast sum?"

She looked at him then, her eyes half-blinded with tears, but she only said stiffly, "You told me, my lord, that I might do as I pleased with the money that I have inherited!"

He waited, his eyes studying her face, striving to read an answer in her expression, but she looked down again quickly without adding another word. When she said nothing more, he drew his hand away and stood up. He was convinced now that someone was threatening her, for surely she had had no opportunity for gaming: the only possible reason that came to his mind for such a demand. But what secret could such a young girl have to hide? All his jealous fears began again to rise. He felt increasingly disturbed and angry, and crossing the room to stand before the fireplace, said coldly, without looking at her, "I will put five thousand pounds in your hands tomorrow morning."

The contempt in his voice and the set look about his mouth were intensely painful to Emma; she rose unsteadily to her feet, a stricken look upon her face as she said haltingly, "T-thank-you, my lord. I am indeed grateful to you." then with a curtsy and a murmured, "Good-night!" she hurried out of the room.

After the door had closed behind her, he remained standing for a long time, staring after her, a frown upon his face.

That night, after Dora had quitted her silent mistress, Emma lay weeping as if her heart would break: the realisation of the possibility of happiness, which had, of late, been growing within her, seemed ended forever. Gradually the storm of tears abated and, exhausted by the violence of her emotions, she lay emptied of all feeling.

Her response to the strange, loveless marriage that had been forced upon her had, over the past weeks been imperceptibly changing; the desperate fear of her husband, that she had at first felt, had been slowly disappearing, to be replaced by trust and respect. His forbearance in the face of her youth and innocence, his kindness towards her, his understanding, all these had made him become to her a dear friend. Alongside this increasing affection, had grown up an awareness of his handsome person, a wish to be near him, which she hardly dared to admit even to herself.

Now all was to be lost. Like some monstrous barrier, her concealment of Richard's demand would forever lie between them and, she thought bitterly, it was hardly likely that this would be the last application that he would make to her for funds.

Out of her misery and black despair, a resolve began to form. She knew that she had not the courage to show Ware the letter, nor bear to let her husband's eyes read Richard's foul lies, lies that were impossible to disprove; but tomorrow she would tell Ware that the money that she had asked him for *was* for Richard; she owed him at least *that* explanation. This resolution made, she felt some small measure of calmness return to her and fell asleep as the first signs of dawn were beginning to lighten the sky.

It was broad daylight when she awoke and she was astonished to find that it was so late. When Dora answered her bell, she learned, in response to her enquiries, that his lordship had issued instructions that she was to be left to sleep until she rang. Emma, touched by this further proof of his thoughtfulness, determined as she drank her cup of chocolate to lose no time in speaking again to her husband.

In the light of day it now appeared to her to be an ordeal which she would have given anything to avoid but her resolve remained unshaken and anxious not to delay for fear that Ware might have gone out, as soon as Dora came to take away her tray she sent a message requesting his lordship to come to her that morning before he left the house.

Ware had woken early in a savage mood. He had for some time past been forced to admit to himself that he had fallen deeply and most unexpectedly in love with his young wife. He had thought he had seen her fear of him begin to be replaced by trust and, infinitely more experienced than Emma in the relationship between the sexes, had believed that she was slowly awakening to his desire. It was, he had until then felt confident, now only the natural diffidence of a very young girl that had made her hesitate to show him that she was no longer indifferent. What had happened yesterday, so unexpected and

268

so inexplicable, had been a shattering blow. One of Emma's most endearing qualities had been her incorrigible honesty: but what was he to think now? To what folly had she been led?

Having sent instructions to his bankers, he had felt unable to remain inactive indoors, and, when he received his wife's message, he was already dressed to ride in the park, so it was in buckskin breeches and top-boots, with his whip and gloves in his hand, that he entered her room.

Emma had not expected such an instant response to her message. She had not yet begun her toilet and was standing, still in her night-dress, by the elegant escritoire in her boudoir with the fatal letter in her hand, when Ware strode into the room without waiting for a reply to his knock. In her nightclothes she looked both young and defenceless and, despite her sleepless night, an adorably appealing sight. Ware wondered grimly if she knew what a desirable picture she presented.

Startled, she hastily hid the letter behind her on the desk, saying in a flustered voice, "I did not realise that the hour was so late – I wished to speak to you, my lord, before you went out." She was conscious of something distant and forbidding in his bearing and could not prevent herself from casting a nervous glance at the whip that he still held in his hands. Perhaps he noticed it, at any rate, he laid the whip down with his gloves upon a chair and asked her in a more conciliating manner in what way he could serve her.

She found it hard to find the words with which to begin. "I should have told you last night, my lord – the money for which I asked you – it is for Richard!" She saw that he was frowning at her, a hard look in his eyes, and stumbled on, "I had word, you see – he faces ruin..." Before she could finish, Ware had stepped forward and seized the letter from behind her; she gasped a frightened, "*Oh no, my lord!*" but it was too late.

There was absolute silence in the room as he read; outside all the everyday sounds of the London streets could be clearly heard. Emma, her eyes watching him apprehensively, stood frozen, At first there was a lightening of tension on his face, but as he read further his expression changed; there was a grim look now about his mouth and she heard the words, "Oh, my God!" spoken softly as if they had been forced from him. She felt her heart beating wildly. He read to the end and then turned his head and looked down at her, and she saw such contempt and fury blazing in his eyes that instinctively she recoiled. Desperately she said, "My lord – let me explain ...." but he interrupted her violently, striking her face a glancing blow with the back of his hand, "For God's sake – no explanations! Spare me at least that!" For one second he stood staring at her, white about the mouth, his face contorted with rage, then, summoning all his self-control, he crumpled the letter in his hand and, turning away from her, went to the window and stood looking out, his breathing uneven, his hands clenched at his sides.

Terrified, Emma stood rigid, her hand to her face where his ring had grazed her cheek, too stunned to say a word.

Slowly Ware turned back to her. Never before had she seen such cold fury. He said, with biting contempt, "So, by God, all that *innocence* was but a sham! You played your part well, my lady – not for one moment, once I discovered that you were Richard's sister, did I suspect you to be other than an innocent girl!"

Desperation overcoming her fear, not caring what he might do to her, she came swiftly across the room to him and, laying her hand upon his arm, her frantic eyes searching his face, she said in a voice that shook uncontrollably, "It is a lie, my lord! Dear God, you *must* believe me!"

He was too enraged to listen; his one thought was to wound her as he had been wounded, for the terrible secret divulged in Richard's letter exceeded all his worst fears of the night before and the recollection of learning from the guileless Humphrey Featherstone of her presence in Richmond Park, while he was away, only served to confirm all that he had just read. He looked her up and down scornfully, his merciless eyes lingering upon the half-open neck of her night-shift, where the soft curves of her breasts were revealed, and upon her tumbled locks, and said jeeringly, "How well you set the scene, madam wife! But your pretty beguiling ways will not avail you now! My God – how I loath and despise you!"

She drew her hand back sharply, her face as white as her shift as she pulled its neckline closer. Observing her involuntary movement, he added with a harsh laugh, "You no longer need fear any amorous advances from me, my girl! Libertine I may be, but even *I* would recoil from one who had committed such a crime! Believe me – I would rather that I had married the merest drab off the streets than a creature capable of such loathsome depravity! Small wonder that you dreaded my embraces when all the time you longed for your brother's illicit caresses!"

His cruel words stung her like the lash of a whip and, as he spoke, she felt a strange, bitter anger rising up within her, casting out her fear. How could he accept such terrible lies about her? How was it possible he could believe her capable of planning this encounter in such a way that she might seduce him with her charms? She looked fiercely up into his face, as angry now as he, and flung at him furiously, "I thought you were my friend, my lord! How wretchedly wrong I was! I did not expect such injustice from *you!*" She was trembling with wrath as she added in a low, bitter voice, "How could *you* – you who know me – believe such infamous lies? How could you prefer the word of such a man as Richard?" She paused, and her eyes filled with angry tears, "I would have killed myself rather than have permitted such a horror!"

He was still staring at her with no trace of softening in his expression; in his fury and disillusionment, her words fell upon deaf ears. She turned away from him and, biting her lip, went blindly to the door of her bedroom; there she turned and faced him again, white-faced, and cried out passionately, "Never, never will I forgive you for believing that I could be capable of such wickedness!"

For one instant he made an involuntary movement towards her, then checked himself; he let her go and remained standing motionless for some time, staring down at the crumpled paper in his hand with an expression of bitterness and anger in his eyes.

CHAPTER 26

By noon Emma's mood had changed from anger to despair; no more tears remained to be wept: hollow, desolate, she felt only a pain in her breast as if her heart were broken. Having been assisted to dress by her anxious maid, she ordered her luncheon to be served in her own apartment; it was unthinkable that she should sit down to eat alone with Ware if he might still be present in the house. Her thoughts returned again and again to re-live that terrible scene, seeing in her mind's eye the harsh, terrifying stranger that her husband had become. Was this the real man, so unlike the one that she had learned to trust?

Used by her half-brother as an un-regarded pawn in his last desperate fight against ruin, she now recognised Richard as a creature utterly evil who would stop at nothing to achieve his ends. But Ware! How quickly, how easily he had believed her capable of such an unnatural liaison! She thought bitterly of his words, of how he had struck her, and a savage anger rose within her again at his injustice.

Soon after noon, two sealed packets were brought to her room by a servant. She noticed listlessly that they had been sent by the bank and, opening one, found within a bundle of bank-notes. She gazed at them with disbelief; could she really, so little time ago, have thought that she would be able to pay Richard this money for his silence and yet conceal her transaction with him from Ware. For the first time she began to realise and to regret her folly – if she had shown her husband the letter at once, was it possible that he would perhaps have believed her?

The second packet, being opened, revealed a small leather box and within it lay a beautifully contrived brooch of pearls and diamonds forming a lover's knot. She sat staring at it as it lay before her, sparkling in the sunlight, and felt tears pricking her eyelids. No doubt, before he had read Richard's letter, Ware had asked the bank to deliver it, intending that she should wear it that night to the ball – that now was certainly impossible – never, never again would she accept anything of his!

The money, being an advance payment of her own fortune, was a different matter, and all at once she knew what she must do. In the extremity of her anger and despair she had forgotten Richard's proposed rendezvous with her that night; she had only known that if Ware could believe her to be so vile she no longer cared what Richard said or did – but now, with this money, she could leave Ware's house for ever and find some hiding-place. She need take nothing of his with her. To where she might go, to what her life might be in the future, she gave no thought; for over-riding all else lay her determination to get away from her husband. How thankful he would then be to be rid of her presence!

For a moment she wondered if Dora would come with her; but recollecting her maid's affection for Thomas and fearing that even Dora might not believe in her innocence, she vowed to herself that she would quit the house the next morning alone rather than endure another rejection.

Recollecting the ball that night, her first instinct was to plead an indisposition that would make it impossible for her to go? She was sorely tempted but upon reflection, her pride would not permit her to do so. Her kind sister-in-law and her husband were to dine with them beforehand – if she made such an excuse would it not appear to show a lack of courage to face the censure of the fashionable world? Indeed, might not Ware consider it to be an admission of guilt?

As she sat gazing at the package of notes upon her lap, she realised that, even though she no longer intended to pay Richard any part of the price he had demanded for his silence, she still must meet him: it was not impossible that, confronted by her absolute refusal and told that Ware had seen his letter, he might abandon his threats. For her, she thought sadly, that abandonment would come too late, her hopes of happiness already destroyed, but nevertheless she could not help but wish to escape the public ignominy and shame that must follow his lying disclosures.

It was soon apparent to Ware's servants that something was grievously amiss. Following his interview with his wife, his lordship descended into the hall with a face as black as thunder and curtly dismissing his groom, sent his mount back to the stables un-ridden.

His butler, making some conciliatory remarks about the weather, had had his head snapped off for his pains, and Willis was thankful, after one look at his master's frowning face, that his lordship maintained a forbidding silence while he assisted him to change his garments. "Never," he reported later in the servant's hall, "have I seen his lordship in such a towering rage! Whosoever contrived to set him in such a passion will suffer for it! Mark my words!"

Ware left the house almost immediately, announcing that he would not return until late in the afternoon. At first he walked he knew not where, neither seeing his surroundings nor aware of those whom he encountered on his way: images of Emma, imagined scenes of Richard in Emma's arms, were ever before his mind's eye, tormenting him beyond bearing.

Since he had attained manhood he had had scant respect for the female sex, but he had thought to have found in Emma a shining exception to the generality of womankind; it had been, above all, her honesty that had led him, imperceptibly, from a desire to possess her, to love. How terrible to have to acknowledge that he had been deceived: that she had been playing a part so skilfully that he had entered, step by step, into the trap that she had prepared for him.

It was all too painfully plausible that Richard had wagered his sister that evening not only for gain, but in a desperate effort to free himself from their unnatural liaison. Ware had been astonished, even shocked, when he had discovered that Richard had attempted to ruin his sister in order to possess himself of her money – now, he thought bitterly, Richard's actions no longer surprised him. In her dressing-room, he had himself known a moment when he could willingly have killed his wife with his own hands – whatever happened she must be removed from his sight. Tomorrow he would arrange for her return to Millford – he would see Pettigrew and discover how he could have their ill-fated marriage set aside!

He went, finally, to his club and there, at Brooks', ate a solitary meal in frowning silence; by good fortune none of his friends were present and those merely acquainted with him did not care to approach his forbidding figure and scowling countenance. He returned home soon after four o'clock and shut himself up in the library.

It was an ill-choice of surroundings. Everything around him reminded him of Emma and of the night that he had brought home the girl whom he had won so recklessly at play. How right he had been, he thought savagely, when his first instinct had been to rid himself of her. Now every cherished memory of the past weeks rose up before him, poisoned by his new knowledge of her past life. His fears that she might have developed a tendre for Edward paling into insignificance beside what he had now learned.

As he sat staring morosely before him, he recollected that Lady Challenor's ball was to be held that evening. Surely he should refuse to take her? Then, remembering with bitterness how he had planned to use the occasion to establish her securely in Society, he decided angrily that she *should* attend it. Let this false, dishonest wife of his see tonight what it will be like to endure the scorn of Society without his protection!

Ware was alone when Sir Peter and Lady Sophia were shown into the drawing-room. He was standing with his back towards them and, as he heard their names announced and turned, Lady Sophia was struck suddenly by the bleak look about his mouth. He greeted them with his usual warmth but there was something preoccupied in his manner. She thought, as she sat down, that he must be concerned about Emma and about the reception that might be accorded her at the ball, and said to him in her kindly way, "You will see, Robert! You need have no fears. I believe that Emma will be the object of universal admiration tonight. She has such happy manners which cannot fail to please!"

She received no reply. Ware, changing the subject, complimented her upon her dress and pronounced her to be looking in great beauty. Pleased and diverted for the moment, she began to recount to him the difficulties that she had experienced in finding just the right shade of blue to set off the magnificent sapphire and diamond necklace that she was wearing. Sir Peter, with a wry smile, remarked that he understood her to have visited every silk warehouse in the Metropolis. "Nonsense, Sir Peter!" she retorted, laughing, "But it has caused me a great deal of trouble so, naturally, I am particularly pleased that Robert approves."

As she finished speaking, the door opened and it was in a moment of silence with all eyes turned towards her, that Emma entered the room. The artful simplicity of her ball-dress set of her slim figure to perfection: composed of ivory spider-gauze, embroidered with pearls, her slender neck and shoulders rose above its low-cut bodice; she was very pale and, with her delicate features and large, serious eyes, there was something touchingly vulnerable in her appearance. She came slowly forward and, as she approached, Lady Sophia became aware of an anxious, guarded expression in her eyes. Rising from her chair, she embraced Emma warmly, her face wreathed in smiles, exclaiming spontaneously, "My dear child! It is *perfect!*" She stood back to admire her sister-in-law and saw Emma cast one quick glance at Ware from under her eye-lashes; following her gaze, Lady Sophia was utterly astonished to find a harsh frown upon his countenance. He said coldly to his wife, "You are not wearing the diamond brooch that I ordered to be sent from the bank!"

There was a set look to Emma's mouth as she replied, "No, my lord!" in a low voice, then, without adding a further word of explanation, turned from him to Lady Sophia. The latter, eager to avert what she saw at once might become a subject of dispute, looked across at Ware and enquired whether he was referring to the famous brooch worn by their grandmother in the Reynold's portrait; when he replied impatiently in the affirmative, she said pleadingly to Emma, "I wish you will wear it, my dear! I believe it will suit your dress to perfection and it would give me great pleasure to see it again!"

Emma's uncompromising expression softened as she replied gently, "If it will please *you*, my lady, I will certainly wear it!" and without looking again at her husband, she left the room.

It might well have been an awkward moment following her departure but Sir Peter, not so alive to the underlying strains in this interchange, was anxious to ascertain Ware's views on a Bill soon to be presented to Parliament and began to question him concerning it. Politeness obliged his lordship to attend to his guest and the moment of constraint was passed.

On Emma's return, Lady Sophia set herself, in her good-natured fashion, to distract Emma from what she believed to be her fears of the forth-coming evening, providing her with a lively description of the various personages whom she expected would be attending the ball. Sir Peter also, in his calm, sober way, was more than willing to support and encourage his new sister-in-law. He had already formed a favourable opinion of her and considered that Ware had been more fortunate than he deserved.

However, it was not a comfortable dinner-party. There was conversation, but the major part of it took place between the two gentlemen upon the one hand and the two ladies upon the other; no word passed between the Earl and his wife and it was a relief to at least three members of the party when the meal at last was ended.

Ware was in the hall talking to Sir Peter when Emma, ready to leave, descended the stairs in her cloak, and as they both turned to look up at her, Ware saw for an instant that her eyes were fixed upon him with an expression of pain and despair. As their gaze met, she looked quickly away, spoke to Sir Peter and moved towards the door; for one moment doubt entered his mind, he looked after her thoughtfully, then his face hardened: was not this just the very way in which she had bewitched him. Surely no innocent would have secretly planned to pay a blackmailer in order to avoid his disclosures.

The long journey to Twickenham was accomplished in two carriages. At Ware's suggestion, Lady Sophia and Emma travelled together in his lordship's carriage, the two men following in Sir Peter's, in order that they might continue their discussion.

At first Lady Sophia had hoped that Emma would confide in her, for it was now evident to her, beyond doubt, that there had been a serious disagreement between husband and wife; but when, having settled herself comfortably in her seat and arranged her voluminous cloak around her to her satisfaction, Lady Sophia said gently, "Dearest Emma, I do not wish to pry – but clearly you and Robert have quarrelled ...." she found herself at once interrupted.

In a low, shaking voice, Emma said brokenly, "I cannot speak of it! Pray do not ask me!" and in the dim light within the carriage, her sister-in-law could see tears glistening in her eyes. Astonished and uneasy,

Lady Sophia sighed and patted her hand, saying reflectively, "Men are strange creatures! They can be such brutes at times! There – I will say no more upon that subject!" After a short, uncomfortable silence, she began to speak of her children, hoping to divert her sad companion, and thus passed the remainder of the journey, absorbed in the subject dearest to her heart.

CHAPTER 27

Sir Frederick and Lady Challenor were receiving the last of their guests when the Earl and Countess of Ware were announced. Eleven o'clock had already struck, for the press of carriages in the street had delayed their arrival, and many of the guests had already passed through into the ballroom, from whence came the lively sounds of music. The reception rooms, however, were still crowded and, as Ware and his wife were greeted by their host and hostess, many heads were turned in their direction: there was a perceptible hush followed by a renewed burst of conversation, several gentlemen raised their quizzing-glasses and, behind their fans, the ladies exchanged excited whispers. All eyes were drawn to the young Countess of Ware. She curtsied low to Lady Challenor, a little bright-eyed, birdlike figure, fond of gossip and famed for her devastating frankness, who received Emma graciously, murmuring, "Why, I declare – you're the merest child! And as Lavinia Sheldon told me – quite a beauty!" and as Ware kissed her hand, she added sharply, "So you have succumbed at last, Ware! You had best take good care of her – the gossips' tongues have been busy!"

As they passed through the reception rooms, it was at once apparent that the rumours that had preceded their marriage had had their effect. Several dowagers gave Emma cold looks and turned away from her, speaking in barely subdued voices of the scandal surrounding her name; only Lady Sheldon smiled approvingly upon Emma as they passed by her and she caught a fleeting glimpse of Mrs Priestley, a turban of magnificent proportions upon her head, deep in conversation with Lady Foster.

The gentlemen were clearly of a different mind for in the ballroom Emma found herself the centre of a group of men: some were friends of Ware who had already been presented to her at the opera, others were those who desired to meet the female who, it was said, had ensnared his lordship. If they had previously believed the stories of this seductress, many were soon doubtful, finding it difficult to reconcile such rumours with the simplicity of dress and perfect propriety of manner of the slim, pale girl standing beside her husband, her great eyes turned gravely towards each speaker.

So great was the interest in the young Countess that it was not at first noticed how aloof and cold was Ware's demeanour towards his bride. It was Edward who was the first to ask her to dance; stepping forward with a glowing look of approbation on his face, he bowed over her hand, saying, "Will you do me the honour of standing up with me, Cousin?"

She did not look at her husband, but quietly acquiesced and they moved forward to take their places in a set then forming for a country dance.

They danced in silence at first; Emma, thankful that Edward and not some stranger, was her partner, was only too happy to be distracted from the distressing nature of her thoughts by the need to be mindful of her steps; he was, initially, content to admire the lightness and grace of her movements but when he became aware, as he soon did, of the unhappiness underlying her outward composure, he felt an uneasiness that he found hard to explain. To distract her, and because it was a subject at that moment so close to his heart, he congratulated her upon the success of her plan the previous evening, adding with great satisfaction, "Called at the Priestleys this morning, coz – received with considerable warmth by Miss Priestley's mother y'know! Saw the adorable Miss Priestley herself too, by Jove!" Parted for a moment by the movements of the dance, as they were brought together again he whispered, "I want you to become better acquainted with her, Emma – she's an angel, you know, so trusting and gentle."

His efforts were rewarded by a smile of infinite sweetness but at that moment, as they moved around the room, Emma had a fleeting glimpse of her husband's tall figure quit the place where she had left him and enter a doorway at the side of the ballroom where, through the open doors, baize covered tables and a crowd of men were visible. Perceiving with miserable certainty the night stretching ahead of her without his protective presence, she felt a renewed anger rise within her at the cruelty of his conduct. Something of her feelings must have been visible in her expression, for Edward, following the direction of her eyes, had himself seen Ware leave the room; as he led Emma off the floor at the end of the dance, he murmured anxiously in her ear, "I hope that you have confided in Robert as I advised!"

She shook her head fiercely, a note of anguish in her voice as she whispered, "Whatever you may hear, Edward, I hope that *you* at least will believe in me!"

For Emma, the evening had now assumed a nightmare quality; the great ballroom, the glittering chandeliers, the music, the banks of heavily scented flowers and the crowd of elegant guests, all had an air of unreality and brooding terror. She was next asked to dance by Mr Featherstone, who, having met Emma at the opera, was eager to renew his acquaintance with this captivating creature. He had been, at that time, struck so forcibly by Ware's remarks concerning her virtue that he felt himself somewhat upon his mettle to discover if such a paragon could not be tempted to stray a little from the straight and narrow path by a little mild flirtation. He found, however, that his gracefully turned compliments fell on deaf ears; no arch looks nor playful words met his discreet advances and he was obliged, disconsolate, to abandon his tactics. He was more than a little surprised that Ware had forsaken his young wife so early in the evening and, being famed for his exquisite manners, at the end of the dance, he courteously led Emma to a chair and offered to fetch her some refreshment.

He had just brought her a glass of lemonade and was standing by her chair making polite conversation, when Emma saw an older, heavily-built man approaching them whose face was vaguely familiar and who said in a loud, hearty voice, "Evenin', Featherstone! I'm come to request your good offices in making me known to Lady Ware! I'm an old friend of her brother's, y'know, and anxious to make her acquaintance."

Mr Featherstone knew Sir James Kent only slightly, and what he knew of his reputation was not good, but he was hardly in a position to refuse his request. The introduction made, Emma found herself looking up into eyes, set in a florid face, that held an expression which made her feel faintly uncomfortable.

Having made his bow, Kent bent forward again and asked, "May I have the honour of the next dance, Lady Ware?"

Emma looked around her in confusion but it was impossible to decline his request and, having murmured her assent, she found herself being led onto the floor.

Mr Featherstone stood for a moment looking unhappily after her. Then, muttering to himself, "Dammit, Ware should take better care of her!" he returned thankfully to his own circle of friends.

The dance was an ordeal for Emma. Her partner seemed intent upon embarrassing her and lost no opportunity of squeezing her hand and drawing her as close to him as the steps of the dance would allow; at the same time he bestowed upon her such ogling glances and paid her such fulsome compliments, expressed in terms that could only disgust, that she scarcely knew where to look.

It did not take long for this strange partnership to be remarked upon by those watching the dancers. Sir James's reputation was bad and his fondness for very young girls had drawn forth, even in that society where so much was condoned, a strong measure of disapproval: he was widely considered 'bad ton' by the fashionable world and was certainly *not* a desirable acquaintance for the young Countess of Ware.

The word spread rapidly: some observers concluding maliciously that Ware had tired already of his bride, others that, beneath her innocent appearance, she was indeed a wanton – fair game for any man. A very few, of a more charitable frame of mind, felt some sympathy for her and said in a whisper that Ware should take better care of his young wife.

When the music stopped, Emma would have been thankful to have escaped from the attentions of this odious person, but he drew her arm through his and, saying to her in a low voice, "I have something very particular to say to you, Lady Ware!" he escorted her into a small saloon adjoining the ballroom. There flashed through Emma's mind the recollection that Sir James had said that he was a friend of Richard's, and the notion that he might be the bearer of some message from him prevented her from drawing back when she discovered that the room was empty. She turned to him, saying in a hopeful voice, "You have some word for me from Richard?"

To her horror, he only laughed unpleasantly and said, "Just a little ruse, sweetheart, to find myself alone with you! I was present, y'know, at that card-party of Richard's! Caught a glimpse of you then and been wishing ever since that it was I who had wagered for you and not Ware!"

She backed away from him then with a stifled cry, but he caught her hand, saying in a thickened voice, "Thought I should like to sample what I missed that night! For it seems to me, he don't appreciate you as he should! You're a devilish attractive little creature, y'know!" and with these words, he seized Emma in a rough embrace and tried to plant a kiss upon her averted face.

She was struggling frantically to break away from him, sickened by his perspiring face and gloating eyes, when, to her relief, a tall woman dressed in the height of fashion came into the room with her partner.

The newcomer, looking more amused than shocked, said with a light laugh, "Why, good gracious! Lady Ware!" and Emma, released suddenly by Sir James, saw to her mortification that it was Mrs Tremayne who was standing before her, clearly enjoying the situation and absorbing every detail of Emma's dishevelled appearance and hotly blushing cheeks, and who added spitefully, "My dear Lady Ware! Your husband is indeed *considerate*, as I remember you once told me, to have absented himself so conveniently from your side!"

Emma, ready to sink into the ground with shame and anger, stammered out, "You m-mistake, ma'am – it is not as you think!" and, with a furious glance at Kent, brushed past her tormentor and went quickly out of the room, almost colliding with a couple passing by outside.

The gentleman, who was revealed to her horrified eyes as Mr Hartley Tremayne, stared at her with astonishment, exclaiming, "Gracious Heavens – Lady Ware!" then, catching a glimpse of Sir James within the open doorway and observing her obvious distress, murmured maliciously to his companion, a stoutish young lady wearing an unbecoming shade of pink, "My dear Miss Talbot, I fear that I should be in your dear mama's bad books if I were to present you to this young lady!" and hurriedly removed himself and the fascinated Miss Talbot from her presence.

A sense of panic seized Emma. Amongst all the glittering throng she could not see one friendly face; no sign of Lady Sophia nor of Lady Sheldon; even the company of Mr and Mrs Priestley would have been welcome. It was then, almost with relief, that she realised, from the general movement of the company towards another room, that supper was being served, and midnight, the time set for her meeting with Richard, must be close.

Glancing around her, she discovered that the curtains of the tall French-windows at one end of the ballroom had been drawn back and the doors opened to the terrace outside to permit some cool air to enter the room, and perceived thankfully that it would not be difficult to leave the house unobserved.

By the time that she had reached that end of the room, most of the guests were making their way to the supper-room and, with wildly beating heart, she was able to slip outside onto the deserted terrace.

CHAPTER 28

Edward was standing near the door of the supper-room talking to Humphrey Featherstone when he caught the sound of Emma's name amongst the babble of conversation around them. At once all attention, he heard a female voice saying, " .... ample evidence, my dear Charles, to confirm the rumours we have heard about Lady Ware! – dancing with Kent and going off into a room apart – *alone with him*!" Looking around, Edward saw that the speaker, at some little distance from him, was Elizabeth Tremayne. She was whispering something into the ear of the man beside her, then they both laughed and he said with a chuckle, "Little baggage! Caught in the act, eh?" adding solemnly, "What the devil made Ware of all people choose to marry a girl of that stamp? Bless my soul, if it don't defy all comprehension!"

Mr Featherstone, who had caught the last of these remarks, frowned and said fretfully to Edward, "Confound it! What in the world has come over Robert! Deucedly inconsiderate of him – leaving that young wife of his on her own! Found myself obliged to introduce that Kent fellow to her! Shocking loose fish – didn't like it at the time – knew no good would come of it!"

As Featherstone spoke, Edward's eyes were searching the room for Emma. At last he discovered her, alone at the far end of the room, and, with dismay, saw her glance around, her face white and fearful, as if to see if she was observed by those nearest to her, then slip out through one of the open doors onto the terrace and disappear from his sight.

Outside, Emma drew her shawl closer around her, for the night-air was cool after the heat of the ballroom; the moon was up and the sky clear and full of stars. Searching the prospect before her with anxious eyes, she saw the moonlight gleaming upon a stretch of water in the distance and, after a hasty glance around her to make certain that she was alone, she went down the wide stone steps, that descended from the terrace, to a broad walk leading away from the house towards the lake.

As she drew nearer to the water, she could see upon her right, partly hidden by some trees, a building with classic columns constructed to resemble a Greek temple. She moved from the path and walked softly on the grass; she could feel the slight dampness through her thin slippers. When she reached the pavilion, she discovered that the pillars of the portico concealed glass doors which opened into a large room with a marble floor and several benches of stone; the ceiling rose high above her, invisible in the darkness; it was very cold inside and Emma shivered.

She had to wait for several minutes in ever growing apprehension, before she heard, somewhere in the distance, a clock striking twelve and, shortly afterwards, the sound of footsteps approaching. One of the doors opened and Richard came in; she could just see his face in the dim light and her fears were at once re-doubled for she could tell by his unsteady gait that he had been drinking.

In her white dress, she was plainly visible and he came straight towards her; he was breathing heavily and the fumes of wine hung about him.

"Thought that you'd come to your senses, little sister!" he sneered as he approached, a triumphant expression on his face "No sense in wasting any more time! Give me the money and I'll be gone!"

She took a deep breath and said in a low voice, "I have brought you no money, Richard!" For a second she hesitated, then she added fiercely, "I have told my husband the truth! You will *never* receive any money from me for your lies!"

He stood staring at her, his mouth fallen open, and repeated her words in a stumbling voice, "Y-you told him the truth?" Then, all at once, as he perceived the misery in her face, his expression changed to one of fury and he shouted at her, "You cursed little fool! He didn't believe you, did he? You and I are the only ones who *know* that it was all lies! And that's something that *you* will never be able to prove! My God, what a crazy innocent you were to trust Ware!" There was venom in his voice as he hissed at her, "Well, you have done for yourself, my girl! I'm ruined now and, by God, I shall drag you down into the mire with me!"

She took a step forward and stretched out a hand imploringly, "For God's sake, Richard! You have already destroyed all my hopes of happiness – can you not be content with that? Tomorrow I shall leave my husband and you will have nothing to gain by spreading your wicked lies!"

Hating herself for being forced to plead with him, Emma was unaware that his attention was not upon her words; her sudden movement had made her shawl slip at one shoulder and the moonlight was glittering upon the diamond brooch at her breast. It had caught Richard's eye and he said suddenly, "Give me that brooch!" and seized her wrist. For a moment he stood staring down into her frightened face, and she saw a most horrible expression compounded of lust and cunning light up his blood-shot eyes. He looked her over in a way that sickened her and said softly, as if it was himself whom he addressed, and in a low voice more terrifying than all his ranting and shouting had been, "You must have pleased Ware mightily that night that he should have wished to make you his wife! Now, my dear, you shall please *me*!" and she found herself seized by clumsy hands, hands that clutched and tore at her dress, and heard him say thickly with a cruel laugh, "By God, it will be a pleasure, my girl, to make my lies become the truth!"

Edward found Ware sitting at one of the tables in the card-room, where play had stopped for the moment while supper was in progress. He had not wasted a moment in seeking him out, for the words that he had heard and the look upon Emma's face as she slipped out into the garden had filled him with alarm and foreboding.

Saying, "A word with you, Robert!" he drew Ware to one side and said in an urgent voice, "I am concerned for Emma, cousin! I believe she has suffered most unwelcome attentions from Kent and I have this moment seen her go out alone into the grounds – that she was grievously distressed, I have no doubt!"

Whatever reaction Edward had expected, it was not that which he received. Ware looked at him coldly, eyebrows raised, and said sarcastically, "Upon my soul, you seem very busy on my wife's behalf. I believe she is a great deal more capable than you think of managing her own affairs!"

Profoundly shocked at this callous attitude, Edward flushed, saying defiantly, "I own that I am quite ignorant of what has passed between you but if you had seen her yourself ....! All I can say is, if *you* will not go after her, Robert, then, by God, *I* shall!"

"And interrupt some rendezvous?" Ware spoke so bitterly and with such barely concealed anger that Edward stared at him in astonishment and retorted with rising alarm, "Are you run mad, cousin? I tell you – Emma looked in despair – God knows what she might do! And out there, beyond the gardens .... there is the lake!" He paused, then added slowly, "Don't you *understand* – I fear for her life!"

For one second Ware stood arrested, staring down into Edward's anxious face from under frowning brows, then, grim-faced, with an expression in his eyes that his cousin found impossible to read, he demanded to know by which door Emma had left the house. Upon receiving Edward's reply, he left him without another word and, crossing the ballroom, went out on to the terrace.

He went directly towards the lake, not following the path, and moving swiftly, gripped by a sudden terrible fear – what might he find? Into his head there had crept, unbidden, the ghastly vision of a dead girl lying in the water, her white dress floating around her slim body; he felt his heart beat suffocatingly for, although Emma's death would deliver him from a wife whom he believed he now hated, even *he* could not contemplate such an event without the utmost horror ....

He was quite near the lake when he saw her in the distance and relief flooded through him for she was moving away from the black expanse of water; but the relief was short-lived for, in the moonlight, he saw her slight figure approach a pavilion set amongst the trees and disappear within. Certain that she could only have come there to meet someone, he at once comprehended with pain and bitterness that that person must be Richard and the very fear that he had just felt for her safety now only added to the murderous rage that swept over him. Consumed by a cold fury, he thought savagely, 'By God, she goes to pay him for his silence .... let them meet then and I will confront them together!'

Desperately, Emma struggled to free herself, to push away Richard's hateful, bloated face, to escape from his clutching hands: she was unaware that she cried out, unaware of everything except her over-whelming fear of this man and of what he sought to do to her; a sicken-ing repulsion filled her, a sensation of defilement at his touch and she screamed again, "Let me go! For God's sake, let me go!" but as she fought to free herself as his grip tightened, she realised, panic-stricken, that she had not the strength to hold him off.

Suddenly she was no longer alone; a tall figure strode across the room and, pulling Richard away from her, seized him by the throat, forcing him back against the stone bench. As the moonlight caught his face, she saw that it was her husband with murder blazing in his eyes....

Richard's fingers scrabbled desperately against the vice-like grip ever tightening. His eyes were frantic as he looked up into Ware's dark face above him: felt powerful arms forcing him backwards, hands chok-ing the life out of him. It was only as Richard began to lose conscious-ness and his movements became feeble that Ware loosened his grip and thrust him contemptuously away so that he fell to the ground and lay there gasping for breath, his hands clutching at his throat. For a moment Ware stood looking down at him and gradually the light of murderous rage died in his eyes; then he turned and saw Emma standing, her back pressed against the wall, on the far side of the room.

She made no movement and, as he came slowly towards her, he could see that she was standing rigid, breathing quickly and in her eyes a look of fear mixed with defiance. She said softly, as if she found it hard to control her voice, and with a pathetic attempt at dignity, "Whatever you may believe, my lord – I am innocent!"

She could not see his expression, for the moon-lit doorway was behind him, his face in shadow; he said gravely, "I overheard every word that passed between you, Emma! I know *now* that everything you told me is true!" he paused, then added bitterly, "How can I ever forgive myself for not trusting you? Dear God, how you must hate me!"

It seemed at first as if she could not comprehend his words; as he came closer, she stared blindly up into his eyes, her face white and taut, then, all at once, she began to tremble and covered her face with shaking hands. He was afraid to take her in his arms, as he longed to do: had she not already endured too many unwelcome embraces that night! Instead, he took one of her hands in his and gently kissed it, saying with concern, "Do you feel able to return to the house alone? I will rejoin you when I have finished with this contemptible creature."

In a faltering voice, she replied, "Yes, I w-will go!" and casting a look of loathing at the figure of Richard lying, groaning, upon the floor, asked painfully, "What will you do with him, my lord?"

"You need not worry your head about Richard!" he answered savagely, "He will never trouble you again, that I can promise you!"

He picked up her shawl from where it had fallen in her struggle and, as he laid it around her shoulders, he observed, his mouth tightening grimly, that her dress was torn at her breast where the brooch was pinned. Seeing the direction of his gaze, she endeavoured to re-pin it to hide the torn silk but her trembling hands made it impossible. Silently, he took the brooch from her and, with gentle fingers, re-pinned it to her bodice so as to conceal the torn ruffle. As his hands touched her, he heard her draw in her breath but she did not shrink back from him; she cast one swift glance at his face then stood looking down as he fastened the clasp. 'Thank God,' he thought, 'at least she is no longer afraid of me!' then, saying, "Find Sophie and stay with her until I come!" he led her to the door, his arm protectively around her shoulder. There, she took one last fearful look at her half-brother and then was gone.

After she had left him, Ware stood looking down in silence at Richard, where he lay groaning upon the floor; then, in a bitter voice filled with contempt, he said, "Get up! I shall not take your worthless life now, though that is what you deserve!" He paused, while Richard stared up at him with the sweat running down his face, his neckcloth undone, and a livid red mark at his throat, then continued harshly, "About one thing let there be no misunderstanding, for you have misjudged my intentions before! If you ever breathe *one word* of your foul lies about my wife, if you so much as hint at any scandal, *make no mistake*, I will seek you out, wherever you are, and kill you with my own hands without the slightest compunction!"

Uncertainly, Richard struggled to his feet and stood, swaying slightly, his gaze fixed upon Ware's face, dazed and silent. There was no mercy in those hard eyes, only such an expression of contempt and anger that left Richard in no doubt that this was no idle threat.

"You will leave here now and return home at once, and, having collected whatever necessities that you require, you will depart tonight for Dover; there you will take passage on the first available ship sailing for France!" He took hold of Richard's collar in both his hands and, looking down into his terrified face, said in a grim voice, "From that moment you can go to the devil as far as I am concerned, but you will not set foot in this country again until at least one year has passed!"

A cry of protest rose to Richard's lips but he did not dare to speak. Fearful of the man before him, as Ware loosened his hold, he staggered to the door and, without a backward glance, disappeared into the blackness of the night.

It took every ounce of courage that Emma possessed to re-enter the house and to find Sophie. It was Sir Peter who first saw her; he had gone to fetch a glass of champagne for his wife when he observed Emma, on the far side of the room, alone and very pale and there was something in her manner, in the expression in her eyes, that brought him swiftly to her side. She gave him a look of relief but found herself unable to speak. Concerned, he drew her arm through his, and, talking gently to her about the disagreeableness of the excessive heat in the rooms, led her to where Lady Sophia was sitting beside Lady Sheldon watching the dancers.

Both ladies had been, at that moment, discussing in low voices the strangeness of Ware's behaviour since his arrival at the ball. Lady Sophia was too loyal to her brother to have introduced the subject, but Lady Sheldon had no such delicate scruples; "My dear Sophie!" she had exclaimed upon sitting down purposefully beside her and wielding her fan in a vigorous manner, "What an unprincipled rascal that brother of yours is! What, in the name of Heaven, can Ware be about to abandon that sweet creature to the unwelcome attentions of a man like Kent? Unless of course he is aware of something that we are not! There was already gossip enough." In a shocked voice she had added, "I have even heard it said by several acquaintances that Ware has already tired of her – yet it was only yesterday that I could have sworn that he was a man deeply in love!"

Lady Sophia, perplexed and alarmed, had been unable to offer any explanation; she was reluctantly admitting that she was totally at a loss to comprehend his behaviour, when she caught sight of Sir Peter approaching them with her sister-in-law leaning upon his arm.

One glance at Emma's white face was enough for her to see at once that the young girl had suffered some terrible shock. She said in a re-assuring voice as one speaking to a child, "Come, sit by me, dearest Emma! No-one shall bother you —Peter shall fetch you a glass of wine and you will feel better almost immediately!" As she spoke, she wondered anxiously where her brother was but did not dare to ask Emma what had occurred. She was horribly conscious of curious glances being cast in their direction and so it was with a feeling of thankfulness that she saw Ware's tall figure coming towards them. Her relief was all the greater when she realised that, whatever had passed between him and his wife, the difference was at an end, for he looked with obvious concern at Emma before making his bow to Lady Sheldon.

After exchanging some civilities with that lady, whose curiosity was by now thoroughly aroused, he bent down and asked Emma in the gentlest of manners if she would do him the honour of standing up with him for the next dance.

Emma would have given anything in the world to have remained safely where she was, for not only did she feel doubtful whether her legs would support her after her recent ordeal, but she was painfully aware that every eye would be upon them, every gossiping tongue ready to comment upon both her appearance and her conduct; but she had no choice, Ware's strong hand had already taken hers in a firm grasp, helping her to rise and leading her on to the floor: it was impossible to refuse. As they took their places in the set, he murmured in her ear, "Good girl! That was bravely done! Soon I shall take you home, but first we must undo some of the harm that I have done to your reputation by my folly."

Emma would have felt a degree of nervousness under any circum-stances in dancing for the first time with this man, whom Fate and his own ruthless determination had made her husband: she would not have wished to show her inexperience, to appear inept or clumsy; as it was, she had to stand up with him, still dazed and bewildered by the frightening drama of that day and, conscious of being the cynosure of all eyes, go through the intricate movements of the dance. All the fortitude that she could command was required to continue to the end of the figure: by good fortune it was one with which she had been familiar since her dancing lessons with the Squire's daughters in Hinton St. Anne. Ware gave her all the support that he could; she felt the strong, warm pressure of his hand and, after a few minutes, he said softly, with a smile, "I might have known that you would be a delightful dancer."

To the surprise of the onlookers, it soon became evident that here was a man who entertained the warmest feelings for his wife and, even those most ill-disposed towards Emma, found it no longer possible to subscribe to the view that Ware had regretted his hasty marriage; moreover, seeing the elegant form and well-bred manner of the young bride, it was becoming all too vexingly apparent to the lovers of malicious gossip that the scandalous rumours concerning the Countess of Ware might well be without foundation. Even some of those persons who had been the first to think ill of Lady Ware were now amongst the most eager in their praise.

When the dance ended, the first person to approach them, as they quitted the floor, was Edward. His profound relief and pleasure upon observing that all was now well between his cousin and his cousin's young wife was clearly evident; evident, too, was a certain shy happiness which even Ware remarked.

Miss Jane Priestley's hand rested upon Edward's arm, and the loving look that she bestowed upon her partner as they drew near told its own tale. There could be no surprise therefore to Emma when Edward murmured in her ear, "Wish me joy, cousin, for Jane has this evening consented to become my wife and I shall wait upon her father tomorrow!"

As Emma softly congratulated him and spoke kindly to Miss Priestley, she could not but envy them their happiness. There might well be some difficulty in gaining Mr Priestley's consent: his sights had seemed to be set so firmly upon some member of the peerage for his daughter, but she felt hopeful that any objections on his part could be overcome.

To her surprise and relief Ware, too, expressed his pleasure. Only *he* knew how deeply he was indebted to his young cousin for his timely warning. When the young couple had moved away, Emma looked up at him anxiously and found that he was smiling ruefully down at her. He said, "How very paltry considerations of family and breeding do seem to me at the moment!" and led her back to his sister's side.

The Earl and Countess of Ware left the ball early. In such a press of people, their departure was not noticed and Ware considered that Emma had already endured as much as she could withstand. How such a seemingly frail creature could have withstood all that had been inflicted upon her that evening astonished him and only served to increase his admiration and respect.

When he mounted up into the carriage and sat down beside her, she was leaning against the soft back-cushions looking pale and worn. Overcome by an immense lassitude, drained of all emotion, her great eyes, dark with fatigue, gazed at him from a face that was fine-drawn with exhaustion. He said, in a voice full of concern, "You may rest now and be easy in your mind, my love. Nothing in the world shall be allowed to distress you." Too tired to speak, she inclined her head and closed her eyes thankfully.

Throughout the hour-long journey back to Grosvenor Square, Emma slept. Ware never took his eyes off her. In the dim light her face was just visible and as she fell asleep, she shed her cares and her unhappiness and looked even younger and more defenceless. A tendril of hair had escaped the confines of her ribbon and lay beside one smooth cheek; her hands were lightly clasped upon her lap and gradually, with the swaying and jolting of the carriage, her head came to rest against his shoulder and remained there.

She awoke when the carriage drew up in Grosvenor Square and, as she stirred, said in a sleepy voice, "Are we home, my lord?" He was infinitely touched to hear her speak of his great house in those terms but when, suddenly becoming aware of how closely she leaned against his shoulder, she sat up in some confusion, he remembered grimly the words that he had overheard her speak to Richard, "Tomorrow I shall leave my husband!"

It was with this in mind that, upon entering the house, Ware drew Emma towards the library, saying gently, "Forgive me, my love, but there is something I must say to you which cannot wait until the morning."

Confused, she allowed him to lead her to a chair and sat regarding him with troubled eyes.

He had withdrawn from her to lean against the mantel-shelf and she could see that there was an alteration in his manner towards her. He seemed to find some difficulty in finding the right words to say to her and stood staring at her as if she was a stranger.

Finally he said in a harsh voice, "I cannot blame you if you cannot find it in you to forgive me for not trusting you – indeed you may well hate me for it and for all that you have had to endure since that fateful wager .... but this I do ask of you – do not leave here tomorrow!"

He saw her start and added swiftly, "Yes, my love, I heard you tell Richard that you would leave me and I know that you now have the means to do so .... but for God's sake, Emma, stay!"

She was regarding him wonderingly, taken aback by the change that had come over him. Where now was the autocratic nobleman, the man who brooked no opposition?

Her silence seemed to further sadden him; he came across the room and sat down beside her, saying, his eyes fixed sombrely upon her face as if to catch every fleeting expression, "I swear to God, child, that if you wish it, I will arrange for you to live separately from me, so that you need only see me when you wish to do so!"

She remained a moment staring at him, incredulous, hardly able to believe her ears, then slowly she said, "For the future, my lord, I hardly know ...." she hesitated, then added, with a catch in her voice, "But I will not leave here tomorrow, my lord, that I *can* promise you."

His relief was evident. He took her hand and kissed it gently, then, raising her to her feet, he escorted her to the bottom of the stairs and stood watching her as she slowly mounted the great staircase and disappeared from his sight.

CHAPTER 29

Willis, as he moved silently about his duties, noticed his lordship's preoccupied air. However late the hour, he could not have contemplated for a moment allowing his master to retire to bed without his assistance and would, indeed, have been mortally offended if he had been ordered to do so.

It was a relief to him to find that the black rage, so evident when his master had left the house, had been replaced by a mood, it seemed, of sadness. That all was not well with my lord's life at that moment he was well aware and would have given a great deal to have had it in his power to lighten his lordship's cares.

Willis had had high hopes of the Earl's marriage, believing that her ladyship, although so young and inexperienced, would have a softening influence upon her husband's character: that he would reform his wild ways and settle down to raise a family and attend to his great estates; but perhaps, he thought shrewdly, that infamous start to their relationship was too great a barrier to their happiness. Who knew better than he how ill it had begun? Often and often, he had remembered that night when he had escorted a frightened, white-faced girl to her bedroom.

Ware's thoughts were indeed sombre. Even if Emma would willingly remain with him, weeks, months or, could it be, even years might pass before he could regain her trust. The time seemed to stretch before him like an eternity. He knew, in his heart, that he could not lay all the blame for his predicament at Richard's door; if it had not been for his own pride and hasty temper perhaps he would not have so quickly condemned her, so swiftly punished her. He should have understood that in her horror and desperate fear she had hoped to avoid telling him of the shocking lie with which Richard threatened her. Was it not true, indeed, that, even if she *had* shown him the letter, there might perhaps still have remained some faint shadow of doubt in his mind if he had not overheard the truth from Richard's own lips?

When he had learned of his wife's innocence he had felt as if some great burden had been lifted from his heart, but how damnably hard it would be, perhaps impossible, for someone so honest, so trusting as Emma to pardon him. Painfully he remembered her words, "I will *never* forgive you!" God! What a fool he had been!

He was deep in these thoughts, as Willis, his ministrations nearly at an end, was helping him into his dressing-gown, when he saw to his astonishment, reflected in the mirror above the mantelpiece, the door behind him which led to the adjoining room open a little way and Emma's face visible for one moment before the door was silently closed again. He did not change his position but said softly, "That will be all for tonight, Willis! You may leave me now!"

Willis was too well trained to allow any surprise to show upon his face at this unexpected and premature dismissal, for he had not yet put his lordship's room in order nor hung up his discarded garments; he merely bowed and said impassively, "Very well, my lord!" and, taking up his lordship's elegant coat, bade him goodnight and left the room.

Left alone, Ware threw himself into a chair beside the dying fire. He was sitting there, his legs stretched out before him, playing with the lid of his snuffbox, a puzzled frown upon his face, when he looked up and saw his wife standing in the doorway.

Upon entering her bedroom after leaving Ware, Emma had found a patient, anxious maid awaiting her and, as she allowed Dora to help her to undress and make her ready for bed, she thought wonderingly of the astonishing conversation that she had just held with her husband.

It had been a relief to Dora to find her mistress no longer the desperately distraught creature whom she had helped to prepare for the ball and she wondered silently what could have happened that evening to have restored her poor lady to a more tranquil state of mind. She had drawn in her breath sharply at the sight of the scratch revealed on Emma's breast but had bitten back her instinctive exclamation, fearful that she might tread on dangerous ground and praying wholeheartedly that his lordship had not been responsible for the injury, for all in the servant's hall were well aware of his black mood that day.

When Dora had finished and helped her mistress into bed and she was once more alone, Emma lay back against her pillows and struggled to comprehend that Ware had actually offered her her freedom – freedom to live separately from him, freedom no longer to feel an obligation to fulfil her duties as a wife ....

Why, she wondered, did she not feel a lightening of her spirits as she now contemplated the end of her strange, shared life with this man. The cage was now open – why did the bird seem so reluctant to fly? Surely she should not even contemplate remaining in the house of a husband who had struck her, who had refused to believe her or to trust her: who had deliberately sought to ruin her by his public indifference and neglect that night at the ball?

She tried to summon up the remembrance of his ruthless overbearing of her wishes since the night that she had driven away with him from Richard's house, but found that these recollections were less vivid than other memories of their past companionship and of the protection that he had given to her, not least by giving her his name. She could not but recognise that most heart-rending of all that had happened that day had been the desolation of losing one whom she had believed to have become her friend.

Like a sudden, over-powering revelation, the answer came to her – she must forgive and stay with her husband because she loved him!

In spite of his overbearing manner, his kindness and generosity had won her affection: of the attraction of his handsome person there could be no doubt – to share his bed, to feel his touch was now no longer a matter of dread and fearfulness but something to be longed for and to be enjoyed. She could never hate him!

She sat up in bed, hugging her knees, almost shocked by the strength of her own feelings, a shy smile upon her lips, her uncertainties vanished. It did not seem any longer to matter that Ware did not love her in the same way that she loved him – how could he? He would be kind and how vividly she knew that he had long desired to possess her – of that she had been well aware from the beginning and had been grateful for his self-imposed restraint.

She thought of the sadness reflected in his face as they had parted that evening and the idea began to form in her mind that she would go to him that very night. Tonight she would repay him with a loving heart for his past forbearance and show him that she forgave him for all that had happened that day. Slipping out of bed, she took her candle and went quickly through her dressing room to her husband's door, her heart beating wildly.

It was a disconcerting set-back to discover that Willis was still with his master; Ware, his back turned towards her, was slipping his arms into the dressing-gown that Willis held for him. She closed the door again softly and stood leaning against it, so sure that she *must* see him that night, that she was scarcely aware of the cold as she stood, bare-footed and in her thin night-shift, waiting for Willis to leave the room.

After a short time there seemed to be silence and this time, when she opened the door, she saw that her husband was alone, sitting by the fire. Then he looked up and saw her ....

As Ware beheld his wife standing in the doorway, his one thought was that he must not frighten her. What, in Heaven's name, she intended by coming to his room he had no idea.

Allowing no trace of surprise to appear upon his face, he felt his heart beat faster as he gazed at this desirable creature before him, his wife and yet not his wife; but he was holding himself on a tight rein and did not move, only saying, "Well, my love?" in a low voice.

He saw her take a deep breath and come towards him and rose quickly to his feet, his brows drawn together in a frown, 'Dear God, had she changed her mind and come to tell him that she would, after all, leave him in the morning!' Nevertheless, he contrived to say evenly, "What is wrong, Emma? Why are you here?"

It was not as simple as Emma had expected. Ware seemed to tower over her, to have become almost a stranger. Now that she was near him her courage was beginning to fail her; she could not look up into his eyes but said awkwardly, "My lord, I came to ask you to come to my bed-chamber tonight!" She paused, feeling the colour flame in her cheeks.

There was a moment's silence; she heard Ware draw in his breath sharply, then he said, in what seemed to Emma to be a forbiddingly stern voice, "And for what reason, my love, do you wish me to come to your room?" 'For God's sake,' he thought, 'let there be no mistake – no misunderstanding!'

At that she looked up at him quickly, then lowered her eyes. She must be honest whatever it might cost her.

"My lord, it is because I have learned to love you as a wife should love her husband!" and, with an immense effort, she added, "Because I wish you to consummate our marriage!"

He put his hand under her chin then and turned her face up towards him; he still looked stern, she could see, but as his eyes looked into hers and he saw the soft appeal in them, the love that was shining there, his harsh countenance was suddenly transformed: she saw an expression of joy upon his face and was vividly aware of his long suppressed desire for her. He stood a moment, staring down into her eyes, then, with a gentle hand, he traced the outline of her face, touched her eyes, her nose and mouth, as if he wanted to learn, forever, every line and curve.

Above all things he did not wish to alarm her: but when, instinctively, she put her arms up around his neck, and drew his dark face down towards her, he swept her into a crushing embrace and kissed her with passionate intensity, feeling with joy her response and holding her so tightly that she could scarcely breathe; but, when she stirred a little, he loosed her at once and stood with his arms around her, looking at her so lovingly and with such tenderness that she put up her hand to touch his face, tears in her eyes and said wonderingly, "Why, my lord, can it be that you *love* me?"

Kissing her again gently, he said, "Dear God, I love you and need you so desperately, my little love! I feared that you might never forgive me – I thought that I should have to wait for months, even years!"

She shook her head, smiling mischievously, "Have you forgotten that you once said that you would make me love you, and now, you see, you have! How could I not forgive you?"

A shadow passed over his face as he said ruefully, "My God, what a coxcomb I was to have said such a thing! When I said that I did not even know the meaning of love!" He picked her up in his arms and, looking down at her, said softly, "Do you trust me, dearest Emma?"

When she nodded happily and replied, "With all my heart, my lord!" he carried her through into her bedroom.

As daylight entered the room the next morning, Emma awoke and lay looking wonderingly at the dark head upon the pillow beside her, conscious of an over-whelming sense of love and of gratitude to this man who, for all his strength, had been so gentle to her the night before. She lay there, filled with happiness, waiting for him to wake. But soon a faint worry began to cloud her thoughts: suppose that upon waking, he should not remember, at first, in whose arms he had lain that night or, even worse, that he should compare his wife to one of his beautiful mistresses and find her wanting!

Her first fear was not realised however, for, before Ware even opened his eyes, he turned and stretched out his arm towards her to draw her closer, murmuring, "Emma, my little love!"

When he was properly awake, he found a pair of anxious eyes fixed upon his face and, smiling lovingly at her, said softly, "What is troubling you, my dearest Emma?"

She looked shyly at him, and answered doubtfully, "I fear that you may be angry with me if I tell you."

"How could I be angry with you when you look so confoundedly adorable." he replied, with a look in his eyes that made her blush.

She said, almost in a whisper, "I fear that you will have found me young and stupid and .... and that you may prefer your mistresses in bed to me." She had not dared to look in his face, but when he laughed, her eyes flew to his; what she saw there was immensely re-assuring.

He said teasingly, "How indelicate you are, my love! But fortunately for you I find your candour quite enchanting!" Ruffling her curls, he added gently, "You need not worry yourself, my lovely Emma, upon that score – those affairs are all finished with and in the past and need not concern you in the least. They were never important in my life."

Emma sighed happily, "I could not bear to share you with a mistress, my lord!" she said simply.

He looked at her with amusement and, seeing beside him her sweet face, with her large brown eyes fixed so earnestly upon his, no trace of guile in that clear look, he said thoughtfully, "I will have you painted by Lawrence looking just so – to remind you, always, that you are the only love in my life!"

It was a year later that two portraits were added to the collection in the long gallery at Millford House. Sir Thomas Lawrence had painted the Countess of Ware standing in a garden beside a classical column; she wears a white dress, which clings softly to her figure, her brown tresses confined by a filet of blue ribbon. She looks out from the painting into the eyes of the beholder with an air of gentle innocence and in one hand holds some flowers, small, white, star-like blossoms with heart-shaped leaves, '*Lunaria Annua*', commonly known as 'Honesty'.

The companion portrait shows the Earl, three-quarter length, seated beside a baize-covered table; he is leaning back a little in his wing-chair, a quizzical expression in his eyes and about his mouth lies a hint of amusement. One arm rests negligently upon the table and near his hand lies a leather dice-box from which have fallen two dice, showing uppermost the five and the four.